The Trouble with Hades

Book Two
The
Hades
Series

TM WATKINS

2023 eBook / 2025 Paperback

This book is a work of fiction. The names of characters, places and incidents are products of the writer's imagination and are not to be interpreted as real. Any resemblance to persons, living or dead, actual events, locals or organizations is entirely coincidental. With the exception of quotes used in reviews, this book may not be reproduced or used in whole or in part by any means existing without written permission from the author.

Cover Design by Brosedesignz.

www.brosedesignz-bookcovers.com

If you wish to contact the author, please visit: www.tmwatkinsauthor.com

ISBN: 978-1-7637195-4-5

SERIES ORDER

The Trouble with Evie
The Trouble with Hades

CONTENTS

CHAPTER 1

I will admit that I am not observant. It's a fault, that is absolutely certain. In this instance, though, it was nothing detrimental. Just a glaring hint about the demon headmaster who had named the football team Hades Demons.

I'd also not noticed that the team tryouts had taken place in the sports field mere steps away from the side doors I use daily. I missed the cheerleader tryout flyers pinned to every noticeboard, but that could have been my mind trying to save me from the horror of it all.

Packing my books, I tried not to groan or roll my eyes. It had been done by the other students, and our teacher had dismissed their distaste with a simple statement that her words were not a suggestion. We were having a study session in the great outdoors while supporting the team, who were having their last training session.

I looked at Anzide, my silent and hidden protector, an outcast Nephilim who was always by my side when I was outside of the protection of my home. He smirked and said nothing.

The enemy Drakkus, a psychotic vampire that wanted to claim the rule of the vampires from me, hadn't made an attempt on my life yet, but I figured it would happen soon. I just couldn't wait.

"Evie,"

Mrs Winslow gestured to come over to her. Lifting my bag over my shoulder, I approached her desk and offered an uneasy smile. She rarely called upon me, but when she did, it was usually only to check I was still awake.

"Mr Harlwood has just sent a message that we have a new student. Would you please go to the office to collect the student and bring them to the field?"

"Sure."

When I looked at Anzide, he gave me a shrug and followed me through the open door.

"Why would they send the new student to bring the newer student to the field that only the jocks and the cashmere brigade know where it is?"

He chuckled.

"Because James knows you so well."

Yeah, James Harlwood, headmaster of the only high school in Hades and a demon. At least he was on my side.

As we turned the corner into the main corridor, I

almost barreled into Kannon. My ex-boyfriend, the vampire who was a member of Drakkus's coven, and my secret nemesis, who was completely unaware of how much I knew. It was always an exceptional moment in my day when we crossed paths and were about as entertaining as watching the grass grow.

"Evie," he said eagerly. "Are you going to the game tonight?"

"There's another tonight?" I said, perhaps sounding a little too snarky.

"Yeah, they happen regularly when we get into football season."

"Then what's the nonsense I'm being made to sit through today?"

"Practice."

I rolled my eyes, which seemed to amuse Kannon.

"I made the team."

Well, that explains the uniform. Did he really need to tell me when it was obvious? I guess so.

"Good for you. It's a little surprising that your owner is allowing you to take part outside of his little clique."

"Evie," he chided.

"Got any idea of when the meathead is coming for me?"

Kannon shook his head.

"Useful as always. Good luck tonight."

Moving around him, I kept a straight path while wondering if Anzide had done anything to antagonize Kannon. It was guaranteed that he would have made himself appear to Kannon while remaining hidden from everyone else. It didn't matter, anyway. Kannon would know that Anzide was always around to protect me.

Feeling an arm slide around my shoulder, I glanced at Anzide and the supreme smile on his face.

"You're so mean."

"You were the one that was mean to him. I just ensure that the wound is regularly reopened."

I tried not to laugh as I opened the door to the office. It would seem odd, considering that Anzide was never seen by Jane, the receptionist. The demon principal, though, that was a different story.

As I walked in, I stopped. James was talking to an older woman and the new girl.

Clearly, mother and daughter, there were limited differences between them. Both had fair skin with rich coppery hair and bright green eyes. Height, body shape, and age were the major differences

"Evelyn," James said eagerly. "Come in."

Giving an awkward smile, I closed the door and hoped that Anzide made it in before the door swung shut because I could not see him at the moment.

"This is our new student, Karina Daniels, and her

mother, Nora. They're vampires."

I looked at the desk and noticed that Jane was not here. That explained mister *blast the secrets* here.

"Cool,"

Nora smiled at me.

"I've already discussed the situation with Nora and told her that her placement in this town weighs heavily on her choices regarding the coven she associates with."

"It is always to the legal owner of the land if you're wondering." Nora interrupted.

I nodded, a little surprised at the sudden statement. James hesitated and gritted a smile at me.

"She's already had a run-in with someone from the Fleming clan."

"Me too," I said eagerly. "He's a char-grilled vampire now."

Nora chuckled, turning to James.

"You were right. She is a riot."

"And the perfect leader for our little town."

"Got to win the war first. With that in mind, I'd suggest you lie low for a while, avoid giving direct answers if they push you to decide, and stay as neutral as possible."

"Numbers will help, Evelyn."

"I know, but for their safety, they should try to avoid

incurring their wrath."

James didn't look impressed but accepted it with a nod.

"Of course. In the meantime, you can show Karina around the school."

"Sure. I need to talk to you later as well."

"I look forward to it. Better hurry, or Mrs Winslow will wonder where you are."

I nodded, holding the door open for the new girl. Her mother smiled eagerly at me. It was not surprising because I was the leader of a vampire coven, and she was a vampire eagerly searching for an association.

"It was lovely to meet you, Evelyn."

"You too, Nora."

We began the awkward walk to the doors. I looked at Karina, and she hesitantly laughed.

"This is weird, right?"

"More so considering I've only been here a few weeks myself."

"Really?"

"Yeah, and everyone calls me Evie."

She nodded. Karina was definitely a girl that walked the same path in life as me. She was yet to receive the uniform, so Karina was dressed in casual clothes. Wearing jeans, a shirt, and a sweatshirt wrapped around her waist, her style was so much like mine it was almost like we were twins. That is if I wasn't wearing the stupid uniform. Karina even topped the outfit off with army boots. I usually wore joggers but wanted a pair of boots.

"It's kind of cool that you're the leader of the Corbin clan after,"

Karina stopped, her fingers pressed against her lips as she stared at me in horror.

"I am so sorry, Evie. I forgot what Mister Harlwood said about your grandfather."

"Great-grandfather and it's okay. Niko was a wonderful teacher, and I am always grateful for the time that I had with him. I can't change what happened, but I am in the middle of dealing with my anger and the vengeance that I promised."

"Mister Harlwood said that there was a blood war going on."

"Does it concern you?"

Karina shrugged. She seemed fairly easy going.

"Seems rather calm, but I guess the other guy isn't about to advertise what's happening. The humans are so blase, aren't they?"

"That's the obscuris veil that Mister Harlwood put over the town. You notice it because you're new, and you're a vampire."

We reached the door in our slow walk. It was obvious that neither of us was eager to leave the quiet corridor.

"We were also told that you're technically not a vampire."

"Yep, a mixed bag of goodies."

Karina giggled, smiling at me.

"Because of Niko, I have vampire traits in me. My great-grandmother was a shapeshifter,"

"Cool," she interrupted. "I wish that I could have met her."

One day, you will.

"Well, you can blame Drakkus for ordering the hit on her and my grandparents."

"He's so lame," she muttered under her breath.

"My grandparents, well, my grandmother was half-half, and my grandfather was human."

"Interesting selections there."

I chuckled, nodding. The smile on my face faded as I thought about my mother.

"Next along are my mother and my uncle Brad. My mother died a couple of years ago, and Brad's been my guardian ever since. He's only just started to take on a fully formed side, which is vampirism. My mother, I don't know. I knew nothing about this life until we came here. She said nothing, and I don't know if she actually knew."

We stopped at the gates. I gripped the pole and looked at Karina. It seemed as if she could sense the tension.

"My father is unknown. The current belief is that because my mother was a prostitute, I result of one of her interactions with a client. As for my father, he is a biblical creature."

Karina stared at me, her mouth agape.

"They call them Eternals, and a Phoenix is created when a powerful Eternal breeds with a non-biblical creature. Apparently, we're a rare kind of Eternal. We're classed as one and should not breed with mortals or immortals, just our own kind. It's the same for all Eternals. If we do, it's a death sentence for the other person. Essentially, my father doomed my mother to death."

"Oh," she said, drawing out the word.

"Yeah, oh. She got in a few years, and it wasn't what killed her, but her life was always ticking away."

"That's terrible. How could he do something like that?"

Karina kept talking as she walked through the gate. I looked at Anzide, who gave me a sympathetic smile.

I suspected he knew who my father was, but I'd made Anzide promise to never tell me because I wasn't interested in knowing my father. Even though it was standard for a phoenix to be trained by their maker, I said no.

Entering the field, I made my way along the wide sideline to the bleachers. Most of the class was seated in the upper section, scattered across the long white wood planks. Mrs Winslow was helping a student with something and was distracted enough to be completely oblivious to the rest of the class.

As we approached the bleachers, I saw Audrey Hartley, my other nemesis. She also happened to be Kannon's secret lover, and she knew the dastardly plans he had cooked up with Drakkus to lure me in.

"Oh, Evie," Audrey said sweetly. "You can't try out for cheerleading."

"What a shame. I guess I'll just have to sit on the bleachers and watch you make an ass out of yourself instead."

Karina giggled, which was probably a mistake. Audrey scowled at her.

"You're not too smart, are you, new girl?"

"Smart enough to realize that you will never win against Evie."

Audrey was stunned, staring at Karina as she turned and climbed onto the first step. When she realized I was smiling at her, Audrey frowned at me.

"It doesn't matter. You'll be dead soon, anyway."

"You're a fool if you believe that."

Turning away, I climbed up the bleachers and sat next to Karina. Anzide was always a step behind and remained hidden as he sat beside me.

"What's her story?"

"That's Audrey Hartley. She's the queen bee of the rest of those girls. I've dubbed them the cashmere brigade. I don't know how they get away with it, but when they're supposed to be in uniform, they alter it with things like cashmere jumpers. Once, they all wore matching black pearls until I insulted them. They were a gift from Drakkus, who was clearly trying to buy them. Audrey's father is a builder who's cut a deal with Drakkus to get himself a little monopolization on the town. He was the one that told Drakkus that there was a crack in our basement wall."

"And sold your great-grandfather out." She murmured. "Mister Harlwood told us about that."

"Well, Audrey kept trying to make me hand over the leadership to Drakkus. When being sweet didn't work, she threatened me, even got a little physical until she saw this."

Karina's eyes widened at the sight of the necklace.

"That's a coven jewel."

I nodded quietly. Karina knew way more about being a vampire than what I did. Niko had given the necklace to me, but I didn't get a chance to ask him about it, and since then, I'd forgotten. It was lucky that Niko wasn't really dead and that I could ask him when I returned home.

CHAPTER 2

James leaned back in his seat, smiling with a shrug.

"Was it wrong to invite them?"

"No, but,"

"But what, Evelyn? They're vampires. Nora wants to know that her daughter is safe when she feeds because Karina has expressed an interest in doing it by herself. At eighteen, it is only natural for a young vampire to yearn for a little freedom."

"I just meant that it seems like you're trying to find a friend for me."

"Well, it wasn't intentional, but I suppose it seems like it was. I made a list of what I wanted for this town. At the moment, my primary focus is to assist the true leader of Hades without actually helping. One aspect of that is to provide support through other people, in this case, vampires. I went searching, and I found Nora. We sat down and discussed the situation and what my expectations were."

"It wasn't a standard lure?"

"No. As I said, I have a primary focus at the moment. It serves a purpose for me, too. Vampires feed, and the departed always find a way to the demon that is waiting for them, regardless of how they die. That list is completed, Evelyn. I have the paranormal residents that I believe will help you in this war. That leaves me with nothing to do, and I detest boredom. So, with that in mind, I would like to return to our conversation regarding the lures. Before that, I must apologize for not stopping by to say hello to Niko. I was a little distracted by the list, but I will visit soon."

"I'll let him know."

"Thank you. Now, Nora has taken over the vacant position as the real estate agent. It might interest you to know that they have also found a cute little house in the next street from your place. Just a short walk through a path between the two properties."

That was rather convenient. It made me wonder if I'd given off lonely vibes. I wasn't trying to, but maybe I had been. Brad might have had something to do with this. He was always droning on about me making a friend. Yes, it definitely reeks of his nonsense.

"And the other paranormals you mentioned?"

"Oh, just the standard people," he said with a vagueness that I found curious.

"Hiding something, James?"

He smiled. "Always. Fear not, Evelyn. I only invite

paranormals who are aligned with my interests. Any in this town that are not that way were the ones invited by Hannah at her master's request. The vile little demon is gone, but we cannot do anything about the legacy she has left behind. The vermin will emerge in the days after the war is over, and those loyal to the Corbin clan will see to their demise or departure."

I looked at James and wondered if he was creating a coven for me. We weren't sure who could be trusted in this town, so he was going elsewhere. Bringing in fresh blood was a good idea. It was also great that he had them lining up to be a member of the Corbin coven, provided that they were actually being honest.

"Now, as I said to you previously, I'd like to modernize Hades just a little. I know you've agreed to it, and I will be mindful not to attract too many humans. When we discussed the new agreement, I stated what I'd like, but you did not offer anything, believing that you had nothing to offer me. It is a technicality, and I can ignore it if I choose, but I believe in friendly relations with all, especially the leader. I don't have to ask you to throw a lure out, but I want your permission. You've given that, and now I feel indebted to you. I've given this a lot of thought, Evelyn. When I approached you with the alteration to the first agreement, I believed that you'd ask that I repair the house. Your request to repair Niko was commendable, and I understand why you requested it. The problem that I have is that if Niko was left alone, he wouldn't have almost died. You would have continued on, and if things had returned to the path that your life was on, you still would have destroyed the house."

It was clear that James wanted me to take something else rather than repairing Niko. The problem was that my great-grandfather was my world, and we needed him. Brad was having so many issues with the alterations in his body, feeding, and becoming accustomed to a new way of life. It was necessary that Niko returned to us quickly.

"My offer is one that I give with pure sincerity because, from the first moment, I saw a great leader in you. You are honest, you are determined, and you will always do what is right for everyone. Just like Niko, you are the kind of leader that I want ruling this town. Therefore, I give without strings. I always will. I would like to discuss this with Brad and Niko as well if you don't mind."

"Of course. I'd like it if they were involved."

"Good. I will visit later this afternoon. Now, what did you want to talk to me about?"

"Larry."

That intrigued James. He sat forward in his chair, leaning on the desk.

"And what of our darling police officer?"

"He pulled me over the other day and said that someone had told him I was driving without a license. I laid it out and told him to be wise about the steps that he makes from now on because I am the leader. Then I asked him if he wanted anything, and he said protection for himself and his family from now until the end of time, I guess."

"Self-serving and noble. What troubles you about this request? It is easily given."

"Is it? I said that the generations of family would have to present themselves, but it's just so daunting when you think about how many people that could be. And I keep thinking it's not enough. Kannon said that Drakkus bought him off with the protection, refit of the station, and a new cruiser. What else is there to give him?"

"Are you still associating with the Lothaire boy?"

"No, this was a while ago. Now I'm just stringing him along for the fun of it."

That amused James.

"And Anzide likes to taunt him regularly."

"Nephilim are good at that."

Anzide got a smile that was full of haughtiness.

"We are, and I do like annoying the boy."

"More like you enjoy creating problems."

With a shrug, Anzide showed his indifference.

"Anyway, what can I offer Larry?"

James shifted his seat closer to the desk, still leaning on the paper blotter.

"Evelyn, Larry was given the opportunity to ask for anything he could think of. He would already know that a vampire would willingly splash thousands, if not hundreds of thousands of dollars to bribe the police. That is why he got so much from Drakkus. Larry saw that fool walk into his world, and he took Drakkus to the cleaners. Clearly, he knows that there is nothing else to ask for, so he went with the only thing that has value to him now—the lives of those he loves. Give the man what he asked for, and if you're worried, set up an account with money in it in case Larry changes his mind."

I nodded but still felt that my commitment was lacking.

"If you start, then Drakkus will also start. The bidding war may begin as small gestures toward Larry, but it will end in the grandest things money can buy. The only one who will benefit is Larry, who will get too big for his britches and then start lording it over everyone in the town. It will arouse suspicion, and the townsfolk will wonder where he's getting the money from. His expectations for a higher level of bribery will grow, and soon, he will not care what kind of light he shines upon the town. No matter what you do, you will always have a competitor in Drakkus. Goad him into a fight, and you will soon find out what kind of a sore loser he is. I have given my advice. Be it on your head if you choose to ignore me."

"I don't want to ignore you. I just don't want to seem like a skinflint."

"Perhaps a return to the subject after the war is over might help ease the conflict in your mind. When everything is done, and there is no opponent to up the ante, you can visit Larry and thank him for his dedication to your leadership. Does that ease the burden?"

"I think so."

James smiled warmly at me, clearly pleased I was listening to him.

As I stood, I pulled the bag strap onto my shoulder.

"So, I'll see you later?"

"Is an hour sufficient?"

"Yep."

"Good. I will see you then."

Anzide was holding the door open, silent in his observations as always. He didn't say anything until we were outside.

"He's determined to oust Drakkus, isn't he?"

"Is it odd?"

"Do you mean from my limited worldly experience as an eternal?"

"Yeah."

Anzide shrugged.

"Demons will always have their own motives, and they usually keep them hidden. In this case, I think that James has reasons that are obvious, with maybe some things that are hidden. It would probably be wise to discuss it with the unseen one as he knew him for years."

"But that was a long time ago," I muttered.

Would Niko know what James was likely to do now

after all these years?

Stopping in the middle of the path, Anzide wrapped his arms around me. I glanced at the field that was still in sight and wondered if I looked odd.

"Are you still hidden?"

"Nope."

"So the vampire standing at the sideline watching us is just a coincidence?"

"Absolutely."

The grin was adorable, and I couldn't resist when Anzide was this playful. He leaned down and kissed me, making a show of it. Of course, he made it worse by letting the hands wander down my back and curving over my backside. I chuckled, ending the kiss.

"You're a monster."

"True, but you have to agree that he deserves it and a whole lot worse."

"I suppose so."

"You suppose? Evie," he chided.

My lips tightened as a curl curved into the corner.

"I see, you're just teasing me."

"Always. Our life is just one big tease."

"Tell me about it," Anzide groaned. "Give a man a taste of Heaven and rip it away from him with family dinners that include a guardian that's no longer needed, giving me a death stare."

"Brad's always needed."

"You're eighteen, and you're an eternal."

"I know, but you're missing the point. I get it. You don't really understand the deeper needs of these frail humans."

"Vampire, and I seem to recall that I was the one that pointed out he wasn't coping with the changes in the relationship dynamics."

"Yeah," I murmured softly as we began the long walk home. "I guess that he's learning. Maybe the additions have helped."

"It is likely to be the reason."

We were about to turn towards the forest when I saw Brad's car in the distance.

"Either he's forgotten that I said we'd walk home, or he's just conveniently driving past at the right time."

Brad stopped, giving us a confused frown.

"I'd say it's a little from each column," Anzide said as he opened the door for me.

When Anzide was in the car, Brad looked at the both of us.

"What are you two doing here so late?"

"I told you that I was going to see James after school.

He's coming over for a chat in an hour."

"For what?" he muttered, turning the car around.

"He's getting bent out of shape about the agreement and how I wasn't supposed to ask him to repair Niko. I think he wants to fix the house."

"Well, that would be helpful."

Brad drove past the real estate agency. Karina was out front with her mother. When she saw me, she waved eagerly. Hesitantly, I waved back.

"Did you make a friend?"

"Maybe."

"Good."

"They're vampires. James asked them to come here. Her mother is Hannah's replacement."

"And she gave a minor slaying to Audrey," Anzide added.

"Seriously, minor."

"But noteworthy all the same."

Brad looked at me, giving me a nod that I guess meant that I should agree with Anzide.

"Well, she stuck up for herself, which is always worth something. They're also eager to join the coven. Apparently, they've already had a run-in with someone from the Fleming clan."

"What a surprise," Brad muttered. "Can we trust them?"

"James searched and found them. I think he's trying to give us a coven of outsiders who he can guarantee are loyal rather than the unknowns that are already living here."

Brad sighed heavily as he pulled into our street. I had to agree. The entire situation was stressful, and there wasn't a single thing we could do to stop the inevitable.

CHAPTER 3

Niko stood near the dining table and shook his head. Putting the only dining chair to survive my anger down, he flicked his fingers and gestured for everyone to get out of their seats.

"Why?" Brad grumbled.

"Because we are going to start conducting proper meetings. Evie is the leader, therefore she sits at the head of the table. Her second in charge, which is you, sits to her right. Anzide should be on the left. Beatrice and I will take the other places."

"Don't you think you should be in the dining chair?"

Niko looked at me curiously.

"You are the leader, Evelyn."

"No, you are."

"I am dead to the world."

"And I'm an Eternal. I should not be allowed to lead a coven. Aren't there rules against it?"

"No."

And with that, Niko ignored my frustration and sat down on the bench seat. Beatrice silently smiled as she sat on the opposite side. Once they'd both slid across the vinyl, Brad and Anzide sat down.

Niko pushed a scrap of paper across the table, nodding at it when I looked at him.

"That's your order of business."

With a huff, I moved the chair closer, sat down, and took the piece of paper. Brad was smirking, which earned him a scowl. He didn't care, which was not surprising.

"Okay, so old business."

I looked up and saw the plain faces.

"Well, this is working well."

"Perhaps we could address your attitude." Brad offered.

"Sure. This is a meeting for the Corbin coven. Everyone in that coven is in this tin can, and they know that Niko is not dead. I'm not supposed to be sitting in this chair. Niko is the leader."

"You are only partially correct, Evelyn. The fact that I am not dead, that everyone in our little coven is sitting here and knows I am not dead, is correct. That's where it ends, I'm afraid. Regardless of your deity status, you are the one who engaged Drakkus in the ending of the blood war. Only you can complete it, and a part of that is that you are the leader of the Corbin clan when you do. I cannot take over as leader until you have done that. If I do and Drakkus dies, we enter into a negative void that will engulf the town. Vampires will leave, and we won't get any new members to enter our coven. There is no physical wall, but one will emerge in the days after the void begins. It will shroud the town in darkness and abysmal weather."

"Wait,"

I sat up, looking at Brad.

"The weather was atrocious when we first came here. Now it's not."

"That's because the void that Drakkus caused when he tried to take the leadership from me has receded. You freed me, and you took leadership of the Corbin clan. I actually find it surprising that the Europeans didn't notice that I wasn't around."

"They did." Beatrice offered. "Drakkus played nice, pretended that he knew nothing about what happened. The idiots left without an investigation or even bothering to interview anyone other than the clan members. I was considered new to town, so they didn't even glance in my direction."

Niko gave an indifferent shrug and turned back to me.

"Is that the explanation that you need to accept that you cannot change things at the moment?"

"I guess."

"When the time comes, I will take back the leadership, and you will be free of the burden. The only thing I ask of you and Anzide is that you remain within the clan as senior members and members of my committee. Beatrice will take on the role of my second in charge, and Bradley will be taking on a senior role as well. Now, if we're done with coven roles, I suggest that we discuss the house. I've noticed there has been talk about the old plans."

I looked between Niko and Beatrice, wondering what they'd think if we suggested that the house, the way it was, wouldn't suit us as we are now or in the future. Anzide looked at me with a soft smile and a slight shift in his eyebrows. The waggle that said I should be brave and just throw it out there.

"Okay, so we're thinking about the long term here, okay? Please don't be offended."

"We won't be offended, darling," Beatrice said.

"Good, because I'm thinking about the many years ahead of us. We're essentially three families because Brad will find a girlfriend, and you guys are, uh, you know."

Beatrice grinned at me.

"In love, like we always have been?"

"Yeah, that's the one."

"Are you suggesting that Niko and I might like to have another child, and perhaps the others around this table might, too?"

"Yep."

Embarrassment central.

Beatrice nodded. She turned to Niko and smiled at him.

"She has a point, darling. We always talked about having another child. Perhaps when the war is over, we might finally be free to welcome more children."

And not have the weight of Drakkus hanging over them. Or any of us.

I looked at Brad. He'd been caught in the lure of a demon employed by Drakkus. She'd gotten close and caused issues between him and me, all while pretending she was interested in him. They hadn't gotten far, but I guess it was enough to make him feel bad about it.

"We could. For now, it will be thought about and discussed again once the war is over. As for this house, it doesn't matter what you build so long as you rest here. The coven leader must reside within the boundary that I marked as the Corbin coven sanctuary. A side note on that, any vampire that is part of another coven cannot enter our land."

"Is that why Kannon doesn't jump the fence?"

"Yes."

"But he used to come here all the time."

"And that was when he made you believe he wanted to be a part of your coven. Now that you know differently, his ability to enter the land has ended."

That meant that, in theory, this was a sanctuary from all vampires who were not in our coven. All I had to do was make it to the property, and I would be safe. It wouldn't stop something from being fired from the fence line, though.

"Does the spell that James placed over the property stop things being fired from the fence line?" I whispered to Anzide.

"Yes. It also stops all vampires. The technicality of the sanctuary is that a vampire who is not associated with another coven can enter the property. James temporarily stopped that technicality."

"What about Nora and Karina if they join the coven?"

Anzide looked at me and offered a shrug.

"I'm sure that if James intended for them to join the coven, he would have altered it to accommodate them. We can check when he visits."

With my lips pressed tight, I nodded. It was information that I found interesting and somewhat helpful. Turning back to the meeting, Niko looked up from the house plans and shrugged.

"You can change the house as you please. I understand your point of view and agree with you. Each of us will enter into a new situation as we progress in our lives, and the house will be inadequate for the future. Which brings us to the subject of money. How do you propose to pay for the build?"

"It will come from my portion of the inheritance." Brad began. "I believe that Evie needs to be seen as financially fluid so the majority of her money will remain untouched. We can keep the other expenses low if we're careful. You and I don't eat food, so it's only groceries for three and other little things like cleaning stuff, I guess."

"Will there be enough now that we plan on making changes?"

"I don't know. We'll have to sketch some ideas, take them to Henry, and see what he says. I can't really do that until you've risen from the dead unless I try and tell him that I want an enormous house for three people."

"Well, for the time being, we will stick to the original house plans. Once the war is over and I'm back in the land of living, we will readdress the issue. In the meantime,"

Niko turned his watch, looking at it.

"James will be here soon. Perhaps we should move onto new business."

"Okay. I guess the new vampires in town might cover that, right?"

Niko nodded.

"So, James said he searched for a few paranormals and asked them to come here. I have only met two of them. Mother and daughter. The mother, Nora, works at the real estate agency, replacing Hannah. Karina goes to school. She's in her final year. Apparently, they live in the next street."

"Interesting. Do they seem acceptable to join the coven?"

"You're not making me decide, are you?"

"I am. You are the leader, Evelyn. They will ask to join our coven, and you must decide if they will join or if they will be sent on their way. Perhaps a wise choice should be made considering the effort James has gone to."

I groaned, rolling my head back.

"I told her that she should remain neutral until the war is over. This kind of information would have been handy *before* a vampire asked to join."

"True. Perhaps you could take a walk and visit Nora and tell her that if she is still interested, she can join our coven."

"But she might come here. Then she'll see you and you," I said, turning to Beatrice.

"Maybe we could cut them off at the door," Brad suggested. "Niko and Beatrice can go behind the curtain, and hopefully, no one will see a thing."

"Fine."

Getting up from the table, I trudged out the door with my handsome personal guard following.

"I don't know where she lives."

"James has just arrived," Anzide offered. "You could

ask him."

Leaning, I looked out the door and saw James getting out of his car.

"Alright."

Anzide followed me to the driveway to greet the intrigued demon.

"Are you leaving, Evelyn?"

"It was suggested that when a vampire asks to join a coven, a yes or no answer is given. Not my, *sit on the fence and remain neutral* suggestion."

He chuckled and nodded. Turning to face the street, he pointed at a house.

"See the green roof over there. That's the house. Shall I delay the conversation until you return?"

"I think you won't be given a choice. He's in a formal mood. Good luck."

James chuckled again. As we walked down the driveway, he crossed the lawn to the caravan.

Taking the path between the two houses, I looked over the low chain fence and saw Nora near her car. When she saw me approach, Nora smiled.

"Hello, Evelyn. Are you here to see Karina?"

"Both of you, actually. I'm kind of new to the whole leader of a vampire clan thing, so I wasn't aware that suggesting that you remain neutral was not how it's done. I apologize, and I am now up to speed with things. If you are still interested in joining the Corbin clan, you and Karina are welcome to do so."

"Oh, it's okay. We're kind of new to things, too. We'd love to join."

Karina appeared at the door. Her eyes widened when she saw me.

"Evie?" she said, thumping her way down the porch steps. "How come you're here?"

"Brought up to speed on vampire etiquette and now making things right."

"I just accepted an invitation for us to join the Corbin clan."

"Awesome. So,"

Karina's eyes slid to the figure next to me. I didn't realize Anzide had appeared to them because I always saw him but never really knew if he was hiding from the world unless he said something.

"Sorry. Things just escape me. This is my partner, Anzide. He's a Nephilim, and he's always around me, but because of Drakkus, you may or may not see him. So, sorry about the deception."

"It's okay, Evelyn. An unseen guard is always wise. Do not be sorry for protecting yourself from a monster."

"Sure. Anyway, my uncle Brad is my second in charge, so if you have any issues, you can go to the property. The house is kind of scattered, but he'll probably be in the caravan."

I expected to see confusion, but there wasn't any. It made me wonder how much James had said. I guess it was necessary to inform vampires that, at the moment, there wasn't a coven house. Just coven land and a pile of rubble.

"Well, we have to go to a meeting, so we'll see you around."

"Sure. We'll stop by to say hello to your uncle."

Anzide and I started the journey back to the property.

"Well?"

"Clear in regards to what you want and need."

"But?"

"But the past is not exactly nice. Let Karina tell you in her own time. Don't push her because their maker was not good to them."

Now it made sense as to why James brought them here. It wasn't about Karina feeding safely. It clearly had to do with the past. I was curious, but I wouldn't make Karina tell me. If she wanted to vent, then I'd listen.

We returned to the caravan as quickly as we could.

Brad had brought in a lawn chair to sit on while James was on the dining chair. When we returned, James was distracted by talking to Niko and Beatrice. Apparently, James knew the secret that she kept because a demon knows all creatures, and the woman that she was didn't make sense.

"Well, where to begin?" James said eagerly. "I thought about the situation after you left, and on the way here, I finalized what I thought would be a good suggestion. I considered two paths, but now that I'm here and see the situation, I will lean towards the house. It is obvious that you're all struggling in this place, and I might add that a metal box is not ideal for vampires during a hot day. You're just lucky that it's started to cool off. Of course, the freezing cold is also a problem, so before the hinges ice up, let's get the offer out there. The house in its original state, while beautiful, is not what you need."

"We were just talking about that. How crazy is that?" Brad said, thoroughly amused.

"Great minds think alike. Anyway, I considered the options. Building bigger is always an option, but you'd be left with no yard and the risk of being too close to the fence line. My suggestion is that you purchase the houses on either side of this property. It would be a long-term plan because the main house needs to be started first. This will remain the Corbin clan house, and when Niko has returned to the rule, Evelyn and Brad can move into the house on either side. Now, you're going to tell me that you don't have the funds for that, which leads me to the second portion of the offer. There is a spell that I can place over a bank account. It has to be with a certain bank, but I will help you deal with that part of it as they don't advertise this account, and if you ask about it, you'll raise a lot of flags."

"But the spell?" Niko asked, sounding a little confused.

"It's a reset spell. Whatever amount you put into this account is the base figure. You can withdraw all but a dollar from it, and at midnight, it will reset to that amount. I can place the spell on the account until the house is built if you like."

Brad shifted forward, leaning on the dining table.

"So, the houses. Can I withdraw all but one dollar and put it into another account and start saving to purchase the two houses?"

"Yes, you can. I would suggest that your secondary account remains at this bank as they are a little, how do I put it? Let's say that they are aligned with the immortal way of life. You bank with them, don't you, Niko?"

"Yes. I'm sure my account has grown rather wildly over the years. Of course, I cannot access it without raising those flags, so for now, it must remain as it is. I must say, I like your offer, James. It's not giving us money, but it's easing the burden that Evelyn and Bradley face. I also like the idea of the two houses. It will allow Evelyn and Anzide to grow as a couple, and in time, Bradley will find a partner, and they will have a home. Close but far enough away to seem adequate."

I looked at Anzide, who gave me a slight shrug. Our own home, completely alone without anyone else around. It seemed exciting and daunting.

CHAPTER 4

James was waiting outside the office when I walked into the main corridor. He gave me a fond smile as he opened the door.

"Good morning, Evelyn. Jane has your new schedule."

"Thank you."

He didn't follow me into the office, remaining outside to greet the students as they walked to their classes. I was a little late, but after the meeting yesterday, James said my schedule was altering anyway, so it would be okay.

Jane smiled at me as she passed it over. With my gratitude given, I made my way out of the office. James was distracted by talking to a student. I moved quickly, noticing that my first class of the day was starting in half an hour.

When I turned the corner, I was surprised to see the second locker door open. It shut, and I was faced with Karina.

"Evie," she said with a beaming smile.

"Uh, hey Karina. Did they stick you in the,"

I was going to say the darkness, but I looked up and saw the light was on.

"Typical," I muttered.

"Is something wrong?"

"Just that they finally turned the lights on in this corridor. They never used to, and the doors open the wrong way for the light coming from the main corridor. I was considering buying a battery-operated light."

"Well, lucky you didn't, eh?"

"Yeah, I guess so."

Opening my locker door, I stuffed the books for the afternoon lessons and shut the door. Karina was all smiles, but it soon faded. Her gaze landed somewhere behind me. Seeing the uneasiness on her face, I turned to see Audrey and the cashmere brigade behind me.

Audrey smiled supremely.

"Oh look, the freak has a friend. Now there's two freaks."

"So ingenious," I muttered. "How do you cope with all that brain power?"

She ignored me, which was not surprising. Audrey tilted to the side, looking at Karina.

"You might have the potential to join our group, but

you need to lose the whole grunge vibe with your make-up and, of course, ditching the loser beside you. You're new in this town, so I'll fill you in. We are the ones that you want to make friends with. I'm sure that you don't want to be labeled as an outcast like someone else has been."

I looked at Karina, who had a fearful look in her eyes. She didn't want to upset me because I was the clan leader, and she was the newly approved member. In all honesty, I didn't care if she was nice to Audrey. If she became a part of the cashmere brigade and started taunting me like Audrey does, then I might be a bit angry. Then, I would be having words with James because, clearly, it would be an issue. I couldn't tell Karina what I knew about Audrey and Kannon unless we were alone. There was nothing I could do about this. I just had to accept that leaving this to Karina to figure out was the only option I had.

"I can't recall if I told you yesterday, but they know about your species."

"Vampires?" she whispered.

I nodded and smiled. Surprisingly, she smiled back. When it was directed at me, the smile was sweet. It soon turned dark as the corners increased and the mouth opened. Her fangs appeared, and the innocent new girl just got bitey.

Audrey and her lackeys stepped back. Their eyes widened in momentary horror and shock.

"I guess you didn't get the memo. The new girl is a

vampire and knows who the true leader of this town is. Run away, little girl. Run before this vampire decides that she didn't have enough for breakfast."

Glancing at me, Audrey waited for something. I merely smiled while raising my eyebrows expectantly. She let out an exaggerated huff, turned on her heels, and stormed off. The rest of the girls followed, though in a less than melodramatic way.

"You'll never be cool now."

"Okay, well one, I am cool because the leader of the coven has the locker next to mine, and I can totally see a friendship forming."

Karina stared at me with a crazy grin.

"Totally."

"Two, I'm going to be here for less than a year, and three, if being cool meant putting up with her nonsense, I'd give it a hard pass."

"Well, so long as you know what you're doing."

With a nod of reassurance, Karina smiled. It didn't last long. She fidgeted in her uniform, frowning as she pulled out a crumpled scrap of paper.

"I hate the uniform. My last school was casual."

"Me too," I murmured.

The crumpled paper was actually her lesson schedule. Karina looked over at mine, which was sitting on top of my books.

"Oh my god. You have the same first lesson as me. Please tell me there's a spare seat next to you."

"Lucky you."

She squealed with happiness as we began to walk to the stairs.

"I did not think that I'd,"

Pausing, Karina looked at me cautiously.

"Probably taking that too far. Never mind."

"It's okay."

"We can be friends, right? The whole leader thing isn't going to cause problems, is it?"

I shrugged. What could I say? In an unknown amount of time, I wouldn't be the leader, and everything would be fine. Sure, blurt out to the world that Niko's not dead. Risk his life and his recovery just to be reassuring.

Anzide, who was clearly hidden from Karina because she hadn't looked at him or acknowledged him, smiled softly.

"I'm sure it will be fine."

"Awesome. So, would it bring down the mood to talk about the past?"

Again, I shrugged.

"I don't find my past so rude that I won't talk about it, but others have found it offensive."

"Oh, sorry, I meant me. But I get what you're saying. Sometimes, we don't have much of a choice in the life that we lead. If your mother couldn't get a job, then maybe it was the only way she could get money. I don't get why people get their noses out of joint about the job. At least they're trying to make money for themselves rather than relying on government handouts or stealing."

I nodded.

"I am open about my mother. I don't think her life or her job was wrong, but there are aspects of our personal life together that were wrong. She was always angry at me, and she hit me. I was always made to feel as if I was a burden on her life. There were times when she would be sober, and she'd offer to play a game of hide and seek. I'd hide, and she'd try to find me. I never understood it at the time, but she always said *you can run, but you can't hide.* I used to think that she meant from her because she would say it when I was hiding somewhere. Now I think that what she meant was from Drakkus."

"You think she was teaching you how to hide if he found you?"

I nodded, feeling the weight of the past bear down on me.

"She wasn't a great mother, but she could be a good one. I think she drank because of what she knew was out there searching for us. No one knows what the truth is, though. She never said anything to Brad, so it's one of those things that will always remain unknown. But that's basically it."

We'd reached the second floor, slowly making our way towards the classroom. There was no rush. Our class didn't start for another twenty minutes.

"Must have been hard."

"She created a survivor, and a part of me likes to believe it was intentional. Learn how to take a beating, get back up, and soldier on. How not to cower in a corner because some scary man is standing over me."

"She made a warrior."

I shrugged. There wasn't much else that I could offer. I had mixed thoughts about the subject. A part of me felt like my mother was a monster because she raised her hand repeatedly, but the other part of me whispered that she knew what was chasing us. The problem was that one outweighed the other. She could have created the warrior with love and support. She could have enrolled me in self-defense classes. Her methods were not ideal, and I had to stop trying to justify her actions.

The door was open. I showed Karina to the desk where I usually sat and showed her the one that was always empty. It was a small class, so there were a few free desks. We were alone at the moment.

"So, I guess you're wondering about me, right?"

I was taken aback for a moment, then shrugged uneasily.

"Look, if it's too difficult,"

"No, no." Karina interrupted. "It's kind of cathartic.

It's just my mother and me now. I don't remember much about my father, but he left when I was young. We were human up until I was sixteen. A vampire abducted us. I guess he wanted to make a family. We were both turned. He kept us locked up, but we escaped. James offered us sanctuary here in Hades. He said that my growth is stunted because a human should not be turned until they're at least eighteen. So, I kind of still look sixteen. It will take a couple of years for me to look like an eighteen-year-old, but once I get there, I'll be fine. I was made to do a test because I missed so many days of school."

"Looked like an overcooked lobster?"

Karina giggled and nodded.

"I'm okay now, but I have to do this year with a lesson plan created especially for me based on the test results."

"Me too."

We compared our lesson plans, noticing that we had quite a few classes together. I smiled at Karina's enthusiasm while silently wondering if a certain demon had anything to do with this.

If James had invited Nora and Karina to the town, I assume that he would have checked them out and made sure that they were worthy to be a part of my coven. He wanted this to be Corbin territory again, and I seriously doubt that he would make such a grave mistake as inviting unacceptable vampires to move here.

The door opened, and the teacher walked in, giving us a warm smile and hello. It was the end of our conversation about parents, makers, and our lives. As some of the other students entered the room, I glanced at Anzide, who was at the window, hidden from everyone but me.

Anzide gave me an uneasy smile. He'd heard it all, but it wasn't the first time he had heard it. Entering her mind had given him a first-hand view of the ordeal, and when I saw the sad smile, I could tell that Karina had left a lot of the details out.

I wondered if it was illegal to turn a child into a vampire. Later, when I was home, I would ask Niko. There wasn't much that we could do unless Nora and Karina offered more information so that we could find the perpetrator, but I was a leader. I figured it was my duty to ensure they understood that justice could be found if it was available to them.

It was mind-boggling. How would we find a rogue vampire without the help of the authorities? There would be no database of information. We'd have to rely on information and maybe let the whispers whip around their hometown to see if we could lure him out.

Then, there was the question of what to do with him. If Kannon was right, it was illegal for vampires to kill each other. I know that Drakkus didn't care about that rule, but I did. Of course, I wasn't a vampire, but I was acting under the instruction of one. I was the leader of a vampire clan, and I had to be responsible for my decisions and actions.

I was definitely going to have to talk to Niko about this. It was beyond my abilities, and I didn't want to say the wrong thing to Karina.

CHAPTER 5

Karina and I were in the cafeteria when Kannon entered the room. He glanced around the tables as he walked through the line and collected his lunch. I thought he'd keep going past our table and sit at the one that the jocks usually sat at. Instead, he stood at the end of our table and nodded at it.

"Mind if I join you?"

"So long as you don't mind lowering your status."

It was the last thing that I wanted, but to complicate things, it was also something that I knew could be beneficial if someone opened his foolish mouth and blurted out secrets. My fingers were crossed.

Kannon shrugged as he lifted a leg over the bench seat and sat down. Karina looked at me curiously, saying nothing as she ate her burger.

Neither of them knew that Anzide was in the room, though both probably assumed that he was there. He saw Kannon sit down and gave me a frown. It wasn't jealousy that earned me the frown, but probably closer to questioning my sanity for agreeing to this. I could say that, technically, I hadn't agreed. I merely offered a statement that offered no answer.

"So, new girl. Where are you from?"

"She's from Nunya." I offered before Karina could speak.

She grinned, saying nothing.

"Nunya? Never heard of it."

"Sure you have. It's the capital of Business."

Kannon looked at me. It was like he didn't get the joke, but Karina's giggling clued him in.

"You're so hilarious, Evie. Nunya Business. I can be curious about the new kid around here, can't I?"

"Well, one, she's not a kid. Karina is eighteen and two, she's also a vampire. It makes me think that you already know who she is and that you've been sent here by Captain Peckerhead to get her to join his coven. FYI, he's too late."

Kannon rolled his eyes.

"Drakkus didn't say anything to me. He's barely speaking to me at all."

I seriously doubt that. The statement made me want to scoff, but I restrained it and all forms of amusement that might follow. Still, I liked to tease, and when given a golden opportunity, I always indulged.

"Aww, did you have a lovers tiff?" I teased in my best

pouty voice.

"Instead of mocking me, maybe you should be looking at your own problems."

I shrugged, ignoring the statement. It wasn't his place to tell me what to do or caution me about the issues in my life. He was full of good advice that came from well-meaning intentions. I had to understand that he cared about me and Brad. We were once something, and despite what had happened, he still cared. It was enough to make me reach across the table, grab a fist full of hair, and slam his head into the plate of food. But I was a good girl and refrained from listening to the devil on my shoulder.

As I tried to tune out Kannon's ramblings, I looked at the line and saw Audrey and her friends. She was watching us, namely Kannon. I guess she didn't like that he'd been sent here to do a task. The scowl on her face said as much.

"You know what I'm talking about, right? You're supposed to be this powerful being, and you're not. It worries me that you're going into this with nothing but a few people who won't be able to help you. Brad's body is still trying to cope with becoming a vampire, and I don't see loverboy anywhere around. Word on the street is that he's a bit of a newbie, too."

Karina looked at me. I could see the frown she was giving out of the corner of my eye. I wanted to say that it was okay, and I knew what Kannon was doing, but I didn't. Silence was my game here. Let him think that he's getting the upper hand.

"Oh, and of course, you. The new girl and her mother. I'm guessing that you were turned recently if you're only eighteen. This is a battle that you're outnumbered in, Evie. I've seen the numbers. I know how many followers Drakkus has."

He reached across the table, and I swear, Audrey almost lost her tray of food. My silent gaze turned back to Kannon, ensuring that I didn't give away a single clue about my mood or thoughts.

"I care, Evie. I don't want to see you or Brad hurt. What about the newcomers? I'm sure that Karina and her mother don't want to be dead just because they believed the lies that you've sold them."

Lies? It was a little offensive to hear the king of lies suggest that I might have oversold myself and my abilities with a few fibs.

"You know that I'm right here. Do the right thing for everyone around you if you don't care about your own life. Leave town."

I picked up the drink container in front of me, giving it a jiggle. Kannon frowned, probably annoyed that I was ignoring him. I wasn't, but I was definitely trying to mess with his mind.

His eyes shifted to the container. Was it fear on his face? I couldn't tell, but I hoped it was.

"Did you get a milkshake?"

Karina nodded, appearing unsure about why I'd asked.

"Mine's empty. Do you mind if I look at yours?"

"Not at all."

Passing it over, Karina smiled with a slight frown in her brows. I'm sure she was probably wondering if her new leader had lost the plot. Sometimes, I wondered that as well.

Removing the lid, I looked at Kannon. His eyes widened. Clearly, word had spread that I was not to be trusted with milkshakes.

Kannon stood, grabbing his tray of food.

"You don't have a lot either. We should get a refill."

Putting the container on the table, I smiled at Kannon.

"Well, it was nice talking to you again, Kannon. I think your friends are waiting for you."

He looked at the table that was full of footballers. They were either looking at us or whispering about something. It wasn't hard to assume they were talking about Kannon sitting at our table.

Kannon looked like he was weighing up the options. Sit back down and risk getting assaulted by the milkshake bandit, or join his friends at the jock's table and desperately clamber his way back into popularity. I'm sure he'd make some excuse, which would be quickly forgotten.

"Yeah, whatever," he muttered.

Karina watched him, then turned to me.

"Why did you let him talk to you like that? You know that he was gaslighting you, right?"

"I know exactly what Kannon was doing, and you needn't fear my actions or intentions. My game is the long con, and I am slowly working myself into a position that will see to our victory."

"Oh, okay. So long as you know what you're doing. Hey, what was the deal with the milkshake?"

I chuckled, shifting to face her better now that I was finished with my lunch.

"Well, not that long ago, I was driving home, and Larry pulled me over. Have you met Larry yet?"

Karina shook her head.

"The town's only cop. Reasonable guy who just wants to survive and happily accepted a deal when I laid out the truth for him. Drakkus was watching, so when Larry was gone, I approached him with the milkshake I'd been drinking. Pulled out the front of his pants and upended the drink into them."

"Oh my god," she giggled. "Was he angry?"

"Furious. Imagine this guy trying to be the big man lording it over a teen girl, and she ignores his attempts only to pour a cold and sticky drink down his pants. His moment was totally gone, robbed in broad daylight."

"Call the police," Karina said with a teasing tone. "We've got ourselves a moment thief. Bet you loved every minute of it."

"It was the best feeling ever, but I kind of threw up a little later. Anzide said it was adrenaline or something."

"I wish I'd been there. I would have loved to have seen the look on his face."

"It was epic."

The bell sounded, and everyone started to file out. Kannon didn't seem to be in any hurry. I guess that was because he wasted most of his time trying to belittle me into believing his terrible words.

When most of the crowd was gone, Karina and I took our trays to the rack and began to walk out of the room. I looked back, seeing Kannon was only now getting up from the table. I guess he didn't want to talk to me again.

Notably, Audrey was still in the room. Her friends were getting closer to us, and I wanted to see what Audrey would do once her friends had passed through the doors.

As soon as the doors swung closed behind us, I grabbed Karina's arm and dragged her to the side. The doors swung open, and the cashmere brigade emerged, too busy talking about their next cheerleading practice to notice that we were hiding in the corner behind the door and that Audrey was not with them.

"Anzide," I whispered.

Karina gasped when he appeared.

"Hide me."

"You're up to no good again, aren't you?"

"Yep."

I needed evidence. So, after turning down the volume on my phone, I looked at Karina.

"Won't be long."

She shrugged, leaning against the wall. Anzide gripped my shoulder as I walked to the doors. Through the glass window, I gathered evidence of Audrey and Kannon as they talked. It wasn't the metal-banging good time they had against my locker, but it was enough to show that they were more than just friends. For two people who pretended to hate each other, they sure liked to make up for it when they were alone.

The picture appeared on my screen, which was new. The last time I tried to take a photo of a vampire, it didn't work. Clearly, it was a spell that was the handiwork of Hannah. With the demon gone, so were her spells, and it seemed as if anything James might have put over the town was either not working, nonexistent, or intermittent.

"Ugh, that's so gross," Karina whispered.

I looked at her. She was up on her tiptoes, holding the door frame rather than leaning on the easily moved swing door.

"Eww, get a picture of that. Bet if the cafeteria staff

weren't there, they'd be doing it on the tables we eat off. Well, not to eat off, but you know what I mean, right?"

"Sure do."

"I'm still eating food, but it will probably end soon. I am beginning to find it tedious."

Kannon and Audrey moved away from the edge of the table where they'd been kissing so hard they were almost on it. Karina lowered so that she was hidden from the window.

"Oh my god, they're coming. Hide me too."

Anzide shifted, and soon, Karina disappeared. We were dragged back from the door to the small gap behind it.

"I can't believe she's being so stubborn."

"You've just gotta keep trying, baby. She'll believe you soon enough. Keep playing the friend angle, and she'll eventually fall back into old patterns."

"We don't have time for eventually. I need to get the placement before Drakkus gets sick of waiting for me to comply with his demands. The longer he has to wait to become leader of this town, the angrier he gets."

Kannon and Audrey kept talking as they continued through the corridor. When they were out of sight, Anzide let go of us.

"That is one neat parlor trick you've got going there, Anzide. When are you going to learn it for yourself?"

Anzide chuckled.

"She's a hard taskmaster. Almost as bad as Mother, right?"

I rolled my eyes. Karina wasn't as bad as Mother, but I'm sure she could be.

CHAPTER 6

Brad emerged from the administration office as Karina, Anzide, and I turned into the main corridor. I knew that he was coming here to discuss the offer with James, but I thought he would have left it a little later than this. James said he would be working until six p.m. tonight, so there was no rush.

Still, it was done, and I was grateful I didn't have to go into the office again. It was beginning to appear as if I was a delinquent or possibly a tattletale. Either way, it wasn't a good look for the new girl to repeatedly go to the office.

Brad waited for us to approach, then gave me a look. The *be polite* look.

"This is my uncle Brad. Brad, this is Karina. Oh look, your mother is here too."

Karina turned to see her mother walking in the main doors. She looked like she'd just finished work. Dressed in a uniform, looking a little wrung out.

"That's well-timed," Brad said as he turned.

Yeah, I was just thinking that. Curiously convenient.

Silence soon hit him. Karina and I exchanged glances. Why? Brad could not stop looking at Nora.

"Are we about to become cousins?" she whispered.

"Maybe." I returned.

I don't think that I could have said a better thing to Karina. She excitedly clapped while remaining subdued enough to not draw attention to herself. Even I found myself smiling. It was from Karina's quiet outburst of happiness, but it was a smile nonetheless.

"Hello, Evie."

"Uh, hi, Nora. This is my uncle Brad. Brad, this is Nora, Karina's mother."

As they began to talk and walk to the main doors, I turned back to see James watching through the glass panel. I tilted my head with raised eyebrows. He smiled with a shrug, then walked away.

"He totally planned this," I muttered to Anzide.

"Yep. Demons will do that. They like to live in a perfect world or as perfect as they can get it. He's got the vampire leader in his pocket, and he's doing everything he can to ensure that she stays there."

He could see the concern on my face.

"It's fine. James is not an issue."

"You know it's really weird to see you talking to no one, right?" Karina asked.

I nodded. "It's weird knowing that no one else will see him. I have to remember not to do a lot of things. Sometimes, he moves through walls, but there are times when he doesn't."

"Physical limitations," Anzide offered. "Coupled with how tired I am, how much energy I have exerted."

"Well, there you go."

Karina giggled, glancing at the void of nothing where Anzide's voice came from.

We began to follow Brad and Nora out of the building. I didn't want to catch up to them. The risk of hearing Brad put his moves out into the world was too much for me.

"You know, if they get together, you guys might move in. There's plenty of room,"

"We can't, unfortunately," I interrupted. "Well, I can't because I have to stay at the coven property, but Brad could. Although, I doubt he would."

"If it means getting laid, he might." Anzide offered.

"Yeah, but where does that leave me?" Karina muttered petulantly. "They're hooking up. You two need privacy, and little old me will be sitting on the front step trying to get my homework done."

"You can always visit,"

Even though it would mean that a certain vampire would no longer be able to hide.

"I wouldn't want to intrude."

"Trust me, you won't be."

Karina frowned, looking confused.

"I know it sounds crazy, but trust me, it's fine."

We stopped and looked at Brad and Nora. She was smiling, and Brad was saying something. My lips pressed tight as my eyes narrowed. Clearly, we weren't leaving anytime soon.

"Maybe we should wander down Main Street and leave the lovebirds to do their thing."

Anzide moved in front of me and stopped. I could see the anxiety growing.

"What's wrong?"

"We are supposed to go straight home. I didn't expect Nora to appear like this. Now he's making gooey faces at the woman. You need to tell Brad that we're having a family-only meeting this afternoon."

"We are?"

Anzide nodded. I quickly caught up to Brad.

"Sorry to interrupt, but I thought you might forget that we've got a family meeting this afternoon."

Brad was silent as he stared at me. With a forced grin, he nodded.

"Of course, I forgot. Maybe we could catch up a little later on?"

"I'd like that. Perhaps a little walk around town to search for a nice place to have a meal."

"Great." Brad gushed.

I wanted to roll my eyes and stick my finger in my mouth to show how sickly this was.

Brad flicked the fob, unlocking the car as he said goodbye to Nora. I waved at Karina, agreeing to meet up at the lockers tomorrow.

Brad huffed as he got into the car.

"If I lose out because of whatever nonsense you two are cooking up, I am going to be extremely cross."

"We all want you to get your end in, Brad, but be serious for a moment."

"Gross," I said, frowning at Anzide. "But it's completely true. She's not going to refuse you because it was extremely obvious that she was into you."

"Good," he grumbled. "What's going on?"

"We need to return to the caravan, and we need a family meeting."

With a sigh, Brad turned over the engine and pulled out of the car space. I knew what was going through his mind, and despite my reassurance, he thought that he wasn't going to get another chance with Nora. He was wrong. She looked at him with hope in her eyes. The second in charge of a coven was a grand position, and to form a relationship with one was just as good. She wasn't going to let this little fish escape.

"Did you discuss everything with James that Niko wanted?"

"Yes. Niko certainly doesn't like being kept out of things."

"You think that he wants the war over so that he can get on with his life now that Beatrice is back?"

"I think he wants to get out of the tin can. It's tiny and hot during the day. We're both in there, but only I can go out under the shade. It would be driving him crazy."

Well, that made me feel a whole lot better.

"But James said he can find us extra helpers to assist Henry with the build. The accounts are set up, the spell has been cast, and I've already done the first transfer. At midnight, it will reset, and tomorrow, I will do it all again. Beatrice is going to shift back into Natalia and take on the daytime duties like going to see Henry about the plans."

"Yeah, you might want to put a hold on that one for a few days."

Brad glanced at me as he slowed to turn into the driveway.

"Why?"

"Well, you're talking about going out on a date, and if you're seen talking to Natalia, someone might get a little bit confused."

"Okay, well, I guess Natalia will have to become a

member of the clan so that she can be properly introduced, and at that point, it can be clearly stated that nothing is going on."

"It would be so much easier if they didn't have to hide."

"Yeah," Brad said as he sighed.

"Speaking of that, it might have to happen anyway. Karina doesn't want to be around when you and her mother are getting busy. It's not a good idea for her to be roaming the streets, so I told her to come to the caravan."

Brad nodded.

"It's not ideal to out Niko and Beatrice like that, but we might not have a choice. I'm sure Niko will agree with you."

The car was stopped, and as the door to the caravan opened, I saw Beatrice looking at us. She'd taken Natalia's form because she was exposed to anyone that was looking that way.

"That's not going to help you either. Nora walks past and sees her, she's going to think that you're hooking up with her."

"Maybe I need to have a word with grandma."

"That sounds so gross, but have fun with it. I want to be a fly on the wall when you do it."

Brad scowled at me, then turned to get out of the car.

"It would be funny, right?"

"Brad would be so embarrassed. Hey grandma, can you not look like your alter ego and stand at the door making it seem like we're boning? There's a new chick in town, and she's totally into me, and you're making this difficult."

Anzide sniggered.

Brad crossed the sunny gap with record speed. I was surprised that he actually ventured out of the house during the daylight hours, but I guess he was probably becoming accustomed to his new way of life. Maybe the vampire had fully settled into his body and was at ease with the world. He needed to be taught how to transfer the money after James created the accounts, but that didn't mean he expected Brad to walk in the sun for it. James would have waited for the sun to set.

As we crossed the lawn, our neighbor on the left-hand side called out to us.

"Uh, hi."

"I was hoping to talk to you and your uncle. Is he free?"

Broad daylight might be fine in short periods of time, but for standing out and talking to the neighbor? Probably not. I could guarantee Brad would start turning pink or that a cloud of smoke might start. In front of Warwick was not a good idea because it would lead to questions being asked. It was the kind of attention that we did not need.

"Sure, come on over."

I turned to Anzide and raised my eyebrows.

"Can you go and tell Brad that we have company?"

Anzide nodded, quickly crossing the lawn.

"Mighty shame what happened to the house. Crazy that the pipes just exploded like that."

"Yeah. We lost almost everything, but I'm just glad that we're okay."

"Oh, absolutely."

Brad emerged from the caravan, standing under the shade that was attached to the side of it.

"Brad," the neighbor said eagerly.

"How's it going, Warwick?"

"Pretty good. I've been speaking with the missus about a few things. She's been itching to do one of those driving tours of the country. We've been looking at campervans and whatnot, scratching out a few ideas, you know."

Brad nodded, glancing at me with uncertainty.

"We were thinking about taking out a loan to purchase the van, and it's still an option, but we were sitting on the back deck this morning, and you know, we can see the yard and how you're trying to clean up. I guess you're trying to save money and make your insurance go as far as it can."

"Yeah," Brad hummed softly.

"Then this idea strikes me from out of nowhere."

Oh, I wouldn't say nowhere. There would be a source, and his name was James Harlwood.

"If you're interested, we could sell the house to you and Evie. Then, you can get out of this tin can and into a home while you rebuild this house. What do you think?"

Brad smiled at Warwick.

"I think it's a great idea. Why don't you get the real estate to do a valuation on the property, and then we can discuss the price?"

"Sounds great. I'm glad that you're able to do this. I'll come back to you with that price."

"Can't wait," Brad replied.

Warwick waved as he turned to walk back to the low chain fence. It didn't take much for him to climb over it.

"Well, I guess that's another thing to tick off the giant checklist that James set for us. Come on, let's get this urgent meeting underway."

CHAPTER 7

Niko was intrigued, quietly watching as we walked into the caravan. I dumped my bag, flicking off my shoes without a care. I was done with hot shoes and socks, which were the next to be removed.

"Is everything okay?"

"We're having a meeting, apparently," Brad muttered.

"Oh, don't act so hard done by. You need to play hard to get. Otherwise, Nora's going to think you're a tramp."

Brad frowned at me, and I did my usual by smiling sweetly as if I was innocent.

"I've been sitting on this for a few hours so that Evie could get the day done."

"It's alright, Anzide." Niko implored.

He clearly figured out that Anzide was stressing out about not telling us this information sooner. It was obvious that Anzide knew me well enough not to say anything because I would insist that we return here immediately if it was as bad as I think it is.

"So, when Evie was talking to Karina in the cafeteria, I knew she was relatively safe, so I decided to check out a few other minds. When Kannon sat down, I utilized Audrey's anger and her distraction to enter her mind. She's cut a deal with Drakkus to become a vampire."

Everyone looked at Niko, who was silent for a few seconds, then gave Anzide a firm nod.

"That is good information. I will relieve your distress by telling you that only the leader of the ruling coven can perform the alteration of species. Drakkus cannot change Audrey unless he is made leader. Now, for a little extra information on that particular subject. It was one of the lessons I'd intended to give you, Evelyn, so please pay attention."

Sure. Not a vampire, but go ahead.

"If a person wishes to become a vampire, as I stated, it must be the leader of the ruling coven that they apply to and, if granted, given a new life by them. If the leader does not agree, or in the instance before Evelyn's arrival to Hades, where there was no official leader walking the streets, a person can go to another town and ask their leader. Most will refuse a stranger. Leaders want to see people be a part of their town for several years before approval. They also usually require a guarantee that the person won't skip town once the deed is done. If Audrey were to approach, she might be lucky and find a leader who is willing to do it and then let her leave, but I seriously doubt it. She would be expected to do her time as a resident of the town, and if she were to bail on her agreement, they would hunt her down and kill her. And yes, they would tell her of the ramifications of her negligence. There is one thing to note about this situation, and it is that Drakkus has a reputation that has spread far and wide. James and I discussed this yesterday. Many leaders want nothing to do with Drakkus at all. When I say many, I do mean it in the largest way possible. It even extends to those who have associated with him and his clan. The followers are seen as untrustworthy."

"Such is the price of their crimes against you, my love."

Niko gripped Beatrice's hand with a loving smile on his face.

"It is."

I turned to Anzide.

"Was there anything else?"

"Just a lot of things that we don't need to talk about. A lot of things that I'd like to have purged from my mind."

"Can you enter Kannon's mind?"

"Previously, I've tried and never been successful, which I assumed was because of Hannah. Now that she's gone, I decided to try again. I could get into his mind, but it was a thin exterior with a strong resistance to anything I tried."

Again, everyone turned to Niko.

"For an eighteen-year-old, that's quite rare. At that age, his mind should still be relatively unstable and easy for you to enter. I would suggest that you try again when you next see Kannon. Perhaps when he is distracted."

"I tried it in the cafeteria today. It wasn't enough."

"Well," I began. "The only other option is the one class we have together."

I suggested it because I knew that Anzide was not going to leave my side while I was at school.

"We're having a test next week. Will that be distracted enough?"

"Hopefully."

Niko looked at me with an almost fatherly frown. It was moments like this that I missed while he was gone. Now that he was back, I wouldn't take anything for granted. I wished for him to return, and that had been granted. Our little family has grown to include another, and if luck is on Brad's side, things might change again.

"What is your plan on how you will deal with Audrey?"

I thought about it and then gave a slight shrug.

"I'll bide my time regarding the information. I will not turn her. She lacks the ability to be nice to me, and she's even been rude to Karina. Audrey has plotted against me, telling Kannon things to help him try to control the path that I take. She couldn't get her way, she was horrible, and she even lashed out at me."

Brad frowned. I must have forgotten to tell him that.

"I can handle myself. After going to some of the roughest schools in this state, I can handle someone like Audrey. She's like a kitten in comparison."

He wasn't impressed but accepted it. I would have thought that after learning about my childhood, Brad would think that I could take on any bully that came my way. Which I could.

"Niko, can I ask you about turning?"

"Of course."

"Karina was turned when she was sixteen. Is that illegal?"

Niko glanced at Anzide, which made me frown.

"What?"

"I told Niko what I saw in their minds so that he understands the situation. If you insist, I will tell you, but I'd rather that you weren't subjected to it."

"What if I say something that triggers her because I don't know?"

"She's right, Anzide." Beatrice offered. "Evelyn is old enough and wise in her years to handle the truth."

"Do you know too?"

"We all do," Brad muttered. "And as much as I don't like gossiping about others, and I'd rather not discuss it at all, I think Evie's right."

Anzide nodded with a heavy sigh.

"Their maker was the leader of the town. Nora and Karina will say that he abducted them because he was lonely and wanted a family, but it's a lie. They were one of many who were abducted for the sole purpose of being feeding and sex slaves for the males of the coven. The leader recruited males of his liking to be a part of his coven. They were free to do whatever they wanted. The females were abducted and kept caged in a warehouse. In Nora's mind, she recalls him saying that Karina would become a vampire when she turned eighteen. Karina was younger than sixteen when she was bitten during one of the attacks. Nora was already a vampire at that stage. Karina almost died, but the leader turned her. They did not escape. James was approached when he was searching the area for vampires in this town. Because he posed as a vampire to help his search, they invited him to the warehouse to become a part of their coven. James walked into the place, saw the situation, and fixed it."

So, James really was their savior. It made me want to search for him and give him the biggest hug I could manage.

"He stopped the clock in a demon kind of way. It appears to be stopped, but it's actually a spell that the demon casts and one that you will learn when you're ready to mess with time like that."

"It can be incredibly dangerous," Niko offered. "But extremely beneficial in situations like this."

With a nod from Niko, Anzide continued.

"Time slows for everyone within the area, aside from

the demon. James would have kept the spell within the warehouse, but beyond the walls, life still carried on as normal. No one can enter, and no one can leave unless the spell caster allows it. James walked the long rows of cages, searched the minds of the women, and formed a really long list of vampires to kill. When he'd destroyed every single monster associated with the coven, he began freeing the women. That's why he was distracted for so long. He had to restart the clock and take the women to various covens across the country to start their lives over."

"So, why just Nora and Karina?"

"I guess they fitted this coven better than any of the other women. Maybe we fit into their lives too, probably better than any of the others. A young woman at the helm who happens to be the right age for the daughter to become friends with. She's had a rough start to her life too, something that they can bond over."

Anzide turned everyone's attention to Brad with a simple hand gesture.

"Then there's the caring father-figure uncle watching over her and guiding her through this crazy life. Because of his caring nature, he's a perfect candidate to ease a scared woman back into the world of dating and intimacy with a man, maybe even more. He's already a father figure to a teenager, so the daughter that could easily become his stepdaughter will be well cared for."

Next along was Beatrice, who smiled softly when Anzide gestured to her.

"In time, they would meet the matriarch, a mother hen figure that will always pull the young under her reassuring wing. And finally, the patriarch, the true leader of the town, a vampire everyone should aspire to be like."

Niko nodded quietly and graciously, appreciating the compliment.

"Where do you fit in?"

Anzide shrugged.

"Maybe I'm the protective brother."

"Maybe you are."

Because he really would be. If something happened, I knew Anzide would protect Nora and Karina just as much as everyone else in this caravan.

It was a terrible tale, one that I wished had never happened to Karina and Nora. Brad was right that it wasn't ideal to talk about people or their problems, but in a way, I was glad that Anzide told me. Now, I would be more careful with what I said in front of them.

"Are there any other concerns about what Anzide has seen?"

Niko thought about it momentarily and shifted forward on the seat, leaning on the table.

"I think it would be ideal to conduct constant observations of their minds, especially Kannon's, once you gain access. Not only will it give you a view of their interactions with Drakkus, but it could even give us an early warning of when they plan to attack. Information like that is pure gold."

"Agreed. It might even give me an insight into the movements Drakkus makes. Pinning him down to a schedule or habits has been extremely difficult."

Beatrice and Niko looked at each other.

"Care to offer insight into him?"

"Times are different now," Niko muttered tersely. "I could tell you that he would spend his Sundays at a particular tavern, but it's no longer a part of the town, so that is rather useless."

"But," Beatrice said, giving Niko a firm look.

"Yes, *but.* He was always a man of habit. It was always to a ridiculous degree, and it often caused a few terse words being directed at me because other followers were not happy with his antics. If you can find him once and track him, then you will have your pattern."

"But that means that Anzide would have to leave Evelyn." Brad offered.

He was clearly not impressed by the idea.

"While that could be true, there could be many variables in the situations. She might be here with us, and he walks past the property. Perhaps she could be in town with you, and Anzide spots Drakkus. Don't be so quick to cast it away when there are options."

"Okay, so I guess if you have the chance and I'm safe, track Drakkus."

Anzide nodded. I don't know if he's going to get the chance to track Drakkus, though. In all the times when I've been out, I've hardly seen him. Drakkus was usually outside the cafe when school finished, which I assume is only because Andross is dead. With his new second-in-charge, a student at the school, it meant that he had to rely on someone else to monitor the area. Clearly, he didn't trust anyone to do that, which could prove to be an advantage.

"You could try it if he's at the cafe. I'll be with Karina, and if you leave, we can go to Nora and stay at her office until you're done."

Anzide nodded, though I don't think he agreed completely. He wasn't about to say that Nora couldn't cope if something happened. I think it was probably closer to him thinking that it would be a failure of duty on his part.

CHAPTER 8

It was Saturday morning, and I'd planned for an entire weekend of sitting on my butt doing nothing. Except that life doesn't work like that. At least for me, it didn't.

A shadow loomed over me, and I lowered the book. Brad looked like he was on a mission, and as much as it was thrilling to learn about the Eternals, I knew that I should be reading it and not doing whatever it was that he wanted.

"What's up?"

"I seem to recall that you owe me a lot of favors."

"I do?"

"You do."

My eyes narrowed. It seemed like this was a setup, and I did not owe Brad anything.

"Alright, I'll bite. What do you want?"

"For you to get dressed and be in my car in less than ten minutes."

"And where are we going?"

"Lunch."

"I see. Where are we going to have lunch?"

"It's now nine minutes."

With a frustrated huff, I got up from the hammock.

"I think that a bit of information would be necessary so that I don't look out of place wherever we'll be having this *lunch*."

Anzide smiled softly, almost like he knew. He probably did.

"Is this some attempt at bonding?"

"No. Eight minutes."

"Nine and a half, at most. Now, keep your hair on and tell me where we are going."

"Nora is making lunch for us. You will behave, sit, eat, and be grateful. No smart-ass comments, no innuendo, or even direct statements. Then, after lunch, you will go with Karina to her room or wherever it is that you two decide that you need to go so long as it is nowhere near me and Nora."

"Or you could just admit that you're planning on porking her and go to her room, leaving Karina and me with the television."

"Turned up loud," Anzide muttered.

"I don't pork anyone."

"Tell me about it," I groaned.

Anzide chuckled despite the mighty glower Brad was giving us. I grinned, and with a fluttering of my eyes, I sauntered off to the caravan.

Niko and Beatrice were playing cards at the dining table when I walked in. Both looked up with smiles on their faces.

"Off somewhere, darling?"

"Apparently, I'm now a wing woman for a horny man."

Niko frowned as he watched me rummage through the basket of clothing that I had yet to put away. Life in a cramped caravan was dysfunctional at best.

"What's a wing woman?" he whispered to Beatrice.

Pulling the curtain across, I turned and almost yelped. Anzide was behind me. The ravenous hunger made me grin. Pressing me against the cupboard, Anzide kissed me hard. Unable to resist, I wrapped my arm around him and urged him closer.

Heavy footsteps entered the caravan, and I knew captain doom was on the warpath again. Pulling away, I looked up at Anzide.

"Date night?" I whispered.

He nodded quietly and then faded out of the area. Dressing into the nicer clothes, I emerged and saw Brad waiting. His eyes narrowed when only I emerged.

"Where's Anzide?"

I shrugged.

"Did you pack your condoms?"

"Evie," he grumbled.

I waved goodbye to the smiling duo and went in search of Anzide. He was on the other side of the caravan, pretending that he'd been there all along.

"Do I want to know?"

"I try to avoid entering minds, more so when it could be something I don't want to see or have burned into my memory. Remember that I still have to look at him after this."

"How true."

"I have previously scanned the area around this street. There is a park we can go to, and it has a rotunda for Karina if the sun proves to be an issue."

"And our friendly vampires?"

"Don't frequent this area unless they're doing surveillance. They've already done their daily sweep of the street, so we should be okay with it. I will still maintain a vigil to keep Brad and Nora happy."

"Or, we could convince them to let us go further into town."

"I guess it depends on how desperate Brad is."

"Are you serious? Can't you smell the aftershave? I'm

drowning. And what kind of lunch can vampires really have?"

Anzide shrugged at me. We turned to face Brad as he approached the car.

"Lunch, are you serious?"

His eyes narrowed at me.

"Don't be difficult, Evie."

"They're vampires," I hissed. "You're a vampire. The only ones who will eat anything are Anzide and me. Do us all a favor. When I suggest that we take Karina into town, you say that it's a great idea. No resistance, and I won't give you a hard time about how you're clearly using me to get closer to Nora."

I held out my hand with determination on my face. Brad let out a frustrated huff and shook my hand.

"How long do you want? Are you a minute man, or do you like to,"

"Evelyn, I swear to god, if you don't shut up."

I grinned like a loon as I climbed in behind the wheel. Brad continued to frown at me, which I ignored by putting on my seatbelt and starting the engine. Shaking his head, he moved to the passenger seat.

"Think of it as lessons in driving that I clearly don't need because I am such a legend."

Backing out of the driveway, I made my way through the streets. Going by road made the journey a little longer, but that was okay. Brad needed to chill out. Otherwise, he'd sweat his way through the shirt.

Pulling up outside the house, I pulled the handbrake on and looked at Brad.

"If you run home now, you can change your shirt and return before we get to the door."

"Will there be a day when you don't tease me?"

"Maybe, but it would be a pretty boring day, don't you think?"

The door opened, and like she was already aware of the plan, Karina skipped down the stairs with a bag over her shoulder and a jacket in her hand. She opened the passenger door, giving Brad a wicked smile.

"Out of the car, lover boy."

Brad grumbled something unintelligible. I leaned over to yell at him.

"Be home by ten, young man."

In true Evie style, he said nothing in response but offered a scandalous one-finger salute.

"Atrocious behavior for my second in command," I said, shaking my head.

Karina settled into the passenger seat. The door was shut, and she turned to the back seat.

"Hey, hey, Zeed."

"Is that my name now?"

"It is."

Plugging in her belt, Karina looked at me with her usual bubbliness.

"Did he say anything, give you a time frame? Dish the dirt."

"Well, he said it was lunch, but that's not really a thing for a vampire, so we cut a deal. I'd lay off teasing him, and he wouldn't object when I suggested the three of us go out."

"Huh. Clearly, nothing like my mother. She was to the point. Get dressed and get out. Don't come back for several hours, and if you're bored, go to the caravan and wait there."

"Brutal."

"Yeah, but that's my mother. She does not beat around the bush about anything. We talked about it. She said that she's interested in taking it further."

"Well, lucky Brad, eh?"

She nodded. I knew what she was thinking. This was the beginning. In the end, we'd be family.

"So, what are we going to do? You guys have been in this town longer than me. What's fun?"

"I have no idea. Most of my time has been spent at the house or school."

Pulling out her phone, Karina searched for places that might be interesting.

"How about bowling?"

"Sounds great."

"There's also an arcade."

"Even better."

Karina guided me through the streets until we reached the bowling alley. There were only a couple of cars in the parking lot, which I thought was a good sign that we'd get a lane. I soon learned that it was not the case. It was league tryouts, and the place was packed.

The man behind the counter was not sympathetic. He suggested that we could try again on Monday or book in for next weekend. All lanes were booked and would be that way until the close of business on Sunday.

"Come on, we'll have fun in the arcade."

"You know, it's rude that you've booked every single lane without a care for the residents of this town."

"Kid, I don't have time for this."

"So why don't you pay me to go away? Tokens for the arcade."

He scoffed but still filled a plastic cup with silver tokens.

"I don't want to hear from you about this again, alright? Subject is over, and you've been paid off. Now, beat it."

With a grin, I took the cup and happily walked away. Karina giggled as she turned to face me, walking backward.

"He caved so easily."

"Must have been seconds from wetting himself, am I right?"

She nodded with a chuckle.

"Definitely scared of you."

Walking through the entrance, I saw nothing but bright lights flashing at me. Everyone was in the bowling alley behind us, and we had the entire arcade to ourselves. Karina tugged at my hand, eager to find a game to play. I turned to Anzide, who gave me a nod.

"Go. I'll stay here. If we get company, I'll come over."

"You can come in, you know."

"I know."

Walking behind Karina, I let her decide where we would go first. She stopped at a claw machine, eyeing off the stuffed toys.

"Well, that's a bit rude."

"What is?"

"There's a stuffed cat that is so cute, but he's stuck under the cow."

"So, you want the cat. Are you prepared to be a little underhanded to get what you want?"

Karina bit her lip, glancing at me and at Anzide, who

was leaning on the door frame.

"Maybe. What about the cameras?"

"We can deal with that. Hang on."

Returning to Anzide, I hoped the plan would work.

"Do me a favor. Disappear after going to the bathroom, come back, and when Karina plays the claw game, rig it so that she gets the cat."

"That's cheating, Evelyn."

"I know, but like me, life hasn't been nice to her, so maybe you can be."

Anzide pressed his lips tight with a smile. He walked to the bathroom while I returned to Karina.

"So, Anzide's going to help out. Just aim for the cow, and the cat will miraculously get caught in the claw."

Dumping the coins into the machine, Karina began to move the claw. It dropped, and amazingly, the metal arms widened enough to catch the cat underneath. Slowly, it rose, jiggling as it made its way to the chute.

"Do you want the cow?" Anzide whispered.

"No," Karina replied.

The cat dropped, but the cow lingered on the acrylic wall, eventually falling back into the pile of toys. Karina eagerly grabbed her cat.

"Thanks, Zeed."

"No problem."

The unseen one returned to us, acting surprised when Karina showed him the cat.

"Come on, we need to document this awesome day."

"It's just a stuffed cat," Anzide said dryly. "I'm sure if you looked on the internet, you'd find dozens of them."

I frowned at Anzide as my arm was being dragged away. He shrugged.

"Come on Zeed. Get your ass in here."

She pushed him into the photo booth, then me.

"Sit on his lap, cuz there ain't enough room for three fat butts."

After loading the coins into the slot, Karina shut the curtain.

"Crazy faces?"

"Sure."

Karina stuck her fingers in her mouth, dragging her lips to the side as she poked her tongue. I crossed my eyes and pulled a silly face. In one of the photos, Anzide grabbed me and licked my cheek. I howled with laughter.

"Oh my god, you're so gross," I said, still laughing.

The machine had stopped taking pictures. Karina pulled the photos from the dispenser, and I looked at the crazy faces that Anzide was pulling. I couldn't see much of him from my position, but he'd done as Karina wanted. Silly faces with lots of fun.

"Which ones do you want, top or bottom?"

I looked at the photos, unable to decide.

The machine began to make noises. We turned to look at it as another row of photos appeared. I looked at Anzide, who offered a subtle smirk with a shrug.

Karina was so happy that we didn't have to decide. We each had a set of images. I don't know how Anzide managed to make it print another set, but he had.

"How?"

"It's digital, Evie. Did you read the large sign that is right in front of you?"

Clearly not.

"Okay, smart guy."

Pulling his shirt, I dragged him down to me.

"Thank you."

With a kiss, he was a happy man.

CHAPTER 9

Brad was quiet during dinner. He wasn't usually talkative, but he would interact with the rest of the family while we ate. Tonight, though, he was either deep in thought or distracted. It seemed as if I was the only one that noticed. With Beatrice and Niko keeping a conversation flowing, I suppose the quiet one would easily get overlooked.

Dinner for Brad and Niko consisted of raw meat. It wasn't a regular thing, but if Niko was in the mood for a family dinner, this was what they had. Afterward, they would go in search of something more substantial. I suppose he could be bored with raw meat and wanted to feed, but I'd learned that when Niko got a bug up his ass about something, there was no changing it. So, family dinners were a thing that could not be shifted.

I said that I wasn't going to tease, but Brad wasn't making it easy on me. I'd lay money on this being about Nora. Maybe they'd decided against going further. It seemed an impossible suggestion, but I could see both of them being worried about it going pear-shaped.

If that was the case and it was about Nora and the concerns they had, it needed to be talked about. Niko would be able to help. He always had insightful words and helped wherever he could.

Glancing at Niko, I raised my eyebrows and subtly tilted my head at the silent one. Niko grimaced, almost like he detested my request.

"Care to share what is bothering you, Bradley?"

His head lifted from where he'd been watching as he pushed the piece of cut steak around on his plate.

"It's fine," he murmured.

"Clearly, it's not, so do us all a favor and call upon your loved ones for assistance."

Brad sighed, leaning back into his seat.

"Nora has concerns about the age gap."

Bingo. Niko frowned like he couldn't understand what they were worried about. I didn't know either. It's not like she was an old woman. She looked young, but it was a flawed statement anyway, considering Nora is a vampire. Maybe she was super old. Could Karina be the late-in-life miracle?

"How old is Nora?"

"Thirty-six."

Oh my god. They were a pair of drama queens. I scoffed, earning a frown.

"Eight years is nothing. You're wasting our time with

this conversation."

Niko joined Brad in frowning at me. I rolled my eyes and returned to my pasta. It was more entertaining than this nonsense.

"You're twenty-eight if my math is correct, right?"

Brad nodded.

"I fail to see the issue."

"Told you so," I muttered.

"It's a bit of a gap, Evie."

"It's not really."

"I'm inclined to agree with Evelyn in this matter. Eight years is not a concern."

"This is a different era," he muttered. "You don't understand."

Beatrice reached out, gripping Brad's balled fist.

"Darling, look at your grandparents. Do you know the age gap between Niko and me?"

He shook his head.

"Two hundred years."

"See? That's an age gap. No one cares, do they?"

Beatrice chuckled, and I shot a challenging smile at Brad. He was not impressed. Did I care? Nooope.

"No, they don't. I found myself a handsome toyboy

vampire and couldn't resist. Don't worry about a paltry eight years. I know that the world is different from what Niko is used to, but you can't be bound by what is happening in one era when you will live through many. Vampires are immortal, and age means little to them. No one is going to concern themselves with your age. Most won't even care to ask."

"You will find that what a vampire will notice is how you two interact with each other, how much love there is, and I don't mean this slobbering nonsense that goes on these days," Niko said with an air of arrogance to his tone. "I mean the subtle hints of your undying affection. If you are concerned about Nora's thoughts, bring her here, and we can talk about it. She's had a bleak start in the world of vampires, so it is easy to assume that she knows little of our ways. In fact, it would be a good idea if Nora and Karina visit regularly so that they can be taught what is ideal for a proper vampire. Send a message to her and invite them to spend the day with us tomorrow."

"It's a little cramped in here," Brad said.

"I suppose that it is. There is little that we can do about it at the moment. If you want to move forward with Nora, have your conversation at her house. I require well-behaved vampires in this coven, so they should still visit."

Brad nodded, quietly sending Nora a message.

"So, what else did you get up to after the arcade?"

"Well, after we annoyed the owner for booking all the

lanes again, we decided to annoy someone else. Somehow, we ended up at this random house that's near a park that happens to have a lot of pigeons in it. I don't know how it happened, but Anzide got onto the roof and unloaded a lot of birdseed onto it while Karina and I tried to pick up the dozens of bags that were just lying around everywhere. These bags had splits in them, and birdseed went everywhere. It was crazy. It didn't take long for the birds to realize. There were a lot of feathers and poop. Karina and I were trying to get away, and somehow, the bags in our hands spilled all over the car sitting in the driveway. It was covered, and the birds went crazy. There were even other kinds of birds, not just the pigeons. The car was a mess but not as bad as the house, though."

I looked up from the plate and saw two faces of doom and another that was quietly smiling. Beatrice said nothing as her eyes lowered to the plate.

"Please tell me you did not do that to Drakkus's house."

"We did not, and I also don't know where it is."

"Well then, it seems as if you've clearly managed to figure out where the Lothaire's live, so it's not unreasonable to think that you could figure out where Drakkus lives. Were they home?"

"Amazingly, no. Crazy, right?"

Niko sighed heavily while Brad shook his head.

"Pranks are not the ideal behavior of a coven leader."

"Yeah, but there aren't many Phoenix, so I'm calling it early on this one. We are definitely jokesters."

"Joke all you want, Evelyn. At the core of this, we are still a coven, and you are still the leader. You should refrain from anything that is considered beneath you."

I stared at Niko as the thoughts rolled around in my mind.

"Is there something you wish to tell me, Evelyn?"

"Not really. Just that, you know, I'll behave. From now on."

His eyes closed as Niko exhaled slowly. When his eyes reopened, I saw an exhausted vampire who was now living in a world with a wise-cracking teenager. It was something he'd never experienced before, and in a modern world, it had to be tough.

"What did you do?"

"So, when I said I don't know where Drakkus lives, it wasn't a complete lie. I still don't know."

"But?"

"But we might have traveled by Anzide Air and did a little decorating at his house. You know that this is normal behavior for a teenager, right?"

"It might be, but your partner in crime is not a teenager."

"Technically, he could be." Beatrice offered. "Nephilim age in a way that is vastly different from anything we are used to. He has the appearance and the mind of an adult, but deep down, he's experiencing life in this world as a teenager would. He's going to school with Evelyn, he's hanging out with her and now Karina. It's only natural for a teenager to get into mischief, and they are both doing what they've missed out on in their early years."

Which was so accurate, it wasn't funny. Sure, I had teen years. They were wild and unrestrained, but that didn't mean they were fun. I did things to survive, to put food in front of myself when my mother forgot to buy it for me. As for Anzide, his life before me was one of service. There was no fun in his youth, as short as it was.

"Alright. I concede that you are enjoying your teenage years and accept that there is little I can do to alter it. I will also add that when considering the life that you endured, I think that a little fun is necessary. All I ask is that if you decide that you want to continue your campaign against our enemies, you ensure that you are safe. Remember that the two of you are eternal, but Karina is only immortal. Death can still shadow her life, and I would not want either of you to bear the burden of that for an eternity."

Wow. Way to kill a mood. Niko was a legend.

"Sure," I muttered.

"This would be the part where you tell me all the other things you're hiding from me."

I looked up and saw Anzide grinning like a loon.

"We can call it a bonding experience between a coven

leader and a new member, right?"

"If you actually accepted your role, then we could, but you won't, so where does that leave us?"

In an awkward situation, sitting at a tiny and cramped table in a small caravan.

"I guess somewhere like where we're at right now."

Niko grumbled softly.

"Continue."

"We let down the tires of his car, used shaving cream to draw indecent images that referenced his trouser snake, put a couple of fake spiders in his letterbox plus a few snakes in the grass. There might have been a glitter fight that got a little out of control as well. We were bored. Blame Brad's devious urges to defile Nora for hours."

Brad glared at me, almost as unimpressed as the one that Niko was giving me.

"And let's not forget how uninteresting Hades is."

Niko opened his mouth, but Beatrice placed her hand on his forearm. His head turned to her, and she gave him a soft smile.

"Enjoy moments like this, my darling. She's showing us what it's like to be a young but strong woman in a modern world. They're also bored. There is a part of her statements that have an element of truth to them. In giving Brad and Nora time alone to forge a relationship, they are left to their own devices. This town has little in the way of entertainment for the youth. It *is* boring in this town. The steps you take can create a firmer foundation, or it can create a mark that will leave a scar and always be there, no matter what you do."

Niko paused, and for a moment, he looked at Beatrice. His gaze turned to me, and as the glare softened, Niko conceded.

"Alright. I cannot say that I am impressed, but I will let it slide. Perhaps the three of you can think of alternatives so that in the future, you can make better use of your time."

"Sure," I said softly.

Brad was still frowning at me. He was probably annoyed that if he wanted us to entertain Karina so that he could have play time with Nora, we'd be up to no good again. I gave him a challenging smile that Brad shook his head at. It was fun, and that's all there was to it.

Secretly, I was hoping to annoy Drakkus enough that he actually did something. I wasn't ready for anything he might throw at me, but this was dragging on. I wanted to get the blood war over and done with so we could get on with our lives.

CHAPTER 10

The teacher called an cnd to the test. There was a collective sigh that whipped around the room. As for me, I was fine. I learned things fairly easily. Sometimes, I studied, but I always soaked in the information. James was right when he said that I could get this done in a short amount of time.

It's why I'd spent the past ten minutes drawing doodles on the back of the test. The teacher was walking through the aisles and saw me drawing pictures. She turned the test over, checked it, and begrudgingly turned it back to let me continue. I guess that meant that I'd passed the exam.

Glancing around, I searched for Anzide. I couldn't see him, but I knew he was in the room. Anzide had warned me that to crack into Kannon's mind, he'd need to concentrate, and that meant that he would have to divert all of his attention and power to what he was doing. Ensuring I could see him while no one else could was a drain. Besides, I didn't really need to see him. I knew that he was always around, no matter what the situation was.

In a classroom or out on the street, nowhere was safe in his mind. Nowhere except the coven property, and that was only as long as James kept the protection over it. We needed to learn how to do that so that when he removed it, we could apply our own.

As Kannon collected his things, he looked at me. A vague smile was offered. I really wanted this nonsense to be over with. Then, I wouldn't have to put up with his ridiculous attempts to be my friend.

The teacher collected my test, moving through the rows. When she reached Kannon, he offered his test and returned his attention to me. I expected him to ask if I'd attacked his house and car with a lot of birdseed. There was no proof and no witnesses. We made sure of that before starting our craziness.

"Hey, I wanted to apologize for the cafeteria thing. It was rude to talk like that."

I guess it was a no to the questions about the bird-seed.

"I get it," I said with a shrug. "You're worried. You know what Drakkus is capable of, but you've never seen me in action. We're both powerful, but I'm untrained. I'm young, he's old. It's okay to be concerned, and I appreciate that you care."

Karina raised an eyebrow at me, saying nothing. She merely collected her things and waited by the door. I could understand her questioning the statement. I often questioned what came out of my mouth, too.

"Sure. Anyway, I thought that maybe you and the new girl might want to hang out at practice this afternoon."

"The new girl has a name, and it's Karina. I can't stay here any longer because I have to get home. Brad's picking me up. That aside, I wouldn't voluntarily go to a practice session anyway, but given that the cheerleaders are always there, I'm going to decline on that alone. I know you're trying to be nice to me, and I appreciate that, but I'm sorry because I am not going to be anywhere near the person who constantly belittles and bullies me. Her father is the reason Niko is dead. You know that, right?"

Kannon nodded grimly.

"Good."

Lifting my bag over my shoulder, I quickly walked to the door where Karina was waiting for me. She smiled at me, almost as if she knew the truth, which she didn't, but it was there. It was a little freaky if I was honest.

"He's such an ass," she whispered as we walked to the stairs.

"Yeah, but what's worse is that I actually liked him. I was considering doing the nasty with him. I kissed him."

"Eww."

Karina screwed up her face and then giggled.

"That's just nasty."

I shrugged.

"For a while, he was the only one on my side. I wasn't looking for someone to hang out with or make friends, but he made life around here easier."

Karina smiled sympathetically.

"It's rough starting at a new school. I guess having enemies right from the beginning didn't make it any easier."

"Yeah."

After grabbing books from our lockers, Karina and I made our way to the side entrance of the building. Anzide appeared to me, but I could tell that Karina couldn't see him.

Brad was supposedly going to be there waiting for us while going through the documents Nora was preparing. It had nothing to do with his sudden interest in her.

I was definitely getting a ready-made cousin, and I think she was thrilled. I wasn't ready to admit that I was, as well. The past still haunted me. I still waited for the day when Brad would say that we were leaving, and I had to say goodbye to another group of friends. It didn't matter that we were now purchasing a place or that we were the owners of the clan property. I could see the roots driving deep into this down, connecting us permanently, but I still fretted that it was only a matter of time.

There was also the fear that she was just a repeat of Kannon, only in female form. My mind would say that it's okay. James checked them out, and he asked them to come here. The thoughts whispered that someone from the Fleming clan had gotten to them.

All that I had was the reassurance from Anzide. He agreed to conduct sporadic checks on them to ensure that they were still aligned with our clan.

Brad and Nora were standing near the car, too busy talking to notice our approach. Karina looked at me with a wide grin as our pace slowed down.

"Has your mother said anything?"

"Just a few little things that I guess could be taken either way."

"Brad said Nora was freaking out about the age gap. I told him that eight years is nothing, and everyone agreed with me."

"Do you think he's worried?"

"Nuh. I know Brad. That won't worry him, but if Nora's stressing over, then he will focus on it. Hopefully, he will be able to convince her that vampires don't care about age. If not, then I'm sure someone else will."

Karina giggled.

"Has your mother said anything to confirm her thoughts?"

"She said he's a nice guy, and it was really sweet that he took you on after your mother died. I tried to covertly push for information, but I think she knew. She just said that they get along and,"

Karina bit her lip as she stopped and looked at me.

"Are you going to tell him?"

"Only if you want me to. Are we playing matchmaker?"

"She said he's cute."

I chuckled.

"What's so funny?"

"He suggested a roster for the caravan."

Karina frowned at me.

"Anzide and I would have to go for a walk, and I assume you'd still be at home."

"Oh," she said softly, then her eyes widened, and the smile grew. "Oh my god."

"I'm going to get a sign that says, *if the caravans a-rockin', don't come a-knockin'*."

She giggled.

We began walking again, soon reaching the road.

"Must be difficult for you and Anzide."

"We cope."

Cope was a strong word. Probably the wrong word. Struggle was likely to be more accurate. It had been a while. I missed him and the intimacy that being alone with him gave me. It wasn't just about the pleasure. It was about growing as a couple. We had our little moments alone as we snuggled in bed. It wasn't the same, but it was better than nothing. I'd go to sleep in his arms, and when I was out, he'd either stay there until dawn or sit on the roof of the caravan, unseen as he meditated.

I always found it to be a curious thing to do, but Anzide said that when he was meditating, it wasn't for relaxation, but it was to multitask. He'd watch over the occupants in the caravan while observing the land for unwanted visitors. Anzide could run on very little sleep. I knew that he had a firm schedule in place. While Brad, Niko, or Beatrice were awake, he'd power down for as long as he could. Then, when it was time for them to rest, he'd wake and take on his sentry position. Knowing that, I tried to either leave him to sleep alone on the bed or, if I was tired, go to bed early.

"You two look like you're up to something." Brad offered.

"Aren't we always?" Karina said.

"Well, I know I'm always thinking about dastardly plans and scheming things."

Karina grinned, then looked at her mother, who was trying to be polite by smiling. It was obvious that she wasn't used to me yet.

"Evie's teasing, Nora. Just ignore her."

Nora nodded with a smile. As she turned, I gave Brad a crazy grin as I drew a love heart with two fingers. He frowned, and as the nose twitched, Brad mouthed at me to shut up.

"Later, Karina."

She waved as she walked into the real estate office.

Brad unlocked the door, still scowling at me. I said nothing as I climbed in.

When Brad shut the door, he sighed.

"Are we in the car, Anzide?"

"We are."

"Great," Brad muttered.

"So, you were talking to Nora."

"I was. What of it?"

"Did you talk about the age thing?"

"We did."

"Good grief, it's like extracting a tooth with you. You know what I want to hear. Did she accept that the age gap doesn't matter or not?"

"She did."

It wasn't until we were halfway down the street that Brad looked at me.

"Go on. I know you want to."

"Brad and Nora sitting in a tree,"

He rolled his eyes and shook his head.

"You're like a five-year-old, Evie."

"Yeah, but at least I'm fun. So, has Nora said anything?"

"Is this genuine interest, or are you trying to gather

information to tease me?"

"Genuine interest. I'm shocked that you'd suggest the other."

"That's because I know you, and yes, she might have said something."

So, I really was going to get a cousin. I could see the writing on the wall with this one. From what Brad had said about his past relationships, they were either extremely fleeting or they lasted long enough to consider marriage. Brad wasn't about to have a temporary relationship with someone who was a coven member, so this was going to become a full-blown relationship.

"Well, that's good, right?"

He shrugged. I looked back at Anzide. He gave me a shrug, too. I understood his shrug. He didn't know a lot about relationships. Anzide was new to the world and was still trying to understand how humans did things.

"Brad, you need to be realistic about Nora. She's a coven member, and if you upset her, she's going to run to Drakkus."

"That's why I'm trying to keep it light and easy until the war is over. Nora understands that my focus has to be on you and helping you through this time. She also believes that even though they are new to the town and the coven, it's her responsibility to help you as well. At some point, they're going to have to find out about Niko and Beatrice."

"Yeah,"

There was a heaviness to my tone. Exposing Niko like that was not going to be easy, and I didn't want to do it. I wanted to keep him hidden. That way, he would be safe and protected from those who would try to kill him again. The past created an irrational fear inside of me, and at some point, I would have to face reality. Niko would walk out of the caravan, and he would be exposed to the world that might try to bring him down again. They'd tried twice now, and I didn't want to give them a third go at killing him.

CHAPTER 11

Set out under the awning was a lawn chair and a large fan directed at it. Brad had managed to rig up a generator to make the many fans operate, but it just proved that this caravan was not ideal for us. Especially the one that cannot leave it.

"We need to order more walls."

"What for?" Brad asked.

"Well, clearly, you have set this up to sit under the cover with a fan on you, which tells me it was hot in the caravan. Is that right?"

"Yes."

Brad followed me into the caravan. The heat hit me instantly, and I knew that being in here was not fun. Being unable to escape was probably a nightmare. Now more than ever, I regretted asking James to fix Niko. Sure, Niko was safe, he was repaired, and he was with his family again, but it meant living in an oven.

"Was there another person who might have felt

the same way but couldn't escape the caravan like you could?"

Everyone looked at Niko. It appeared as if he didn't know how to sweat.

Dressed in a shirt and pants, he seemed peculiar to me, considering I'd only ever seen him dressed in long pants and a long-sleeved cotton shirt.

"I cope, don't worry about me."

"Nonsense, darling," Beatrice said in her soft, husky tone. "We can get a marquee and create a large area for you to rest in. With the walls around them, no one will see you."

"Get the right type, and they can even be air-conditioned. Toss some flooring down, bring in the furniture that survived the nightmare that is me, and you're all set."

Niko gave an uneasy smile.

"I am grateful, but it's not necessary."

"Honey," Beatrice said as she reached across the table. "No one will see through the walls. It won't blow away. You will be safe. We will make sure of that."

"Done," Brad exclaimed loudly.

He looked up as silence hit the caravan.

"Done what?" I asked cautiously.

"Ordered a marquee. Fast shipping should have it here in a couple of days. The place even sells the flooring and all the bits needed for the air con unit."

"And the unit, right?"

Brad rolled his eyes at me.

"Yes," he groaned. "As if I'd want to be stuck in a hot tent without one."

"Okay. It's just that you were rather fast."

"It's hot, and I want it here as soon as possible. If it means that I don't research prices, then that's how it is."

"Well, I guess we'll wait to see what it's like and how big it is."

Niko didn't look overly impressed but seemed to be okay with it. I understood his fear, and I wanted to say that I was worried too, but he couldn't stay in this little hot box during the middle of the day.

The heat wouldn't be here for much longer. Soon, the cold would arrive, followed by snow. Getting out of this place was necessary for all of us.

"How was school today?" Beatrice asked.

"Eh, boring as always. As much as it's great that I can soak information, it kind of makes things like school into a dull waste of time."

"You don't have to go if you don't want to."

"In a way, I kind of do. I mean, I get to see Karina, and I can keep James in the loop of what's going on if I need to. Then there's the infamous duo who are always in need of watching, and at the end of it, I'm rewarded with going to the prom. So, like all things, it has its pros and cons."

"Well then, if you're happy to remain there, then you do just that."

Brad turned and looked at Anzide, who looked like he'd checked out. It reminded me that Anzide said that another meeting was necessary.

"You said something earlier about a meeting?"

Anzide sighed as he ran his fingers through the thick black hair. The tension was heavy in the air.

"Kannon is not eighteen."

"How old is Kannon?"

"Twenty-one."

"Well, that's a rather large lie," Brad grumbled.

"Vampires tend not to focus on age once they get past eighteen." Niko offered. "After all, we are immortal, and if we tried to keep track of the number, we'd get sick of the time that passes us by. To avoid depression, we state the year that we were born, perhaps the day and the month, but we don't offer an age."

It was a strange thing to consider when thinking about a vampire. Depression and, perhaps, all of the issues that humans face. Were they all subjected to them, or was it just the fixation on the constantly growing number?

"Audrey's actually nineteen. She was held back in her

early years when her family moved to the town. They met about six months ago."

"What's his reason for being in school?" Beatrice asked.

"He's the intel for Drakkus. Everyone in the clan has a task. Kannon's is to be a part of the youth demographic, control any issues that arise inside the school, and be the ears that Drakkus needs. Curiously though, he did not tell Drakkus about James."

That was odd. I wonder what was stopping him.

"Kannon knows that he's fooled James into believing he's eighteen. He doesn't want Drakkus to discover that James is the demon because it could cause problems. More so when you think about the long-term plan. Kannon is about to end his schooling. When he's done that, Drakkus will need a new spy in the school. If James is wary about every vampire because of the distrust that he has since learning the truth, they might not get a shot at sending a replacement into the place."

That made sense.

"We should tell James, though," I said. "He should know the truth about Kannon, but we can ask that he refrains from saying anything or treating him any differently."

"I agree," Niko interjected. "If given the information with a reasonable request, James will be benevolent. After all, this will suit his long-term plan. If he rocks the boat regarding Kannon, it could cause little ripples that may just become large waves. We will tell James about Kannon's true age and ask that he does not act on it to ensure that our plans for the future are not put in jeopardy."

Everyone nodded, and I gave Anzide a nod. He still looked anxious.

"The other part of this is that Kannon considers himself to be bisexual. He has been in a relationship with Drakkus for as long as he's been an adult. It is a fully consensual relationship, and Kannon did not have any concerns about Andross. There were no memories of animosity, but there was also nothing about him being a part of their time alone."

"It's called an open relationship." I offered.

Anzide sat down on the dining chair, looking as if he was thinking about it.

"I don't know the concept of that."

"Those in the relationship have an agreement that allows each person to pursue others."

"I see. I suppose it makes more sense now that I know that. In Kannon's mind, he sees himself as the main partner of Drakkus. Does that mean that Andross was one of the others?"

"It sounds like it."

There was a heavy frown on Anzide's face. It looked like he was thinking about it and still couldn't understand. In time, it would become a part of the facts in his mind.

"Don't worry about that part of it for now. You'll become accustomed to the different relationship situations in time."

"Okay. So, the official agreement that Drakkus made with Audrey and Kannon is that he agreed to turn Audrey once he was the official leader. Kannon's payment is that he's made the second in charge. There's also a second agreement in his mind, one that Kannon and Drakkus made in secret. A constant and willing lover in his bed whenever he demands it. I guess that's what doesn't make much sense to me. There are no memories in Kannon's mind of a fight or any reason as to why Drakkus would demand that when he already has it."

I shrugged. There were only two in this tin can that could tell us how Drakkus's mind worked, and I doubted that they knew anything about what went on in the bedroom, so what they would know would be limited.

"Kannon asked that it be kept from Audrey for the time being. I think he plans to keep it a secret for as long as he can manage."

Well, that's definitely not going to blow up in his face. I never understood why anyone thought they could get away with that kind of nonsense.

"I remembered what you said about the leader only being the one that could turn a vampire. Kannon doesn't know that rule. He thinks that Drakkus isn't going to do it until the war has been won and is holding out to ensure that Kannon remains loyal. In his mind, he thinks that Drakkus will win because Evie's,"

"Young, untrained, weak?"

Reluctantly, Anzide nodded.

"We don't agree." Brad insisted.

"Exactly," Anzide said. "He hasn't seen how well you're reaching the portal now. He's got no idea how far you've come in just a short amount of time. Let him think it, pretend if you want. He'll never know unless you want him to."

I shrugged. Playing mind games with Kannon was always fun, but I was worried that at some point, he might make me angry enough that I let slip. Or worse, turn him into a flaming blue chargrilled vampire.

"I have no intention of telling him anything."

"Good. When I saw the thoughts about the leadership and the nonsense Drakkus has been feeding him, it made me wonder about everything that was going on. How could Kannon not know about the leaders and turning humans? Kannon was born in this town. I thought he was from another coven, but I was wrong. His mother was pregnant when they moved here. They haven't said anything because he's never discussed the deal with them. It also means that anything they said to you about knowing Niko is an absolute lie. They were not a part of this town when he ruled. Now, here's where it gets interesting. I was curious about what Audrey thought about the deal, and so I entered her mind and dug a little deeper."

"You didn't find it the first time?"

"Entering a mind is not easy. The younger the mind, the more scattered the memories. Audrey's mind is a jumbled mess, and finding anything worthwhile is a feat. Knowing there would be more, I searched for a little longer this time. It was easier because she was concentrating, whereas last time she was not. So, in her mind, there is a memory of entering the Fleming clan house with the expectation of a meeting with Drakkus and Kannon about their agreement. She was told to wait in one area, and when she was left alone, she wandered. Audrey saw and heard more than she should have and knows that Kannon is willingly cheating on her and has no plans to stop in the future. She knows about the secondary agreement, and she is not a happy young lady. Audrey has concocted a plan to kill Drakkus once he has turned her into a vampire, and Kannon is made the second in charge."

Wow. That was a dark thought for such a bright and bubbly girl like Audrey.

"For the record, she has no idea how to kill a vampire correctly. She thinks that a stake in the heart is enough. She also knows about the blood war and that you must kill Drakkus to end the war. Audrey does not care. She is that angry."

"Well, she's not going to get the chance." I returned. "I don't care how angry she is."

"I think you fail to see the opportunity here, Evelyn," Niko began. "In this girl, there is an opportunity to bring her to our side. If she is angry, then she can be shown compassion and understanding. With that, you might see a difference in personality."

"It's a big *might*, Niko."

He shrugged, indifferent to the statement.

"We're not looking to alter her species, nor are we out to make her into a friend. All we're interested in is turning her against our enemies. Anything is possible if you keep your mind open to everything."

I wasn't sure if that was the path that I would or could take. I suppose that Niko was right. Anything is possible. It's not as if I'd spent years enduring Audrey's nonsense. In fact, I could probably count the incidents on two hands. Given the time frame, it was a little unsettling, but she had an agenda, she was being manipulated, and I stood in her way. It was only natural that she'd mount a grand offensive against the blockade that I was.

CHAPTER 12

It was Sunday, and the day was turning out to be glorious. The sun was out, but the breeze cooled the temperature quite a lot, so it was rather brisk. Despite the sun, we were wearing jackets. It was vastly different from the past week when it had been crazy hot. I guess it didn't help that the caravan amplified the heat.

Anzide and I were walking around Hades, taking a tour of the streets and buildings. We looked like a pair of tourists, mostly because I had my camera. This wasn't a casual stroll for sightseeing or to learn the layout. This was a vampire population count for Niko.

We'd discussed the vampires in this town. Niko knew that there would not be a single one of them that was on his side. He said that it was simple. There was no doubt that Drakkus would rule with an iron fist, and if a vampire didn't do what he wanted, they'd soon find his wrath. If that ended in death or compliance, Niko wasn't sure. That's why he wanted to know who was left.

Beatrice was proof of the determination that Drakkus held to maintain complete control. When she returned to the town and posed as her alter ego, Natalia, Drakkus, and his cronies tried to get her to enter the coven. Her refusal was met with many attempts to kill her. It just made it all the more clear that any vampire that didn't join his coven was dead and that every single vampire in this town was on his side. We could not trust anyone.

Anzide was my guide as to where I should point the camera. At a distance, I couldn't tell if someone was a vampire or not. The only reason I'd managed to get the other vampires so easily was because I'd seen them in the forest attacking Niko.

Turning down a side street, I'd become distracted by the view. I hadn't been down this street, and it was rather pretty. Trees lined the center strip, and they were showing the first sign of fall. Soon, they'd turn a little rusty with pretty browns and oranges, and then the cold would continue to grow. I couldn't wait for the snow to arrive.

"Have you seen snow before?"

Anzide looked at me, giving a shake of his head. His attention on me didn't last, and Anzide turned back to the path ahead of us. I frowned. It was unlike Anzide, and I wondered what was going on.

Before I could ask, his hand went on my shoulder, and his free hand rose to his face, his index finger pressed against his lips. With a flick of his head, Anzide gestured further down the path. I could see what had made Anzide quiet. It was Audrey.

The more I watched her, the more I realized how

strangely she was acting. Her head was always turning back to see what was happening behind her. It looked like she was checking to see if anyone was following her.

Stepping out onto the street, Audrey quickly crossed to the other side. There was a gap between buildings, enough for pedestrians but nothing else. Interestingly enough, Kannon was waiting for her.

The area was too open for anything scandalous, but I found it curious that they were secretly meeting like this.

"We'll stay here. Change the settings and take photos."

"For what purpose?"

"Rainy day savings."

At this distance, the click of the camera would not be heard. Altering the camera, I waited until they were in focus and began taking the photos. At first, they were harmless, but it soon changed.

"And here I thought a public use path would make them behave."

"It's only kissing, Evie."

"Yeah, it's where it begins. Soon, those panties will hit the floor, just like last time. You know, I don't want to see them do the wall shuffle again, thanks."

"Then take a few photos as a backup before it gets too gross, and we can go. I thought you'd want to know what they were up to."

"Yeah, I guess. Why are they hiding? Wouldn't everyone already know that they're together?"

"You supposedly don't."

"Yeah, but I'm not here, am I? What's their excuse?"

"No idea. Maybe this is about the thrill."

Lame.

"I've had enough. Let's go."

We walked to the end of the street, and as we turned, Anzide let go of me. I reappeared on the street, and no one noticed a thing.

"It doesn't make sense."

"They're probably hiding it from Drakkus. Don't stress over the little things, Evie."

I huffed, putting the cover on the camera. It was a slow learning process with the camera, considering I'd only ever used the one on my phone. With a little practice, I was getting there. My pictures weren't perfect, but so long as they were focused enough for Niko to see who was in them, then they were enough.

Hearing a tooting horn, we turned to see a familiar red car slide up next to us.

"Oh look, it's grandma," Anzide said in a cheeky tone.

The window lowered, and in her form as Natalia, Beatrice leaned down to look at us.

"Hey there, kids, want a lift home?"

"That would be great."

We climbed into the car. It was small, probably enough for Natalia in her old life. Not sure what Niko would think about this car. Or modern cars.

"I got everything on your list."

"Awesome."

The view next to and behind Anzide was nothing but paper grocery bags. This little car had an open cavity for the trunk, so we could see everything she'd crammed into it.

We'd offered to help, but Beatrice said that she was fine to do the groceries on her own. Because there wasn't much space in the caravan for a lot of food, she shopped every few days. I suggested that she and Niko could stay at her place, but both of them refused. Their home was here, and they were not prepared to leave it or us.

"Plus a few little extras."

Natalia nodded at the bag at my feet with a conspiratorial smile. Warily, I lifted it and opened it, seeing a packet of condoms.

"Wow, like that's not weird."

She chuckled.

"Brad said that you're all good for the education part."

"Yep. Want some pointers like I gave him?"

Natalia laughed as she shook her head.

"I'm all good, thank you."

The amusement died, and even though there was a smile on my face, I knew that deep down, I shouldn't be happy about it. I was too young when I learned everything, barely into my teens. It was information that I wasn't ready for. But, my mother thought that being informed was better than an unplanned pregnancy or a disease. Now, I could see that she was right, but it was wrong in so many ways.

"She could have said the basics, you know?"

The smile lowered as Natalia looked at me. It was strange to see her in this form when I knew that beneath the false view was Beatrice, my great-grandmother.

"Instead, I got a gory explanation about oral sex, positions, and great places outside of the restrictive walls of a house. How to be pleasing but never the suggestion that I should expect it from my partner. She had a warped view of everything."

"This has not been an easy life for any of us, Evie. In the times that I got to see your mother, I could see the brightness fade over the years. The last time I saw her, she was a shell of her former self. She'd been told what was waiting for her."

"I guess that's why she never told me," I murmured.

"You've got a fighting spirit, just like your mother used to have when she was a little girl. Even in her early teens, she was still a fireball of energy. There was talk about returning to Hades to end the war, but your grandmother wouldn't have it. She had a family to protect, and that was a job that she took seriously. I could see it in your mother's eyes, Evie. She wanted to come back and fight Drakkus. She wanted to be free to live her life, but her mother wouldn't hear a word of it. That's probably when the spark began to die. She knew that if she didn't kill Drakkus, her life would always be spent looking over her shoulder."

The car pulled into the driveway, slowly chugging up the slope until Natalia stopped it and turned off the engine. She faced me with a sympathetic smile.

"I shouldn't have left. When Niko said to take Victoria and run, I should have argued with him that it was better to stay and die in his arms than to live a life without him. I know that Victoria harbored a lot of resentment towards this town and Drakkus. She hated that she had to grow up without her father. There were many years of arguments, tears, and temper tantrums. In the end, she gave up on holding any hope that she would see her father again. I wronged them for letting this happen. If we'd stayed,"

"You would be dead or behind the wall with Niko. Either that or Drakkus would have gotten what he wanted. Which I think he probably would have killed you and Niko anyway."

With a sad nod, she accepted it.

"One time when I saw your mother, we got to have a little chat without your grandmother around. She was ordering our meals, and we had just one small moment alone. Your mother said that she was going to have a little girl, and when she did, she wasn't going to make the same mistakes as her mother. Her daughter would be the one who ended the war, and she would not stop her."

"She raised me to be the one that did what she was not allowed to do."

"Yes. I know that your life was not easy with her. She should have told you, but I understand why she didn't. It's been rough, and we couldn't do anything to stop what was going on with this town. This town is connected. The roots drive deep into us. Any one of us could have come back here and killed him, but the void would consume the town again. Patience almost killed us, but we've reached the end of the path. You've engaged Drakkus in battle, and now, you will end the blood war. Just like your mother believed that you would."

I nodded, then turned to get out of the car.

Over the years, I'd always thought that there was something wrong with me or that I was just a bad child. Since coming here and learning the truth, I started to understand that my rough childhood was just one little piece of a large picture. There were better ways of doing things, but like I always said about my mother, she had a warped view of everything.

Maybe it was madness caused by the monster that hunted us. Maybe it was the drugs. Maybe she really did want to make me into a strong warrior who could stand up to Drakkus and win the war.

I stood next to the car and looked at the caravan. I could see Brad sitting in a lawn chair. He was stretched out under the awning with a large metal fan pointed at him. When I looked at Brad, things started to make a little more sense. At least if I looked at it from my strange mother's point of view.

Her baby brother.

The innocent one who knew nothing about the dangers of their past and their family. My mother probably knew that Victoria wouldn't tell Brad about the past. She had to protect him when their mother wouldn't.

It was guaranteed that she would see him as a kid who couldn't do anything to save himself because, in her twisted sense of reality, she would think that as a secondborn, he was a rare and useless creature.

Everything she did was to protect him, and when I arrived, her attention turned to creating the end of a vampire's cruel reign.

CHAPTER 13

Stepping beyond the fence line was always done with trepidation. Sometimes, it would only be minor. Other times, it would be large. Leaving the safety of the property after seeing what the vampires would do to us was not easy. When I watched Niko and Brad leave to feed, I always worried. Fear would consume me that the vampires would try to kill Niko again.

Anzide suggested a walk through the forest to calm my mind before making another attempt to reach the portal by myself. Mother was impatient, and I was taking too long. Drastic measures would be taken if I didn't improve. So, this was Anzide's answer.

Shade lowered the temperature. I knew it would be cooler, but there was a chill that warranted at least a light cardigan or jacket. I'd left the caravan, not thinking about it. It was a foolish move, and now I paid the price for it.

Anzide held my hand as we walked through the vegetation. We were off the track for a few steps but soon turned onto another path.

It was nice to get away from the constricting caravan. The thought of everyone being trapped in the caravan just made my mind spiral out of control. It was my fault. Sure, things were getting out of hand, but I let the emotions take control. I should have remembered that it was my emotions that caused Andross to burn.

"Maybe we should try and find a second caravan."

Anzide stopped and looked at me. I suppose that my random statement was confusing, given that I was supposed to be relaxing and clearing my mind.

"It's a little crowded," I muttered.

"I know, but I don't think that you're going to find another one in this town. Even if one could be purchased, I think you might get outvoted. What brought this on? Why is the marquee not enough?"

"It's hot. Soon, it's going to be cold. We wouldn't be in this nightmare if I could control myself. The shed is so full of furniture that it's about to explode. Then there's all the stuff still sitting on the lawn. You know it's going to start raining again really soon, right?"

Anzide sighed, pulling me into his arms.

"Don't worry about the furniture. I have it on good authority that someone wanted to replace a lot of things anyway. What's gone into the shed are the things that have been agreed would be kept, and the items on the lawn are things that are not wanted. Trust me when I say that those who you are most concerned about are, in fact, the least worried about those things."

Leaning back, I looked up at Anzide.

"You worry needlessly."

"Promise?"

"Absolutely."

"Well, okay then. If you're wrong, you'll be in trouble."

Anzide chuckled, then took my hand again.

Walking through the forest was an odd kind of relaxation. The sunlight filtered through the canopy like gold rays, giving it a magical vibe. It was a mixture of varied-sized trees, deciduous and evergreen. I'd learned that from Niko.

Inhaling deeply, I drew in the divine scent of the pine trees. It was always going to be the marker of this place and this time in my life. The incredible memory of this place and the family that I'd been given.

Stopping, I looked to my right. I could feel something. Almost like I was being drawn to the witch's ring. I'd never felt anything like it before, and I was curious and anxious.

The ring was like a consuming vice around me. Vines wrapped around me, slithering over my skin and creeping higher. Constricting me until it covered me entirely.

Anzide shifted to face me, distress rippling through his features.

"Evie?"

"The ring," I whispered.

Then I turned to the path. There was a lure that was enticing. The closer I got to the ring, the more the veil relented on me. It was like the witch's ring was calling me, commanding that I approached it.

"I'd rather we didn't go there."

"I know, but I just feel drawn to it."

"It could unbalance you."

"It's finc, drama queen."

Anzide huffed, following me along the path. When we reached the witches' ring, I could feel the energy.

"Do you feel that?"

"Yeah," Anzide said in wonder. "It's raw power emanating from the circle. It feels like there's a large wall around it."

His hand reached up like it was pressed to an invisible wall.

"It's never been like this."

"No,"

Anzide turned to face me again. This time, there was a vast difference from his previous concern. His eyes shifted in all directions, turning to look around but never letting go of my hand. The free hand was still pressed to an invisible wall, pushing against it as if there was something physically stopping him.

"It's been used recently."

"Mardyl?"

"No. He left town not long after the incident. This," he paused, glancing back at the ring. "This was used by a woman."

"How can you tell?"

He shifted behind me, resting his hands on my shoulders.

"Close your eyes, focus on the power that you feel. Let it soak into your body and consume you. Can you feel the incantations?"

I did as Anzide suggested and let the power into me. When I actually submitted to the ring's power, the constriction changed. Now, it was like a soft veil that floated over my body, wrapping around me before slowly seeping into me. The power focused on my arms, hands, and fingers. It didn't take long before the veil changed and turned into little tendrils that emerged from my fingers. They searched. They found.

"It was a woman," I whispered, opening my eyes. "And she's still here."

"Ooh-kay. That means we're leaving."

Anzide turned me around and pushed me away from the ring. His hands on my shoulders were not as relaxing as I'd like them to be. It was the shortest walk back to the property, and I knew that Anzide had a lot to do with it. My feet probably weren't on the ground at all.

Opening the caravan door, he frowned as his head flicked. Restraining my distaste, I climbed up the metal stairs, greeted by Niko.

"You're back early. How was the walk?"

"Witchy."

The smile dropped, and Niko frowned at us.

"What does that mean?"

"Evie was drawn to the ring because it had just been used. I think that we disturbed the witch because Evie said that she found her."

"Found her?"

"Yeah," I said, sitting next to Beatrice at the dining table. "I could feel the power. Anzide said the witch was female, and he showed me how to search for the power. I searched, and I found her. Then we left because Anzide freaked out."

"Witches are dangerous," he grumbled.

"They are," Niko responded. "But it can depend on the circumstances. Most will not engage by choice. If you didn't see her, then that is the reason. She chose to hide until you left. They will lead a quiet, almost hermit lifestyle to avoid any confrontational situations. Many suggest that the past haunts them, ingrained into those who survived, and passed down through the generations, but the reality is that witches have always been a solitary race. Of course, that doesn't mean to say that they won't seek out a partner to love, create a family, or even have friends. Those that do venture beyond the norm always keep the circle tight."

Niko shifted forward as he leaned on the table. The frown deepened.

"Please listen to me carefully. We will not engage the services of a witch who uses black magic. It is a path that is complicated and unnecessary. Your skills will be more than enough."

I scoffed, rolling my eyes.

"Yeah, provided that I can actually learn something. I'm still trying to get to the portal by myself."

"Mother is not a happy lady." Anzide offered with a grin.

Niko leaned back, glancing at Anzide.

"There is only so much time that they will grant her before they deem your lessons to be unworthy. When that happens, Evelyn, you might be faced with a situation that you do not like. Those that oversee the portal do not like novices, nor do they like the untrained to take weeks to learn something that should be ingrained in them."

"How do you know so much?" I asked.

Niko dragged a book out from the pile, pushing it to me. It was one of the many books that James had given me. The demon was a hardass, too.

"This is your father's fault. He would know that you exist. Perhaps he does not know where you are but would know you're alive. Isn't that right, Anzide?"

I looked at him as he nodded, giving me a grim smile.

"Those that manage the portal would have hauled him in already. It is surprising that they haven't suggested that he takes over."

"They have. I said that Evie doesn't want to know about her father because of the whole killing her mother thing. They accepted it but only on the proviso that I can get the education done within a certain timeframe."

"How long have I got?"

"Friday."

Two days. Two whole days.

"How come you didn't tell me?" I snapped.

"Because you've been doing really well. Mother said that you're almost there. I didn't think you'd have issues because you are actually reaching the portal by yourself."

I sighed, sinking back into the seat. Yes, I reach the portal every time, but that boat is still too slow.

"Until you complete the entire process efficiently, they deem you incompetent. That means that no matter how easily you can get to the portal, you're still burdened by the delay once you're in there."

"They see it as one whole process?"

Anzide nodded.

"Well, I guess we'd better get on with it," I muttered,

getting up from the table.

Stepping out of the caravan, I felt the cool breeze whip past me. Temporary covers had been put up, creating a lot of shade over the caravan, but it was still warm in there.

The gap between the caravan and the walled area was only small, but it was enough to be exposed. As soon as I stepped out from the cover of the caravan, I could feel something watching me.

"Anzide, I don't think we're alone."

He looked at the forest and frowned.

"I can feel something out there, but unless I go and actually look, I won't know for certain. That means I'd have to leave you to sit and twiddle your thumbs while you wait for me to return. So, what's more important? The silent stalker or the portal?"

Huffing in frustration, I walked to the walled area.

"The choices are the witch who has decided to check us out and make sure we're not a threat, a minion of Drakkus, or Drakkus himself."

"None of which are good, right?"

Anzide shrugged.

"All have their pros and cons."

"Drakkus will see me coming out of the portal in my weakened state. That's not good."

"But the good thing is that he won't know what you

get up to while you're in there."

Pulling the cover over the gap, Anzide enclosed us into the little room that would hopefully shield me from those who watched from the forest. The bonus of the situation was that once I actually entered the portal, I did not have a worldly presence. It was a perk of actually being capable of getting into the portal myself. I had control over my body and mind, meaning that I could actually bring my body to the portal rather than just my mind.

With positive thoughts, I sat down and tried to calm myself down. The figure in the forest didn't matter. All that I had to concern myself with was getting to the portal and to Mother as quickly as possible.

CHAPTER 14

I reached the portal in my usual time, which was reasonable, according to Anzide. The boat ride, however, was still my downfall. To be fair, I'd lessened the time in which it took me to reach land, but it still wasn't good enough.

Mother silently shook her head and walked away. Anzide looked at me, then at Mother. He chased after her, and even though they were some distance from me, I could still hear everything. It was like she wanted me to know. Maybe Mother thought it would help me improve if I realized where I was failing. I knew, though. I understood that there was something wrong with my ability to guide the boat quickly and efficiently.

"You're wasting time, Anzide."

"She doesn't want to know her father. Just give Evie a couple more days."

"No, on both counts. Phoenix always knows their creators, regardless of the situation surrounding the conception. The creators are the ones that guide them in the path to the portal. It is their job to instruct their young in the ways of this world. You've gotten her far, be proud of your efforts, and do not be so harsh on yourself or Evelyn. You are young, Anzide. You are not meant to be a teacher at such a tender age. It is done. The creator will be sent to assist."

"Wait," I begged, stepping closer. "Anzide said that I had two more days."

"You've had weeks. What difference would it make when your improvement has been limited?"

"Well, maybe I work well under pressure."

"This deadline has been looming, and you have been fully aware of it. I see no reason as to why it or anything will change enough to make me agree to the upgrade of your status."

Mother stared at me.

"Own your failings, but understand that you are young and were not raised in this world. You can't be blamed for not understanding how this world works because every single eternal that has been created was done so in this world. You are the only one who was not, and now you suffer for it. This is not the end of the path, Evelyn. It is just the beginning. You tried, and you have accomplished a lot in such a short amount of time. Time is not on your side, and that is why we have ruled that you must complete your training with your father."

When I looked at Anzide, he smiled softly, and an eyebrow raised, one that Mother would not have seen.

He was telling me to get my inner Evie out and let her loose, just like I had with the Nephilim and Drakkus.

"I can own my failings, as you say, but I was told that I still had time to get this done, and now you're telling me that it's not happening. I was granted the time until two days from now, and you will honor that."

Mother tilted her head. It was hard to see it, but in the corner of her lips was the tiniest smirk.

"Oh, I can honor it, but you will not like my terms."

She inhaled sharply, and for a moment, her body straightened. Leaning on the tall staff, Mother looked at me with pure amusement. Clearly, she thought that I would not like whatever she was concocting.

"So be it, Phoenix. You are permitted to make one more attempt tomorrow, thus completely ending your remaining two days. After that, we will send your creator to take over the instruction, regardless of whether his influence is welcomed or not."

Mother turned and began to walk away.

"Had I thought that I would have to put up with another, I would have banned your father from walking the Earth. So much like him."

Anzide smiled at me, and then a frown quickly formed. He chased after the hobbling woman who was rather fast on her feet. After a few words, Anzide returned to me.

"What did you ask for?"

"Time on the lake. Get in the boat."

"Seriously?"

"Absolutely. The only issue that you face, in Mother's eyes, is your ability to get to land quickly and efficiently. She said that you can access the portal in an acceptable time frame. Your worldly presence follows you into the portal, so all you need is that boat."

I huffed and walked back to the boat.

"But it's not always going to be like this, is it?"

"No. The boat is like an alternative view of how we navigate this area. If they just plonked you into the water, you'd think that you were drowning."

Anzide stepped out onto the water to show me how it was really done.

"Wanna try it?"

He held out his hand with hope on his face.

"You're crazy. I can't move the boat properly, and you think that I'm going to step out of it and onto the water?"

Anzide shrugged and slid backward over the water.

"Follow me."

Sitting in the boat, I calmed my mind and focused on Anzide. It wasn't easy, and the boat still wobbled like I was standing and about to lose my balance. Distraction was the worst, and when I heard something, the boat shifted to face it. Anzide moved around like he was gliding on ice, effortless and perfect. It didn't help.

"There's something that you can look at if you follow me over here."

I followed the sound of his voice. The fog was thick, and I'd lost sight of Anzide. There was no concept of time here, at least none that I was aware of.

The boat hit a wall, and I was almost knocked out of it. As the fog began to dissipate, I saw Anzide sitting on a ledge. Behind him was a large window.

With a wiggle of his fingers, the boat turned, and I was dragged closer. Holding out his hand, Anzide helped me onto the ledge.

"Okay, I'm here. What's so great about this place?"

"There are quite a few of these. They're called viewing platforms. They used to be the way that the portal master would check that the world was ready to receive someone. Now, the system is different, and they don't need it, but the windows are still here. Guess what this place is?"

I shrugged, unable to see much through the dark glass.

"The land of the Phoenix."

Anzide flicked a panel down and altered a few of the controls. The glass changed to a screen that showed everything.

"Are you going to show me my father?"

"There may be a chance that he's here, but I doubt it. I won't point him out."

"You know who he is?"

Anzide nodded, giving me a sympathetic smile.

"When they started telling me that you weren't learning fast enough, they let slip his name."

I didn't want to admit that my curiosity was growing. He shouldn't have been with my mother. The inevitability of his actions weighed heavily on her life and probably on mine, too.

The screen shifted as Anzide moved the controls. It was a path through the lush valleys of a land that was bright and full of beauty. Soon, the view reached a small town that looked like it was built to replicate a quaint English village.

"It's pretty," I admitted. "But you can't enter it, can you?"

"That's a complicated one. We can visit the towns of the other species, but we don't reside in them. I don't know why, but I assume it's to stop cross-breeding. We're not supposed to,"

"Because it creates an unholy mess that's like you and me?"

Anzide nodded.

"Yep. The Nephilim that's half angel and half demon."

"And the Phoenix, that's also a vampire, shapeshifter, and human."

"I know it seems harsh and extreme, but there are reasons for it."

"Like me?"

He looked at me, and I could tell that Anzide was deciding whether he wanted to answer that.

"It's okay. I get it. I'm not a full Eternal, and I've probably still got vampirism and shapeshifter in me, which is causing problems. The alterations are there, and I can feel things changing, which is probably why I can soak a book in easily but struggle with things like the boat."

Anzide smiled as he wrapped his arm around my shoulder.

"But you are advancing enough to indicate that it's almost fully complete. It's probably one little thing that's holding you back."

"My mind?"

He nodded, laughing softly.

"Yeah, that mind. You keep thinking negatively, and you're not going anywhere. Optimism needs to be your best friend. So, with that in mind, get back in the boat and take it for a spin. See what other worlds you can find."

Anzide helped me off the ledge and into the boat. It still wobbled, but I didn't end up in the water.

"What about the Nephilim world?"

"Yeah, it's here, too."

"And the land where your parents are?"

"A little more complicated, but yes, there is a window for that too."

Sitting down, I thought about it and looked up at Anzide.

"Can you go and see them?"

He sighed, and with a flick of his fingers, thc boat turned towards the lake.

"I could ask to visit, but I won't."

"Can I ask why?"

"You can, but the question is, should you?"

"I should. Why don't you want to visit your parents?"

"Because what they did was wrong, and I was punished for their actions. They served time for their side of the punishment but never bothered to take on more for what I was given. They could have, you know? My parents could have asked that the time allocated to me be added to their time so that I would be free of the service. As soon as they finished, they left. I was still bound to my punishment, still considered an outcast for a crime that I did not commit. Do you want to know how punishment works here?"

"Sure."

Because clearly, Anzide was angry and needed to say it.

"The time of service is decided and split between those involved. In this case, there are two groups that are considered. The offender and the product. They split the time between the offender and the product. That means that my parents had half, and I had the other half. It's unfair that I am forced to serve half of the sentence, yet they get to split their half between the two of them."

Which meant that they only served a quarter of the sentence. I couldn't understand why the product was punished. They didn't ask to be created.

"You said that they've already passed over."

"It's a way of saying that they scammed the system. They found out that a leniency request could be made. Usually, it's done on behalf of the product because they are not the ones who committed the deed. They applied together as the offenders and took the deal when offered. If you're wondering why I dislike demons, that's your answer."

"Oh," I said softly.

"Yeah, oh. My father knew the workings and figured out that they could get out of their punishment in the original form and take it as a different form. They're now working as household staff for someone higher up the chain. It's not something that anyone considers punishment, if you're wondering. The perks are so good that there's actually a waiting list to be a part of the staff for these places. They get time off, isn't that wonderful?

Holidays, fully funded by the staff management. They actually get paid, too. I never got paid or had a holiday."

Reaching out, I took his hands and pulled him closer.

"But maybe you got something better?"

Anzide stopped, and the frown melted away.

"Yeah, I did."

I giggled when he climbed into the boat. It rocked from side to side because he wasn't supposed to be in it with me, but neither of us cared. We kissed and ignored the wind that whispered a warning that we were wasting time. One little moment wouldn't hurt. I hope.

CHAPTER 15

I lay on my back, staring at the bright blue sky. The grass was soft, but there was a twig digging into my back. Did I care? Yes, but I lacked the energy to deal with it.

Anzide interrupted my view of the blue and the white fluffy clouds, giving me a smirk.

"You're wiped."

"I'm always wiped. What's your point?"

"Grandma's on her way over."

He sat back on the grass next to me. As Anzide helped me sit up, Beatrice pulled back the material and gave me a smile.

"Wow, okay. I was going to ask that you pick up the parcel at the post office, but I guess not."

"I'll be fine. Just give me some time to recover."

"Well, it's almost five, so we don't have time. It's okay. I'll go."

"Is it the marquee?"

"Yeah, that's why they're not delivering it. They said it's too bulky for their poky van. Not sure how we're going to get it here."

"Maybe we should all go," Anzide suggested, rising to his feet. "Take both cars."

Helping me to my feet, Anzide held on. I could feel the giddiness and was grateful that he saw it.

"I know what's going to be said."

"It's fine. Once we've got the marquee set up, no one will see a thing."

Anzide held onto me as we emerged from the walled area and into the yard where I was exposed. It was just a few steps, but everyone agreed it was too much.

Brad was standing at the doorway, shaded by the cover. There was a mighty frown on his face.

"We have discussed this, and we agree that you are risking too much by this kind of exposure."

"Well, we're about to fix that, so chill out."

Brad huffed and turned back into the caravan. Inside, I saw Niko at the table. It seemed to be his favorite place, but in reality, there wasn't much of a choice given how little space there was. I hoped that the marquee was large enough to give him a little more freedom.

"Okay, into the cars."

I was in the car with Beatrice in her alternative form while Brad drove Anzide in his car. If I weren't so tired,

I might have been able to drive, but Brad was adamant that it wasn't happening. So, he risked the sunlight and drove to the post office.

We'd packed Brad's car as much as we could, then put the smaller items into Beatrice's car. Both were loaded, and the postal worker agreed to bring the rest of the items when he finished work in half an hour. We had the marquee pieces, so we would start setting it up when we returned to the property.

"Hey, look at that. It's Drakkus, and he clearly has no idea that we're here."

"He's distracted." I offered.

Anzide nodded and then grinned like he had a terrible idea.

"When Brad comes looking for me, tell him that I'm on a mission and will find my own way home."

Fading from sight, Anzide left me in the car. It wasn't for long. Brad opened the door and leaned down to look at me.

"Now, I thought that I saw Anzide in the car, but he's not here."

"He's somewhere over there near Drakkus and said to tell you that he's on a mission and will find his own way home."

"Alright."

Brad stepped away, and Beatrice climbed in behind the wheel.

"This is exciting, isn't it? A huge tent."

"Yeah."

There was no merriment in my tone. As she turned onto the street, Beatrice glanced at me.

"Okay, spill it. What's going through your mind?"

"That Niko wouldn't have to sit in the hot tin can all day if I hadn't destroyed your house."

"Oh, honey. It's okay. We understand that you couldn't control your powers."

"Still can't. How can I defeat Drakkus when I can't make these things work?"

I looked at my hands. No matter how much I tried, I couldn't willingly make the powers work. It was only when I lost control of my emotions that my body took over and unleashed everything within me, causing problems.

"Maybe Mother is right. Maybe I do need my father to help me."

"If you search your thoughts and feelings, you will know what is right for your life. No one wants to dictate anything to you, but some will want to guide you because they believe that they know what is right."

"It doesn't matter anyway. The house is destroyed, and it's going to cost a fortune to rebuild it."

As Beatrice slowed to enter the driveway, I looked at the footpath and saw Nora and Karina. I guess they were visiting.

"They don't know about Niko, do they?"

"No, and I'm not sure if I'm ready to expose him like that. I keep thinking it needs to happen, but I don't want anything bad to happen to him again. Has Niko said anything to you?"

Beatrice shrugged.

"Just that he feels better. He's ready for anything, Evelyn. Niko remains unseen so that the future takes a particular path. You have to be seen as the leader of the Corbin clan, and if Niko is exposed, then a demand will rise, and the vampires in this town, regardless of whether they follow him or not, will expect that he is placed as the leader. It will cause disharmony, and while it won't disrupt the land or cause a void to be created, it will begin. Little waves at first, but over time, the void will grow."

She stopped the car on the grass near the caravan. With the engine still running, Beatrice faced me.

"I know you're at odds with everything that happened, but please understand that Niko does not find it upsetting. What he does find upsetting is that you are stressed regarding it. You're not focusing on the more important things like entering the portal or your schoolwork. Talk to Niko if you must, but I assure you that you'll only get a repeat of what I said."

I nodded.

"Now, the newcomers. Shall we be introducing them

to our beloved Niko?"

"Let him decide that."

"Alright."

Getting out of the car, I moved to the rear and lifted the first of the items out. Karina was all smiles as she approached.

"Hey, hey. Need some help, amazing leader?"

"Sure. Hey, have you guys met Natalia?"

"Uh, yes," Nora said, looking at the caravan door. "Doesn't she work for the Heritage Trust?"

"Yep."

Hearing my name, I turned to see Natalia urging us over.

"She's been in the town for a while, right?"

"A few years."

"And she's not a member of the other coven?"

I stopped and looked at Nora. The concern was obvious.

"Ah, I get it. You're worried, and I understand. We have ways to figure that out, and that's why you're about to enter the caravan and learn a few things. Are you ready?"

Karina nodded eagerly, and Nora gave me an uneasy smile.

I climbed up the steps into the caravan and saw Niko standing behind Natalia. When the two newest members of our little clan were in the caravan, they were silent as they stared.

"So, we'll start with introductions. This is Nora and Karina."

Both were given nods and smiles from the silent ones.

"And this is probably going to blow your mind, especially considering that you said you'd like to meet my great-grandmother."

Karina's eyes widened as she looked at me.

"No," she whispered.

"Yes. Natalia Eastwell is actually Beatrice Corbin."

She shifted into her true form to the sounds of gasps.

"And the lovely fellow behind her is Niko."

"Thank you, Evelyn. You are always too kind." Niko said as he stepped out from behind Beatrice. "No doubt, you're wondering why I haven't returned to my former position as leader of the Corbin clan. It is because Evelyn has engaged Drakkus in the end battle of the blood war. To successfully complete the task, she must be the leader. I remain hidden to ensure this town does not plunge into a void of darkness. As such, I would appreciate it if the two of you could keep the secrets that we have revealed to you today."

"Of course," Nora said. "We would not want to expose you to the enemy or this town to any form of darkness."

"Excellent. Now, I believe that Anzide has returned with information. Please, let us conduct a mini-meeting to listen and discuss."

Niko looked at me and gestured to the floor with his eyes. Yep, I was meant to find the chairs and sit at the head of the table again. Now, though, we had two extra bums to find seats for.

While Brad and I searched for chairs, Niko organized the seating arrangements. Nora and Karina were on one side, with himself and Beatrice on the other side. Brad and Anzide were at either side of me as I sat down.

"Okay, the mini-meeting has begun. Anzide, what did you find out?"

"A couple of things. First off, Drakkus does not know who the demon is. He has no idea that Kannon is aware of the truth. Drakkus knows there would be a demon, but he could not find out before Hannah left."

"That is good," Niko responded. "The less he knows in that respect, the better. Carry on."

"Alright. So, the main thing that was in his mind, the most prominent, was his future as the leader of the Corbin clan."

"The what now?" I asked.

"Drakkus understands that to lead this town successfully, and rightfully, he needs to be in the Corbin clan. I don't know how he came to that conclusion, but,"

"He is correct." Niko interrupted.

"Yeah. Drakkus also knows he cannot breed with Evie because of her deity status. There is only one option left, and that's Brad. Obviously, he's unable to impregnate a male, so his plan is to find a suitable woman who will conceive the child. Once the girl is born, Brad will be removed, and the child will be raised by the woman alone. When the child is an adult, Drakkus will force her to marry him."

"But that doesn't make him a ruler. Does it?"

Niko shook his head at me.

"That doesn't mean that he won't rule over this woman and the child with an iron fist to ensure that they are compliant with his every desire. His end goal would be to have the leader in the flesh, but in reality, she would be nothing more than a puppet. He would be the ruler."

"And I'd be dead," Brad said as he looked up at me. "You too."

"And therein lies the problem." Niko offered with a devious smile. "How does one actually kill an eternal?"

"They can't," Anzide responded. "No matter what Drakkus thinks he's capable of, he will never be able to kill Evie. That means that no matter what, she will always be able to be the ruler of the Corbin clan. He has not figured that out, if anyone was wondering. Drakkus firmly believes that he can kill Evie and that he will win the war."

"Let him think that. I can accept his foolish belief if

it means that he's not looking at me or trying to figure out how to kill me. Which, how is he thinking that will happen?"

Anzide shrugged uneasily.

"Same as a vampire."

Niko chuckled, shaking his head.

"Oh, I'd almost forgotten his lack of ingenuity."

"And his distaste for books," Beatrice added.

Niko nodded.

"If he'd bothered to pick up a book, he might have found one or two that contained all that he needed regarding Eternals."

"But his gusto is understandable, right?"

Everyone looked at me like I was crazy.

"For this war to end, one of us has to die. Drakkus is doing exactly what any of us would do if we were in the same situation. He's trying to remain positive and thinking that he will win."

The group nodded, and as the mood shifted into a grim reality of the future, I thought about Drakkus. It was not surprising that he was thinking about life beyond the war. It was probably the only thing that was keeping his mind positive.

CHAPTER 16

Once the marquee was set up, we quickly installed the air conditioning unit. The caravan was moved into place, and in the remaining area, flooring was installed.

It was long, consuming most of the width of the property. The reality of the situation was that it was the perfect size. We had space to move around in, the caravan was put at one end, and we even created a sectioned-off area for me to practice entering the portal.

It wasn't a perfect area, but it was enough. Niko was able to move outside of the caravan during daylight hours. Even the area that was shielded had a leisurely feel to it and, thankfully, didn't seem to constrict. We had to be mindful of the workers who had started the clean-up and reconstruction, so an area was created. It was a walled-off section that shielded the view of the caravan from the only entrance into the marquee. We also ensured that the walls would not fall down or blow away. I think Brad went a little crazy when he purchased extra pegs and rope. This thing was not moving.

The area was large, and I knew that it would benefit

Niko a lot more than what he was ready to admit. He didn't hit his head on the ceiling of the caravan, but it was close. He always bent over when walking out of the bathroom and the back bedroom area. Like always, Niko said it was fine and that he didn't mind the situation and everything was okay. I didn't see it that way, and every time I saw him sitting at the dining table, I saw the constricting walls that seemed to creep closer each day that passed us by.

As much as the caravan was small, it wasn't that bad. I was surprised that Henry was so willing to give it away, to be honest. I'm sure that if Brad couldn't find anyone to give it to, he'd return it to Henry. And, it would be returned in a better condition than what we received it.

When the workers weren't here, and we didn't have to worry about Henry walking into the marquee to discuss something with us, Niko had the freedom to walk anywhere within it. The bonus was that all the unwanted furniture had been brought into the marquee, creating pockets of areas and giving it a more homely vibe.

The parts of the material walls that could be opened to create windows were tied down and covered with fabric. Anzide pulled on all of the ropes and pegs to ensure that it was strong enough to withstand a heavy wind.

"You know, this is large enough to create rooms."

I grinned and waggled my eyebrows at Anzide.

"That's true. I vote that you suggest it to your family and see what they say while remembering that it's just one large room, and no amount of being quiet will hide what we're doing."

I huffed and closed my eyes again.

"Okay, going in now."

"Good luck. Remember to concentrate, remember everything you've been taught. I'll be waiting for you."

This was it. My last chance at doing this with Anzide's help. As much as I was curious about my father, I didn't want to know him. The past burned holes in my heart, a pain I wasn't sure could ever be repaired. If I didn't get this right, there would be no choice. He would be forced to enter my life and teach me what Anzide could not. There was also the whisper in my mind that if I failed, Anzide would blame himself. I didn't want that. If anything, I had to succeed so that he wouldn't try to lay blame.

Darkness shrouded me. As I opened my eyes, I felt the cool veil brush over my arms. The fog had descended. The murky view offered nothing. It was like Mother had ramped up the fog just to push me to the limit. I'm sure she meant well, but it was a pain in the backside.

Focusing my mind, I urged the boat to turn and move. I could not feel Anzide's presence, and it was disarming for me. He was my beacon, and it was like he wasn't here even though he said he would be waiting. No matter where I searched, I could not find him or the island. I was lost, and morose thoughts began to consume and dominate. The boat moved, but I knew it was floating aimlessly. I was failing despite the focus I held.

"Half an hour," Mother called out in the darkness. "The time allocated for finding the island port is over."

"Half an hour is hardly enough," I grumbled.

The boat moved with speed, knocking me off the seat. The water that sloshed around the sides of the boat gave way to the sand. I sat up, faced with a glowering old woman.

"It should take a minute at most." she snapped harshly. "You have been given more than necessary, and I have been far too lenient. Go home and wait for your creator. He will be sent to you, and pray that you learn faster than you have in the past because my patience has worn thin."

Instead of shuffling away, Mother disappeared. Anzide helped me stand up.

"Sorry," he murmured.

"For what?"

"I know that she shielded me. She said it was for your own good, and I had to accept that this was how it had to be."

"It's not your fault. You tried to teach me. Why did she hide you?"

"Because you need to learn to find this port without me as your beacon. What if you come here without me?"

"I won't."

Anzide frowned at me as if to say that it was foolish

to think that he'd always be by my side. I'd like to think that he would be.

"Come on, let's go home and warn everyone that we're about to get a visitor."

We reappeared on the little cushions in our mediation area.

"What do you think about that?"

I shrugged as I stood.

"Conflicted. He killed my mother, but a part of me wants to know what he's like."

"Hoping for a jerk so that you feel okay when he leaves?"

"Yeah, maybe."

Anzide gave me an uneasy smile, and it was then that I knew that my father was not a jerk. I had a feeling that this was not going to be what I expected it to be.

Everyone was seated in the outdoor setting when we emerged. Hope was on their faces, but that soon changed when faced with my disappointment.

"So, be prepared to meet my father. They're sending him here to teach me."

"I know that you don't agree with us, but it is for the best." Niko offered.

I nodded.

Anzide shifted to face the internal door, which was

the only thing that stopped a visitor from seeing Niko.

"We have company."

Well, that was fast. I'm sure Mother had him waiting in the portal, expecting that I'd fail.

Brad stood and walked through the door. I stood behind it, listening to what was going on.

"Henry,"

"Uh, hey Brad. There's a guy out here that says he's here to see Evelyn. Says he's her dad."

It sounded almost as if he was worried that this was not a good situation. Maybe he thought I lived with Brad for a reason and was now concerned that he might have to call Larry to intervene.

"Yeah, it's okay. Send him in."

I looked at Anzide. He gave me a warm smile that I guess was his way of reassuring me. My stomach was turning itself over, making life difficult for me.

"Is it him? Is this really my father or another imposter?"

"Now that we know the truth about you, we can see everything. We are no longer blinded by the belief that you're a landbound immortal."

Brad appeared at the doorway, holding back the scrap of material that was more of an annoyance than a shield.

"Be brave and say hello. Ask him questions and learn the truth, but do not assume you know it. There are only two people who can tell you what went on between your parents, one is dead, and the other is just a few steps away. Would you like me to go with you?"

I nodded. Brad stepped aside, holding the material up for me to pass through. Anzide was a step behind, mostly because I'd taken his hand and would not let go.

A tall man stood in the middle of the area, dressed in slacks and a skivvy. The black-on-black combination made his fair skin and auburn hair stand out. He smiled, but it was reserved, probably full of fear that I'd react harshly.

"Hello, Evelyn. I am Carsten, your father."

I smiled weakly as my hello escaped. Carsten turned his attention to Anzide, and with a nod, he continued to Brad.

"You must be Bradley. Nancy talked about you a lot. Thank you for taking care of Evelyn after Nancy's passing."

"Uh yeah, no problem."

"I understand that this is not an easy situation, Evelyn, but those who manage the portal have ruled that you must learn how to navigate it efficiently. I wanted to honor your request that I stay out of your life, but they insisted it was not open for negotiation. With that in mind, I suggest we get the education done quickly, and then I can leave you to continue with your life without my interference."

Brad turned to look at me. His eyebrows raised, and

his eyes widened. The wordless message that I should maybe rethink that idea and try again.

"I've already been to the portal today, and I'm weak from it."

Carsten nodded quietly.

"Maybe we can talk," I suggested.

"You have questions?"

I nodded. Yes, I had questions. Maybe he had the answers.

Brad and Anzide left us, returning to the area behind the wall. I gestured to the lounges.

"This is quite a setup you've got here."

"Newly installed. We've got issues,"

"Evelyn," Carsten interrupted. "Forgive me, but when whispers began to grow in the portal surrounds, I made a few inquiries."

"Whispers?"

"The unknown entity who ordered the Nephilim around as if she were the one who controlled them. The one that barked orders at them, stood her ground, flattened the very same ground, and unfortunately, the house as well. The Nephilim are a stubborn bunch, and I'd suggested that I might be the father of this person, but they claimed to have the right person, so I was sent on my way. I happened to cross paths with someone that you might know—Renuge. He said that he's never met anyone quite like you and that, in many ways, he was reminded of me."

Carsten smiled as he looked at the shock on my face.

"Mother said something like that yesterday."

"Well, of course, she would. She knows her own child."

"What?"

"You weren't told? That happens quite a lot, but Mother is actually my mother and your grandmother. The portal is full of beings that are related to or know someone, somewhere in some roundabout way. It is widely believed that at some point in the distant future, we will hit the limit, and it will become necessary to seek out partners from other sources. I think that is why they were so lenient on you."

"And not my people skills?"

Carsten smiled. I had to admit he was easy to talk to.

"So, you made inquiries?"

"Yes. I knew you existed, but I didn't know where you were. It is extremely difficult to find an underaged being regardless of their species. Your mother was determined to hide, though I don't know her reasons."

"Drakkus."

"No, not in that respect."

Carsten inhaled deeply, slowly letting the air out.

"I will take you back to the beginning so that you understand everything. Are you ready to hear about the past, Evelyn?"

CHAPTER 17

"I met your mother when she was nineteen. At that stage, she did not have any siblings and always believed that she would be an only child. She was lonely in terms of her alter ego. There were a few friends, but none that knew the truth. All she had up until she met me were her parents, the occasional visit from her human grandparents, and the woman who she believed was her maternal grandmother but was told differently. They'd lived a nomadic lifestyle, never settling for too long in one area, always looking over their shoulders. She knew the truth because your mother was fiery and demanding. Nancy wanted the truth because she knew that something was wrong."

So the apple really didn't fall from the tree. Or, in this case, two trees, apparently.

"Was she a vampire or shapeshifter?"

"I never saw her consume blood. She never mentioned which way she leaned, so I would assume that she'd taken the path of the shapeshifter."

I nodded, accepting the answer that seemed reasonable if it were the truth.

"I'd decided to live on Earth for a few years, and because I'd spent too long outside of this world and never really engaged in it, I was not accustomed to the technology that had grown in my absence. I decided to hire someone to do the jobs around my house, and I would observe. Your mother was one of a few who rang, but after meeting all of them, I decided on her. Not only was she knowledgeable about the other side of this world, but she was a wonderful person. I didn't have to hide anything because your mother already knew about Eternals. She was happy to show me how to use the various pieces of equipment, and as the days became weeks and months, we formed a friendship."

It was clear that I had everything wrong. I guess that happened when there wasn't enough information.

"Your mother liked that she could tell me everything without fear. She could ask for advice and often came to me for a discussion where she wanted my thoughts on a subject. Once, she said it was cathartic to let go and talk to me. Her mind was stressed out because of everything happening here in this town. I questioned the reasons she worried about a town that she had never been to, and your mother told me about the blood war. She could have ended it, and she wanted to, but her mother would not allow it. Nancy said that her mother refused to return to the place where her world fell apart. All that her mother wanted was to live with her parents, and that had been taken away from her. She wasn't prepared to lose her daughter to the same monster that ripped her father away from her. The years passed by, and one day, out of the blue, Nancy told me that she was about to become a sister. She said that it was quite a shock because they always believed that the Corbin line only ever had one female. I pointed out to your mother that her grandparents never truly had the time to create another child before Beatrice took Victoria away. It was then that your mother started talking about having a child."

"Wait, she wanted to have a child?"

Carsten nodded with a warm smile on his face.

"Very much so. I suppose that it might seem a little odd, but when your mother and I talked about her having a child, she always believed that her daughter would be the one that ended the war. She was determined to raise a strong young woman who would do everything that she was not allowed to. The years continued to slip past us, and every now and then, your mother would talk about her baby brother. I could see beyond the words, I could see that she was worried about his future, far more than her own. The life she had been living, the one full of fear, was taking its toll. The bright spark that I met a decade earlier was fading. She smiled, but there was nothing behind it. Then, one day, completely out of the blue, your mother asked me for an important favor. She asked me to impregnate her."

Well, that just blew everything out of the water. It wasn't an accident. I was created by choice.

"I sat your mother down and told her that while I was honored and would love to give her a child, I could not because Eternals are not meant to breed with other species. Your mother replied that she knew the consequences of the deed, and she knew that it would end in her eventual death. Nancy said that she was a walking target anyway and no longer cared. What she wanted was to give the world a vampire killer. Her daughter would end the war."

"What happened after you got her pregnant?"

"Nancy disappeared. I woke up the next morning, and my bed was empty. There was a note that said that she would return when you were five so that your training could begin. She said that she would keep in contact with me and that she would involve her brother to ensure that he was adequately prepared for the future. I waited. I was in the same house for many years, but I never saw your mother again. There was no way of finding you, and your mother was determined to hide. I suppose from me, but definitely from the enemy. Perhaps she changed her mind about our agreement for your training. There was no way that she would have died from our interaction for a few years, but I feared that something else might have happened. Knowing that you could not have died, I searched the orphanages to no avail."

Well, that was certainly a tale. I just wished that my mother had been sober enough to tell it to me. I suppose there were a lot of things that I could wish for, but knowing what she was like, I knew that not one of them would come true.

"Tell me about your life."

"Well, our life was always on the go. She lived her life on the street corner, or at least, that's where I thought she was. I really have no idea where she went at night. I'd come home from school, and she'd be walking out the door."

Carsten was shocked, almost horrified.

"I learned how to cook thanks to a neighbor who could smell the burning food and was banging on the door, begging me not to burn the apartment building down. She figured out that my mother was hardly ever home and made sure that I knew she was always around if I needed her. It would have been great, except a month later, we moved. I think she called child services, and my mother got wind of it. Anyway, I'd wake in the morning, and my mother would either be in her bed or on the lounge suite. Either way, she was always passed out. I'd have breakfast, get ready for school, and then leave. She was always angry. I couldn't do anything right, and everything she shouted at me contradicted what she'd yelled at me previously. When I didn't do the right thing because I didn't know what was right or wrong, she'd hit me."

Carsten's head turned as his eyes shut tightly. His fists balled on his legs. Slowly, he exhaled, and when he returned to me, I was faced with a much calmer being There was still a lot of pain on his face, but he'd shut it down to listen to me.

"I always thought that I was a bad child. Nothing was ever right. Everything was always wrong. We moved constantly, and I began to think that I was the reason. I got in trouble at school, with the law, I never had friends, I was always the outcast. Nothing ever made sense until I came here. Pieces have been falling into place, and I keep thinking there was a reason for everything she did. You might agree with that, but I don't. I was trying to sanctify her abuse, but I can't do that anymore, especially not when I now know that she could have honored her agreement with you. She could have left me with you. Then, I would know everything that I need to know right now. I wouldn't be floating aimlessly in that stupid rowboat."

"I don't agree with your mother, Evelyn, and I am sorry that you endured that life. If I could have found you, I would have. I know that it will mean little to you, but it sounds as if Nancy had lost her mind. The past that you have spoken about, the person that she was, that was not the woman that I knew. Yes, the light was fading from her eyes, and yes, she believed that she would be found one day, but not once did she ever show a sign of that kind of life."

"Do you think she was trying to make a warrior out of me?"

"Perhaps in her sick mind, yes. If Nancy had any sense, she would have returned to me. I would have brought the two of you into my home and life. Your mother would have been safe within my walls, and you would have been prepared for this moment. That is what I'd planned to offer her when I woke the morning after. It wasn't love, but it could have been. We'd been friends for many years, and I always enjoyed her company."

That was the life that I should have had. It was far better than the one that I'd endured. As I thought about it, I wondered how the rest of my life would have been shaped. There would be no Anzide, at least not in the way that we'd met. We might have met in the portal, or maybe I would have found someone else.

Would we have returned to Hades? Yes, but under what circumstances? At what point would we have come across Niko in his jail cell, which was more like a poorly constructed tomb?

I had no answers, and I wanted to say that everything happened for a reason, but at what point was I supposed to stop making excuses for her terrible behavior and admit that she was an awful mother?

"I have a meeting to go to. Well, not really a meeting. I'm looking at the rental property across the road."

The house that Mardyl had stayed in when he was here in town, lying his ass off to me and the Nephilim.

"Some fellow named Tom Garrow. Do you know him?"

"Yeah, kind of. He rented this place to us before we took over as owners. He's a nice guy, kind of overdoing the spray tans and teeth whitening, though."

Carsten chuckled as we stood and walked to the door.

"If you like, I can return afterward."

"Sounds great."

"I know it's not easy for you, Evelyn. I understand

your apprehension, and I am not offended by it. As I said earlier, I will do my duty to you, and then I will leave."

Our walk to the front of the property stopped when Tom got out of his car. He looked over at us with a slight frown and then an uneasy wave. I waved back.

"He won't understand the situation."

"And he should be kept in the dark. I look too young, and to suggest that you are my daughter would seem impossible to his mind. I am merely a man who arrived early, saw the curious situation, and decided to say hello."

I nodded, giving Carsten a smile.

"Okay, normal man. I guess I'll see you later."

"Until then."

I watched him walk away for a few seconds and then turned back to the marquee. My walk across the lawn was quick because I needed a little insight before he returned.

CHAPTER 18

"So, what do we think?"

"That is not for us to decide, Evelyn," Niko responded. "He is your father."

I dumped myself into the chair with a huff.

"Well, he's really nice, and he explained everything. It makes sense. I don't know if it's the truth, but,"

Anzide cleared his throat, frowning at me.

"Eternals lack the ability to lie."

"I can lie."

"You're not completely there yet. Wait until the last of the immortals leave your body and see how well you can lie after that."

Great. Let's hope that didn't happen before I was done lying to Kannon and Audrey.

"So, everything that he said was the truth?"

Anzide nodded.

"Okay. I guess that means that, at some point, my mother actually wanted me. She created me to end the war."

"Your mother sacrificed her life to give you to us," Niko said.

Yeah, she did that. She also did a lot of other things too.

"Carsten said that my mother wrote in the note that she left him that she would return when I was five and that she would involve Brad as well."

"A wise idea, but unfortunate that she did not continue with that plan."

"I feel like I'm betraying her by even talking to Carsten, but the reality is that I don't care. Every single punch that she threw reminds me that she doesn't deserve anything from me."

I was done thinking about it. The past couldn't be changed, and if my mother thought that the answer to making me a stronger person was hitting me constantly, then that's how it was always going to be. Nothing could have changed that.

"Hey, did you know that Mother is really Carsten's mother?"

Anzide smirked.

"And that she's really your grandmother? Yes, she might have mentioned it. That's why she was always so lenient to you. Want me to blow your mind?"

"I seriously doubt that you could after everything else that has been thrown at me, but why not? Give it your best shot."

"Carsten is not her only child. There are many."

I sat up in the chair.

"Okay, mind blown. How many cousins do I have?"

"A lot."

Did it make any difference to Carsten being in my life? No, but to have a family beyond this group was certainly intriguing.

After half an hour of discussing Carsten and my extended family, Anzide perked up.

"Company."

Was I excited? I wasn't sure. Maybe it was a mixture of excitement and trepidation.

Anzide was with me as I walked through the door. Carsten smiled as he approached.

"You were right about Tom in every way. Lovely fellow but needs to tone down the view. Still, if it makes him happy, then I say, why not? On my path here, I had a little bird nattering in my ear that they'd like you to try again today. I told them that you were tired from the previous effort, but they were rather insistent. So, how about it?"

"Sure. We've set up a little space over here."

We walked over to the area and settled in. Carsten

waited for Anzide to enter.

"It was suggested that you observe so that future endeavors are less time-consuming."

"That's an abysmal assessment of my efforts."

"The suggestion was not meant to be a report on what you taught Evelyn. Besides, we have to begin somewhere."

Carsten turned his attention to me.

"Evelyn, I want you to look at me and observe what I am doing. See my hands at my sides as they move. Pretend that they are the instrument that steers the boat. It is my mind that tells my hands what to do."

"How come Anzide or Mother never said to do that?"

"Because the mind of an Eternal does not retain what comes naturally to them. We learn, we understand, and then the learning process fades. I have kept the thoughts with the belief that at some point, you would return to me, and I would teach you about everything that you have missed out on."

"Like flaming blue hands?"

Carsten's intrigue grew as he looked at me.

"Sounds like the Unholy Burn. I also noticed the scorched land at the front of the property and, of course, the lack of a house. That looks like the result of an Infernal Pyro Typhoon. You've been casting like a witch with abilities that you have because you're an

Eternal but shouldn't be using because you're incredibly undertrained. I cannot blame your mother entirely, Evelyn. I should have looked harder."

"It's fine."

"Is it?" Carsten challenged. "I see a property that is missing a house, and I heard the tale from Renuge. Your mother might have left, but I stopped looking. I shouldn't have, and this is the exact reason as to why. Perhaps this is something that should be discussed at another time. It is imperative that you learn how to access the portal in a timely manner. Back to my hands and watch as they move."

The hands moved back and forth. As I watched them, I felt the darkness consume the air around us. I was in the boat.

"Use your hands as I showed you, Evelyn," Carsten whispered through the wind. "Guide your hands with your mind."

I closed my eyes and searched for the land. There was nothing, but I still focused and continued to search. My hands moved, and I heard the water slosh around the boat as it rocked in the water.

Opening my eyes, I was faced with fog. I stopped and looked around. In an instant, my head snapped to the side. I'd found the land.

Turning my hands to shift the boat, I kept focusing and moving. I don't know how long it took, but when the water gave way to the sand, I was extremely happy.

Carsten stepped forward and held out his hand.

"Well done."

Hearing a huff, I looked past Carsten to see Mother.

"As always, you are too generous."

"Mother," he grumbled. "Be nice to Evelyn. After all, she is my only child."

Mother rolled her eyes dramatically and then began to shuffle away.

"Admit that you are impressed, Mother."

"Perhaps it is true."

"And perhaps she could be granted that meeting, hmm?"

"She could be."

"Less than a minute. Far better than any of her previous efforts. A reward for her efforts would be nice."

Mother stopped walking. She turned to give us that stink eye.

"You're as bad as your father. Alright. Evelyn will meet the passage master."

Carsten smiled as he turned back to me.

"Come with me. I'll take you to meet Benicio."

Leading me over the land, Carsten took me further than I'd ever walked before. Mother was moving in a different direction to us.

"Hey, when will I learn how to do those spells by choice?"

"We can start tomorrow afternoon. You've used most of your energy accomplishing this task, and technically, I can't get you into the sparring room until Benicio has shown you around the areas."

"I've got school tomorrow."

"We can start in the afternoon if you like. The room runs on a different time length. An hour here or in the sparring room equates to ten minutes on Earth. It's designed to give us maximum workout time with little loss in the real world."

"Cool."

The sandy land connected to a wall. As we got closer to it, I could see a faint light that shone over the door. It opened, and a shadowy figure waited for us.

"Welcome back, Carsten. I see that you have brought me a friend."

"Yes. Benicio, this is my daughter, Evelyn. Evie, this is Benicio, the passage master."

He held out his hand with a warm smile. The man reminded me of Santa Claus with his cheery smile, robust frame, and wiry white beard. The only difference was that it was clipped short rather than the lush, bushy beard that seemed to be the standard view.

"Welcome to the passage, Evelyn. When you are more at ease with entering the portal, you will actually find it easier to move around the land to either side here. That way, you won't get sand in your shoes."

With a wiggle of his fingers, my feet and shoes were sand-free.

"Come with me."

Entering the new area was like stepping out of the darkness and into pure light. The doors behind us closed, shutting out the foggy shadows.

"This is technically the portal. Out there is the gate. We call it the portal to avoid confusing the newcomers, but now that you're used to it, you should start using the correct terms. The portal is like a hub where everyone passes through to get to their lands. As an eternal, you are free to enter any area you please. A house will be created in the land of the Phoenix, and you will be notified when it is completed. This is the mail center where you should visit every couple of days."

Benicio walked up to the counter.

"Evelyn Newton."

The man nodded and turned to the wall of pigeonholes. A wad of envelopes was pulled out and passed to me.

"Uh, thanks."

"No problem."

"Continuing on, this is the notice board which you should check. There is a library over there, management to your right. A rather ordinary food court, but that's just my opinion, and those large doors ahead of us are the access to the train station. It's not the kind of train that you'd be used to. Come, we'll take a quick look."

We passed through the almost empty area that was like an outdated mall. Bland white tiles that looked like they were installed a hundred years ago.

The glass doors opened, and it was a view of the same, only set out differently. In front of us was a train, but it looked much smaller. Almost like it could fit a few people in it.

Benicio approached, and the doors slid open for him.

"They are self-driving. All you need to do is select the land, and once everyone is in the cart, press the close door button, and then this big green button. In an emergency, you can press this red button under the plastic cover. Any questions?"

"Yeah, you said I'd get a house in the Phoenix land. Can Anzide live with me in this house?"

Benicio glanced at Carsten.

"Anzide, the outcast Nephilim?"

"That's him."

"No. He's an outcast, so he is limited to the land of the outcasts, the portal, and no further."

"Huh. Okay. Thanks for the tour."

Turning, I walked out of the little train and through the glass doors.

"Evelyn," Benicio called out.

I stopped and turned to face him.

"Yes?" I said sweetly.

"You shouldn't be associating with an outcast or a Nephilim."

"Oh, but I am. He's my partner, and I've already been through this with the Nephilim. I am the reason that Renuge returned to this world with his tail between his legs. Don't think for a second that I will treat you any differently if you try to take Anzide away from me like he tried to do. If Anzide cannot join me in the land of the Phoenix, then I don't want to go there. If you won't grant him passage, then you can stick your offer of a house up your ass. My life is with him, and if the powers that rule this world cannot accept that, then that's their problem, not mine."

I stalked through the passage and entered the gate. Mother was standing near the entrance with a smile on her face as she leaned on the staff.

"You could have said that you were my grandmother."

"I could have."

"All I've ever wanted was a family."

"And in this world, you have one. Is this the hill that you wish to die on?"

"Yes. When we broke the rules, Anzide made a deal to save me at the cost of his own life. He saved me when

I was exposed and vulnerable. He brought me to this world, and it was my fault that I couldn't get to the land."

"We are aware of the issues, Evelyn."

I wiped the tears away, preparing myself for what I saw as the inevitable. Becoming an outcast like Anzide.

"I accept my fate. If Anzide cannot come with me, then I am not interested in the land of the Phoenix."

Mother sighed heavily.

"For someone that has no interactions with her father, you sure are like him. The matter will be discussed, and the ruling will be waiting for you in the mail center. Give it a couple of days. Nothing seems to move with speed around here."

I nodded and faded back to Earth. The future and everything to do with the portal and the land of the Phoenix now hung in the air, waiting for a group of nameless creatures to decide my fate.

CHAPTER 19

Karina was waiting for me near the side doors. In the shade of the building, she was shielded from the morning sun and almost hidden from view. I approached, unsure of how much I should say in the open setting of the school. Ears were everywhere, and they were always listening.

"Had a rough night?"

"More than just a night. What's new?"

"Not much, but I might have actually been inside where it was cooler, but then it got a little too perky, so I decided to come out here. The view is rather cute."

Karina nodded to the field where the football team was practicing.

"All I see is a bunch of guys."

"Well, yeah, but there's a new guy."

She was leaning on the wall with a dreamy look in her eyes. I scanned the group, searching through the guys I'd seen before while trying to figure out who the new one was.

"Not seeing it. What's his number?"

"Ten."

That made it easier. Mostly because he was looking at me. Even at a distance, I could tell that he wasn't human.

"He's cute."

"I'll take your word for it."

"Oh, come on, Evie. Admit that he's cute."

"Well, sure. He's reasonably good-looking. Not my style, though. Besides, I have a partner, and I'm happy where I am. I can't screw normies anyway, remember?"

"Oh yeah." she hummed. "Even if he's not a normie?"

"You can feel it, too?"

Karina nodded.

"He's most likely a vampire that's spent enough time acclimatizing himself to the sunlight so that he can cope with human schooling."

"Maybe he's something else."

Because James did not elaborate on what he meant when he said he'd brought paranormals to the town. Paranormals could mean a few different species.

"I wouldn't worry about it for now, though. Come on, I've got to find a safe space to tell you what you missed out on."

"Sounds intriguing."

As we walked through the doors, I looked at the field. Curiously, Kannon was not out there. It seemed odd, considering he'd made a point of telling me that he was in the team, which indicated he was excited about it. Maybe he just wanted to keep nipping at me to make me crumble into believing we were friends.

The new guy was still watching me, and I didn't know what to make of it. Anzide was close by, and I knew that he was unseen because Karina hadn't acknowledged him. She knew that if she didn't see him, I didn't want her to say hello or anything like that. If he was hidden, she had to pretend that I was alone.

"When's your first class?"

Karina looked at her schedule.

"Ten. You?"

"Same. I swear Harlwood did this intentionally."

"But it's sweet, right? It means that he cares."

"Or that he's trying to make me into his best friend. It doesn't bother me. I just find it weird."

"Everything in this town is weird."

I chuckled.

"That's what I thought when we first moved here. Oblivious people that don't notice the strange things that happen. It rained relentlessly for a week, and then, all of a sudden, it stopped. Of course, I know why now, but back then, it was the strangest thing I'd ever seen."

We were taking a slow walk through the empty corridor. The first class of the morning had already begun, but for us, our first lesson didn't start for almost an hour.

"So, I met my father."

Karina stopped and stared.

"Everything that I thought was wrong. My mother knew what he was and that it would kill her. She wanted to have a child. She also took off after they slept together, so he had no idea where I was."

"She did it intentionally?" Karina whispered.

"I think she was trying to create the ultimate weapon."

Karina smiled.

"And she did. I've been doing a lot of reading since coming here. Harlwood's been quite helpful with directing me to the right books."

Why was I not surprised?

"You're going to win."

"Easier said than done."

"It's fine. I'll be your cheerleader. I'll stand next to you and fight until there's nothing left."

"At the cost of your own life?"

Karina shrugged.

"My life is in this town. When James found us, he offered us a life in Hades. He told us about you and Brad, who you were related to, and how amazing you two are. Then he told us that you were stuck in a terrible situation, and while you had the ability to win, you needed a little backing. We would enter this town that was about to endure a vampire blood war, but we shouldn't fear anything because no matter what, he would protect us. All we had to do was commit ourselves to you and your leadership. He warned us that the other clan would try and tempt us, maybe even threaten us. We had to be strong because there was nothing better than the true leader of the land. Not the imposter, not the treacherous followers he governed. James said that we could refuse. He would happily set us up with an easygoing clan like he had for,"

Karina paused, giving me a pained smile.

"There were other women who were abducted like us. James helped a lot of women that day and killed so many horrible men."

I know.

"I'm sorry to hear that."

Karina wiped away the tears.

"I wasn't sixteen," she whispered. "James has tried to age me to what I should be because the alteration did a lot of damage. He can't do anything more, though. I'm at the limit. He said that I just have to wait, to keep growing and to take on the blood diet as soon as my body can handle it."

I didn't know if it would cause issues, but with the hope that because I was female, she would find it easier. I opened my arms and offered a hug. Karina sadly smiled and accepted the hug.

It ended quickly, and as much as she probably needed it, I was grateful. I didn't need Audrey to see it. It was guaranteed that she'd make some snide remark, and I'd punch her for it, which would kill any chances I had of bringing her to our side of the fight.

"I'm glad we agreed to come here."

We started walking again, reaching the corner to our lockers. One was open. It slammed shut, and the honey-colored eyes of the new guy met mine. His hair was wet from the showers, pulled back into a tight bun. On the field, it had hung loose to his shoulders.

Pulled away, though, it highlighted the rich olive tone of his skin and the defined cheeks and jawline. Up close was even better.

He smiled, leaning on the locker.

"Cooper, but everyone calls me CJ."

"Evie, which is short for Evelyn, and this is Karina."

He nodded with a deeper smirk. I watched as Karina's cheeks glowed with a soft pink hue. Behind Cooper stood an outcast Nephilim. The deep purple eyes bored into the back of his head as Anzide concentrated on his mind. All I had to do was keep Cooper engaged in a conversation. Hopefully, it will be enough.

"You managed to get into the showers and dressed rather quickly."

Cooper shrugged, not making any form of statement or giving an answer. I was dubious now more than ever. He was far too quick, and I don't know how he managed to wash himself, dry, and dress so fast that he could reach the lockers before us. Sure, Karina and I walked slowly, and had a deep and meaningful conversation, but it still didn't make much sense.

"So, what brings you to Hades?"

"The principal suggested that it was a great place to live."

"Is that right?" I hummed. "Would that be because you have something to offer the town?"

Cooper smiled as he lifted from the locker.

"Maybe."

He leaned closer, which was a lot for the tall footballer.

"I know what you are," he whispered.

Karina's eyes widened with fear as she sucked in a lot of air.

"And I know what stands behind me. Search as you please because I hide nothing. I know what is coming, and I know what you need. We are here because the demon thinks that you need more backing than what you've already got. You want something from me? The deal has already been cut, Evelyn. We are here for you."

Cooper leaned back, and I heard footsteps.

"And, of course," he said in a normal tone. "We just couldn't resist the idea of coming to Hades."

His eyes lifted to behind me. I turned to see Audrey and her friends. She smiled at Cooper and sneered at me.

"CJ," she said eagerly. "Why are you here?"

"This is my locker."

"Oh, you should ask to move down with the other footballers. Then you won't have to associate with these two losers."

"Audrey, go be a sullen cow to someone else."

She gasped and then frowned at Cooper. In a huff, she stormed away. I smiled as I turned back to Cooper. I think that I like the new guy.

"You were saying something about being here for me?"

"Well, kind of. It's about fifty-fifty if I'm completely honest. We were offered a deal to hide here until certain issues with the Nephilim passed. Everyone has a differing opinion on cross-breeding and what the Nephilim will accept. Once my parents realized that we could be in trouble, we went underground to hide. We were told that it's a big no-no to cross-breed. Who knew, right?"

"I know," I said with a mighty grin. "So, what are you?"

"What? Your guy hasn't figured it out?"

"Oh, he has, but I'd like to hear it from you."

"My mother is a witch, and my father is a werewolf."

Well, I think that we just found the witch that had been using the ring.

"I guess the whole showering thing makes sense now."

"I guess it does."

Karina, the silent one, just stared at Cooper. She was so obvious that it became clear that we needed to discuss how to play hard to get.

"So, we were talking about a certain person who suggested this was a great place to live."

"James tells us that cross-breeding is generally okay, but because my mother is a witch, it's an issue. They're the one species that are not permitted to cross-breed because it creates unstable abilities in the child. So, he checked us over and said my brothers and I were fine. The werewolves had dominated us already. No witchiness to be found. He said to come here and lay low because something was brewing, and once it boiled over, things would be fine. So, I take it that you were that something?"

"Yeah. Most things around here have something to do with me or my family. No issues with the Nephilim anymore?"

"All good."

I nodded. It would seem that my little showdown with the Nephilim helped more than just myself. That was rather pleasing, in my opinion.

"So, have you met any of the vampires around town?"

"Oh yeah. We had a run-in with them a couple of days ago. We actually have a family friend who lives with us, and she's a vampire. That head guy,"

"Drakkus,"

"Yeah, him. He said it was abhorrent that a vampire co-existed with werewolves and half-breeds. Then he suggested that if she wanted to amend for her misdeeds, she could leave the house and request to join his clan. Can you guess what she told him?"

"I have a few thoughts."

"She told him to find the tallest tree with the widest trunk and shove it up his ass. It was beautiful to hear and to watch his reaction. He told her she'd rue the day she came to Hades."

"Sounds like a true villain. Well, I'm the leader of the Corbin clan and the true ruler of Hades. I don't care if your friend is living with another species, and if she likes, she can apply to join our coven. In fact, you all can because I don't care if you're not a vampire."

"You need all the backing that you can get."

I nodded because I couldn't have put it better myself.

CHAPTER 20

We hadn't moved far. Cooper's first lesson was in the room opposite, so he walked a few steps down the main corridor to the rooms. The teacher was late, and rather than sit in the classroom with the other students, he decided to stand outside and talk to us. Karina and I still had half an hour to wait for our lesson to start.

Kannon approached. I didn't know his lesson schedule, but he was carrying a math book, which meant he'd be climbing the stairs behind us to the next level.

He stopped with a nod to Cooper.

"Hey, you're CJ, right?"

Clearly, he missed football practice. They hadn't met yet, which I found a little odd, considering CJ's already had a run-in with Drakkus

"I am."

"Kannon. You know, the new paras always check in with the guy running this town."

Karina rolled her eyes, which made me smile.

"You'd be better off to join his group."

"You're a little late to the party, Kannon." I offered. "Someone's already played that card. In fact, Captain Peckerhead actually called Cooper and his siblings abhorrent, so your suggestion that they join the Fleming clan is rather pointless."

His eyes turned to CJ, probably trying to figure out what he was.

"I'm pretty sure I can convince him to change his mind if you're interested."

"You're sounding desperate."

"Evie, mind your own business."

"Seriously? You approach this group who were talking, you invade our conversation, and you make a pathetic attempt to lure Cooper to your clan. How is it not my business?"

"You're not going to win this war. I'm just trying to save lives."

He was so delusional.

If I thought that it couldn't get any worse, I was wrong. Audrey and her friends were drawing closer, and it was clear that she intended to be a part of this.

"Maybe you and your mother should reconsider as well."

"We picked our side, and I'm not interested in changing," Karina said firmly.

"Yeah, I have to agree with Karina on that one," Cooper added. "Being called abhorrent is low, but the way that you speak to the true leader, *your* true leader, is just pathetic. Clearly, this faux leader that you seem to worship has shown you a poor representation of what is right and wrong. I don't want any part of that."

"Then you will die with the rest of them."

Karina scoffed a laugh, shaking her head. That didn't help Kannon's growing anger.

"Evie, I know that you think that you're this all-powerful being, but I know what Drakkus can do. You're going to lose. Brad's a dead man walking."

I inhaled sharply. He'd just threatened Brad.

"Are you threatening my family?"

Kannon was silent for a moment. Behind him, Audrey smiled supremely.

"Yeah, maybe I am."

I nodded and decided that I was done with him. I was no longer interested in toying with him, stringing him along with false information, or anything else that came with the fake friendship.

"Okay. I'm done. Here's a little info blast for you. I know that you've got secret plans with Drakkus to formally become his second in charge, not this lie that you've tried to make me believe. I also know that you've been screwing him for years and that you have no intention of changing that in the future. I know that you've been cheating on Audrey because I know that you've been in a relationship with her, too. If you think that I am wrong, know that I saw you screwing her against my locker. I've seen a lot of things. I also know that you were in that relationship with Audrey and Drakkus at the same time that you were attempting to start one with me. Which for the record, I am fully aware that it was nothing but a ploy to get into the house. I know that you're not eighteen and that you're actually twenty-one."

There was a collective gasp behind him, which I found odd, considering that I'd just said that he was cheating on Audrey.

"And while we're on the subject of Audrey,"

Her eyes widened as she stared at me.

"I know about her secret plans, too. She plans to kill Drakkus once you're made his second in charge. Naturally, that won't happen because he won't win."

I smiled at her. It was full of silent sarcasm. The look of karma coming to bite her on the ass.

"Let me be the one to tell you that when I win the war, I won't be turning you into a vampire."

Audrey lunged with an angry look on her face. Cooper stepped in front of me and growled. I looked up at the back of his neck. Just above the sports shirt at the base of his neck, the little hairs stood on end.

I leaned to look at her when Audrey gasped with shock. She stared in horror as she backed away. The friends were already at the stairs, ready to race up them.

Kannon moved, but Anzide appeared.

"Little boy, do not bother."

Now the friends were really freaked out. They screamed and ran up the stairs.

I thought that we'd have onlookers after the cashmere brigade started screaming, but crazily enough, James was the first to appear. He looked at the view and turned to Kannon.

"It seems as if you and I need to have a little chat, Mister Lothaire. My office, now."

James waited until Kannon started to walk down the corridor.

"Miss Hartley, please go to your class or join your fellow bully."

Quietly, she walked up the stairs. James turned to face me and raised an eyebrow.

"Quite the drama creator, aren't you?"

"He started the fight, and I ended it. Well, Cooper did, but he was doing as you demanded of him, right? My wolfie protector."

James said nothing as the smirk filled his face. The door to the administration slammed shut. James glanced at it and turned back to me.

"I do what is necessary to ensure the longevity of this town and those who inhabit it. Now, that nonsense."

He gestured to the far end of the corridor.

"I'd like to end the drama, but I need grounds for it. Give that to me, and I can stop it and send the spy away."

"He's actually twenty-one. Anzide entered his mind and found out that interesting tidbit. Now that Hannah's not around to block his thoughts, maybe you should have a little dig in there, too. There is one little issue, though. He hasn't told Drakkus who you are, so maybe tread carefully."

"One little vampire does not frighten me, regardless of the delusions of grandeur or the insanity of the mind."

"Well, that's your call. Also, Audrey and Kannon are a thing, so your need to remove the spy might be pointless."

James nodded slowly, probably thinking about the predicament.

"One doesn't need the piece of paper, but the other does. Removing Miss Hartley would be unwise."

I shrugged.

"That's your call."

Footsteps and whispers could be heard from above. Notably, Anzide was no longer visible. James looked up and frowned.

"Return to class or receive detention," he shouted.

They scattered, leaving the area empty except for one person. Audrey's plain face indicated nothing to me. Not a scowl, not anger. Just nothing. I didn't know what to make of it. She walked away without a word said.

James looked at his watch.

"Your teacher should be here soon, Mister Jackson. Perhaps you should wait with your class."

He nodded.

"See you later."

When Cooper was in the classroom, James turned back to me.

"I will consider the facts and what may arise if I decide to punish Audrey now that I am fully aware of her antics. It would have been a good idea to tell me she was being difficult towards you."

"Please, she's nothing compared to what I'm used to."

In fact, Audrey wasn't a bully when compared to some of the ones that I'd seen over the years.

"That is not the point. Your mind should be on other things, not her. As for the other issue, he's not going to be a part of the school anymore."

With a nod, James turned on his heels and began the long walk to his office.

Hearing a heavy sigh, I turned to look at Karina.

"Changing your mind about being my cheerleader?"

"Not a chance. That was intense, though."

"Speaking of intense, what's your deal with Cooper?"

Karina stuttered, and her cheeks bloomed in the prettiest pink.

"I think that you should lay a few hints out. You said he was cute, and it's not like he wasn't looking at you."

"He was?"

I nodded, hoping that things worked out for them. Cooper seemed like a nice guy, and Karina was just adorable.

The door to the office opened, and in the distance, I saw Kannon. He turned to face me, and I knew the mood was dark. It was a blur as he moved with speed. In seconds, I was slammed into the locker, his hand around my throat.

"You think that you will win," Kannon hissed. "But you won't."

He was dragged off me and tossed to the floor. As his body skidded over the worn linoleum, Anzide appeared.

"Leave now before I kill you."

Kannon stood, straightening his clothes.

"In fact, you should leave town because you're not wanted here. Isn't that right, Evie?"

Lifting from the locker, I stood firmly.

"Absolutely. You should leave. Go home, pack your things, and leave town."

"You don't have any say in my life. You are not the leader, regardless of what a dead vampire says. He had no power in this town, just like you don't."

He looked at me with cold indifference.

"This is not over, not by a long shot. You won't win, and I won't be going anywhere. I will be there at the end, and I will stand over your dying body with a smile on my face, reminding you of this moment and how you had the chance to walk away. Be prepared to die, Evie. Death is coming for you."

Kannon turned on his heels and took off. I'd never seen him move with such speed.

Other things were moving with speed. I could feel the rise of breakfast. Racing through the corridor, I ignored Karina and Anzide and ran to the bathroom.

I was in the middle of throwing up when Karina entered the bathroom.

"Anzide wants to come in, but I said it's a no-go zone for the dinky pinky club."

I groaned with a laugh.

"He also said that you like to puke after the adrenaline stops. With that in mind, I'm going to make an end-of-war pack for you. A little electrolyte replacement, a barf bag or two, maybe some wipes in case you miss the bag, breath mints because pee-ew. Oh, and a hair tie because, this,"

She held up a strand of my hair that was wet. I

flushed the toilet and moved to the sink so that I could clean the vomit out of my hair.

"I didn't puke when Audrey lunged at me."

"Maybe because Cooper diffused the situation before it escalated. Kannon was pretty fast, and I guess he took you by surprise, too."

Standing upright, I pulled the paper from the dispenser and tried to dry my hair.

"Anzide's pretty annoyed that Kannon got that close."

"No one could have predicted he would act like that."

I opened the door to see Anzide standing at the threshold.

"Did you hear me?"

He huffed and then nodded.

"It's done, and I'm okay. We learned something, though, didn't we?"

"That he can move like most vampires?"

"I can't move like that."

"What about your mother?"

Karina shrugged.

"I don't think so. She would have said something if she could."

"It's probably because he's a born vampire and has been learning for many years. You and your mother are a different story."

Walking out of the bathroom, I wrapped my arms around Anzide's waist and looked up at him.

"Are you done sulking?"

"I failed in my task. They," he paused, giving me a hard look. *"They* gave clear instructions as to what was expected of me. Now you've got discoloration on your neck that I guarantee will turn into bruises."

"Do you realize that this is only going to get worse?"

Anzide's frown didn't change.

"No matter what you do, I am always going to be in harm's way. What I think that was requested was that you protected me from serious danger or being abducted. The bruising may not happen, and if it does, then everyone has to accept it. Kannon has always been full of hot air and idle threats. No one could have predicted this sudden change."

Footsteps grew louder. Anzide faded from sight, leaving my statement hanging without a response. Our teacher passed, giving us a flick of his head.

"Move along, please ladies."

I was hesitant to leave the safety of being near the bathroom. The sudden urge had dissipated, but I feared that it would return. There were only two choices that I had here. Either go to class or go home sick. At the moment, I didn't feel sick or that hot flush that always hit me before. It was just a queasy feeling in my stomach.

With a sigh, I caught up to Karina.

"I really hope that I don't get sick in the middle of the battle. That's the last thing that I need."

"Yeah, I can't imagine that Drakkus is going to stop attacking just to let you throw up. The alternative is that you go with it and puke all over him. I'm sure he won't expect that, and it's certainly an upgrade from the milk-shake."

I couldn't help but giggle. Karina was crazy fun, and I loved it.

"Maybe you need to learn how to deal with the hard fall from an adrenaline high."

"Is there even a book about that?"

Karina shrugged as she pushed open the door. The library in the portal might have had an answer. If only I hadn't burned that bridge. Still, I would have to return to see what their decision was so maybe I could go to the library. It wasn't a part of the various lands, so I guess it might be alright.

CHAPTER 21

We decided on a little tour of Hades after school that wasn't really a tour. The idea had been there, but we felt hungry, so our little group went to the local diner, and that's where we stayed.

It was almost like a get to know each other situation, and it could be considered a double date because other than Anzide and myself, it was just Karina and Cooper. Almost. For Anzide and myself, it was definitely a date because any time away from the property was a date for us. As for Karina and CJ, it was debatable. Karina's cheeks would turn rosy red if I said something about it being a date. I'd be quietly scolded, but underneath it all, there would be the sweetest smile that spoke the truth.

Karina was seated next to CJ at the table, quiet and unassuming. With only two long bench seats, she had no choice. Also, she'd sat down first, which meant she was against the wall. I guess Karina might have assumed that I'd sit next to her, but she was wrong. I was playing cupid.

I ordered a milkshake, hoping the cold milk would

offer a little respite to the soreness around my throat. Turning to Anzide, I gestured to my neck.

"Is it bruising?"

"No bruises as such but a bit of redness. Give it time. The skin is just irritated."

We had time because I was in no hurry to leave. Walking into this place was easy, but leaving was not. The problem was that this was the diner that Drakkus used when he was watching what happened at the school. To the uninformed observer, he appeared to be a pervert, but to those of us in the know, we knew exactly why he was at this diner.

As for him being a problem, it was because he'd decided to sit in his usual spot to conduct his daily observations. He was out there, right now. I quietly sipped my milkshake, watching him. It was obvious that he didn't know that we were in there. This place offered table service, so as soon as he sat down, someone was out the door to take his order.

Technically, we should have still been at the school, but I only had two lessons today. Karina and Cooper were let out early because the teacher they had for the first lesson was also the one they had for their last. She was sick, and James could not find a replacement in time. So, they were out of school ahead of schedule.

To get out of the diner, we had to leave through the front door. Drakkus was at the first table, and there was no way that we could sneak past. Anzide could help by making us disappear, but the people in the diner would see us and then not see us, which I knew would create a lot of issues.

We were sitting in the booth, trying to figure out how we would get out or whether it was just easier to sit and wait for Drakkus to leave, when I saw my father. Drakkus looked at him but said nothing. There was a mighty frown on his face, probably trying to figure out the new guy in town. He was something, but what? Will Drakkus ever figure it out? Probably because I was going to eat humble pie and ask my father for help.

"Come on."

Emerging from the booth, we moved quickly to the door. Drakkus saw me, and instantly, his body went rigid. I opened the door and smiled at Carsten.

"Hey. We need your help."

"Of course, Evelyn. What's the problem?"

"Tell you later. Be ready for anything, though."

Carsten held open the door to let everyone out. As we walked away, I looked back and saw that Drakkus was standing next to the table. He watched us, and I knew I'd just made him curious.

"Alright, now that we're away from the big, bad vampire, how about you tell me what's going on?"

"You knew he was a vampire?" Karina asked.

"Of course I did. I am an extremely old Eternal."

She frowned for a moment, glancing at me.

"Okay, introductions. This is my father, Carsten, he's an Eternal. These are the two newest recruits, Karina, a turned vampire, and Cooper, who is half-werewolf, half-witch."

"Lovely to meet you," Carsten said with a smile. "Now, the vampire?"

"That's Drakkus."

"Oh, *the* Drakkus. His curiosity certainly makes sense now. I suppose he will try to figure out what's going on. Best not to give him too much to work with. Come along, Evelyn and friends."

We began walking to the end of Main Street. I knew that Anzide was a step behind. As for Cooper and Karina, they were walking beside each other ahead of us.

"He will start to pay closer attention now, Evelyn. I know that you have issues with the portal, but for the time being, please put them aside so that we can begin training. It is going to be your best asset to hide how advanced your skills will become. We will start when we return to the coven land. The sooner you can control your skills, the safer you will be."

"And everyone else," I muttered.

Carsten looked at me curiously. I gestured to the forest at the side of the school.

"The guy that was the second in charge for Drakkus attacked me in there. I killed him but have no idea how I did it. That was the blue flame thing."

"Unholy Burn."

"Yeah, that. I don't know if I can knowingly kill someone. I mean, Andross doesn't count. That was an accident."

"Then perhaps you should consider the alternative. If you don't kill him, then he wins. You will still be alive because there is nothing that he can do to end your life. Everyone else, though, that's a different story. From those two who are on the cusp of a romance that could burn bright through the ages to those much closer to your heart. You know who I speak of, and trust me when I say that when it comes down to a blood war, the winner will kill all of the loser's family to ensure that they are seen as the strongest. Bradley and I discussed the recent events. He told me how you mourned the loss of Niko greater than what he expected."

Carsten stopped and looked at me.

"Are you prepared to lose him again?"

"No."

"Then that is your guide, Evelyn. When you think that you cannot kill Drakkus, remember what he did to you and what he took from your life. Remember that he will do it all again, only this time, it won't just be Niko."

We reached the property, and I asked Anzide to keep everyone outside of the tent while I checked on the occupants. I didn't want to just invite Cooper in without checking with Niko first.

His eyes lifted, and as always, I got a warm smile.

"How was school today, Evelyn?"

"Interesting. We've got a new person at school."

"Another?" Beatrice said, sounding amused. "James has been busy."

"Yeah, I guess so. Anyway, his name is Cooper, and he's a half-werewolf, half-witch. He's also out there."

Niko and Beatrice exchanged glances. When Niko looked at me, he relented with a sigh.

"I suppose that you've already invited him into the clan."

"I have. I should have checked, right?"

"Perhaps, but James has asked him to come here, so there is that to consider."

"I think James wanted him to be a more visual protection rather than the one that always hides from view. In fact, Cooper actually stopped Audrey from lunging at me today."

"Then he serves a valiant purpose. Half-witch, you say?"

I nodded, and Niko got an intrigued look on his face.

"His mother?"

Again, I nodded.

"I took a moment to inspect the ring. She is wiccan, so I have no issues with her presence in this town or as close as she would be when using the ring. Has Anzide checked the young man's mind?"

I shrugged, and clearly, he heard his name because Anzide appeared next to me.

"Cooper is a young hybrid. He has a strong mind for such a young age, but I was able to enter all sections. During the initial contact with Evie, he acknowledged my presence even though I was hidden, and he offered his mind freely. I found the meeting with James, and there is confirmation that the demon asked him to be the visual protection for Evie. I am the unseen. He is the seen. Cooper has moved to this town with his parents, two younger siblings, and a family friend who is a vampire. They have already had an altercation with Drakkus. He suggested that the friend could join the Fleming clan to make amends for her sins of associating with the abomination hybrids and their parents who should be jailed for their crimes. She politely told him to find the tallest tree with the widest trunk and shove it up his ass."

Niko and Beatrice giggled like children. I had to admit, it was funny.

"They are on our side. There is no doubt in Cooper's mind about that. I am yet to locate the rest of the family to confirm their allegiance, but I doubt that James would invite them without having complete faith in their compliance. It is clear that James is determined to remove Drakkus but knows that for this war to end successfully, it has to be Evie who does the job."

"Then that is how things shall be. The newest of our recruits shall be more than just vampires."

"I'll go and get them," Anzide said as he turned away.

"What's going on at school that Audrey's lunging at you?" Brad asked, giving me a mighty frown.

"So, Kannon was being a dick because he'd tried to tempt CJ to his side, and when he threatened you, I did an info blast that included what I knew about them and her plans to become a vampire. When I told her that I would not make her a vampire, she lunged, and CJ stepped in between us."

Taking a deep breath, I braved the other part of today. The part that I knew they would not like.

"Kannon attacked me because James booted him out of the school, and I was the reason. Anzide pulled him off me, and that's it."

We'll gloss over the part where I puked my guts up in the bathroom. It was not necessary. Not when Brad was looking at me as if he didn't know whether to be worried or angry. Niko and Beatrice had a similar kind of confusion.

"He was seriously fast. One second, he was at the door to the office. The next, he was at the lockers. Just a big blur. Can you move like that?"

"I can," Niko said. "Did you tell James what he did?"

"No. I don't need to go running to James all the time, you know. Telling you guys is bad enough. Anyway, we've got company."

Pulling back the curtain, I waited for everyone to

enter.

"Everyone, this is Cooper Jackson. My uncle Brad, my great-grandmother Beatrice, and my great-grandfather Niko."

He nodded and said hello to all of them, smiling brightly.

"You need to remember that it is believed that Niko and Beatrice are dead. Beatrice is a shapeshifter, and in this town, she usually poses as Natalia Eastwell."

Beatrice shifted her form so that Cooper would know her alter ego.

"So, if you see her in this form on the street, you know it's all good. Just remember that the secret has to be kept until after the end of the war."

"Sure."

CJ sat at the table and started talking to Niko and Beatrice. Naturally, Niko was curious about the newcomer, his past, and his plans for the future. All I wanted to know was that I could trust him to keep the secret.

CHAPTER 22

I entered the gate quicker than I had yesterday, earning a nod from Mother. Her silent approval meant a lot, considering it had been so different not that long ago.

Carsten was ahead of us, talking to Mother as we walked towards the doors to the portal. Slowing down, I pulled on Anzide's hand. He turned and tilted his head with a curious look.

"Why do we need to have houses in the portal?"

"They are there if we need to leave Earth, like when they're fighting. If something happens and we're the only ones left standing in an area that is home to the losing side, we're going to be in trouble. They made a rule that if we're living in an area that is experiencing unrest, we either have to move to another country or return to the portal. Technically, though, we're supposed to live here and visit there. You're one of only a few who have a connection to the land-based immortals."

"So, now that the blood war has begun?"

"In theory, we should return, but it has been discussed and noted that for the war to end, you must be present for it. Otherwise, the land will enter into a void, and it becomes extremely taxing upon any Eternal in the area."

"But you were in Hades during the void."

"Yes, and how often did you really see me?"

I shrugged, remembering how we thought that Brad had upset Anzide by highlighting the truth, and he left because of it. Now, though, I wasn't sure if it was the case.

"How do you think James coped?"

"From my understanding, not very well. You heard what he said. He was missing out on all those souls. James has taken on a reaper role. It's not like the human vision of the grim reaper but more like a collector. The duty of a demon reaper is to collect the souls of the dead, consume them, and take them to the beyond. To ensure they do a proper job, a demon reaper is altered to feel a sense of fullness when they consume the souls. Most demons say that they feel hungry but that's just them being dramatic. With Hannah taking all the souls, James was left with virtually nothing. It was not her duty. James had been assigned Hades. She could have been in a lot of trouble if James decided to create waves."

"Do you think it's why she left without saying anything to Drakkus?"

"Undoubtedly."

Mother turned off to another path, leaving Carsten waiting for us at the junction. He smiled and gestured to the doors to the portal that were opening for us.

"Today, we're actually going up the stairs. To the left is the sparring room, and to the right is the training room."

We entered the portal, and I checked in at the mail-room. No mail was waiting for me, and I made Anzide check for himself too. I didn't know what to think or feel. Was no news good news? Did I really care?

"Hey, the library. Does it have any books about adrenaline?"

Carsten turned and pursed his lips, clearly thinking about it.

"I'm not certain. Why do you ask?"

"Every time I get a surge of adrenaline and it drops off, I end up throwing my guts up. I just wanted to know if there was something that I could do to stop it from happening."

"Well, I don't know for sure, but I will put a request in for you later. For now, we have to get a move on because we have been allocated a time, and if we're late, they won't extend it."

Reaching the top of the stairs, Carsten turned to the left.

"I thought we were training."

"Sparring offers a real-world view. We're going to

simulate the forest near your house, as it was agreed that it is likely that Drakkus would want to hide the war from the humans."

He opened the door, giving me a vague shrug.

"There is only so much an obscuris veil will hide. Now, we're all in this because someone is just as much a newbie as you are, so the both of you can get your coveralls on."

Anzide said nothing as he pulled a pair off the shelf. There was a slight smile on his face, but it didn't offer much of a hint as to what he was thinking.

"In this area, we can administer blows that will knock our opponent off their feet, but they will remain unharmed. These coveralls are designed to show where we take a hit and what kind of attack it was. This here is a chart that you can look at and see the colors of the various attacks and how they will appear on your coveralls. At the end of it, the coveralls will be compared and graded. Also, you will notice the glass at the top of the room."

"We're being watched?"

"We are. There are many who are intrigued about this new girl. Whispers are rampant, and when it got out that I'd booked us in, there was a rush to get a placement in the observation room."

"Great. I'm still a learner here."

"I doubt they care."

"It's not going to be much of a show."

Carsten shrugged as he pulled the screen over the shelving.

"Why do Eternals need spells?"

He stopped moving the screening and looked at me.

"It just seems strange to me. Aren't you all supposed to be about love and the goodness in the world?"

"Not necessarily. As for the spells, these are designed and created for use in the real world if necessary. It is expected that we try not to intervene, but if the situation warrants action, then we are permitted to do what we can to ensure that all is well. Generally, though, we try to let things run their course."

I nodded, though I wasn't sure if their limited interaction was acceptable.

Near the latch point was a panel. He pressed a few buttons, and we were plunged into the forest. I couldn't see the pale walls or the row of black glass that surrounded the room.

"Anzide," I whispered. "How can I do any of this?"

"Well, think about what happened when you did it involuntarily. How did you feel?"

"Angry. Like spiders were crawling all over me."

He moved behind me, gripping my shoulders. In the forest, I could see a shadow moving through the trees.

"Drakkus is here," Anzide whispered. "He's killed

Brad and made quite a show out of taunting his death in front of you. Beatrice is dying at your feet because of him, too. He learned her secret identity and said that it made her death all the more sweeter because no other vampire had been able to kill her. Yet here she is, seconds from her untimely end. Blood coats the forest floor, a vile reminder of the monster that is still hunting your family. Now he's stalking Niko, and there's nothing that you can do to stop him. He's already taken your uncle and your great-grandmother. Now he's hunting your beloved Niko again. Drakkus is going to take him away from you again."

Tears rolled down my eyes because I could see Brad and Beatrice dead at my feet. Karina was here too, as was Cooper. Everyone was dead except Niko, who was nothing but a shadow in the trees. There was another shadow stalking him, and I knew it was Drakkus.

"What happened that day, Evie? Tell me how the vampires took Niko away from you."

"They cornered him and stabbed him with a blade that had been soaked in holy water from the Vatican. There was blood everywhere. I couldn't save him."

"He did that, Evie. He murdered Niko. Feel the anger. Let it grow inside of you. He took your mother from you. Drakkus is the reason she lived a life on the run. She was always trying to hide from him. Nancy vowed to protect you from Drakkus, but her resentment towards him grew because she knew she would never have a normal life. He caused the anger in her. He is the reason that she beat you. Every punch you took, it was his fault."

Anger boiled. I couldn't hear anything but a ringing static noise that was loud. I screamed, and everything exploded. The static was gone, replaced with something that sounded like a bellowing boom.

When I opened my wet eyes. The lush foliage of the forest was now gone. The trees were bare, and the once beautiful forest was coated in black. At the far end of the forest was Carsten. His coveralls were black, head to toe, completely covered.

"And that is what they call The Dragon of Thunder," Anzide said with an appraising smile.

He was covered in black, too. It wasn't just the coveralls. Just like Carsten, he was covered in what looked like a dusty black powder. It was almost like he'd taken a dunk in a vat of printer toner. The powdery substance puffed from his body when he moved.

I looked around the room. It wasn't just the trees. The walls and the glass panels were coated, and it made me wonder if those who were in the viewing room could see anything now.

"Essentially, you burned everything with a fire spray, like a dragon would, but it sounds like a thunderstorm. It's not the kind of fire that you'd be used to. This is an oxygen-depriving spell that turns everything with oxygen in it or emitting it into a black powder. That's why it's affected the trees. Touch one of them."

Warily, I walked over and touched a tree. It went up in a puff of black powdery smoke.

"Works well on those who need oxygen to live, not so much on the likes of us. If you're alone with your enemy, it's a good one to use, but if the likes of Karina and Cooper are around, I would suggest that you do not use it. Most spells work well with emotions, but the dragon, she burns through the anger. Remember that when you're in the war. Drakkus will use everything he has against you, and you can retaliate as you please but you need to remember who is with you."

I nodded. I didn't want Karina or Cooper to suffer because of my actions.

Anzide turned to Carsten, who was removing the coveralls. They were hung on the wall with the ones that Anzide removed. The pair put another set on, and the room was reset. For a moment, they discussed something that I could not hear. Anzide nodded, and they separated.

"Your father wants us to work as a team for the next attack. We're going to try Chaotic Energy. This is a two-person attack where we bounce it back at each other. The idea is that the enemy can be herded into one spot. So, for example, if Drakkus has himself and five others with him against just you and me. We could use Chaotic Energy to group them into one space. Once we've rounded them up, we can attack them with something else. Any questions?"

I folded my arms, narrowing my eyes at him.

"What's going on?"

Anzide hesitated. "What do you mean? You're learning how to harness your skills."

"Yeah, but it's supposed to be my father teaching me, not you."

He paused and then sighed as his body sagged.

"So when you were doing the tour with Benicio, I was approached with an offer to teach others."

"And I take it because you're teaching me, you accepted the offer?"

"They said that I showed remarkable skill in teaching you how to access the gate, and if time was on our side, I would have eventually gotten you through to the portal. It's not common for an outsider to teach someone. Everyone is taught by their parents. They'd watched everything and said that it was something that I'd be good at."

"I see. Well, congratulations."

"I haven't accepted the role yet. Firstly, I said that protecting you through to the end of the war was my top priority. They agreed. Secondly, I said I wanted to talk to you about it first because it's not just my life that it affects."

"Will you live here?"

Anzide shook his head.

"Not if you won't. I will travel when I am needed."

"So, is this a test or something?" I asked.

"It is."

"Are you going to pass?"

"I hope so."

"Would it be wrong if I hugged my teacher?"

"I don't know."

"What about kissing him?"

"Probably."

I chuckled. "Too bad."

Wrapping my arms around Anzide's neck, I kissed him. I didn't care who was watching. The moment was too important to worry about trivial little things like that.

CHAPTER 23

The hammock had been set up under the trees, and when we returned from the portal, I climbed in and enjoyed the cool afternoon. It wasn't at all planned, but I fell asleep. When I woke up, the sun was setting, which was a little disappointing. As much as I've slept, it felt like I'd been up for days. It wasn't a good thing and I knew that it could be problematic if Drakkus decided that he wanted to end the war right now.

Anzide was sitting on an outdoor chair. When he saw me struggling to sit up on the hammock, he rose to his feet and helped me.

"You were out for a while. Carsten asked me to tell you to find him when you woke up."

I nodded and went in search of my father. He was talking to Brad at the house. The frame was up, and it was beginning to look a lot better.

When Brad saw me, he gave me a smile and returned to the marquee. Carsten waited for me.

I walked into the newly forming house, realizing

Anzide was not with me. I guess that Carsten must have asked for a private conversation.

His hands were behind his back as we took a slow walk through what had been the dining room.

"Evelyn, I asked to speak with you privately about something that concerns me. I know that you put in a great effort today, and I must say that I am not alone in how proud I am about how far you've progressed. It may please you to know that there is a waiting list for those who want to see you in the sparring room."

I smiled, though I felt worried about what was concerning him.

"Lethargy is common in those who attempt spell attacks. It is less common in those who are able to access the portal because to do that, they are a strong person, and spell attacks are not nearly as draining. I try not to pry, Evelyn, but when I see you emerge from the portal and almost collapse into the hammock, I become concerned. When I first arrived, you said that you were weak from entering the gate. You hadn't entered the portal, but you weren't far off it which meant that you should have been stronger than you were."

"So, what's wrong with me then?"

Carsten's mouth opened as he looked at me, but all he managed was a sigh. He grimaced and turned to walk through to what was the lounge room.

"You also said that you wanted to gain information about adrenaline. There is nothing about spikes and dips, sudden drop-offs, or anything of that nature. However, there was information about vomiting."

He gave me an uneasy smile.

"Evelyn, I think you might be pregnant."

I felt winded, gripping the frame as if I was going to fall down from the shock. It was like I could feel the blood draining from my face.

"I can't be," I whispered, leaning against the wooden frame. "I've got to finish school and the war. I can't be pregnant and fighting off Drakkus as well."

"Of course you can. Why on Earth would you think that you can't do any of those things just because you are pregnant?"

"But I might not be."

"The chances of that are slim. With that in mind, I purchased a test for you. It is in your school bag, as I suggest you conduct it away from this place."

"Why?"

He shrugged.

"More private, less eyes upon you when you emerge. It is up to you. If you'd like to take it now, I can easily retrieve it and put it in your pocket. I will even distract the others while you're busy."

I nodded. Gripping my stomach, I felt queasy. Carsten saw the uneasiness and gripped my shoulder.

"Evelyn, no matter what happens, you will cope. You

are strong and resilient. If that's not enough to ease the thoughts in your mind, then consider the family around you. They will not falter. They will stand beside you as you walk down this path. All of us will."

I got the message loud and clear. If I wanted him here to help, he would do it. With a nod, I gave Carsten a weak smile and walked back through the house.

Returning to the marquee, Carsten sat at the table with Brad, Niko, and Beatrice. Anzide was hanging around, probably wondering what Carsten wanted to say and why I was as pale as a ghost.

Moving my hand over my jeans, I felt the box in my pocket. As I walked into the caravan, I could feel Anzide's eyes on me. I didn't know what to say to him or what to think. Would he be okay if I was?

After reading the instructions, I took the test and waited. It was the longest five minutes of my life, and when that second line appeared, I cried.

This was not the right time. Clearly, I was suffering from morning sickness, though thankfully, it was sporadic. I dreaded a time when it would become regular.

"Evie?" Anzide whispered. "Is everything okay?"

"It's fine."

"You're crying in the bathroom. Somehow, I don't think it's fine."

Wiping away the tears, I pocketed the test and opened the door. I tried to move past, but Anzide gripped my arm.

"You can talk to me. If the sparring room was too much or if I was too hard on you, then say something."

"I'm just worried about things, that's all."

Moving past him, I walked to the door. Anzide pulled me back by my arm again.

"I know when you're lying to me."

"I wasn't lying. I am worried about things."

Pulling my arm free, I walked down the stairs. My family, who had been sitting around the table talking, suddenly grew quiet. I looked at Carsten. He gave me a sympathetic smile because even though no words had passed between us, he knew.

"Evie," Anzide called out just as I reached the doorway out of the hidden section. "Stop bottling everything up. Just say whatever is troubling you and let others help. Keeping your emotions inside of you only leads to problems, and you know what happens then."

Angrily, I turned. He was right, but that didn't mean he should keep at me like this. It would only cause an outburst. Thankfully, I was calm enough to keep the outburst to words and not any form of a spell attack.

"I'm pregnant." I snapped.

Anzide stared silently, joining the others in their silence. Turning, I walked out of the marquee.

I found myself at the stairs that cut through the front

lawn to the street. Sitting on the top step, I pulled out the test and looked at it.

I didn't consider this to be a mistake or unwanted. It was just poorly timed. But, like always, life threw a curve ball at me. Carsten might think that I was able to fight in a war against an egotistical and psychotic vampire, but I didn't. All I could see was this happening when I was eight months pregnant with a massive mound in front of me. Slowed down by the extra weight, I wouldn't be much of a problem to bring down.

Then there was the other issue. I wasn't ready to become a mother. At eighteen, I'd barely started my life. But I had to suck it up and accept it. This is what happens when I misbehave.

Hearing footsteps, I turned to see Beatrice in the form of her alter ego, Natalia.

"May I join you?"

I nodded, moving over for her to sit down next to me.

"Are you okay?"

"I'm fine. I don't mind that I am."

"You're just worried. We understand, Evie. You've got this war looming over you, and we can all see how easily you would worry about this and the baby. But you know that as an Eternal, you don't have any issues or complications."

"Just throwing up."

"That will pass in time."

"What if it drags out so long that I'm either heavily pregnant or that I've had the baby? God, what if I go into labor during the war? How can I kill Drakkus while suffering contractions?"

Natalia smiled, nudging her shoulder against mine.

"Like all great women who find themselves in situations like this. Harness the pain and send it out to him. Carsten mentioned that there are a few great spells that you can utilize in such a situation."

I hummed, thinking that giving Drakkus labor contractions might just be fun.

"How's Anzide?"

"Shocked. I think that out of everything he expected you could have said that was the last on the list. He wanted to come here and I suggested that perhaps a little grandmotherly love would be far better. I think that he might have wanted to get away from Brad and Niko who were looking at him like he should have known better."

I smiled, but my heart wasn't in it. When I looked at my great-grandmother, she knew.

"You will be a great mother, Evie."

"I've never seen a great mother, so how is that possible?"

"Because you're a great person. You're worried, and I understand that. You endured a horrible childhood, but you've come out the other end as this amazing young woman. You've shown a lot of resilience, and you will continue to do that by winning the war and giving birth to a beautiful baby. You'll be a wonderful mother because you know what it takes to avoid being a terrible one. You won't repeat the past."

I nodded, wiping away the tears.

"Would you like to know a little secret?"

"Sure."

"You're not the only one who is pregnant."

"Really?"

She nodded with the happiest smile I'd ever seen on her.

"That's so awesome."

As I hugged her, I realized that our family was growing. There was another life to protect, one that was far more vulnerable than anyone else here.

I knew I had to buckle down and learn to harness my abilities. Getting this war over and done with had to be my number one priority. That is after I talked to Anzide.

Brad decided to pay Nora a visit, and my father returned to his home for the evening. Niko and Beatrice went for a walk in the woods so that he could feed. That left me alone with Anzide.

I wasn't worried about how this would turn out, but I was concerned that he might have misinterpreted my reaction.

He was lying on the bed when I entered the caravan. As I climbed up, Anzide turned his head to look at me.

"I wasn't upset because of it."

"I know. You're worried about Drakkus."

"What do you think?"

He shrugged and then shifted to allow me space on the bed beside him. As soon as I was on the mattress, his hand went under my shirt. Anzide smiled and stopped at the top of my stomach.

"There's our girl," he whispered. "She was hiding from me."

Anzide sighed. Leaning on one hand, he kept the other on my stomach, closest to the baby.

"You know that I can't lie."

"Am I going to get upset at what you say?"

"No. At least, I hope that you won't. This is something that I never expected. Well, never thought of, I suppose. I joked about it not that long ago, but I didn't think that it would happen so soon, which is probably the stupidest I've ever been."

"We should have been more careful."

"Nothing could stop what is meant to be."

I looked up at Anzide, fearful that he was hiding what he really thought. He might not be able to lie, but that doesn't mean he couldn't hold his tongue and refrain from saying anything negative to spare my feelings.

"I am okay with this."

"Promise?"

"I promise."

Anzide kissed me. Slow and needful, it was everything that a stressed-out person needed.

CHAPTER 24

Beatrice gave me a list of things to collect from the shops when I decided I wanted to see James about the schedule. He needed to know that life was going to alter for me, and it wasn't a little hiccup. She was going to be a screaming poop machine that would demand my attention constantly.

With most of the items in the cart, I wandered down the candy aisle, searching for something to make me feel better. It wasn't the right answer to the problems, but I didn't care. Something deliciously chocolate would be perfect.

Anzide wasn't much better. He'd found out how amazing this aisle was not that long ago and often put too many naughty things into the cart. I looked at the contents and grinned, shaking my head. He'd already stashed a stack of cookie packets as if he wasn't going to be back here in a couple of days.

"Don't they have these things in your hometown?"

He turned, giving me a vague shrug.

"Probably not. They're not big on the whole food thing. That's why the food court sucks."

"And what about groceries?"

"There are places to purchase various items within each of the areas."

I nodded, quietly thinking about the portal.

"Do you think that it would get boring?"

"As in how and why?"

"Like if there was an apocalypse and it was our only choice. What would we do to stave off boredom?"

"Well, as I am a new resident of the town and my bosses have kept me busy since my working life began, I haven't had time to be bored. I get the feeling that it's not a problem. Everyone in the town is used to the situation and what is expected of them. You, however, I can see you finding it as dreary as this place."

"Yeah, I can see that too."

Done with filling the cart with too much chocolate, Anzide pushed the cart to the register. The girl began bagging it, giving us a questioning look but remaining silent.

Back at the car, I looked up at the sunny sky and sighed.

"Hopefully, there will be a shady park available at the school. Otherwise, the chocolate is going to melt."

Closing the lid, Anzide smirked like something incredibly feral was going through his mind.

"Let me guess, something about melted chocolate and me naked?"

He nodded, and I chuckled. Yep, feral but fun.

Returning to school was not my idea of a good time. At least, at the moment, it wasn't. Once this ridiculous situation was over, I would be okay with coming here. The lessons were becoming a bit boring, but there were perks, like hanging out with Karina and having a moment of freedom from the constricting walls of the coven property.

Glancing around the car park, I searched with a fear that we were being watched. Well, me and maybe Anzide. I don't know if he made himself appear in times like this. Usually, he didn't.

Entering the office, I found James leaning on the hutch of Jane's desk, reading through a file full of papers. His gaze lifted, and the file was closed and tucked under one arm. Like he knew what was on my mind, James offered a sympathetic smile as he opened the door to the back corridor of the office area. When we were safely sealed in the privacy of his office, James sat at his desk and leaned back like he always does.

"I know,"

I was a little shocked at first. There was a lot he could say, but that wasn't something that I thought it would be.

"You know what, exactly?"

"So as not to spoil it, I'm going to write it down, and when you tell me, I will reveal it."

Pulling the notepad off the desk, James wrote something on it and then put the pen back on the desk. Holding the notepad against his chest, James offered a smile.

"Fire away."

"I'm pregnant."

He turned the notebook around to reveal the words *bun in the oven.*

"You're hilarious."

"I know that too."

"So, how did you know that I was pregnant?"

"Because I'm a demon. I see all forms of life. You and your baby daddy will be able to do the same when the two of you age up a little. I suppose that you're here to wrap your head around it and the schedule for the future."

I looked at Anzide, who gave me a shrug.

"I was actually wondering if I'd make it to the prom or if I'd end up looking like a beached whale."

"It would depend on how long you gestate for and when I set the date for the prom, which is usually at the end of April. The Eternals vary in their gestation length. You are probably only a few weeks along, so I'd say that it would put you in a bit of a predicament. The problem you face is the Winter Ball, which is usually held in

November. There is a possibility that you will be okay to attend, though I am not certain."

"Well, it was a great dream while it lasted," I muttered.

"It can vary depending on the dominant species. You should remember that this child is Nephilim and Phoenix, an extremely rare combination. We can take it back even further, considering that Anzide's parents were angel and demon, and yours were angel and human. Take that back even further, and you've got vampire, shapeshifter and human. Naturally, those won't count for much when the others are far more dominating but you see my point that there is quite a mixture going on in there. Generally, the species of the mother will dictate the length of gestation. Your mother would have conformed to a human pregnancy rather than anything your father might have provided regarding his species. You should read this book, Evelyn. It will help you understand yourself, the world that we inhabit, and other little things like your pregnancy."

The book was pushed across the desk. Not overly fancy, just a deep green linen-look hardcover book with one word in embossed gold font. *Gestation.*

"You are incredibly rare. In fact, if my memory serves me correctly, you are the only phoenix that is born to an angel and human. All the others are demons and humans, and none of them have partnered with a Nephilim. Demons interacting with humans is fairly standard. They tend to be the more scandalous of the two. Usually, they stop before anything happens, or they use adequate protection. Phoenix also tends to be rare because of what happens to the human beyond the act. Most refuse to entertain the idea, but there are always circumstances that warrant such an acceptance. The problem is, as you will read in the book, is that the information is limited. What is there is based on what they've already seen, and while it might be similar to your situation, it is not the same. So, I would suggest that you read it but use it as a guide, not as fact. It will give you a lot of information about the other Eternals which I believe you need. As for the prom, would you like the good news or the bad news?"

"That sounds ominous. Hit me with the good first."

"You will be able to attend the prom. The bad news is that bubs will probably be out in a couple of months."

Oh.

"Gestation for a phoenix is estimated at five months. I would suggest that you take the first interaction as your guide and count from there as it is guaranteed that it is the date of conception."

I nodded, thinking that this baby would be out sooner than I'd anticipated.

"Now, I have something that I wanted to talk to you about."

James pulled pieces of paper out of a folder that he'd been looking at when we arrived. Laying them out on the desk, James arranged them so I could see them. They were my tests and the results I'd not seen until now. I passed all of them.

"Your teachers are thrilled they have such a genius in their class. It takes a lot of effort on my part to ensure that they don't overthink it. I do enjoy it, though, if you're wondering."

"Sure."

The smile on his face was devious enough to show that he probably had a grand old time tinkering with their minds.

"But I look at these, and I see someone that will soon grow bored of her classes. A bored mind is unfortunate, but a genius and bored is unforgivable. I know that you've got far too much on your plate already, so when I suggest this, please keep in mind that I propose this for the long term future. You're talking about the prom so that means that you intend to stay here for the rest of the year. Either you're keeping to the schedule that I set and eventually grow bored in your classes or you're taking on extra lessons."

"After the war and the baby is born?"

"Yes."

I nodded, wondering what else this place could offer me.

"The classes are a little boring. So, what are you suggesting?"

"Anything and everything. If you want, you can do every single class in this school. There are enough days left in the year, and you have the brain power to do it. You want to go to prom? Fine, it's done. Will you be sane, or will you have grown so bored that you're causing me problems and creating mischief? Bear in mind the company you keep. They are not so lucky with their lives like the one born to an Eternal father."

"You think I'd corrupt Karina and Cooper?"

James chuckled.

"Evelyn, I *know* you'd corrupt them."

When the amusement left us, I quickly thought about it. Seeing the results, I knew I could do this without much issue.

"Alright. When the war is over, we'll talk about it again, but I will spend the year doing whatever I can in the time that I have. I will have to find someone to look after the baby because I assume that my unseen protector isn't going to believe the world is safe."

"We will cross that bridge when we come to it. Maybe your family could help out."

"Sure," I said, looking at James.

He smiled softly, almost like he knew that Anzide's plans to ask certain family members to help out was unlikely.

"In the meantime, this is a list of the subjects and the breakdown for each of them. I've highlighted the ones that you're currently doing and crossed out the ones that would be pointless, as they are the level below the ones you're already doing. Learn your power, Evelyn. Take this book and soak the information in. Go on, put your hand on the cover."

I could do this. It was easy. My hand rested on the cover, and I let the information flow through me. With it came raw power and a sense of accomplishment. I knew that my little lady would be here in just a few months, like James had said. It wasn't a guess. It wasn't any form of estimation. Five months on the dot.

I could take all of the dates that Anzide and I had been together, but that would be pointless because, like James said, the very first time. The book also informed me that the female always dictated the duration of gestation, the fertility cycle, and when she would be ready for another child. It was almost a relief to know that several years would pass before that happened. Eternals were extremely fertile, but that was only when the female was ready.

I also learned that it was the human side of the equation that caused the death every hundred years. The Eternal overrides it and creates a rebirth into a new life. It was strange, and because there were so few of us, the life cycles and what happened to a phoenix were still being documented. It just made things more complicated, but I was used to it. My life has been nothing but complicated.

CHAPTER 25

Audrey was in the corridor when I emerged from the office. She was alone, just like I was. Well, at least in her eyes, I was.

She smiled supremely at me, almost like she thought that I was defenseless without Cooper here to step between us.

"You're not going to win, you know."

"What makes you think that?"

"Because you're just a pathetic little girl who isn't even a vampire."

Jeez, it sounded like I was faced with Drakkus. *Pathetic little girl,* his words echoed through my mind. It didn't bring me down. All it did was make me all the more eager to show him that there was nothing about me that was pathetic. As for him making it sound like being a girl was a downfall, I was going to show him how wrong he was.

Playing the game, I nodded with a plain face.

"You're right. I'm not a vampire. I have vampire blood in me because my great-grandfather was a vampire, but I don't have fangs, right?"

Audrey smiled like she'd won the argument.

"But then there's that other part of me. Did they tell you that?"

"Who?" she asked in a snarky tone.

"Kannon, Drakkus, whoever it is that is whispering these statements in your ear."

She faltered for a second before returning to the smile that she thought hid her fears. I wasn't a fool.

"My father is a biblical creature, which makes me one too. That's why Drakkus knows that he can't use me to create a child with and claim the Corbin line."

"Why couldn't he? That makes no sense."

"It would kill him. That's part of the reason that Kannon's angry at me. We didn't know what I was, and he was so close to having sex with me, completely unaware that it would have started the clock ticking away at his mortality."

It appeared as if Audrey was trying to comprehend what I was saying. Without more information or time to digest, it wouldn't be easy.

It didn't matter, not really. What did matter was the opportunity that I saw.

"You know that we have the same goal, right?"

"Kannon?"

"No." I scoffed. "A dead Drakkus."

Audrey shrugged as she folded her arms.

"That may be true, but you lost your chance at anything when you said that you would refuse to turn me into a vampire to be with Kannon."

"He's cheating on you. Did you hear me say that? He's screwing Drakkus constantly and has no intention of stopping. You shouldn't accept that kind of behavior."

"You just want him for yourself."

"No, I do not. One, I already told you that I'm a biblical creature, and I cannot have sex with mortals or immortals unless I want them to die. Two, he lied far too many times to me, he sold me out, and he is associating with the vampire that killed Niko. I'd rather he left town completely, and I've told him to do so many times. And finally, three, I have someone. Would you like to meet my partner, Audrey?"

She shrugged uneasily.

"Anzide,"

He appeared at my side. Audrey looked at him and then at me.

"The guy from yesterday?"

"Yeah, the very same. He's Nephilim."

"What's that?"

"I am the child of an angel and a demon. Such creatures were not permitted to breed, but they did, and I was the result of their actions. My task in life was to deliver messages to those who had committed sins of the flesh. One such task brought me to Hades and, in particular, to Evie. Her father was an unknown entity, and her mother was human. We knew that she was a hybrid due to an incident, and I was sent to deliver a message of warning that my overseers would be coming to deliver their verdict against her and the father that we located. Evie stood up for herself and we soon learned that the man we thought was her father was not. It was another, and his actions doomed her mother to an untimely death. Unfortunately, a certain vampire beat the clock and murdered Evie's mother. You might know him. His name was Andross. In fact, Andross also murdered Evie's grandparents and great-grandmother. All because Drakkus wanted easy access to the rule of this town."

Audrey was clearly stunned. Her arms dropped to her sides, and I saw the defenses lower.

"Kannon said that you're in love with him and jealous of our love. What was I supposed to think? That he was lying to me? I never thought he'd do something like that. Now you're telling me that these vampires are murdering people just to take over the leadership of this stupid town?"

"We are telling you that, but you don't need to get stressed out over it. This is my battle with Drakkus. Do you remember what the weather was like before I came here?"

“Yeah,” she said uneasily.

“Drakkus did that. When he tried to take over as leader, it caused a void in this town. A blood war between Drakkus and Niko began. If neither of the original parties is willing or unable to end the blood war, it falls to their descendants, who can end it. I can do that but to end the war and to stop this town from falling into another void, I have to be the one that ends his life, not you, not anyone else.”

“Oh,”

Audrey’s voice was soft, clearly thinking about it. As much as I liked cold weather and rainy days, the sun was good for the soul.

“As for Kannon, I liked him in the beginning, tolerated him in the middle, and now want to kick him into the sun. It’s understandable that he’s trying to make me out to be your enemy, but it doesn’t have to be this way. If you back away from your alliance with Drakkus, I will reconsider my resistance.”

“I can become a vampire?”

“Your actions between now and the end of the war will answer that. For now, you should let things cool off between the two of you rather than a complete cut. Don’t draw attention to yourself or your family.”

“But how can I do that and still be on your side?”

“I have my ways of knowing things. Start with laying off the attitude towards me.”

Audrey stared for a moment and then nodded, giving me an uneasy smile.

"I'm not a bad person, Audrey, and I know you're not either. We just got off on the wrong foot."

"And they've been telling me stuff. I guess it's all lies."

"Yeah, it is. Niko was a good man, and he didn't deserve the painful death that he endured. My great-grandmother was beaten in a fake break-in. My grandparents were in a light aircraft crash, and the aviation authority ruled it as foul play. My mother was pumped full of drugs and vampire venom. Because she knew what chased us, desperate to kill us, my mother couldn't handle her life. She drank herself into oblivion, barely cared for me, and hit me constantly. I've spent years being dragged around this continent, hiding from something I didn't know existed. He did that to us, to me. When I came here, the only family I had left in this world was Brad. I might not have known who Niko really was, but he felt like he was my family. Drakkus took that from me."

Pain surfaced on her face, and I guess she was thinking as if it were herself and her own family. How one family could be destroyed because of the delusions of a psychotic vampire.

"I'm sorry you've endured so much suffering and loss."

"Thank you."

The bell rang, and within seconds, the empty corridor

we were standing in was inundated with students. Audrey gave me a soft smile, and with a slight wave, she turned to walk away.

When she was out of sight, I moved to a side corridor so that I was alone.

"Well?"

I couldn't see Anzide, but I knew he was there. He appeared in front of me.

"Smart move. Bring the mean girl to our side. You never know. She might just end up being a spy for you, too."

"Great. What was going on inside her brain?"

"Visions of those who were whispering in her ear. It's not just Kannon. His father's been telling her things as well. Mostly, there won't be a marriage if Drakkus is not the leader. No second-in-charge job for Kannon means no money for their family, which translates to no wedding, no Audrey the vampire, and no bright future as the wife of the second-in-charge. After the run-in, Kannon added to that by saying that with you as the leader, she'd never become a vampire. After all, you made it quite clear that it was being taken away from her, so Audrey had the confirmation that everything they said was right. You changed that, though."

"She believes me?"

"Yeah, she does. At the end of it all, she was really feeling sorry for you. She knows that she's led a privileged life with her perfect family. Audrey's never seen what it's like for someone to struggle with their life. Now she has, and she's also seen how someone can rise through the pain and persevere. I think that, in a way, she actually looks up to you."

"That's just so weird."

Anzide shrugged.

"As for everything before that, it was clear in her mind that she had no idea you could kill Kannon like that. Kannon kept telling her that you were in love with him and desperate to destroy her so that you could be with him. She liked the idea of taking your side because no one, not even her friends, said that Kannon cheating on her was wrong. There is a constant theme in her head, and it's one that was not helping you. All her friends comment about how cute they think Kannon is and how lucky they believe she is to land him. Audrey has the opinion that if they were given the chance, they would screw Kannon behind her back."

"And that's why she had so many issues regarding me and him."

"Yep. Your reluctance to be around him now works in your favor. Audrey doesn't think that you're interested. She appreciates your efforts to make her see the truth about Kannon cheating on her. You were the only one that said it. In an instant, her opinion changed, and she began to see you in a different light. She wants to earn your approval, and she worries that if she doesn't distance herself from Kannon enough, you'll use it against her. You will begin to see a difference, and I would suggest that you use that to show her your growing approval. If she thinks that it's stagnating, she might just flip back."

Accepting Anzide's statement, I turned back into the crowded corridor. At the far end, I could see the pretty pink cashmere that was like a beacon amongst the white shirts. I would keep Audrey on my side as best as I could. I didn't want to turn her into a vampire if she was going to continue to be horrible to me, but if she changed her ways, I would reconsider.

There was no real reason I would say no if she was pleasant to me. I didn't expect miracles, but I wanted an improvement. I'm sure Niko would demand more from her, especially considering there is a strong chance she'd leave Hades to go to college. I couldn't deny her the alteration if she met my requirements, and if Niko had a problem with it, then I guess he'd have to suck it up and accept it.

A conversation needed to happen once the war was over. If Audrey was leaving Hades, permanently or temporarily, she would either have to let go of her desire to become a vampire or find a coven that would accept her. I think that if she behaved, I could convince Niko to do the alteration and organize a transfer for her. She might come back to Hades. After all, her family was here. The problem was that she called this place stupid. It meant that she found it as boring as what I did.

This would be discussed later, and hopefully, it won't come back to bite me on the ass.

CHAPTER 26

Walking up the driveway, I was surprised to see how much the builders had done today. Henry gave me a wave as we approached.

"Afternoon, Evie, Anzide."

"Hey, Henry. You've been busy today."

"Yep. Lots of hands on deck today. We're hoping to get everything watertight before the snow starts."

I looked at the rusty-colored trees. I'd not paid attention to them, too busy trying to make sure that there was no one hiding in the shadows watching us. The thought of winter's approach made me realize that not only was the hunting ground that Niko and Brad used about to become a barren, frostbitten nightmare, but Christmas was also looming.

"Yeah, I guess it won't be long."

"I'm just grateful that we've had such incredible weather. Usually, I spend weeks waiting for the rain to stop."

"I guess luck is on our side."

Henry chuckled with a nod. One of the other workers called out to him, so Henry excused himself. Anzide and I began walking to the marquee.

"Could you imagine trying to get the house rebuilt with a void hanging over the town?"

"It wouldn't be easy."

Holding the flap aside, Anzide waited for me to enter the marquee. Brad was sitting on a lounge chair reading the local newspaper.

"How was school?"

"Interesting."

Giving him a flick of my head, I continued to our little meeting room. We had the dining table set up for everyone so there would be no lawn chairs or squished together on the bench seats in the caravan.

Niko emerged from the caravan, looking a little flustered. It was a peculiar sight, considering he always seemed refined and calm.

"You're home early," Niko said with a smile.

I looked at my watch. It was four-thirty pm, an hour and a half after school ended. I'd talked to James and Audrey, and we'd walked home. I suppose we were early, all things considered.

"Yeah, I guess we are."

Dumping my bag, I sat at the head of the table and

waited for everyone to sit down. Beatrice emerged from the caravan, curiously hooking the door back. I glanced at Anzide, who had a subdued smile on his face. Brad wandered in, talking about something in the newspaper and distracting Beatrice and Niko.

"What?" I whispered, leaning closer. "Why are you smirking like that?"

"Because you look like you're going to bust a vein."

Leaning into my ear, Anzide whispered what I wasn't seeing.

Brad was at the far end of the marquee for a reason. Niko was in a fluster and not his usual self because of that reason. Beatrice appeared to be quietly pleased, showing a soft smile that rose into her flushed cheeks.

"Oh," I said dryly.

"Yeah, oh. So how about you stop squinting at everyone now that you've figured it out?"

I rolled my eyes at his statement. Where was the fun in that?

"Is there something that you need to tell us?" Brad asked as he folded the newspaper. "I was comfortable."

"If you don't want to be here, then please go back. No one is stopping you."

"I might," Niko interjected. "Please start, Evelyn."

"Okay, so Audrey tried to bail me up again, but I turned it around. Anzide checked her mind while everything was going on."

"You've created an ally?"

"I have. She was being fed a lot of lies and now knows the truth. I've asked her to draw away from Kannon but not be obvious about it."

"And what Evie neglects to tell you all is that it's all good. Audrey is on the path to becoming a better person towards Evie and other students at the school. She sees her in an extremely positive light because Evie was the only one who pointed out how wrong it is that Kannon cheats on her constantly. Audrey thinks that her friends are lining themselves up for a round in Kannon's bed. If ever she asks, it's the truth."

I scoffed, shaking my head.

"Well, then that certainly explains why they're not interested in telling her that his antics are wrong."

Anzide nodded and then frowned as his head turned to the door.

"We've got company. Human company."

Brad stood and walked through the door while Niko and Beatrice returned to the caravan. Curious about who was here, I got up and looked past the cloth door. It was Audrey.

Turning in shock, I frowned with a bewildered smile.

"Audrey's here."

"I know. I can feel a lot of fear and anxiety, so I will

be coming with you."

When we emerged from the makeshift room, Brad was talking to Audrey. He gestured to the lounge and turned to see us approaching.

"I'll leave you to it."

"Thanks."

Audrey gave me an easy smile. Her eyes were red, and her face was blotchy from crying.

"What's wrong?"

She smiled, but I could see the tears were ready to emerge. The sleeves of her precious cashmere jumper had been pulled over her hands, looking ratty from where she'd wiped the tears.

"I'm sorry, I didn't know where to go. I should go to see Larry, but he's being paid off by Drakkus. Dad won't understand, and I know he'll tell me to ignore it."

"It's okay. Why don't you sit down and tell me what's happening?"

Audrey nodded. When her back was turned, I looked at Anzide. He gave me a grim look as he shook his head.

"Bad?" I whispered.

"Really bad."

I sat on the lounge next to her. Anzide sat on the coffee table in front of us.

"So, after school, I was with Kannon. He said that we

had to go to see Drakkus about the agreement. Drakkus was so angry,"

Audrey wiped the tears as the weepy words escaped.

"I didn't know what was going on. Drakkus kept demanding that Kannon showed his loyalty to the clan and his leadership."

"Has he faltered in his loyalty?"

"Not that I know of. I mean, Drakkus has been getting antsy about the leadership, but he knows that he's the only one who can do anything about it."

"Maybe Kannon said something he shouldn't have, and Drakkus reacted."

Maybe they'd finally realized Drakkus was a few bricks short of a house.

"I don't know. I'm not even sure if Kannon knows. Drakkus demanded that Kannon show his loyalty to the clan and his leadership by executing Jess. When Kannon refused to do it, Drakkus got really angry. He lunged at Jessica with a knife and stabbed her."

Teary eyes looked at me, and I knew that whatever was in her mind would always remain. I could see her crumbling before me, and there was nothing I could do to help her.

"Then he cut off her head."

Audrey burst into tears, sobbing that she couldn't get the image out of her head. I wrapped my arms around her and looked at Anzide. He pressed his lips tight, morosely looking at me. I wanted to ask if there was anything that he could do, but deep down, I knew that we had nothing.

I gestured to her, and Anzide raised a finger as he stood and disappeared. Seconds later, Anzide reappeared with my father.

"Hello, Audrey," Carsten said in his smooth tone.

She lifted from my arms and wiped the tears from her face.

"I'm Carsten, Evelyn's father. Would it be alright if we had a chat alone for a few minutes?"

"I guess."

Freeing myself from Audrey's vine-like embrace wasn't easy. I never thought that she'd get so personal this quickly.

Taking Anzide's place on the coffee table, Carsten faced Audrey. She was tucked up on the lounge, gripping a pillow like she thought it would help her.

"Why?" I asked when we reached the other side of the marquee.

"Because your father is an extremely old Eternal. There is a soothing quality about Eternals, and the older they are, the better. Didn't you wonder why Audrey latched onto you so easily?"

"Yeah, what's the deal with that?"

"You're an Eternal, and you've shown her compassion and understanding. You are a beacon of light and hope in the fog of despair."

I sighed, wrapping my arms around Anzide.

"This is so awful. I liked Jess. She didn't deserve this."

"While there is truth to that statement, remember that she was a part of the group that was actively deceiving you up until they were caught. She knew what her brother planned to do and even helped him plan your abduction. I'm not trying to make her into a monster, but you shouldn't create a martyr either."

After a few minutes of waiting, I got fed up and sat down. Anzide sat on the lawn chair next to mine, and we waited while trying to avoid watching too much. Audrey wasn't crying anymore, and she seemed quite relaxed. Carsten was doing all the talking. Occasionally, she would nod, and a few words were said as the minutes passed by.

I was a little shocked when my father offered his upturned hand. Audrey reached out, turning her palm up as well. Carsten gripped it with one hand and began pointing at things on the palm.

"What is he doing?"

"It's kind of like a spell. I would have thought he'd go for something like a permanent erase, but that's the temporary one."

Anzide shifted to face me, frowning softly.

"And it's not a memory chant either. It just disconnects the heaviest of emotions from it. She will still have the memories, she will see the event in her mind, but she won't get so upset from it."

"I guess he can't wipe it completely. Otherwise, they'll know that she was here."

"Good point. Anyway, this will allow her to move on and not go insane from the memory rerunning through her mind."

"When everything is over, can we remove the memory completely?"

"It can be done. I would recommend that you hold a meeting to discuss it, though. There may be implications surrounding it, and that kind of change warrants all to know what is happening."

When Audrey and my father stood, I got up and crossed the gap between us.

"Audrey is feeling a little better now. She understands that the memories will be strong for a long time, but I've helped her with a few techniques that will help her think of other things and forget the event. Audrey also understands that she must not tell anyone of these techniques because if she does, they will know she has been here to see us. Once the blood war is over, I've asked Audrey to come back and see me for another chat. I'm going to do a little research to help her in the future so that it will become a distant memory."

"I'm glad to hear that."

Audrey smiled at me and began to walk to the door.

"I'm glad that I came to you. I know that the past few weeks have been difficult for you, and I want to apologize for everything that I've said and done. I shouldn't have listened to them, but they're so charismatic."

We walked to the driveway. Audrey had driven here, and the flashy red car was parked on the street.

"Would it be wrong to keep it after everything that's happened?"

"I, uh, don't know what you mean."

"That," she said, pointing to the car. "It's the bribe that Drakkus used to keep me quiet."

"He had a car ready to bribe you with?"

"No. Apparently, it was going to be a gift for when I joined the coven. Kannon said that I'd seen too much and said he needed to buy my silence. Something about the Europeans."

Audrey shrugged, not noticing when I glanced at Anzide.

"Well, I think that if you refuse it, then they will wonder if you're going to say something or if you have already done that. I would suggest that, for now, you keep it and maintain a view that makes it clear that you're going to be silent."

With a nod, Audrey smiled at me.

"You're right. Thanks for everything, Evie. I'll see you tomorrow."

"No problem."

Audrey walked down the driveway, waving at Karina when she reached the end of the footpath. Karina frowned as her head tilted. When Audrey drove off, Karina crossed the road, gesturing to where the car had been.

"What's the deal, and why was she here?"

"We had a chat after school. She's now secretly on our side. After school, she went to the Fleming coven house with Kannon. Something rather dark and horrid happened. She came here in tears. My father subdued the emotions so that she could keep going."

"Dark and horrid, huh?"

"Do you really want to know?"

Karina shrugged.

"Know your enemy, right?"

"Yeah, you say that now. Drakkus wanted Kannon to kill his aunt as a show of loyalty to him and the coven. When Kannon refused, Drakkus stabbed her and then removed her head. All of it in front of Audrey."

Karina winced, shaking her head.

"What a monster. No matter what's going on, we're feeling sorry for her. No one should see that."

I nodded in agreement. The sooner Drakkus was gone, the better.

CHAPTER 27

Karina followed us to the tent. I looked at Anzide, silently questioning him, which earned nothing more than a confused frown. When I pointed at my belly and tilted my head towards Karina, Anzide shrugged.

"You're so useful."

"Or perhaps I like to annoy you. Makes life interesting. Go ahead. She's going to find out soon enough."

"Find out what?"

"There's a reason I throw up after the adrenaline spikes."

Karina looked between us, silent as the thoughts ticked through her head. Then came a whopping big grin.

"You are not serious."

"We are."

"You're pregnant?"

"It's true."

"Oh my god," she squealed, thoroughly happy as she hugged us.

Yep, poor old Zeed was dragged in with an arm around his neck. I didn't escape either. Karina's hugs were a little wild and crazy.

"That is so awesome. What do the oldies think of that?"

"Happy and not impressed."

Entering the back area, I saw empty chairs and family waiting for us to sit down.

"We were just discussing Audrey's visit. Please, sit and join us." Niko said. "In particular, Carsten told us that Audrey heard them talking about the Europeans."

"She has no idea what they're talking about."

"What Kannon would have been referring to was the fact that Drakkus killed Jessica, and Audrey is a witness. If the Europeans come through here, they will scrutinize everyone associated with any vampire in this town. There was a rumor floating around a number of years ago that they had an Eternal of some form working for them. If it is true, then this would allow them to enter the minds of anyone who crosses their path. They might speak with Audrey, but if they can read minds, then there is no need to. The Eternal would see everything. Of course, Kannon wasn't thinking like that if he'd suggested that Drakkus bribed Audrey with the car. I think that, in this instance, Kannon is trying to stop Audrey from telling you. Without him in school every day, he has no control over who Audrey interacts with. Kannon probably thinks that it's only a matter of time before the walls come down, more so because of Anzide's abilities."

"I won't wipe her memories until it is confirmed if they are coming or not." Carsten offered. "Though she may need to return if the dampening spell doesn't stick. I had to keep it low to avoid anyone noticing. Make no mistake, Drakkus and Kannon will be watching her over the coming days. Audrey needs to struggle with the memories and what happened today. She can't be perky and act as if nothing happened. They will suspect."

Niko handed me a notebook, giving me a firm look.

"Enough of this subject for now. It is important that you start learning what is necessary to complete the future. Read these passages, and memorize them, but do not say them out loud. These are the statements that you must make when the time is right. The first is your charges against Drakkus, then the Lothaire family, then your abdication and passing of the rule to me. If you say the first two out loud, nothing will happen, but the third will alter our status."

Flicking open the cover, I read the first page, which was the charge against Drakkus. Now that we have evidence, we could move forward on this being done correctly.

"We will practice the trial as much as we can. As it won't affect anything, we can keep going until you know it without any problems. A timeline will need to be created so that everyone knows their place and what they need to do."

"But we don't know the big picture. How can we plan anything when we don't know where this will happen or when?"

"You are right. There are certain aspects that can't be planned. However, things like the trial can be. You will start by identifying yourself as the leader of this clan and the rightful ruler of Hades. Once you've identified yourself, you will state that under the code of vampires, Drakkus has broken numerous laws. We would be standing around for days and nights if we listed every single crime, so we will go with the worst and what carries the heaviest punishment. Now that we have Audrey's testimony, we can focus on Jessica's murder rather than trying to list things that we don't have evidence for. So, you state that the list includes the crime of murdering a vampire, which means instant death, to be administered by the ruler of the town. As it is a trial, you need to ask if he wants to say anything in his defense. I doubt that Drakkus has changed in our years apart so I would imagine that he'd taunt you with his belief that you don't have evidence."

"So, we bring Audrey in?"

Niko nodded.

"That is why the timeline is imperative here. As there are variables, I would suggest that your father is the one who collects Audrey. He has the ability to be anywhere within seconds and can bring her to wherever you are equally as fast. Carsten also has the ability to alter things if she's interacting with someone when we need her. Everything needs to be flexible. Everyone needs to be able to move around this town quickly because we don't know if it will happen in the forest behind this property or in the middle of town."

"Would he really do that?"

Niko offered a shrug, looking at me with a vagueness that I'd not encountered from him.

"I want to say no, but I don't know how sane he is. The Drakkus that I knew was intelligent but had moments of sheer stupidity. He would also know that there is an obscuris veil over the town, so there is an element of freedom because of it. There is also the belief that you'd be like me or any vampire and want humans to be completely oblivious, so you would do all that you can to avoid a public war. That doesn't mean that walking down the street can be done without fear. It just means that he's likely to draw back to engage in a more private setting. I would suggest that you do the same as well, if such a situation occurs."

Niko turned to Carsten.

"When you were in Audrey's mind, did you find any resistance to being on Evelyn's side of this war?"

"She fears for her life, undoubtedly because she's seen how easily angered Drakkus is. Audrey knows that he doesn't care about her. She even thinks that he doesn't care about Kannon and questions the dynamics of their relationship. There are thoughts that constantly run through her mind that Kannon is being emotionally abused by Drakkus, and that has created a type of Stockholm Syndrome situation. He's not bound by walls or a cage, but there is an element of captivity in their relationship."

Carsten paused, looking at my horrified face. With a smile, he shrugged.

"Want me to tell you he's fine?"

"I guess."

He nodded. "I understand. Regardless of what has happened between you and him, it's in your identity to be caring towards him. That's the nature of our race. For the record, Kannon is not suffering, nor is he being abused. He has a lot of control in the relationship to the point where they often fight as one or the other tries to regain control. It's almost like foreplay for them because it always ends one way."

"Too much information," Niko muttered. "When did you go digging to get that kind of information?"

"I take all opportunities when they are given. Entering a mind can be dangerous, and it is recommended that we avoid it, but when the payout is grand, I find that it's worth it. If we are careful, we don't cause damage. I am waiting for Drakkus to emerge. Unfortunately, it seems that he is aware of what I am and is taking great care to avoid me. It means I have not been able to enter his mind, and therefore, I don't have anything to give you."

"Shame, I'd really like to know what the meathead was planning."

"Plans can change, more so for someone as irrational as Drakkus. Consider the situation that Audrey witnessed. What happened that made Drakkus question Kannon's loyalty? Did Kannon expect the events as they played out? Because it seems to me as if he didn't. Why would he bring Audrey to the coven house if he knew that Drakkus was going to act so violently? As a human, she is not a part of the coven and, therefore, not bound to the rules. To me, it says that this began as a simple interaction, and something changed. It also shows how unreliable Drakkus is. He is volatile and impulsive."

Carsten agreed with Niko.

"If I get the opportunity, I will do a little digging in his mind. The problem is that I can't find him. I know where he lives, I have been there several times, yet I cannot find him. It's likely that he has a secondary house that is hidden from everyone, followers included. As for Audrey and if she's likely to resist, I cannot see anything like that in her mind. In her head, there are two lines of thought. The first is all about Evie and how Audrey thinks that she's wronged her over the past few weeks. Audrey is determined to make things right now that she knows the truth, and she appreciates how candid Evie was with her regarding Kannon's misbehavior. The second line of thought is about justice for Jessica. Audrey liked Jessica and saw her as a sister figure. She is going to mourn her loss for a long time. I will monitor Audrey's mind to ensure that she is prepared and willing to give the testimony that Evelyn needs, but I don't see there being any issues."

"Good. I'd hate to see Evelyn in the middle of the

war and not have the backing she needs to make this legal. It seems inconsequential when one looks at the broader picture, but it is guaranteed that the Europeans have already been notified that something is amiss in this town again. They will be here, and with any luck, this mess will be over, and everything will be wrapped up in a nice, legally sound way."

The pieces were falling into place. With Audrey's testimony, it could be completed without issue. I hated that he murdered Jessica. As much as she was aware of what her brother was up to when he was planning on abducting me, I knew it was probably only because they wanted this nightmare to end. It sounded as if Drakkus was becoming unpredictable and clearly dangerous to be around. Becoming the leader might solve that problem, but I doubted it.

"Do you know how old Drakkus is?"

Niko thought about it, frowning as his lips pressed tight.

"I don't ever recall him stating an age or the year he was born, but once he mentioned going to see a game at the Colosseum. He claimed that he was seated in the senatorial class, which means that he was a senator. Drakkus never mentioned if this was a night game, but if he was old enough to cope, he could withstand certain situations."

"He probably ensured he was in the shade." Beatrice offered.

Niko nodded, then turned to me.

"Why do you ask?"

"I was just wondering if he's gone mad from an extremely long life."

"For a vampire, an unhealthy mind usually comes from a predisposition, not the length of time walking this planet."

Something occurred to me, and it made me wonder why I hadn't asked.

"So, what about you? When were you born, and where? Tell me about when you two met. I want all the dirt."

Beatrice chuckled, looking at Niko, who narrowed his gaze at me. Karina was eagerly waiting for the information as well.

"I can start," Beatrice offered. "I was born in France in 1493. My mother never said what she or my father feared, but it was enough for them to uproot the family and flee to England. We maintained an ordinary life, posing as the middle class. Moving around constantly meant that money was needed, so everyone worked. I was on my way home one evening when I happened to cross the path of a devilishly handsome vampire. By the time Niko and I married, things were changing. Everywhere we turned, there was too much risk of getting caught. Wars meant the risk of conscription, and for a vampire, it's not exactly the wisest of places to be. So, we agreed to move. We found this lovely little patch of land and Niko created the coven."

Beatrice looked at Niko with a smile that I'm sure was her way of telling him to behave. With a soft huff, he relented.

"England, 1693. I'm sure that a lot of our family are still there, lurking around the corners."

"Speaking of lurking around corners, did you happen to see a certain famous serial killer by any chance?"

Niko scoffed, rolling his eyes.

"Thankfully, no. That entire situation was a travesty and just proves how easy life was for a vampire back then."

"Was he a vampire?"

"Going by the reports, it is doubtful. As he was never caught, I cannot say for certain."

Niko flicked his fingers dismissively.

"Enough of that monster. We waste our precious lives discussing someone who doesn't deserve even a thought."

I looked at Karina, who pursed her lips with an uneasy smile. Clearly, she detected the shift in the mood. It was almost like Niko didn't want to talk about it because he knew something.

I thought about what Beatrice said. My gaze shifted to my father, who was watching. Stretched into his seat, he rested his head on one hand. The smirk was obvious. It was almost like he was goading me into continuing the inquisition. This one was bad for my health, and he was undoubtedly trying to get me into trouble.

The more I considered the situation and the timing, the more I began to realize that it wasn't adding up. Beatrice was trying to help her family survive, so that meant that she was working long hours. She said that she was going home in the evening, and as a shapeshifter, she wasn't bound to a life in the shadows like most vampires were. It was likely that she worked in a factory or something.

"Did he attack you?"

Silence hit the table, and I grimaced because I didn't want everyone to focus on the conversation.

"No," Beatrice offered. "However, it was the same night I met Niko, and it was a close call. He saved me that night, and the would-be attacker took off. Neither of us saw who it was and we don't know if it was him. I worked in a factory that offered a morning and afternoon shift. The afternoon shift always meant that I was walking home in the evening, but it never truly worried me until that night. Fear was growing, and it wasn't an ideal place to be a vampire so we left."

"A lot of vampires left the area. Too much light shone on the streets, and what was once an easy hunting ground became a farce. But feel free to go there. As a bloodline Corbin, you are entitled to hunt throughout the entire suburb."

Well, if I were a vampire, it would be okay, but I'm not. I didn't even own a passport.

CHAPTER 28

We'd been talking about possible situations and what plans we could make when there were so many variables when Carsten paused. As he sat forward in the chair, his eyes lifted, and he frowned deeply.

"We're being summoned to the portal."

"I guess this means that they've decided."

My father gave me a grim smile.

"It's going to be okay. You are my only child, and I am the creation of two extremely powerful and well-connected Angels."

"Yeah, but that means nothing when it comes to my smart mouth."

Carsten chuckled before saying goodbye to everyone and fading out of the marquee. With an uneasy smile and wave, I entered the portal.

Benicio was waiting for us at the entrance to the portal. He gestured to enter as he turned. Anzide took my hand, and we walked into the portal, following Benicio.

Guiding us to a large room on the second floor, he held open the door.

"This is the meeting room. Please take a seat."

In the vast room, a long table was lined with many people, Mother being one of them. Benicio called this a meeting room, but it was more like an auditorium. The chairs surrounding us rose high, and all were full of people who had clearly come to see the spectacle that was me. I would have thought that this should be a private meeting, but I guess I was wrong.

My father was next to me, which I found strange.

"How come you're here?"

"Because I have offered to counsel you if necessary."

"Okay, but just be aware that I'm not changing my mind. If they won't let Anzide into the land of the Phoenix, then I'm not interested in the house."

"If you don't take the house, then you will be one of the outcasts."

"Then I can live with Anzide, right?"

Carsten looked at me and smiled.

"I suppose you would."

"None of this matters when I can't bring the rest of my family," I muttered.

"That is also a part of their discussion. You are one of only a few who have a connection to immortals, but they are beginning to realize that the more we grow as a species, the greater the chances of this happening again become. Yet again, you revolutionize the way that we think and do in this world."

"And that is not as ideal as you think, young one," Mother interjected.

I shrugged, giving her and the ones around a challenging look. It did not wither as I'd hoped.

"Good afternoon, and thank you for attending at such short notice. I am Delray, the portal master. We have convened to advise you regarding the outcome of our discussion and hand down the decision. You stated to Benicio that you are not prepared to reside in the land of the Phoenix if the outcast known as Anzide cannot reside with you. Is that statement still true, or do you wish to recant it?"

"No, it's still true."

Delray nodded, leaning forward on the table. His hands clasped, and a smile was offered. It was the kind of smile that was designed to make me feel small and insignificant.

"What makes you think that you, a mere half-caste, can dictate the rules to us?"

It felt like snakes hissed with rattlesnakes wildly flicking their tails in my mind as the anger burned. I stood, the chair scraped against the floor. In the seats behind, I could see Renuge. His eyes went wild as a huge grin crossed his face. Yep, he knew that this was going to get crazy.

"Don't you dare use that offensive term against me."

The smile on Delray's face lessened as he shifted back from the table. Mother had a subdued smile on her face as she rolled her eyes to the ceiling.

"And I don't recall ever dictating anything to Benicio. I stated the facts. I don't need to live in your precious land, nor do I need your dictatorial rules and segregation of those that you deem to be unworthy. What makes Anzide's value less than yours?"

Delray stared at me, mouth agape.

"He's being trained to teach others, so that means that he must hold some value to this place. So come on, tell me his value compared to yours."

When he didn't answer me, I leaned on the table and stared back at him.

"Let me make this perfectly clear to you. I will always stand against you if you don't change your ways. The Nephilim are not the monsters that you see them as and do not deserve the treatment they receive. The punishment forced upon the Nephilim is unjust, and the fact that no one in this place has said that is something that you and everyone else here should be ashamed of. I'd rather walk a barren wasteland for an eternity than return here if this is the company I'd keep. You can stick your precious land up your ass because we are done here."

Anzide and my father stood to follow. Mother remained silent, still smiling at me as if she knew that this little fireball would not sit quietly.

"We are most certainly not,"

Anger swelled inside of me, and I turned to Delray. His eyes widened, and in the darkened rows above him, gasps could be heard. Even those beside him at the table began to leave their seats.

"What are you doing?"

I struggled. Those spiders were back, and now, they had ants for company. They must have been racing through my veins because I could feel them wriggling throughout my body. By the time I'd fully faced Delray, the anger had surged and become something that could be dangerous.

Could I level the portal like I'd done with the house? Maybe I'd inflict some kind of damage on Delray. I couldn't hurt him, but I probably could knock him off his feet like I'd done with Renuge.

Delray was thrown back against the wall. The onlookers screamed and scrambled to get away.

Delray was pinned to the wall with a rainbow goo that dripped down his body and the wall like a thick slime. He was dressed as a clown with a colorful wig, bright red nose, and thick white face paint. Above his head was a neon sign that said *loser* with large arrows pointing to him. The word loser was repeatedly said, sounding as if it was a computer or maybe a robot.

I smiled, lifting my hand that was glowing with a rainbow flame. It had to be the prettiest thing I'd ever seen. Looking at Delray, I blew out the flames and turned to walk away.

It wasn't until we were at the gate that someone said something.

"So, educate me," Anzide said to my father. "Because I have no idea what that spell was."

"I have no idea either. Someone just learned how to create a spell."

Carsten turned to me, thoroughly amused.

"And what a spell it was. Harmless but effective. You made your point without resorting to violence. Passive,"

"But perhaps dangerous, hmm?" Mother interrupted.

Carsten and Anzide turned as she slowly ambled out of the portal and into the gate.

"It has been a long time since we've seen someone that can create spells. A creator has limitless power and could cast grand things but could also forge a darkness that no one could survive."

She kept hobbling towards me, keeping her gaze firmly pinned.

"Everyone fears a spell creator. Do you know why, Evelyn?"

"No,"

"It is because they think that if the creator is unhappy, they will cast a spell to change things to suit their desires. It could be something as simple as a kitten to play with, or it could be the destruction of a race that does not agree with them. They think they have to walk around on eggshells to stop the creator from becoming angry at them. Already, they've seen what mild anger does. A creator stood before them, unknown until she unleashed a spell that had never been seen before. Now, they fear you. Is that something that you truly wanted, Evelyn?"

"No. I just want equality for everyone."

"I know that you do. Unfortunately, you've dug a deeper hole, and now you are considered an outcast because no one feels safe around you."

"I do." Anzide interrupted.

"As do I," Carsten added. "Mother, you stand there without fear, and I think you agree with us."

"Of course I do. I know my own flesh and blood, but I am only one being in this place. Evelyn has stated that she does not wish to associate with anyone here because of how they treat the Nephilim. They're more than happy to accommodate that statement."

"Are you really just one being in this place, or is there more that would stand beside Evelyn because they are her family?"

"I cannot speak for others."

"Then perhaps you should ask them to speak for themselves. Let the beings who rule the portal see how foolish they are being. Evelyn might be a creator, but it is not as detrimental as what they make it seem. I've been in her company, and not once have I feared her reaction to my presence. Even during that first meeting, when she was hurt and upset because she thought I'd killed her mother, she still did not lash out at me. That rubbish in there, that was a setup. Evelyn was angry because of one foolish being who I am almost positive was trying to goad her into that exact situation. Tell me that wasn't a setup. Evelyn challenged the way that this place has operated and the way that we treat the Nephilim, and it wasn't taken well. They wanted to remove her and to do that without repercussions upon themselves, they had to make her bite back."

Mother sighed, leaning on her staff.

"As always, you make a valid point. We will see what happens from today. Be prepared for the worst. That way, you won't be disappointed."

She turned, shuffling back into the portal. It left me with a sinking dread that I'd made a big mistake.

Feeling morose, I looked at my father.

"What now?"

"Evelyn, I know that it seems bad, but being a creator is something that is incredibly rare. You're untrained, and that is why they are worried. If you'd been found earlier, we could have taught you how to control the power and turn it into skills that can be used in a real-world setting. Now, though, it's a little different. You'll still learn how to control everything. You'll still be around here. Until you've got that control though, people are going to be wary. You just have to accept that and not let it get to you. Fear creates monsters in all of us."

"How long will it take me to learn?"

Carsten shrugged.

"Basic control could be done within a day if you've got the right attitude. The problem that you will face is that they will want the highest level of control from you before they give any leniencies."

"That was a lot more controlled than when she flattened the house. She's still all over the place, but it was not dangerous, whereas previously, her spells have been."

Carsten hummed as his eyes narrowed.

"You are right in your thoughts, Anzide. There is an element of understanding within her. It's not enough to make the powers that watch over this place to be more lenient, but it's better than it could be. The largest of issues is that it is an undocumented spell, which meant that up until it was fully unleashed, they had no idea what would happen. They will argue that many lives were at risk because it could have turned deadly. It doesn't matter if it didn't. They're talking about the lead-up to the casting. At any rate, it's done and we cannot change what has happened. All we can do is wait and see what they say."

And that was as grim as it could get.

"For now, you've got bigger problems, so we will focus on them first. Ignore the likes of Delray. I have no doubt that he goaded you into that situation. He knew that you would bite back. Mother will stand in your corner. She may not appear to be a champion for you, but I know she will not let her kin fall."

CHAPTER 29

It was Saturday, and I was grateful for a day to do nothing. I'd woken late, feeling woozy and not interested in getting out of bed. Usually, Brad would say something, but I think he's decided to take a step back at the moment. Not only was I pregnant and could suffer morning sickness at any moment but I'd come out of the meeting at the portal with less than good news.

I could say that I only had myself to blame, which was the truth, but I knew that my father was right. They'd set me up to fall. It was rather pathetic, but I wasn't going to say anything more about it. I'd given up. The reality of it was that I had bigger issues to deal with. Drakkus was still walking around with his head attached to his neck, I had to get through school, I was about to have a baby, and it was almost Christmas.

I groaned, and Anzide turned to look at me.

"What's wrong?"

"I forgot to ask about Christmas."

He thought about it for a moment as he walked away

from the door to my side. Leaning on the edge of the bed, Anzide had an inquisitive smile.

"That's the religious holiday to celebrate the birth of Christ. I didn't think you were religious."

"How can I not be? I'm a biblical creature."

"Well, technically, you're classed as an eternal, not a biblical creature. That term is used when talking to immortals and the mortals who are aware of us. Would you celebrate it the way that someone in the portal might, or would you adhere to the traditions of this world? Because they are not the same."

"The portal and I are no longer friends. And not the same how?"

"Well, for one, the jolly man in the red suit. The milk and cookies are strange, but I get the carrot for the reindeer. Of course, one carrot for nine reindeer is a bit stingy. I guess it could be counteracted by stating that they would eventually get one, but then he'd have to remember which ones were waiting and I would have thought he'd have enough on his plate. The tale about Rudolph is curious. Has anyone else said that those bullies were gaslighting him?"

I gave a vague shrug, unable to answer.

"I wasn't aware that reindeer could fly."

"It's magic," I offered.

Anzide looked at me like I was the crazy one. As if.

"Sure it is. Then we could go onto how it's curious

that the gifts are given for someone else's birthday."

"Okay, captain bringdown, the party is dead, and it's time for you to leave."

"I'm only partway through my research on the subject."

"Of course you are. Please don't kill Easter. I like chocolate."

His eyebrows raised, and his eyes widened with the obvious wonder that was growing.

"That does sound interesting. I would like to know the connection between the resurrection and chocolate."

I huffed, rolling my eyes. At least I could still buy chocolate on an ordinary day.

"Can I ask you something?"

Warily, I sat up and slid down from the bunk bed. I didn't go far, the world began to sway, and I sat down out of fear that I'd fall over.

"That sounds ominous."

Anzide sat down beside me, offering a vague shrug.

"Say it's three thousand years into the future, and this world is not like it is today. Humanity has become extinct, and with that, the vampires go by the wayside as well."

"Dark thoughts for this hour of the morning. Carry on."

"What if it really is a barren wasteland like you said yesterday? Would you still want to be here?"

I shrugged, unsure of my answer. What kept me tied to this land was my family. If they were gone, then there wouldn't be much that would keep me here.

"Will they be gone in three thousand years?"

"I have no idea. We don't possess the ability to see the future. I was just curious about how stubborn you would be if things turned bad."

"Well, now that I'm considered an outcast, I guess I could live with you."

Anzide smiled, leaning his side against the cushion. His arm lay along the back of the lounge, curling a strand of my hair.

"You say that without seeing it."

"I'm sure it would be enough to make my blood boil."

"It would."

I sighed, moving into his arms. Anzide wrapped me into his embrace as I closed my eyes. It was nice to be in his arms. Maybe if the world ended and it was nothing but a wasteland that was void of human life, we might find somewhere to live.

"I don't know. I wouldn't want to return to their snide comments or mocking remarks that I couldn't even keep my word, but if this place is barren, then it would be rather hot and too sunny. We could walk the land and try to find a tree, but I'm sure they would be gone too."

"Evelyn, I'm going to tell you something that might just change everything."

I sat up, intrigued and wondering what it could be.

"There's a ruling that no eternal higher being, an angel, demon, phoenix, or Nephilim, can be refused entry or cast out of the portal. It is one of two rules that cannot be altered and will always be permanent. The other is that all eternal higher beings must be granted a place of residence within the land of the Eternals. That's the entire land, so don't be concocting a plan to catch them out on that one."

"So, they have to provide a house to me, and no matter what, they can't kick me out or refuse entry? Didn't they lock you out of the portal?"

"Yes, but that was because a hearing was pending. Once it was over, they opened it again. The Nephilim and the outcasts have been given a section of the portal that has been altered to be a part of the Eternals land but technically not."

I frowned, struggling to understand what Anzide meant.

"So, the place where your house is and where my house will be if nothing changes from what it is at the moment is the land of the outcasts, right?"

"Yes."

"And you're telling me that it's a part of the portal made to appear as if it's a part of the Eternals land, but really it's still the portal?"

Warily, he nodded. I guess Anzide wondered if he'd foolishly opened his mouth and started something that was going to cause problems. He was right.

"But the ruling says that all eternal higher beings must be granted a place of residence within the land of the Eternals."

I looked at the book that I'd been reading last night. A curious definition had remained in my mind, and I knew it could be helpful. Picking up the book, I decided that it would join me in the journey to the portal.

"It does."

I stood, and Anzide quickly rose to his feet.

"What are you doing?"

"Getting dressed. I'm in my pj's."

"Are you going to cause problems?"

"Don't I always?"

Anzide groaned his response as I walked into the bedroom. We used it as a dressing room rather than as a bed. There was enough space to accommodate everyone with the other beds, so it wasn't necessary in its original form.

"Is there a place where these rules are written?"

"I don't know if I want to answer that."

"If you don't, then I'll ask my father."

Anzide poked his head through the curtain, keeping it tight to his body for my privacy.

"Do you enjoy causing problems?"

"You know, I think that I do. Maybe it's more along the lines of ruffling the feathers. Standing up for those who don't or can't do it for themselves."

Pulling the shirt over my head, I wandered over to Anzide. Gripping the material, I kissed him softly.

"Why didn't you stand up for yourself when you realized the land is in the portal?"

"There has never been any point. No one ever listens."

"They will now."

Moving aside, Anzide smiled at me as I pushed the curtain across the rail. Wrapping his arms around me, Anzide grinned as he bit his bottom lip.

"You know, as much as I dread the trouble you cause, I think that I secretly like it."

"So, what you're saying is that you intentionally told me about the rules so that I would do something about it."

He nodded, still grinning.

"That makes you either crazy, lazy or a coward. Which one is it?"

"Crazy."

I chuckled as he pressed me against the wall.

"But to be fair, I haven't been around for long."

"Alright, I will grant you a minor leniency."

"Just minor?" he whispered against my lips.

I nodded, pulling him closer. The kiss was indulgent and far too scandalous for such a setting. I didn't care, too wrapped up in the playful dance of our lips. Anzide's hands slipped under the back of my shirt, sliding over the skin.

"I have a thought," he murmured against my lips.

His hands found my bra, teasing under the elastic.

"Is it a good one?"

He grinned, nodding as he kissed me again.

Hearing noises, Anzide stopped moving. In an instant, his hands were off my body, and there was a gap between us. I pouted at him, but all I got was a shrug.

Brad walked up the steps and looked at me curiously.

"You look like you've got something on your mind. What's going on?"

You interrupting our moment. That's what's going on. Or not going on, apparently.

"Not much. Just going to cause chaos in the portal again. We need to discuss Christmas."

"What about it?"

I shrugged, pulling on my sneakers.

"Are we buying presents? Where's the tree and the decorations? Are you going to buy a bigger one now that we've settled?"

"I have no idea."

"Well, can you check with Niko and Beatrice while I dismantle the government?"

"We've got plenty of time, but sure, I guess I can."

"You're a legend, Bradley. Bye."

Brad smiled as he shook his head. I wandered down the steps and waved to Niko and Beatrice, who were sitting on the lounge with swatches around them.

Entering our little portal room, I sat on the mat and waited for Anzide to close the curtain.

"Are you really doing this?"

"I'm here, aren't I?"

Anzide said nothing as he joined me on the floor.

As I focused on the portal, I found my entrance to be fast and precise. I was standing at the entrance to the portal. No boat, no fog. Just a doorway waiting to open for me.

When Anzide appeared at my side, I smiled.

"It's going to be okay."

"I know."

I stepped to walk through the doors, but Anzide held me back. Before I could say anything, he held up his hand, and a light began to glow around the darkened area. Above the doors in front of us and the windows that showed the lands of the Eternals was an inscription carved in stone. It was the rulings, the two statements that said that supposedly could not be altered. But they were. We were proof of that.

The doors opened, and Mother appeared.

"She returns so soon."

The light from Anzide's hand faded, and Mother raised an eyebrow.

"I know what is on your mind, Evelyn. What you believe is not entirely the truth, but you're not wrong either. It has weighed heavily upon mine for longer than I care to admit. For too long, it has been acceptable to say nothing and maintain the course. Then, a rebellious firebrand walks through these doors, and her words create waves in the once-calm sea. She is so loud that it has reached the top, and now the waves are no longer a ripple. The tsunami is coming for us, Evelyn."

She smiled, one that looked like she was full of pride.

"I hope that you are ready for it."

CHAPTER 30

Like they knew what was coming for them, the occupants of the portal were already assembled in the meeting room. Mother slowly ambled to her seat, glancing at the door as it opened again. My father looked around, and after closing the door, he moved quickly to us.

"Is this the hill you wish to die on, Evelyn?"

"I'm pretty sure you know the answer to that. The rules are clear, yet the beings that run this place have been disobeying them."

Carsten nodded with a heavy sigh. He moved to his seat, still beside me as my support and counsel if needed.

"We haven't decided your fate." Delray offered.

"I'm not here for that. Can you tell me what the rulings are?"

He glanced at the other beings at the table. The one next to Delray offered a shrug. With a heavy sigh, Delray turned back to me.

"The rules of the portal and higher beings?"

"The ones that are inscribed in stone around the gate. Please tell everyone listening what they say."

"Uh, no eternal higher being can be refused entry or cast out of the portal."

"And the other one?"

"All eternal higher beings must be granted a place of residence within the land of the Eternals. I really don't see,"

"What is defined as a higher being?" I interrupted.

Delray huffed, frowning heavily at me.

"Angel, demon, phoenix, and Nephilim. Outcasts do not count."

Holding up the book, Delray's eyes widened a fraction. Clearly, he knew what I was about to say. It was sad, really. I would have thought that this place was about unity.

"By definition, this book about the Eternals states that an outcast is a term that refers to one of four Eternal beings that have been punished. It goes on to say that it is not to be considered a new species because the term will not be permanent. Your statement is incorrect. Tell me, where do the Nephilim reside?"

"In the land of the outcasts."

"Is that within the land of the Eternals?"

He was still staring at me. The beauty of this was that

he could not lie.

"Technically, only a portion of it is."

"But the majority?"

Delray gave a vague shrug.

"So, you're breaking the rules of the portal, is that correct?"

"It appears that you're correct."

"It appears? Yes or no answer, please."

"Yes. Is there a point to this?"

"Of course there is. You're going to change things now that someone has finally stood up and said this is unacceptable. The Nephilim must reside in the land of the Eternals. I expect that when you finally decide my fate as an outcast, you will tell me that Anzide and I will be given a home in the land of the Eternals and be free to travel to any land because no eternal higher being can be refused entry."

"You have no authority in this place, nor can you hold us to ransom with your spells or threats."

"I'm not holding you ransom, and I've never claimed to have any authority. I'm here to remind you and everyone else in this place that your segregation is illegal. If you ignore me, then I will only get louder. *That* was a threat if you were wondering."

Walking out of the meeting room, I took a deep breath and calmed down. I could feel the anger growing, and if there was any chance of persuading these people to do the right thing, it would be done without a show. Anzide was next to me when I turned to the sound of my father. He wasn't alone. A lot of beings were moving out of the doors.

"I shall remain here while they discuss it. They are holding a meeting about it, which many are not eligible to be a part of. I am so I will be here to remind them of what is right and to be your voice when you cannot be here."

"Thanks."

"It is not a problem. Why don't you two go for a walk around the place? Perhaps you could go to the gate and look at the land of the outcasts before they alter it."

"Uh, sure."

Carsten closed the door, leaving me a little bewildered.

"They'll alter it? I only want them to move it into the land of the Eternals."

Anzide shrugged as he took my hand.

"Maybe you need to think like your father. He probably believes that no matter how much he argues and fights for your cause, you will end up in the land of the outcasts because of me. After all, you made it clear that you were not interested in the Phoenix land if I couldn't be there, and he's old enough to know that those bureaucrats are stubborn."

We began to walk down the stairs now that most of the other beings had left. Some were mingling in the courtyard, but the rest were queuing for the train. Those who were still in the courtyard turned to look at me. I could see the whispers and the secretive smiles.

"I can't say as I enjoy the audience."

"Some are calling it a fan club. There are a few who are not impressed by the name or the fact that it is true. You actually have a fan club. Crazy, right?"

"That I'm so awesome to have one? I thought you loved me."

Anzide narrowed his gaze, pressing his lips tight. His feigned mood didn't last, and soon, the smirk took control.

"You know it."

"Good save."

He laughed, pulling me into his arms. Our walk towards the gate was slow and a little awkward because I wrapped my arms around his waist.

The path to the entrance of the land of the outcasts was a small corridor between the portal and the mail-room. It was tucked away, almost hidden from sight. In fact, I'd never noticed it until now. When I saw the small sign that said *outcasts*, I understood why. They were being hidden, sent through a door before they got too far into the portal.

"This is so wrong."

"And now you understand why your father is becoming so vocal about it. He thinks that nothing will change their minds, which means that this will be your home. No one wants that for their child or their grandchild. He might not think that there's a future with you because of the past, but that doesn't mean he won't try to help you reach a better path in this life. Now, I know your father said to look at it from the gate, but would you like to see it for real?"

"Sure."

The smoky black glass slid open, and a wave of hot air hit me.

"This is hell, isn't it?"

Because it certainly looked like it. Well, a broken metropolis bathed in red. I couldn't believe that anyone thought that this was acceptable. Compared to the lush green valleys of the land reserved for the phoenix, this was appalling. I understood that this was supposed to be punishment, but why did it have to be this extreme?

"It's not what humans have depicted as their hell, and no one in this place considers any part of the portal to be hell."

"But if there were one, this would be it."

"Yeah," Anzide said with a sigh. "But at least we can come and go as we please. Come on, let's go to our place."

There were no verdant green valleys with picturesque English-styled cottages. No bright and beautiful land with wildflowers or lush trees. It was like a small town with a few tall buildings surrounded by a large ring of houses.

"So, where exactly is that? Is it over there in Dead Tree Valley or down there in Rats Nest Hollow?"

Anzide chuckled.

"Your names are interesting. Should we put them forward as permanent?"

"Sure."

"Why does it look like the buildings are about to fall down? Why are there dead plants everywhere?"

I stopped and frowned.

"Is that a rat?"

"There are no vermin here. It was probably just a demon."

"Still, I can see that this place needs a lot of the ol' Evie touch."

Anzide grinned as he looked at me.

"Crusader for rights?"

"Darn tootin' I am. This needs to be exactly like all the other areas."

"It's supposed to be a punishment, you know."

I rolled my eyes. Anzide accepted it because he believed there was no other choice. He was subdued and forced into a controlled environment that ensured he would remain downtrodden for his entire existence. It was not acceptable, not for Anzide, not for anyone.

"Most of the houses are empty. They're used when two of the outcasts get together and do the one thing they're not supposed to and create life."

"You're kidding, right? They set up houses even though they said don't have sex with each other. Makes perfect sense."

"They know it cannot be stopped, no matter what they say. Those who dwell in this land are already being punished, and there's nowhere else to go. What are they going to do to us?"

"Fair enough."

Anzide pointed to a little house in the distance. It was cute but small.

"That's where I grew up. When my parents made their deal, I was given an apartment."

"It's not a big place."

"Yeah, I suppose I should have seen the writing on the wall. They had no intention of staying, so they picked a place that was enough to raise me until I was old enough to be given my own home."

We began walking along the street, moving toward what I thought was a bus stop. When Anzide sat behind the wheel of a golf cart, I was rather amused.

"Seriously?"

"Oh, absolutely. We're not entitled to a proper transportation system."

"Sounds like another battle for Evie to wage," I muttered as I sat down.

"I wouldn't worry too much about it. Most either like it or don't care. Personally, I like it because I think they're kind of cool."

"Okay, so I guess no battle then. Do they just get left around like that?"

"Yep. We're supposed to take them to one of the transport stops, but sometimes, there will be a few left in odd places."

The closer we got to the central point of the ring, the more I began to realize how similar this place was to Hades. There were lots of buildings that varied in height, but nothing went over three levels. They looked old and in dire need of a little care.

"Do we need to discuss the maintenance?"

"Not at the moment."

Anzide pulled into a side street and parked the golf cart next to a long row of other carts.

"Almost home."

We began the short journey back to the main street. I looked around at the empty streets that were void of life.

"Where is everyone?"

"Well, they were at the meeting."

"They assembled pretty fast."

Anzide looked at me with uneasiness.

"You're kind of in this limbo area where those who are the caretakers of the portal have marked you as unruly, which means that when you reach the gate, an alert goes out. In your case, it's like a beacon for everyone who wants to see what kind of craziness you bring."

"Were your parents there?"

"I wasn't looking, but it is likely."

Gesturing to a green iron gate, Anzide smiled.

"This is us. Green gate on Fourth Street."

"No numbers?"

"Yeah, I think it's something like forty. Mail doesn't come here. We don't get deliveries."

"But if there was another green gate?"

Anzide looked at me as if he'd never thought like that.

"All I know is that this gate is the access point to my place."

I smiled, saying nothing more about it. Anzide pushed open the gate and stepped aside.

"Welcome home."

CHAPTER 31

Anzide's apartment was small. As much as I'd like to say that he picked it because it was this way, I knew that I couldn't. He didn't want to live in a small place, and I knew that because he had made a few comments about the cramped conditions of the caravan. The progression of our relationship had become stagnant, and I think Anzide blamed it on where we lived. At the moment, he had to accept it like everyone else, but I think that if he had the choice, this place would be a lot bigger.

When he spoke of this place, Anzide said that he was told that he was being given a studio apartment. This was his home, and that's all that was on offer. As a Nephilim, he was told he was the lowest of the low, and to be given something was in itself remarkable. It just made my blood boil with anger.

Anzide wasn't the only one in this situation. When I looked across the road to the other apartments, I could see what appeared to be an almost mirror image of this place. A small studio apartment that, while functional, was not enough. It was also one of many buildings that were nothing but a repetitive view. Bland, boring, demoralizing. I could see through the facade of this place. It was vile, and it was going to change.

They made it seem as if it was too much to create a larger space. Like they didn't have the land for it. In the distance, I could see a lot of vacant land. There was no reason for a small apartment. It was nothing but an excuse for appalling behavior.

Mindful of his mood, I kept a smile on my face as I glanced around the areas I could see. To my right was a galley kitchen, and to my left was the door to the bathroom. Opposite the kitchen was the living room, and the only thing separating it from the bedroom was a thin screen.

Walking to the far side of the room, I looked out the window at the buildings that were on the verge of crumbling. This was going to change. There was no way that I was going to let this continue to be what they lived in. This was a disgrace, and every single eternal being in the portal was to blame. And yes, I included my father and Mother in this. They did nothing. Everyone would know what this place was like, and they ignored it. They don't care, and it was a crying shame.

I could be positive easily. The place was clean, it looked sturdy, and it wasn't cluttered. I wasn't overwhelmed, even if I was annoyed. No, I wasn't annoyed. I was angry. Hiding it was the only option at the moment.

I turned, only to find Anzide watching me with a huge grin.

"Go on, say it."

"Say what?"

"That it's tiny, or it's terrible that I was made to live here."

"Well, it is terrible that they forced you to live in a place rather than letting you pick."

"I was given a choice of locations."

Turning me back to the window, Anzide pointed to the view beyond the buildings opposite. There was a mountain that, while it looked dark and ominous, was rather pretty against the ghoulish red.

"I picked this place because of that view. As a single man, I had to go into a studio apartment. I know it's not big, and if we're made to stay in this land, then we will end up in one of the houses, so it won't always be so cramped."

I shrugged with mild indifference. There was no choice in the decision, even if Anzide tried to sugarcoat it.

"I've lived in worse. At least you don't have cock-roaches to keep you company at night."

"True. Now, are we talking about ridiculously small apartments and pet cockroaches, or are we utilizing our time alone wisely?"

I hummed a soft chuckle as I dragged Anzide closer. He complied, pushing me against the wall. My moan was muffled by the intense kiss. Removing clothes from each other as we did the awkward walk to the bed created a trail from the window to the bed.

Sliding my hands over the firm chest, I continued a languid path over the abdomen. Sliding the hair off my shoulder, Anzide kissed his way over my jaw and neck as my hands kept going. He groaned, and I could feel the smile against my skin.

Anzide lifted my hands to his shoulder, then raised my legs to wrap them around his waist. Then he pressed himself against me. I groaned at the pressure from the delectable sensations of our bodies. A teasing and playful dance had begun not just between our bodies but in our kisses. The intense embrace endured, and with every movement he made, sparks began firing deep inside of me.

Lifting me from the wall, Anzide turned to the bed. With a flick of his hand, the duvet was pulled back. The scent of fresh linen hit me as Anzide lowered me against the sheets. I didn't feel a thing, too preoccupied with other sensations, but Anzide had unhooked my bra. I gasped when he reached the base of my neck, the fingers traced over the hardened skin as he pulled the bra away. It was flicked over his shoulder with reckless abandon, and when I lifted my head from the mattress, I saw the sinful smirk as he licked the skin.

Anzide knelt between my legs, lifting them to his chest. It glistened from the heat that was growing in the room.

"Open a window. It's hot."

"Won't make much of a difference. It's always hot here."

Dragging my panties over my legs, Anzide cast them away and then stood from the bed. He pulled a remote from the wall and cranked up the air conditioning. It was an outdated window rattler, but it was better than nothing. At least there was airflow now.

Returning to his position between my legs, Anzide lowered and kissed my stomach. He didn't say anything about the baby, which I thought he might have.

My body bucked from the first touch, already anticipating an incredible orgasm. We might be new at this, but it was always amazing. It gave me hope that as the days and months became years, we would nurture our love and find all forms of happiness in our times together.

He taunted with a delicate touch before slowly delving deeper. With a devious grin plastered on his face, Anzide began what I'd come to describe as divine torture. He took his time, extracting as much ecstasy as he could manage.

My breathing was rough as the blood pulsed through my veins, and my heart raced. A meek moan escaped when I looked up and saw the smirk on his wicked lips. He was making a meal out of me and enjoying every single moment. My brows knitted tight as pleasure sparked. Watching Anzide was always a dangerous thing to do.

The amusement in his eyes told me he was enjoying every second and that he welcomed making me a quivering mess.

In the sultry heat of the room, I gripped the linen as the pleasure grew. My body writhed with every movement of his lips and tongue. The bed was a mess, balled up white linen in my tight grip as the ecstasy finally broke. My body arched off the bed, and I groaned loudly, something that I found to be incredibly cathartic.

As Anzide kissed his way over my body, I shivered. The tender touch, coupled with the close proximity of his body, created an intense sensation that jolted throughout me.

Gripping me under my ear, Anzide lifted me a fraction for a kiss that could only be described as potent. He was intoxicating, and I craved more of him. The demanding embrace was like nothing we'd shared before.

It made me realize that our life in the caravan was crushing us as a couple. We had to get out of the place before it caused lasting damage. It was clear that returning to this place was necessary, even if it was just for a moment alone.

I didn't want to be obsessed or dismissive of the time I spent with my family, but if this relationship was going to last, it had to be strong in every single aspect. The other side of this coin was that we weren't the only ones that needed time alone. It had been over sixty years since Beatrice saw Niko, and as much as they had time alone together, I knew that there was a difference between being the only ones in the lounge area and being completely alone.

Then there was Brad. He was forging a new relationship with Nora. It was a time when they would be trying to figure things out, getting to know each other, and ensuring that the dynamic grew to something that would sustain an eternity.

So yes, coming here might have its advantages.

Anzide shifted onto his side next to me. I rolled onto my side, smoothing my hands over his ribs and onto his back. The warmth of the room was creating far too much heat, and the air conditioning unit was useless.

As we returned to the ardent embrace, I thought about the looming winter in Hades. I couldn't wait for it to snow.

Anzide hissed, moving away from me with a mighty frown.

"Your hands are like ice. What's going on?"

He turned to the window, the frown deepening. Getting up from the bed, Anzide pulled his pants on and moved to the window. Carefully, he pulled the material aside to ensure that no one saw the naked woman on the bed.

The frown fell away, replaced with shock, as he turned to look at me.

"Uh, it's snowing out there."

My lips pressed tight as I smiled.

"And your hands are like ice. Did you do something?"

"Oops."

Anzide chuckled.

"Oops is right. It never snows in the land of the outcasts."

"Well, it was too hot. I can't enjoy our time alone if I'm too busy thinking about dehydration from sweating too much."

"Okay, frosty. You need to warm your hands up, or you are getting a pair of gloves to wear."

Picking up the remote, I turned off the window rattler.

"Open a window and get under the blanket with me. We can snuggle in a different kind of warmth."

With an intrigued hum, Anzide obliged my request. A soft breeze floated through the window, bringing in snow and leaves. Pulling the duvet over the bed, I held it up with a growing need to continue what we started.

Anzide took my hand, feeling the warmth return to my fingers.

"I am in awe of you," he whispered. "You just randomly thought it was too hot, and now it's snowing outside?"

I shrugged. Anzide smirked as he kissed the fingers.

"You'll have them wetting their pants in fear."

"Good. You might think it's okay to live in a rundown city, but I don't."

He chuckled as he moved closer to me. Frowning, Anzide looked down.

“Well, this has never been a problem before. Will it be uncomfortable if we continue in this position?”

“Probably.”

Anzide grinned, biting his bottom lip. Shifting, he laid on his back and waited. The devious grin grew as he helped me sit up.

“Okay, now I’m too cold.”

Getting up, I closed the window. Anzide leaned on his elbows, watching me with amusement. As I climbed under the duvet, Anzide and I looked at each other and giggled. Our time alone was not meant to be this unsettled and such a mood killer, but it was fine. We had a long life together, and it was only going to get better as the years passed by.

CHAPTER 32

I sat up in bed with a strange feeling. Jostling Anzide, I waited until he rolled over and looked at me.

"I have this strong feeling that I have to go somewhere, but I don't know where. It's hounding my mind, politely demanding that I get dressed and,"

I frowned, shifting on the bed.

"Is there a place called the vestibule?"

"There is. I can't take you there. Your father might be able to, but if you're feeling a call, then you need to follow it now rather than delaying it by searching for him."

"What is this place?" I asked as I stood to dress.

"It's a meeting place."

My eyes narrowed at Anzide.

"You're being rather vague. How about you educate me so that I know what I'm going into?"

He sighed, getting out of bed. His pants were on, and

Anzide moved to my side, sitting on the mattress in front of me.

"It's higher up but probably only next level higher. If you're being summoned, then it would be a representative that you will be speaking with."

"What do you think it's about?"

"Could be any of the subjects, but I don't know why they'd get involved. Anyone that walks those corridors usually doesn't care what goes on in the portal."

"So long as there's harmony, right?"

Anzide shrugged, pulling me closer. I leaned down and kissed him.

"How do I get there?"

"Fade and let the feeling guide you. There's no path that you can walk. When you're requested to join them, they provide the link to access the area."

"And you can't come with me?"

"I'd only be sent away with a harsh reprimanding. Your naivety will mean nothing to them. They will say I should have told you how and left you to it. I've done that and in their eyes, there is nothing more than I can or should do to help you. Just fade like you always do to get to the portal. Let the feelings dictate where you move to. Think positively, and you will get there."

I nodded as I sat down to pull my shoes on.

"Will you be here?"

"I think you might find it easier to return to the portal. Besides, your father will probably be waiting for us to return."

"He's going to be upset that he couldn't be with me, isn't he?"

"Absolutely."

Anzide leaned closer, kissing me softly.

"Good luck."

"Thanks."

I faded out of the room and let the sensations guide me. A cool wind floated around me, gently guiding me along a path that I could not see. Everything was white, not overly blinding, but difficult to look at. It was almost as bad as being in pure darkness. The view was endless and offered nothing but the possibility of pure madness if I stayed here too long.

Something appeared on the horizon, small at first but quickly growing in size. It didn't take long for me to realize that it was a being. The figure was tall. I wasn't good at measurements, but he was inhumanly tall. The lean figure was dressed in a dark blue fitted jacket that reached mid-thigh and was decorated with gold embellishments. The swirls and curves appeared metal but flexible enough to move like material. Beneath the jacket were pants that matched the blue material but had no embellishments.

I began to slow as I got closer to the figure. Now, I could see that the impossibly tall figure was extremely gorgeous. The kind of masculine beauty that would have the angels singing in cliche harmony when he appeared. Strong cheekbones and jawline, perfect pout with flawless skin. Dark wavy hair with blisteringly bright blue eyes.

And if the fancy clothes and jaw-dropping beauty weren't enough, then the crazy nonsense on his head might be. It was like a crown, but parts of it sat on his head without connection to the other pieces.

When I stopped, I narrowed my eyes and moved around him, looking at the peculiar headdress. The figure turned to watch me, raising an eyebrow. Reaching the other side, the figure turned to continue watching me. His head tilted, still offering a heightened brow.

"Are they horns?"

His lips twitched, restraining the smile.

"No, it is a crown."

"Are you God?"

"No, I am Belial."

"Why do you wear a crown?"

"It is a sign of status. Don't you fear me, Evelyn?"

My eyes rolled to the nonexistent ceiling as I sighed.

"Look, man, I've gone against Nephilim who wanted to punish me, a demon that was casting spells over my uncle to try and kill me, a psycho vampire who still wants me dead, his loser helper that tried to kill me but failed miserably, more helpers that were planning to abduct me and probably a whole lot more that I don't know about. You need to join the queue if you're going to dole out punishment for something I've done."

Rolling on my feet, I looked around the relentless white void as my hands went into my pockets.

"This your place? I like what you've done with it. You must be big on minimalism."

"Do you always make jokes to deflect your fear?"

"Do you always waste people's time by dragging them into the unknown for a conversation about nothing?"

"You lack manners. Clearly, your parents are to blame."

"Is that some kind of sick joke?"

Belial looked at me. His brows began to press together as he stepped forward.

"I might lack manners, but you clearly haven't done your homework. Call me when you're actually aware of the person you face."

I smiled as I began to fade away, giving him a mocking wave. Belial didn't react like I thought he would. A hand reached out. As it clenched, I stopped fading. It was then that he smiled at me. Belial turned, holding his clenched hand at his side, dragging me behind him with his nonexistent rope.

I scoffed, rolling my eyes.

"Lame."

"Mind your tongue, child."

"Uh, not a child. I'm eighteen."

"And to me, you are a child."

"How old are you?"

"I don't know. I was here at the beginning, and I shall be here at the end. Will you be here, Evelyn?"

"Phoenix are eternal."

"Only in the lands of the mortals and the immortals. Those who dwell in these lands can easily remove you if that is what pleases them."

Well, that certainly changed a few things.

Belial chuckled.

"And now we hear silence. How interesting."

"Why am I here?"

"For a conversation."

Dark walls surrounded us. As the white faded, warm lights from globes lit up the area. The dark walls were a rich and deep green. Plush black lounges lined a wall, and little tables were placed along the row with single-seat chairs in front of them.

"Please, take a seat."

When Belial said that, I felt a tightness loosen around my waist. I was free to move, but I knew that I couldn't fade out of this place. I was here until Belial was done with me.

I sat on the long bench seat with one of the tables in front of me. Belial sat on one of the chairs, crossing one leg over the other as he reclined. On his face was a smile of pure arrogance.

"Why are you trying to take my outcasts from me, Evelyn?"

All I could do was stare in disbelief, struggling to figure out if I'd heard him correctly.

Belial raised his eyebrows, watching me with a haunting smile that mocked me but somehow managed to keep me enthralled.

"Have you gone deaf during the previous minute?"

"No," I murmured. "I was just confused because it sounded as if you think that you own the outcasts."

"That's because I do."

A woman approached with a gold platter. On it were two tall glasses that rattled due to her shaky hands. Carefully, she placed it on the table and set the drinks on the table. Stepping back, she waited with fear in her eyes as she looked at me. There was something so familiar about her. Something that I just couldn't figure out.

Belial smiled. His hand lifted, gesturing to the woman.

"Forgive Sharma, she's new to my world. She's still figuring out how to be a servant, but she's learning quite well."

I nodded quietly, picking up the glass. The liquid was black, fizzing like soda would. I was curious but not overly interested in drinking it. As I lifted the glass from the table, a folded piece of paper fell onto my lap. Belial was distracted by dismissing the woman, so I quickly scooped it up and kept it hidden.

Sniffing the drink, I detected cola. Returning it to the table was met with intrigue, and Belial tilted his head.

"Is it not to your liking, Evelyn?"

"I'm not consuming caffeine at the moment."

"Oh, that's right. Your little bundle of joy. Perhaps water would be a wiser choice?"

With a wave of his hand, the liquid changed. It was clear, and I was grateful that I'd lifted the glass and found the note because if I hadn't, it would now be visible. As for the contents, it would remain in the glass because I was not going to drink it.

"So, this ownership you think you have?"

"I don't think,"

"You know," I interrupted. "I was only curious about why the Nephilim aren't in the land of the eternals because the rules inscribed on the wall of the gate say that they should be."

"I could change that."

"No, you can't. They are the rules that can never be changed. Why did you really drag me here?"

Belial paused, his lips parted as the smile slowly formed.

"You need to end your campaign regarding the land of the outcasts because it should remain in the portal."

"The outcasts are classed as Eternals and should reside in their land. You clearly have an ulterior motive, and given how easily angered Delray was, I'd say that the two of you have formed some kind of agreement that might be illegal."

That made his smile die. Sensing that I really needed to read the note, I shifted my legs and knocked the table. The glasses toppled, and I gasped, pretending it was an accident. Water spilled as the glasses smashed on the floor.

"Oh no," I said, moving away from the liquid and broken glass. "I am so sorry."

"It's alright, Evelyn."

Belial stood, flicking his hand over the water that had soaked his jacket and pants. Now that I was further along the seat and away from the mess, I waited. Belial was distracted by waving his hands over the mess, cleaning everything up. I opened the note and frowned.

Do not agree to anything.

Tucking it into my pocket, I gritted a smile when Belial looked at me.

"You know, I think that we've gotten off on the wrong foot. We should start again. I am Belial, and I have requested that you join me here to discuss the land of the outcasts. I would find it extremely pleasing if you agreed to stop your campaign regarding the location of the land. What do you say, Evelyn?"

His hand stretched out, and Belial shot me a charming smile. It was the most perfect thing I'd ever seen.

"Will you agree to let it go?"

I looked at the offered hand. The nails were trimmed, and the palm looked soft and inviting. Beyond the hand, I could see the veins as they stretched through his wrist. The pulsed close to the surface, a bright red that stood out.

Lifting my gaze, I looked at Belial. The red veins began to show at the collar of his jacket as they slowly crept higher.

Dread began to fill me. Even without the warning, I would have sensed that something was wrong here. The alarms in my head were sounding so loudly that it was deafening. I had to get away from him, but I knew that it was impossible.

CHAPTER 33

I stepped back, shaking my head.

"No."

Belial's lips pressed tight with a forced smile. He took a step forward, moving closer to me.

"I had a lot of hope that you would agree, Evelyn. Are you sure that you won't change your mind? Maybe there's something that I could give you in exchange."

At best, he was a demon. I didn't dare consider the worst of the possibilities. Belial was determined to get me to agree to this, which left only a few candidates. Or one.

"There is nothing that you can offer me."

"Oh, I wouldn't be so sure about that. If that is what you truly think, then perhaps we should flip it. What can I take from you?"

Belial took a step forward when I moved back. The door to the endless white was behind me. I could escape through it, but what then?

"The family you're creating on Earth, maybe the lover in your bed or perhaps what is growing in your womb."

"You cannot take from me."

Belial laughed. As he threw his head back with the taunt, I used his distraction to my advantage. Turning, I raced to the door. My hand pressed against it, pushing the wood. I could feel Belial dragging me back. The laughter had stopped, replaced with a growl of anger.

Facing Belial, my eyes widened at the sight. The veins had reached his jawline. He was still the epitome of male beauty, but the veins were freaky. My back hit the wall, and I gasped. Fear hit an all-time high, and as my hands raised to the advancing monster, I unleashed a spell.

Red flames barrelled towards Belial, engulfing him. Pushing through the door, I ran out into the white. Hearing my name whispered, I turned around to see Sharma near the door frame on the outside of it. She urged me over, still with fear in her eyes.

"Hurry now,"

We were behind the door but not in the building. It seemed incomprehensible.

"Why did you risk the note?"

"Because you are so young and innocent."

She took my hand, putting a locket into it. With a pained smile, she looked up at me with tears in her eyes.

"There is no escape once you agree. Run while you can. Stay out of the land of the outcasts and fight to gain land with the Eternals. Keep Anzide by your side forever."

"Who are you?"

"Just someone who understands that love has no boundaries."

Her hand reached out, brushing my hair out of my eyes.

"I'm so glad he found you."

I was about to question why she wanted Belial to find me and why it made her happy, but then it hit me like a wrecking ball.

"Oh my god. You're Anzide's mother."

Everything began to shake as an angry roar echoed. The white land started to crack. Sharma's eyes widened. Large gray wings emerged as she grabbed hold of me. The door was swatted away, and Belial, who was now twice the size he was previously, turned and saw us.

His hands parted, forcing Sharma to let go of me. She was thrown into the distance, and I began to fall. I screamed as I plunged into the darkness, only to drop onto something bouncy. The inky black snapped away, and I saw the bland tiles of the portal.

As I was lowered to the floor, I saw the ceiling of the portal was still broken apart. Scrambling back, I realized I was not alone. Mother stepped out, her hands raised above her lowered head. Others joined her to keep Belial from entering the portal.

Something touched my shoulder. I yelped and saw Anzide. There was so much fear on his face.

"I'm sorry, I didn't know," he whispered as he hugged me.

Behind him, pacing the floor, was my father. He looked just as frantic.

"Where was I?"

"Not the Vestibule." Carsten offered.

He helped me off the floor, but as soon as I stood, I felt pain in my stomach. I winced, doubling over.

"The trauma might have brought on labor," Carsten murmured to Anzide.

I looked up at the ceiling that was almost repaired.

"Your mother was there. She helped me escape."

"It wouldn't have been my mother. She's living a great life serving,"

"Sharma," I whispered, putting the locket in his hand.

The crack was still open, and the pitiless black called me, demanding that I stand up and fight the battle that I'd begun. Carsten stepped in front of me, blocking the view.

"Evelyn, listen to me, not anything else. Focus on me and my words. Ignore everything else, and if you feel a connection, sever it now."

"He wants the land of the outcasts to stay in the portal."

I could feel my legs giving out from underneath me. Anzide held me up as the tears from the pain rolled down my cheeks.

"Why is it so important to him?"

"We will find out, Evelyn. Ignore what is going on and tell me about your friend Karina."

"She's so sweet. A bundle of energy that finds something positive despite everything that has happened."

"And what about the new guy, Cooper?"

"Fiercely protective of me,"

Mother appeared, looking frantic as she stared at me. Her eyes turned to Carsten, and pushed him aside.

"Where is it?"

"Where is what? I don't understand."

"Were you given anything?"

I nodded, pulling out the note. Mother took it, and I looked at Anzide, gesturing to the locket.

"Drop it before it consumes you."

Anzide dropped the locket onto the floor. Mother placed the note at the top of her staff and then used the tip of the wood to lift the chain. She returned to the group of beings who were struggling to close the crack. Standing below the crack, Mother turned, and with a flick of the staff, the objects were sent flying.

I couldn't see them, but the crack was soon repaired.

The pain subsided, but it wasn't over. Delray appeared, looking like he'd spent too many hours sunbaking under a blisteringly hot sun. He was angry at me but stopped when I gripped my father's jacket, dragging him closer to me.

"I cast a spell at Belial. It was red." I whispered.

Carsten turned to look at Mother, who had returned to his side. With a flick of her staff, Delray was cuffed in glowing bonds.

"An investigation will begin immediately," Mother announced loudly. "Take Evelyn to the infirmary to ensure she is alright. Benicio will collect your statement, and Carsten will remain as your counsel to ensure that your rights are adhered to. The portal will remain locked until this matter is settled."

Anzide lifted me into his arms. I wrapped my arms around his neck, holding on as tightly as I could manage. There was no time to think, but I could have lost this. Just a moment in his embrace.

"Where was I?"

"It's a place called the void. There are only a few who can access it. Belial is one of them. Most don't bother with the area because creating rooms is a strain and takes a lot of concentration."

Anzide walked through the door to the infirmary when Carsten held it open for him. Staff bustled around in preparation for what I assumed was going to be a lot of tests. When he passed by a desk, Anzide stopped.

"Can I have a notepad and pen, please?"

The woman held out the objects that I took. Anzide continued down the corridor after Benicio and Carsten.

"It's easier to explain with a diagram."

Entering a room, Anzide put me on the bed and sat on the mattress facing me. With the notepad and pen, he drew a sphere with a crescent around it.

"This is not to scale or accurate, but hopefully, it will help. The sphere is the portal, and the crescent is the land of the Eternals as a whole. From the sphere, we've got a little gate here and then another small passage directly opposite that leads to the train line. The line runs between the sphere and the crescent. At the tips of the crescent, there are two areas that connect and lock the sphere and crescent together. They're generally referred to as the pins. The land of the outcasts is one of those pins, and the other is the Hallowed Halls. It's where the hierarchy lives. As you know, we use a door to access the land of the outcasts and some say there is a door to the Hallowed Halls in a similar location on the other side, but no one has ever found it."

Anzide stopped scribbling on the notepad and looked at me with an uneasy smile.

"So, I have since learned a little more about the past

and how things happened. The pins were always meant to be for the hierarchy, and the eternals were supposed to reside in the crescent. Then, some naughty beings created life which was against the rules, so it was ordered that they were punished. It was not going to be a permanent punishment, something closer to a sentence that had to be served and once it was done, they could return to normal life. They agreed to set up the unused pin as a jail that had open doors and nice houses. It apparently still fitted into the inscription because, as you can see, the pins connect the crescent to the sphere. To do that, it has to intersect the crescent."

"So, the land of the outcasts is a part of the land of the eternals?"

"For a section, yes."

"And where's the void?"

Anzide drew lines from the exterior of the pins to the gate. It was a narrow space that hugged the sphere.

"It's designed to be a buffer around the sphere. That's why there is nothing in there. No one could locate you at first, but then something happened, and you appeared."

"I was outside the room when I escaped. Sharma moved me behind the door to hide from Belial."

"Well, that's when Mother located you. She cracked the ceiling and broke open the void to pull you back to the portal. It was the only way to get you out of there. No amount of training would have helped you."

"Not when you're going against someone like Belial,"

Benicio muttered. "You're lucky to be alive, kid."

Pressing my lips tight, I tried to smile as if I was grateful, but I don't know if I was. I was still trying to figure out why Belial wanted me there.

"That's the fun part of the explanation. We now move onto the rest of it, which is not as nice."

I glanced at Benicio, who was leaning against the wall. My father was standing at the window, looking at something outside.

"You are technically correct in saying that the land of the outcasts is not where it should be, but it's something that is not discussed because it's a rather large problem. It's actually been shifting and reshaping over the years, and it has been happening so slowly that no one has noticed. That's a problem that is now being rectified and should return to the way that it was within a couple of days. It's not the biggest of issues, though. The outcasts are sentenced, they're sent to this land, but they never see an end to their sentence. It has become an eternal sentence, which is not what was originally ordered. Do you remember that I said that my parents were given a deal to serve someone above us?"

"Belial?"

"Well, yes, I suppose it would be him. He's the one who runs the area. My parents wanted to escape, so he offered a job, and they took it."

"They agreed," I murmured. "Is he the Devil?"

That amused Benicio.

"There is no devil," he offered. "But if there was to be one, it would be him. Aside from Delray, you would be the only one in the portal who has seen him. It's not a bad thing, if you're wondering. It's just unheard of."

The door swung open, and a doctor entered, followed by a nurse. Silence hit the room as Anzide rose from the bed and stepped aside. The nurse began ushering everyone out of the room, insisting I be given privacy.

"They can stay," I said.

"Nonsense," the doctor began. "We have to check that the baby is alright. That means you will need to disrobe from your clothes."

"I don't care. I want them to stay."

Carsten turned from the window. I knew that he'd seen the feather fall from under her skirt when he looked at me. Carefully, he flicked his head, and I raised mine, hoping he would understand. We were being deceived.

CHAPTER 34

Benicio turned back, sensing that something was wrong. Carsten didn't waste time, acting before he needed to react. The doctor and the nurse were pinned to the wall with a glowing green haze that consumed their entire bodies. It didn't take long for their masks to fall.

Belial looked at me with a devious smile, one that made it extremely clear that he would do anything to get his hands on me. Sharma wouldn't look in our direction, and I suspect it was because her son was shooting daggers at her. Out of the both of them, she was the worst. Her involvement was shameful. Belial wanted power, but she was prepared to destroy our lives just to help him get what he wanted. I hoped she felt ashamed of her actions, but I doubted she would.

With a sigh, Benicio shook his head.

"This is a dire turn of events. Hold on, Evelyn, things are about to get a little crazy."

Anzide was back at my side, his arm around me and holding me tight. Benicio had moved as far back against the wall as he could manage. It seemed odd until winged soldiers entered the room.

The feathers were the whitest I'd ever seen. They made Sharma's look dirty by comparison. Metal armor clanged as they marched into the room. The soldier closest to me had sandy blonde hair that was long and curly. Pressed against her forehead, a crown curled at the sides and curved upwards over the temple.

I felt a lot of scrutiny as her golden eyes washed over me. Her lips curled in the corner, slight and barely seen. As she continued past the bed, her attention turned back to the front. Two lines of soldiers entered the room, three on each side. In unison, they turned. Metal clanged, feet stomped as they turned to face each other. I could only see the three on each side, but I figured there were more outside the door because the metal clanging was loud.

In the gap between the two rows, a figure walked towards my father and his captives. Like the other soldiers, his wings were the brightest white, which seemed impossible for wings. The metal of his silver armor looked like it had been polished for hours. This figure was tall and lean, probably packing muscles, but it was hard to tell. His height matched Belial's as did the other soldiers.

When the new figure passed the bed, he glanced at me. It was then that I noticed that the crown he wore matched the soldiers, but it was not pressed to his head like them. It sat off the skin and hair like Belial's did. He was like Belial, and the thought in my mind did not make this any easier.

The figure turned his attention to the captives. With a flick of his hand and disinterest on his face, the figure ordered the soldiers to take custody of the fake doctor and the nurse. It was obvious what they intended to do, considering Belial and Sharma were in their true form but dressed in scrubs.

The pair were marched out of the room, bound in the green glow. It wrapped around them, keeping their feet several inches off the floor. Belial struggled, but it was clearly pointless. He tried to say something, but no words came out of his mouth. Just blissful silence.

Belial looked back at me, and I smiled sweetly as I raised my middle finger at him. He scowled and turned away.

Hearing an amused chuckle, I looked at the new figure. His head tilted as the challenging smile was offered.

"Aren't you the little troublemaker? Defends the weak, blows up houses, kills vampires, befriends a demon living in exile,"

I did what now? Was James in exile?

"Changed the weather in the land of the outcasts. Argues with nephilim and sends them packing with fear mounting. Argues with masters, leaving them questioning everything they've ever known. Every time an alert was sent out, we watched in silence, taking note of everything you said, every move you made. Unfortunately, Belial ensured we could not see what he was up to. We knew that something was wrong when you disappeared from our sight."

"Wait a minute," I muttered, narrowing my eyes at him. "Were you watching everything I did?"

He raised an eyebrow before glancing at my father, who was hiding his smile beneath his hand.

"There was a portion of time that went unseen."

"Uh-huh. Get a good view, did ya? Record it for later on, maybe?"

The figure rolled his eyes.

"No. As you are not aware of this world, you are yet to learn the way that things work. When there is any nudity or actions relating to partial or full nudity, a modesty spell filters everything surrounding the eternal. It is a spell that covers every single part of the portal. Are you satisfied that no one spied on you?"

"Maybe."

He scoffed, rolling his eyes again.

"We do not have the time for this, so I shall carry on with the analysis. You openly mocked the figure in front of her when you knew he was higher up on the chain, argued with him, and when you tried to escape, hit him with a spell that has never been seen before. It had a flow-on effect, highlighting the underling that was assisting him. Which leads us here."

"Who are you?" I asked.

My father, who was back at the window, leaning against the frame, smiled. He knew who this figure was. I knew not to fear this man, but given the day I'd had, it was difficult not to.

"I am Galeth, General of the Soldiers of the Hallowed Halls."

"Cool. Can you go back to the part about the demon in exile?"

"What of it? This is not a subject to be discussed with a third party. If the demon in question wishes to divulge the information, then that is for him to decide, not for me to openly gossip about."

I rolled my eyes.

"Sure, okay, mister stuffed shirt. Why are you here?"

Galeth appeared to be a little affronted, glancing at Benicio, who shrugged at him.

"Because you have displayed certain attributes that have sent up a lot of flags. That is why Belial was determined to get his hands on you."

"So, it wasn't my killer qualities and awesome personality?"

"No."

The tone was clearly unimpressed. I guess he didn't have a sense of humor. The rod up his ass must have killed it.

Moving his hand to the side, Galeth swished his hand over the air, and a clipboard appeared. Pinned to it was a piece of paper with writing on it. I couldn't see what it said, which was frustrating.

"Creates spells. Casts newly created spells with precision. Casts known spells with ease despite still learning. Lineage of the line of the first."

Carsten's smile dropped as he lifted from the wall.

"No, Mother is not the first."

"She is, and if she neglected to tell you that, then it is not my problem."

"What does it mean?"

My father looked at me with anxiety. I glanced at Benicio, who was also oddly quiet and was probably trying to inch his way to the door.

"It means that Inisia was the first of the beings to exist. Your father was the first of her creations, and you are the first of his. In the grand scheme of things, it means little. Inisia and Carsten have learned spells as they aged, lived their lives in this world, and meshed with the others around them. They are just one of the masses. You though, you're vastly different. Raised outside of this world, you've got too much of humanity in your attitude. It can be dealt with if we actually care. What is concerning is your ability to create spells. Those who create usually spend years learning how to craft. They plan their spells, put pen to paper, testing their work before putting it to use in the real world. They have to do that because if they don't, there is risk. Your spells are off the cuff, and even though there is no planning, they are perfect for the situation."

The clipboard disappeared, and Galeth stepped aside

as a screen appeared. Delray appeared, glued to the wall in the rainbow goo, dressed as a clown.

"This shows what you think of Delray. No harm came to him or anyone else in the room. It was effective and the best kind of spell for the situation."

The view changed to Belial burning in a red flame.

"And here we have the recent event. Belial was not harmed, but he was trapped in the flames. This allowed you time to escape. What Belial didn't know was that this spell had a second layer."

Pushing the screen, Galeth turned it into a split screen. On the other side was Delray. He appeared normal.

"We shall hit play so that you can see how this spell continued to work."

Belial roared with anger, shaking the flames away. That's when everything started to rumble. It looked like the portal was suffering an earthquake. Everyone was looking around as if it had never happened before. They weren't panicking, but it looked like it could happen at any moment.

Delray looked around with a frown on his face. As Belial began to discard the flames, Delray started to turn pink. By the time Belial stepped through the door, he was fully free of the spell, and Delray was the shade of a cooked lobster.

"The second layer was to show his accomplices so there would be no doubt for those who would point the finger."

Galeth swiped the screen away.

"But I'm sure you already knew that and would probably prefer that I get to the point. You are a rare creature. As a member of the line of the first, you are powerful. You are also a descendant of a born vampire and shapeshifter, something that, despite your dominating species, still lingers in your veins. You are also what we call a revered soul. The purpose of your creation was to assist others. Animals create because that's what is ingrained in them. They are hard-wired to breed and continue their species. Your mother didn't create you to have a child to raise. She laid down her life to give you to the world. She died so that you could live. That creates a revered soul, one that the world would cherish."

Yeah, but what about the rest of it?

"It has been made clear to us that you must be nurtured and protected. Belial was wrong for his actions, and we expect that this was a one-off incident, but that doesn't mean that others won't think that your power could be harnessed by manipulating you into a drastic situation. Make no mistake, Belial wanted your power. He was trying to drain it from you."

"Wouldn't he be stronger than me already?"

"Power can be weakened by external forces."

Between the fingers of both hands, Galeth held up a scroll. It was wrapped tight with a gold ribbon and sealed with black wax. My father gasped as he stepped back, hitting the blinds. I could feel Anzide moving on the bed, his hand shifting over my shoulder. I looked at him and saw the same shock as what was on Benicio's face.

"This is an offer. It is a placement as a spell creator in the Hallowed Halls, and it is yours so that you can put your skills to proper use. We understand that you have a connection to the immortal family you have and are in the middle of a ridiculous war with a foolish vampire. Things that tie you to the land and not to where you should be. We can accept that to a certain point, provided that you learn to control your powers. You have adequate teachers who will continue to guide you to that place. At some point, you will have to return to this world and enter the cycle of renewal. You will need a place to do that, and you have stated that you will not enter the land of the eternals unless your partner can join you. As one of the creators, we can grant that. Of course, you would ordinarily be granted residence in the halls, but until your outcast partner serves his time, he cannot pass through the gate. When it is done, your residence will change, and he will be permitted to join you in the Hallowed Halls. Provided that you set those terms when you accept the job."

Galeth smiled at me, raising an eyebrow.

"What do you say, Evelyn? Do you want to take the job as a spell creator?"

CHAPTER 35

My father was standing behind Galeth to his side, giving me a wide-eyed nod, suggesting that I should say yes. Anzide shifted to face me, pulling weird faces like he thought I'd understand. Even Benicio was acting odd.

"You're all making faces and nodding at me like I should accept this but fail to remember that I've just endured an attack where another one of his kind wanted me to agree to something. Captain Pervs-a-lot even has the same hovering crown as Belial."

Galeth frowned at me.

"That is a fair point," Carsten responded.

"And one that I understand completely. You're still distressed, you're unsure of me and everything that I represent, and of course, the doctor who should be checking you hasn't shown his face yet. Benicio, would you mind finding a group of soldiers and asking them to search the cupboards?"

Benicio nodded before walking out of the room.

"This offer is not going to expire, Evelyn. We want you to take the offer under your own terms where you can negotiate many aspects of your life in the Hallowed Halls. If you refuse, then we will set the terms with minor allowances because we do not know what you truly desire. It is an offer that, essentially, you cannot refuse. The reality of your situation is that you can't be left to roam around with these powers that will continue to grow. You've created and cast two spells on your own, and we know of your efforts on Earth and in the sparring room. Now that you've turned eighteen, your skills are growing and we cannot sit back and do nothing. We will give you a day to decide on your terms. In twenty-four hours, we will expect an answer from you."

The door opened, and Benicio returned with a doctor who looked a little ruffled. Galeth nodded and walked out of the room with the soldiers who had found the doctor. He pulled the curtain halfway around.

"Mother has a bee in her bonnet." the doctor muttered. "Benicio hasn't sent his report because of interruptions, and this poor old doctor was knocked out and stuffed into a cleaning closet. The portal is pure chaos, and your father has been ordered to remain at your side until everything is dealt with, which means she's down one being who would ordinarily be tasked with many important jobs. If you would lay down please, then I can check everything and tick one of the items off Mother's list."

Once I'd laid down, the doctor poked around my stomach, asking if I felt any discomfort. The door opened again, and a nurse wheeled in a trolley stacked with equipment. Anzide moved to the other side of the bed.

"We're just going to check what's going on in there."

My stomach was slathered in goop, and the nurse ran the wand over the skin. The sound of her heart echoed through the room. After everything that has happened, it was the greatest sound in the world. It sounded healthy.

Stopping, the nurse turned the screen.

"There's the baby. Did you want to know the gender?"

"We know it's a girl. The vampire side of my family always has girls first."

The nurse looked at me and then at Anzide.

"It's not a girl?"

She shook her head and moved the wand to show us we were having a boy.

"Trust you to be different," Anzide said with a chuckle.

"I thought you could see her."

"I thought that too. Guess I was wrong."

"Oh," the nurse said softly. "Maybe that's why."

We turned back to the screen. She offered a cheesy grin as she pointed to the second baby.

"Twins?"

"Yep, and there's your girl."

"It might be a good idea to check for any more." the doctor suggested.

With a nod, the nurse began the search. I looked at Anzide, who was incredibly quiet.

"I can't see anymore."

Handing me great wads of tissue, the nurse packed everything away. When she was done, I was given two little printouts of the babies.

"No wonder I'm always tired."

Anzide was still quiet. It was concerning because he always had something to say. The doctor pushed the curtain back to the wall, and my father gave a smile.

"So, two of them. That's interesting."

"It is?"

He nodded, as did Benicio.

"In these parts, we have one child for each pregnancy, but you've got other species in you, so what is standard for us could be the norm or the complete opposite. Perhaps we should get the statement done so that my mother can stop stressing about everything and reopen the portal?"

Benicio nodded, dragging a chair closer. I glanced at Anzide, who offered a smile, but it wasn't the same as what he usually gave me. It was like he was struggling. I was, too. The problem was that we couldn't talk about it at the moment.

Benicio began asking questions. I answered and then gave him a complete rundown of the events. When I mentioned Sharma, Benicio glanced at Anzide. I got the feeling that he believed that she was not as scared as what she made out to be. To me, it seemed extremely clear that she was more than willing to play her part. Belial was probably giving her something as payment.

When I thought about Sharma's involvement, I began to wonder what Anzide's father thought about it. Was he involved, too?

"Do you know if it was just Belial and Sharma?"

Benicio looked at me, and his gaze shifted upward to Anzide. As the tension grew, Benicio's eyes turned back to me.

"I take it that you are referring to the demon known as Malthe?"

Shifting, I saw the anger on Anzide's face.

"Is that who I'm asking about?"

"It is."

Benicio sighed.

"Malthe has been located and taken into custody as part of the review process. The portal records everything, but because there are so many views, it is going to take time to search through everything. He will be under house arrest and fitted with the same device that Belial and Sharma will have on them. It's wrong to presume guilt over innocence, but given the situation, it's the best thing to do. They will move fast to ensure he is released if he is innocent."

As much as I didn't want to condemn someone, I hoped for Anzide's sake that his father was kept away from him and our children. This was the best and easiest option.

Benicio returned to asking questions. When it was done, I felt a little relieved. Benicio accepted what I said, but that was probably because he thought that I couldn't lie. I wasn't about to tell him any differently. It's not like I was making this up, and it was pretty obvious that something happened. I just didn't need his accusatory frowns.

"I'll see you out, Benicio."

Carsten looked at me, giving me a firm glare. I was on the clock here, and if I wanted privacy for a conversation with Anzide, I had to be fast.

"Are you okay with this?"

"Of course I am. What makes you think that I'm not?"

"You're acting odd. You're quiet, and you're freaking me out."

Anzide sighed, flicking off his shoes to lay on the bed next to me. Wrapped in his arms, I wasn't going anywhere, which was clearly what he wanted.

"I don't have any issues about this. I'm quiet because my mother just helped an elite angel to abduct you, drain you of your powers, and risked the lives of our unborn children. Twice. Not only did she screw me over when she took the deal, but she's trying to do it again by taking you and our children from me. Now I learn that my father could be in on it as well? Of course, I'm going to be freaking out. Let's face it, they don't need to conduct an investigation. He would be a part of it and I'm sure he helped Belial plan everything."

Anzide huffed, holding me tighter. He was quiet for a moment, which I suppose was his way of calming down.

"But it's over, and by the time Galeth is done with them, they won't be able to come near us again. My issue is that we don't have a house or at least one that I'd trust or is structurally sound. Those babies are going to be out soon, and we have nothing for them nor do we have the means to get stuff for them. This slacker doesn't have a job yet."

"What happened to the training job?"

"Still pending because of the blood war. They said it was probably a good idea to focus on maintaining a watchful eye over you rather than worrying about a job. It will be waiting for me."

"Don't worry about the baby stuff. I've seen the bank account now that Brad's doing the money transfer thing. We're good for anything and everything."

"And the house?"

"Well, I guess that depends on the neighbors getting the valuation done. We're able to pay cash for it, so it's just a matter of Warwick getting his butt into gear. Anything else?"

"Not that I can think of, which is just as well because I hear footsteps."

Anzide shifted on the bed to sit up as my father walked into the room.

"So, I guess you'd like to know the finer details of the offer."

"Yeah, the offer that's not really an offer."

Carsten shrugged as he sat down.

"At the core, it is an offer. Their terms are what are considered a tad restrictive. You have to understand that they need to ensure that your powers don't hurt the innocent. There is also a concern that if you are not guided to the right path, you could turn dark."

"What do you mean *dark*?"

"Think along the lines of a deadly evil villain in a superhero movie where the protagonist fails with catastrophic consequences. If you reached that point, they would send their best after you, and you would not survive. That is not their goal for you or for the future. What they want is another brilliant mind creating spells, testing them in a safe environment, and once they've gone through rigorous trials, they would be documented and released for general use."

"How often is anyone in this place going to use my clown spell?"

"Oh, I don't know. It could be used quite a lot if the circumstances were right."

"I'd like to see it used on Drakkus." Anzide offered.

Carsten chuckled.

"It would be a sight."

How true. If only I could remember how I did it.

"Will I be taught how to understand what I'm doing? Because it just happens. I don't have any control over it."

"And that's the problem they want to fix. To answer you, yes. Upon acceptance, you will enter a training phase, which will last until you are deemed ready. Given that you're still in school, I think they will suggest that you finish your education and then take up the role. This is what Galeth was trying to get across to you. They don't know what you want for the future. At the moment, they would be assuming, and if you refuse to negotiate, they're left to continue to do that. It is not in your best interest to leave this up to assumption. What do you want for your future, Evelyn?"

"A happy life with my family. It's all I've ever wanted."

Carsten gave a grim nod, quiet for a moment.

"And what about your friends? You've got Karina, and now Cooper's going to be hanging around. You might even manage to find a friend in Audrey."

Yeah, and pigs will fly, too.

"You've got to think of the big picture here. Galeth

will return, and he will expect that you will have a long list of demands for him. Let me make this clear for you, Evelyn. They will comply. You are so rare that they will be frothing at the mouth. I want you to think about everything you might want, form a list, and see how quickly and easily Galeth will bow down to you."

CHAPTER 36

What felt like an entire day in the portal was only an hour in the real world. That in itself was a problem because the time differences meant that Galeth would want an answer soon. I knew that there wasn't much of a choice, and if I wanted control over the appointment, I had to be a little more compliant. That meant that mischievous Evie was about to be locked in a cupboard, and replaced with business Evie. She was a good girl.

For now, though, it was meeting time. We started with the photos of the babies. The good before the bad.

Everyone was shocked to learn that I was carrying twins. With the joyous news revealed, it was time for the dark side of our update. It came with a slice of happiness at the end, so it wasn't so bad. Or it was considering that I'd been abducted and almost drained of my power. What made it worse was that Anzide's mother was in on it. I wasn't going to sugarcoat it or pretend that she was a captive. Sharma was playing a part, and she completely fooled me.

I think that it angered Anzide more than what he was

letting on. Not only had she done the dirty on him when it came to his punishment, but she aided Belial's attempt to drain my power. She risked the lives of the babies and her grandchildren. I think that if Sharma came near us, Anzide would destroy her.

"So, what are the chances that this guy escapes, makes his way here, and does it all over again?" Brad asked.

"He has been found guilty of the crime and fitted with a device that cannot be removed. Cases like this are rare, so there will be a lot of eyes upon him and his associates. It will be more like a case study, but the bonus of it is that, more often than not, there will be many eyes upon them. There will be restrictions placed upon them, one being that they are bound to the land of the outcasts. I don't know if there will be a time to serve, but for a certain time, they will be completely bound, unable to leave. Anzide's possessions have already been collected and placed in storage for the future. One would assume that it is because of Belial and Sharma being bound to the land of the outcasts or Evelyn's position as a spell creator, but it is actually because of his teaching role. It would seem that you've advanced in the world."

"Who would have thought, eh? An outcast nephilim that is actually considered to be worth something."

"The past has been wrong, Anzide. No one wants to discount your thoughts and feelings, but the past is always behind you, never in front. Look forward to your future because it is filled with so many wonderful things, and if you're looking in the wrong direction, you might never see them."

Anzide looked at me, his eyes passing the photos on the table. The future that was now and coming for us at a ridiculously fast rate. I wasn't told when the babies would be born. The nurse and doctor neglected that piece of information. But it wasn't that far away.

"Hey, do I have to give birth in the portal?"

Carsten paused. A slight frown filled his face.

"I would assume yes. Of course, that takes away from your moment with your family and leaves you with a bunch of strangers. Does this town have a hospital?"

"A small one," Niko offered. "Victoria was born in it. I don't know what it is like now, though."

My father nodded as he returned to me.

"In that list that you're about to form, perhaps you can state that for the health and well-being of yourself and your children, you would like to give birth in the portal but would also like family and friends to visit. It is not standard for immortals to enter the portal, but in this instance, they might make an exception."

"We have company," Anzide said as he stood.

He was through the door before anyone could say a thing.

"Not taking it well?" Brad asked.

I shrugged.

"It's all so overwhelming, and the rest of everything that happened. Plus, that whole thing about his mother being involved. It could have hurt the babies, right?"

Carsten shrugged.

"It would not be detrimental to their overall health, but yes, the extraction process draws their power as well. Anything that could have been in their future would have been passed over. Thankfully, everything is fine, and no damage has been done. As for Anzide, he blames himself. He thinks he was wrong to let you leave like that, but he was right and did everything as expected. When we are summoned, we do not take friends or any form of company. We do not delay or think about it. We are summoned, we leave immediately, we follow the path, and we go alone. I've tried to tell him but he won't listen. Give him time because the reality of Anzide is that he is equally as young and naive as you are."

My ears perked up when I heard Karina.

"Well, I guess that's the end of your list," Carsten muttered.

"How long before Galeth turns up?"

"You've probably got an hour."

"Great."

"Perhaps it would be a good idea to continue writing the list. You can still be sociable with your friends, but the list is important. Galeth is not patient."

Taking the pen and notepad, I wandered out into the main section of the marquee. Cooper was with Karina, giving me a smirk and a nod as they approached.

"Anzide said you had some trouble."

"Yeah, just some guy tried to take my powers because, apparently, I'm a super rare spell creator. I've got to make a wish list of demands for some guy that's going to be here soon to get my answer regarding a job in the portal."

Karina was stunned, and Cooper was just as quiet.

"And I had to be checked because he tried to drain my powers. They found out that there's two in here."

"Shut up," Karina said with a huge smile. "You're having twins? That is so cool."

"Yeah, it is pretty cool."

"We need to go baby shopping soon."

Really soon.

I nodded as I sat down on the lounge chair. Karina was already on her phone searching for the nearest baby store. Putting pen to paper, I began forming my list based on areas of my life that I felt were important.

"So, what's going on in town?"

"Not much. Been sniffing around, found a few hits of Drakkus but nothing too strong that would indicate he's been out and about for longer than necessary."

"They'll probably lay low this week because of the town festival."

I looked up from my notebook with interest.

"Town festival?"

"Yeah," Karina said with a wry grin. "There are flyers plastered everywhere. Hasn't your grandmother's alter ego been busy with it?"

I shrugged. Beatrice was taking on Natalia's form less now that she was hiding here with Niko. If there was a town festival, then she might have to participate if she's still working for the Heritage Trust.

"Anyway, it's Friday, and Cooper's playing a game."

I'd been too distracted to notice how close Karina was sitting to Cooper. It appeared as if he didn't care either, which was awesome. When she looked at him, her hand gripped his forearm. Cooper smiled and lifted the arm around her shoulder.

My eyebrows rose as I lowered my gaze back to the notebook, saying nothing but grinning from ear to ear.

"You're going to be there, right?"

I looked up again and smiled.

"Sure. Wouldn't miss it for the world."

"Even though you hate sports and the cheerleaders?" Cooper asked.

"I can put aside my opinions to show support to you, and as for the cheerleaders, that might just be changing. Don't go saying anything or acting weird around Audrey. You two don't know anything."

Cooper was frowning, his eyes darting between Anzide and myself.

"She's a friend now?"

Clearly, Karina hadn't told him.

"I wouldn't go that far just yet. We spoke at school after she made another attempt to drag me down. I pointed out the obvious, and she realized I was not the enemy. Later that day, she came here an absolute wreck because she'd seen something terrible at the Fleming coven house."

"Drakkus murdered Kannon's aunt." Anzide offered. "I saw the vision through Audrey's eyes, and I'm not surprised that she wasn't coping. It was enough to make me wish I hadn't entered her mind."

Cooper sighed heavily, shaking his head.

"That's awful. As sad as it is, I'm not surprised. Even after one interaction with him and the followers, I saw he was dangerous."

"Oh, he's that alright. Audrey was not coping with what she saw. Dad talked to her and helped her calm down. It's going to be a slow path, but at least she might stop harassing us."

Cooper scoffed, rolling his eyes like he didn't believe it. I guess it was one of those things that had to be seen to be believed.

"Are you coping, though?"

Because it occurred to me that Anzide's mood might not just be his mother. Maybe he thought it might be my future.

"I'm okay now. Carsten showed me the spell he used. I know the memory is there, I can see it in a vague sense, but I am disconnected from the emotions surrounding it. Now I can think about it and not want to violently empty my stomach anymore."

"Oh," I said softly. "That bad, huh?"

"More than you'll ever know because I will not put the thoughts in your head. It's bad enough that we know how she died. We can leave it at that."

Pressing my lips tightly, I nodded and let the subject go. I didn't want to hear it, and Anzide was getting agitated. Turning to the other lounge, I saw Karina and Cooper were talking. They hadn't heard what we'd just said, and I guess we missed out on a few things on their side as well.

When they realized we were watching, Karina and Cooper turned to look at us. Karina gave Cooper a soft nudge with her shoulder, then looked up at him. The shy smile had grown.

"So, there's been a development."

"I can see that."

"Oh, not this," Cooper said with a wide smile on his face. "This is a thing that's being played cool because Nora's extremely protective."

Understandable, given the circumstances.

"At least, if she says something, it is." Karina offered.

Okay, message received.

"Is that a request to keep a secret?"

"Not really. She knows, but there have been a lot of restrictions placed on us. I think a lot of it has to do with the blood war, and she's always worried about what Drakkus and his goons will do."

"Which is why there's been a development. Until the war is over, we've set up camp in the spare bedroom. Well, me and Sebastian. James has put protections over the property, but we discussed it, and I could see that Nora was stressing over it. So, this was what we all agreed upon."

"It's going to boil over soon." Karina offered. "I can feel this weirdness in the air."

"That would be the ties between Drakkus and Evie," Anzide responded.

"Connected through the blood war, it affects all of the followers. Probably why Kannon's been getting in our faces whenever he gets the opportunity."

Cooper's thoughts were probably right. If Karina could feel it, then it would affect everyone in Drakkus's coven as well. As much as I wasn't ready for this war, I knew that it had to happen soon.

CHAPTER 37

Galeth looked at the list, glancing at Carsten.

"Did you read this list?"

The list was flapped wildly at Carsten, who remained stoic, staring at Galeth.

"I did," Carsten replied.

"And you thought it was wise to let her proceed with this?"

My father smiled, almost looking as if he was proud that he'd created me. It was hard for me to think it was real, considering it felt as if my mother thought the opposite.

"She is an extremely talented spell creator, the likes of which you have not seen in at least two centuries. Creators like her don't just turn up every day. She is rare, and you want to ensure that her talents are not left to flail in the wind. You need her."

"You informed her to create a list of *this,*" he grumbled, yet again waving the piece of paper at my father.

"It is an agreement, Galeth. If you do not like what Evelyn has requested, then you should negotiate with her. Are you brave enough to go against an untrained spell creator?"

"Her talents do not scare me, nor do your thinly veiled threats."

He huffed, straightening the paper.

"Category one, the house. To submit plans for the house that Evelyn and Anzide want on their choice of land. Subject to site inspection. For all children to be assured the same level of property. Two, transportation adequate to the situation and their growing needs."

Galeth glanced at me and, in particular, my stomach. He growled softly as his attention turned back to my list.

"Three, children. All children are to be birthed in the portal, with the best medical staff and private accommodation allowances for Anzide. For the immortal family and friends to be given the ability to visit after all births. I hardly think that's,"

When our eyes met, I gave Galeth a challenging look. Shaking his head dismissively, he lowered his gaze.

"The best education for all children. Four, Anzide's punishment is to be terminated immediately. Five, for Evelyn to review annually to ensure that she and her family are granted the best of everything, extending to her children when it comes to their time to negotiate their future. Six, Evelyn retains the right to inflict herself upon the Soldiers of the Hallowed Halls to ensure they know how valuable she is to them."

Galeth scowled at me, but all I gave back was a sweet smile as I fluttered my lashes. He was not impressed.

"I will take this list to decide with my peers and return within twenty-four hours. Don't be surprised if it has thinned considerably."

Galeth disappeared, and Carsten rolled his eyes.

"He acts like you asked for the world."

"Well, I kind of did. It also feels a little lacking. What if I missed something?"

Giving me a reassuring smile, he gripped my hand.

"That is the reason I suggested an annual review. It gives you the opportunity to renegotiate your contract and structure it to suit your situation. We constantly change in this world, Evelyn. There is no way to predict what you will want and need in fifty years or even in five years. As for Galeth, pay no attention to him. It was nothing but an attempt to make you wilt under pressure. He knows it will not work, and he will take the list to his peers with the knowledge that you know what you want. That is what he expected of you."

"And yet he acted like a drama queen."

"That is standard for those who loiter in the Hallowed Halls. I hope you won't become like them."

"Ha," Brad said with a mocking smile. "If anything, she'll make them change their ways."

"Do you think that I overdid it?"

"Not at all. If they wanted to restrict you, they would have set a budget or limitations. Ignore Galeth."

Beatrice leaned over with a magazine, curling the left side behind the right. I looked at the prom dress and thought it was rather pretty, but it would not suit my growing belly. Yes, I had a bump.

It was small, looking more like I was bloated, but it was there. My jeans were tight, and upon investigation, I found a slight alteration to my shape. They were now held together with a hairband thanks to a little ingenuity from Beatrice.

The slimline halter neck dress glistened in the light. It appeared as if the material was stretchy, which was great, but given the changes that were coming my way, might not be a good idea. I was having twins, and I was going to be huge.

"It's, uh, pretty."

"Something to think about."

"It probably won't fit."

Hearing noises, I got up to see what was going on. Our early detection system hadn't said we were about to get a visitor, so whatever was going on was outside the fence line. Peering through the gap between the canvas wall and door, I saw Warwick and his wife moving boxes into a large truck. Anzide stopped next to me to watch the neighbors.

"Do you think it's wrong that James has interfered in their lives like this?"

"No."

Letting go of the panel, I turned and frowned at Anzide.

"Why?"

"Because James can suggest until he's blue in the face. If they don't want to leave, then they won't. Demons have the ability to suggest, but they can't force when a human has a strong hold on something. If they've willingly let go like they have, it means that they were either not interested in the house or where they live. You might even find that they were already thinking it, and James merely suggested that offering to sell it to you and Brad first would be a charitable thing to do."

"Are you sure?"

"Yes, and it will be the same for the other neighbors. If he's suggested it, then it means that James has already checked to see if it is possible. Brad is ready. All we need is to go through the motions, apparently."

"Not too sure?"

"No. The concept of land ownership is rather odd to me. How is it that I will own that land one day soon?"

"With the help of the local demon,"

I gasped and turned to see James behind us.

"Jeez." I groaned. "Since when do you sneak attack us

like that?"

"Since I heard that a little chaos maker was getting a little curious. As for you and your lack of presence in this world, you would need this."

James held out an envelope.

"What's this?" Anzide asked as he lifted back the flap.

"A gift from a demon who has created the documents and history you need to continue along the agreed path. It was something that I forgot to mention and is extremely necessary. Now, you have questions about me?"

"Did that drama queen tell you that?"

James chuckled as we walked to the lounge.

"Oh, I think you've hit the nail on the head regarding Galeth. However, in this instance, I received the alert like everyone else did. You are quite famous. Perhaps infamous is a better term. No, that is not right."

He hummed for a moment and then smiled.

"Infamously famous, perhaps?"

I chuckled with a slight shrug.

"Sure, whatever."

He sat down, putting two more envelopes on the table that was between us. I guess they were for Niko and Beatrice. Identities that were current.

"To answer your curiosity, I chose exile because life in the portal and the land of the demons was rather dull.

Occasionally, there would be a hiccup that would give us a bit of entertainment, but overall, it was boring. Like many demons, I chose to remain here on Earth and take up the role of a soul catcher. There are roles that I could take up without requiring exile. However, it is always based on returning to the portal. Remaining on Earth meant that I chose exile. I can return at any time. I still have a house in the land of the demons, and I, on the odd occasion, return to see family. This place is too exciting to ignore. I might return one day, but there would have to be a world-sized catastrophic event for that to happen."

"Yeah, I'm inclined to agree."

"But of course, there are times when I regret the decision. The infamously famous one has seen to that with ease. My phone has been going crazy. With the alerts and the messages from family and friends, I am constantly updated whenever you move in that place. It makes me wonder if I should return for a few weeks."

"Nah, life here is far more entertaining."

Brad rubbed his stomach, grumbling about missing doughnuts as he stood.

"If you will excuse me, I am feeling rather peckish. I'll let Niko know that you're here."

"Thank you, Brad."

For a moment, there was silence. I turned and saw James looking at me with curiosity.

"Karina told me. I know that it has happened and

that it could always happen again, but why haven't these Europeans done something about it?"

"Because the vampires that associate with each other in those kinds of situations don't want them finding out, they don't want anyone to know, so they're extremely particular about who they tell and invite. The Europeans haven't done anything because they don't know. You can put the call in if that makes it better in your mind, but be aware that if they think it's happening in one city, they will assume it is happening in every city. That will force their hand, and teams will be created that will sweep through all covens. It will be done with speed to ensure that word does not spread. Some covens will survive, but most won't. They are extremely particular about what they see as the perfect coven and will act on anything that is wrong. It will be with extreme prejudice, and few will live to see another day."

"Are we perfect in their eyes?"

"Mostly. If the Europeans walked into this town, they would state that the Corbin clan is acceptable because they will understand that you, as the leader of the clan at the time of engaging Drakkus, were not identified as an eternal. They will accept that you are still the leader even though Niko is alive based on the rules surrounding a blood war. However, they will dislike the time that has passed for the blood war to end. They will state that you are taking too long and prolonging it unnecessarily. You will be accused of refusing to end the war to keep a hold of the leadership, perhaps even colluding with Drakkus to ensure it drags on. There is also the issue that it is your word against Drakkus, and he could easily say that you murdered Niko to obtain the leadership. Of course, if they have an Eternal, the Europeans could easily see the truth. Also, if they think that you've aged enough, lying might not be possible for you anymore. Which, as a side note, that may be just around the corner, if it hasn't already changed."

I frowned, wondering if I could lie. Looking down at my shirt, I decided it was the easiest to lie about.

"My shirt is,"

I couldn't say it. My mouth opened, but the false word would not come out. No matter how much I tried, I could not lie and say that my shirt was green. With a heavy sigh, I rolled my eyes.

"My shirt is black, apparently."

James smiled.

"And there we have it, a fully-fledged Eternal. Congratulations, Evelyn."

"Thanks. Do you realize how much of a pain in the ass this will be? I might need to lie to save myself."

"There are always ways around it. Learn how to deflect and divert. If you are wise, then you will learn how to draw the attention of the other party to something else. Compliments tend to work well. Shift the focus back to the person and talk about them. Feed their ego, if necessary."

I liked talking to James. He made anything seem

possible. It made me realize why Niko liked him as well. Despite the negativity surrounding his species, it seemed as if James was vastly different. I hoped it would always be like this.

CHAPTER 38

Even though it wasn't our house yet, we had access to it. Warwick and his wife had moved out, handing the keys over to Nora. They were happy for her to let us start preparations to move in because it was clear that we were not going to back out of the deal.

Because our lives were about to change dramatically really soon, Brad suggested that we take this house rather than the other, which we had also started to purchase. He didn't care which one, and neither did we. There was only one thing that altered the situation, and that were the two little babies that were growing madly.

I had stopped wearing my jeans. Now, I was in a pair of sweatpants that were tight across the belly that had gotten bigger. If I wore loose clothes, it couldn't be seen easily, but my pants were tight and my shirts always slid up over the mound.

Beatrice was going to take me to the shops later today. I was secretly excited because I had a sneaking suspicion that she'd invited Karina and Nora as well. A girl's day out for one who had never done something like that before and two who needed love and affection in the form of a friendship.

Anzide and I walked through the house that desperately needed a makeover. It was old and tired, and the color scheme was dated and boring. We walked up the stairs and found that there were only three bedrooms.

"So, I guess we're stopping at the twins, right?"

"Maybe they might want to share with their siblings."

"I seriously doubt it."

Entering one of the smaller bedrooms, I looked out the window to the separate garage. Between it and the house was a covered walkway on a slab.

"We could extend it to include another floor over the garage."

"Sounds like a headache for Henry."

"Or maybe keeping him busy and employed, something that I think he struggled with thanks to Ryan's monopolization."

"I suppose planning for a long future with many children would be a good idea. Isn't it standard for children to leave home when they become adults?"

"In the past, yeah. Now, it's a mixed bag. We can continue to buy the houses on this street, slowly picking them off over the years. Then we'll rename the street."

"Vampire Lane?"

"Eternals Way," I said with a grin, wrapping my arms

around his waist.

"How about Corbin Avenue?"

"Now that has a nice ring to it."

Anzide leaned down, indulging me with a kiss.

"I have something for you."

"Really? Might be a bit cold on the wooden floor."

"Hilarious as always, but not what I meant."

Taking my hand, Anzide led me down the stairs and through the side door. Taking the keys, he opened the garage and turned on the light.

A silver minivan gleamed under the fluorescent light.

"Did the previous owners leave their car behind?"

"No."

"So, you got me a minivan?"

"No, again. That's actually a gift from your family for us because apparently, now that we've gone from two to four, we're going to need a big car."

"Great. My first car is a family van."

This was the price that I paid for submitting to temptation. Of course, he was too irresistible to ignore, so I was always going to be tempted. Probably going to be pregnant for the rest of my eternal life.

"I said that you wouldn't be impressed."

Flicking off the light, Anzide locked the door and moved behind me, pushing me to the driveway. Brad was standing in front of a small red car, holding out the keys with an unimpressed look on his face. Beatrice was here but in Natalia's form. I think that Niko was probably close, too. I couldn't imagine that he'd want to miss out on this.

"And that's why I said that maybe a smaller car would be ideal. Especially for the time leading up to the birth and anytime afterward where you might want to go out with Karina or Beatrice."

"Niko agreed, so our granddaughter gets a belated birthday present." Beatrice offered.

"No longer going with the great?"

She gave a vague shrug.

"Niko and I have missed out on many things, and we thought, if it's alright with you, that we referred to you as our granddaughter."

"It's fine. I was only teasing."

I took the keys, only for Anzide to snatch them away.

"We're going somewhere."

Beatrice took the keys to lock the house while Anzide opened the passenger door.

"I thought you didn't like driving."

"It occurred to me that the belly might grow too large to fit behind the wheel, so while you were sleeping, Brad took me out for a long lesson. We also conducted a little reconnaissance while we were out. I need more lessons so, get in. You can drive home."

Brad frowned at me in response to the complaint he knew was brewing. Yes, I was frowning, too, and I was about to protest. So, I accepted that maybe this wasn't just a drive around town and that somewhere was a particular place.

Except, I was in ill-fitting track pants and an old sweatshirt. Anzide always wore long pants and a shirt, which made me wonder why I didn't notice that he was wearing a cotton shirt that I'm almost positive I've never seen before. The long sleeves were rolled to the elbow, and the shirt was neatly tucked into a pair of jeans that looked brand new. My eyes narrowed at the scuff-free shoes.

"Should I change?"

Because it became clear that something was going on.

"Maybe." Brad offered.

"Some warning would have been nice," I muttered, turning back to our property.

Like she was a part of the plan, Beatrice was waiting at the caravan.

"It's hanging on the rail."

"Thanks."

I stopped, glancing at Beatrice, who was smiling at me.

"So, we're not going shopping this afternoon?"

"We are, but it depends on how long you take."

"Yeah," I said, sighing heavily.

Closing the curtain behind me, I changed out of my pants and sweatshirt and pulled on the long blue dress. Sitting on the bed was a shoe box with a pair of black flats. Grabbing a light cardigan, I draped it over my bag and walked out of the caravan.

"Offering any information?"

"Nope," Niko said without lowering the newspaper. "Aside from the fact that you look lovely. Have fun."

Hearing silence, Niko dropped the paper and smiled.

"Do you like the house?"

"It's great."

"And the cars?"

"They're awesome and efficient."

"Good. Happy belated birthday. Now off you go."

"Thanks, I think."

Brad passed me as I walked through the yard. His only words were to have fun and behave myself. It was standard, and I couldn't pick apart the statement for information.

Climbing into the passenger seat, I gave Anzide an uneasy smile. He chuckled, shaking his head.

"We're going to get lunch, captain freakout."

"You've clearly learned new words from Brad."

"And you, and Karina, and now, CJ."

The ability to drive had come quickly to Anzide, not that I expected any different. When I thought about the Eternals and their abilities, I realized that Galeth hadn't returned.

"Oh my god, what about Galeth? He said he was returning."

"Carsten said he would deal with Galeth. You don't need to be there while they're still negotiating."

"How long will this go on for?"

"Generally not too long, but Galeth might try to remove some of your demands. I think your father is eager to see how much he can get from them on your behalf. Don't be surprised if your list grows."

Anzide turned through the streets, driving like he'd spent years behind the wheel. He looked at me, and I could see a fraction of anxiety.

"What?"

"Have you thought about what's going to happen after the war is over?"

"What do you mean?"

"Your father."

I shrugged, still unsure of everything. It was hard to

understand how a parent might actually love me.

"You know the truth now. Doesn't that count for something?"

"It does, and it's not him or what happened between him and my mother. I think it's my inability to accept that he's not like my mother and that he thinks that I have value in his life."

"Are you going to say something before he leaves?"

"Of course I will. He's done so much for me. How can I let him leave without saying what I think?"

I stopped, trying to restrain the heavy emotions.

"How can I let him leave?" I whispered.

Anzide reached out, taking my hand.

"By asking him to stay. He would do that for you. All you need to do is speak your mind and ask him to be a part of your life."

Taking back his hand, Anzide pulled the car into a parking lot and carefully slid into a free space. Faced with a brick wall, I looked up and saw the large sign for the restaurant. It was an Italian restaurant.

"Brad said that you love a good lasagna, and Niko said that this guy has been in the town for years, which apparently means a lot."

"For a small town, it probably does. No restaurant will survive if the residents don't spend their money at their place."

"Well, the only person that could give me a review was Beatrice, and she admitted that on occasions, she'd change to a different persona and visit the place without the threat of Drakkus and his followers seeing a supposed vampire consuming food. She said this place was incredible. Apparently, the pasta just melted in her mouth. She then asked to bring back a few meals for her."

Entering the restaurant, I noticed a few patrons were already seated, some eating, others still deciding. The host showed us to the back of the restaurant, a section that was a little secluded. With the dining area in a L shape surrounding the kitchen, it gave a bit of privacy from the door in this area.

My stomach rumbled when I looked at the menu.

"So, I guess we'll be ordering a starter?"

I grinned. "Maybe."

We agreed upon the bruschetta for a starter, and I picked ravioli for my mains. Anzide decided he wanted to know what was so good about the lasagna. When the host left, I tilted my head with a challenging smile.

"So, what's going on?"

Anzide stared for a moment and then huffed, sounding like he was frustrated.

"I would have said something eventually," he muttered. "But because of the job offer, they've reduced my sentence."

"You're free?"

"Yep. No longer an outcast. I'm still classed as Nephilim."

"It's a name for what you are like I'm a Phoenix. It can't change."

"I know. With everything that's changing in the place, most of the Nephilim won't be doing what is expected of them anyway. They're still trying to figure out what to do about the witches and cross-breeding, but that's not the concern of the Nephilim anymore. Those above us are trying to find roles for everyone, but I am the first to actually get a job and no longer an outcast. So, I guess Galeth will knock the request to end my sentence off your list."

"Congratulations."

"Thanks. It also means that I can live with you when you decide on the house in the Hallowed Halls."

"We decide. It will be our house, so *we* will decide."

Anzide nodded, but I sensed that there was something else. It was almost like something was eating away at him.

"Anzide?"

"Niko said something, and it had me wondering if he was right. I don't want to force anything upon you, but he pointed out that as members of the coven, we have to be the representation of what we expect from the followers."

"I don't understand. What did he say?"

"That we should get married."

CHAPTER 39

I stared in silent shock. I couldn't even say if it was better or worse that Anzide reached into his pocket and pulled out a little box.

"I don't have any expectations, but I thought you might."

"It concerns me that there are external sources that are forcing you to do this."

"I'm not being forced into anything. It can be suggested until the world ends. If I'm not ready, then I'm not going to take this path or any other. This is where I am, and it is true that it was suggested but I am not opposed to the idea and think that it would be a fun thing to do. I would like your thoughts on it though as it is a foreign concept to me. And obviously, your response, which you don't have to say yes."

Anzide continued to grin at me like he knew how painful this was.

"I will tell you what I see from my point of view and from what I know. Us Eternals, we don't have wedding services. Most of us aren't even allowed to form relationships, but if the rumors are true, that will be changing as well. Apparently, someone has shown them how amazing a hybrid can be."

A wicked smile filled his face.

"And, of course, there's you," Anzide said.

"You're a monster."

"I know. So, if we form a partnership, it is obvious to everyone around us. We are considered a couple, and in an odd way, it is our own peculiar version of marriage. However, you have not been raised in that world. You've grown up where marriages begin with a wedding."

The server was making his way to us with our drinks. I moved and looked up, hoping Anzide would realize. He turned and leaned back on his seat, taking the box with him. When the server left, Anzide put the box back on the table and pushed it towards me.

"I've been told that it is common when people are growing up to dream of grand and romantic proposals with fairytale weddings. They actually argued about it. Niko said that it was romantic to get down on one knee, while Brad said that you'd be mortified, warning me against it. Brad said that your childhood probably didn't have much space for flights of fancy, but that doesn't mean you don't want something."

Yeah, Brad was right. Technically, Niko was too, but I wasn't the kind of girl that welcomed attention like that.

"Please don't get down on one knee," I whispered.

Anzide grinned as he leaned his head on one hand. The box sat between us, and I could feel my body tighten when I thought of reaching out to take it.

"You haven't opened it. For all you know, it could be a pair of earrings."

"But given the conversation so far,"

"Yeah. So, if you accept, then you'll have Niko breathing down your neck about it. He suggested sooner rather than later, considering that you're already showing. It was also said that a church service is acceptable, but does not know what denominations are currently in this town. I asked if something could be done in the portal, to which your father said that anything is possible. That's the reason we were kicked out before Galeth returned. Your father is going to add it as an optional item on your list, pending your acceptance and thoughts."

I don't know why I was so apprehensive. It's not as if I didn't want to spend my entire life with Anzide. We were about to have twins. We're in the process of buying a house. What made this so difficult?

"You know that I love you, right?"

Looking up, I nodded.

"Probably since the moment you walked into the room. I struggled between doing what was expected of me, what was right, and what I wanted while not knowing what to do or how to fix the mess I'd created. Every time I opened my mouth, I made it worse. It didn't help that in the beginning, everyone thought that you were an immortal which meant that we couldn't be together. Then everything changed. You opened a door, and I could fix the mistakes by walking through it. I still make mistakes, and I probably will for a long time. It comes with being a newborn Nephilim."

I huffed a laugh.

"That sounds so weird. There's nothing newborn about you."

Anzide smiled back at me, but through the smile, I could see the anxiety. It was new to him, the concept was foreign to the Eternals, but that didn't mean he'd take rejection well. He wasn't about to assume that just because we were about to live together with our babies meant I'd say yes. But I would though. I'd be mad to say no.

"Anzide,"

I took hold of his hand, weaving our fingers together.

"It's okay to say no."

"I know that,"

"Don't worry about your family."

He paused, giving a vague shrug.

"Or the code of vampires that we'd be damaging. Just ignore Niko."

"Anzide?"

Warily, he winced.

"Shut up. I would love to marry you."

Taking the box, I opened it and smiled. It wasn't ostentatious. The ring was beautiful, the diamond was larger than I'd anticipated, and the rows of chips set into the band were equally as flashy.

"Beatrice helped," Anzide said as he took the box.

The ring came out, and Anzide turned it to show the white gold surrounding the main diamond.

"I was looking at ones that had little claws holding the stone. She said that if I was going to select one of them, I should be mindful of how easily they can break and pick one that looks strong. They were nice, but I saw this and thought it would suit you better. Do you like it?"

"I love it because you picked it."

As Anzide slid the ring onto my finger, I heard a squelching, sliding sound. It was followed by a squealing that was extremely distinctive. Looking across the restaurant and out the front window, I saw our excited onlookers. Karina and CJ were at the window.

Excited was probably underselling Karina's mood. CJ, though, it was fairly accurate. He had a smile that clearly said he was happy for us. Beside him was a jumping bean that now had the other patrons in the restaurant looking at her.

"How is that possible?" Anzide muttered. "They did not know."

"But it's highly likely that Beatrice invited her to our afternoon out. Did you plan to take me back to the property so I could return with Beatrice?"

"No, she's coming here to collect you."

Anzide sighed.

"And I guess they decided to get lunch. If you want them to join us, I don't mind."

"Are you sure?"

"Evie, they're your friends,"

"*Our* friends."

Giving them a flick of my hand, Karina eagerly walked towards the door. CJ followed, looking a little reluctant. Almost like he'd told Karina to be quiet and tried to avoid this happening. I didn't mind.

Turning back to Anzide, I smiled.

"Sure you're okay?"

"Absolutely."

Karina, in all her loud glory, squealed with happiness as she crossed the room.

"Oh my god. This is so cool."

As she squeezed the life out of me when she hugged me, I realized something about Karina. She would always be my friend. No matter what happened, no matter where we were in the world, she would be there for me. I'd resisted friends after the sting that came from losing so many. Now that we were settled in Hades and there was no chance of being uprooted again, I didn't have to worry about saying goodbye.

Karina took my hand and looked at the ring.

"Well, Zeed, it seems like you do have good taste."

"You're so kind. Are you two joining us?"

"We shouldn't," CJ mumbled. "I did say that we should keep moving, but I was elbowed in the ribs and told to be quiet."

CJ grinned, rubbing the side of his torso.

"It's okay," Anzide offered.

To make it clear that we were alright with it, Anzide got up and added chairs to the table. Then he went in search of the host to add to our order.

"So," Karina said as she sat down. "Made any plans yet?"

"No, but Niko's already told Anzide that it should happen before the babies are born."

"How long have you got?" CJ asked.

"November."

"Ouch, that's almost here."

"Well, the end of November, so that gives me a bit of time. Hopefully. Given that there are two of them in there, I'm inclined to think that it's going to be sooner."

Anzide returned with the host, sitting in the seat next to me. While Karina and CJ were ordering their meals, I felt something twinge inside me. Anzide tilted his head when I looked up at him. Taking his hand, I pressed it to the skin and waited, not daring to move. I hoped the twinge was movement, but I wasn't sure. His head lowered, waiting with me.

When it happened again, Anzide's eyes lifted to mine. He smiled, a beaming look of pure happiness.

"It was the boy."

Shifting his hand, he moved to the left side, pressing down.

"And there's our little lady. Just hanging out."

"Unlike her brother, who has decided to test out his leg muscles."

When I looked at Karina, I saw her twiddling the cutlery while biting her lip. She wasn't looking at me, but I could read her like a book already.

"Oh, come on," I grumbled.

She grinned, reaching to my belly.

"You want to get in on the action too?"

CJ smiled, shaking his head.

"I'm all good, thanks."

"You're not getting any ideas, are you? CJ might run for the hills."

Karina blushed as she smiled, pulling away her hand. The baby had kicked for her.

"I think I can live vicariously through you for a few

years."

"Good call. You can hand them back when you've had enough."

She giggled and returned to toying with the cutlery. It made me wonder if something else was going through her mind. I wasn't going to say something now, just in case it had to do with CJ.

"So, what's new?"

"Well, my afternoon is free. I think Brad might have messaged my mother and hinted that a little freedom would be extremely welcomed. Personally, I think that other things were suggested, which is just blah."

I chuckled. She was right, of course. No one needed to know that kind of information.

As we enjoyed the moment of amusement, I happened to look out the window. Passing by was a sight that made me uneasy. Kannon glanced in, saw us, and as he scowled, he turned away. Then his pace quickened.

Silence hit the table until CJ cleared his throat.

"So, I might have heard a rumor. Because he got booted out of the school and there is no insight into what you're doing there, someone is not a happy vampire. They turned their attention to Audrey, who told them that she doesn't have classes with you, and during the lunch break, she's always practicing in the gymnasium with the cheer squad. Apparently, she made it quite clear that you were not interested in joining the squad, and there was no place available, even if you changed your mind."

"She has nothing to tell them." Anzide offered.

"Audrey and I do share a class. Was it Kannon trying to save himself?"

"Nope."

"Alright. I have to know. Where did you hear the rumor?"

CJ grinned, glancing at Karina. She scoffed, rolling her eyes.

"A little bird in pink cashmere told me."

"She's just trying to get herself a bit of wolfie love."

I frowned at Karina and CJ. He was smiling at first until he saw my unimpressed stare.

"Oh, not me. She's chasing Sebastian."

"That's good. I guess I don't have to subject you to a waxing when you're in your alternate form then."

Karina giggled.

"That would hurt."

CJ's eyes were wide as he thought about it.

"Yeah, it would. We get rather furry, so you'd be busy, and I'd be in some serious pain."

"Well then, you know what will happen if you ever misbehave."

"Aww, Evie, you're such a good friend." he cooed. "Bet Zeed's sweating on it. Lucky you don't have any fur, right?"

All eyes swung to him, and he stopped eating his meal.

"Well, I wasn't planning on misbehaving, so I don't need fur or anything like that. Zeed's a good boy."

Yeah, he sure is. I was a lucky girl.

CHAPTER 40

Beatrice, in her alter ego, turned up after lunch. We decided to part ways, although I think Anzide was having trouble leaving. He would always worry regardless of where I was or who I was with. But this was the arrangement. A day out dress shopping with Beatrice and Karina. So, he took Beatrice's car home, as well as a lot of meals that Beatrice had ordered from the restaurant.

I'm sure he would be greeted with a freaked-out uncle and great-grandfather because I was going to drive home. Their concerns were that I still wasn't competent, and neither was Anzide. They also worried about getting into an accident and the health of the babies. Beatrice said she would deal with them and to not worry about it. After all, we were both Eternals, and learning things came quickly to us. They worried needlessly.

I was grateful for their concern, and I wasn't about to ignore it or be dismissive. It wasn't just me or Anzide on the road. We had to be mindful of everyone else and the actions they would take.

As for the rest of our company, that was CJ, who was

still here. I didn't mind. He was waiting for his mother to pick him up, and she was running late. So, he was sitting on the window ledge of the shop, playing the acoustic guitar that had been a prop. It didn't make much sense to me, but there were a lot of things that were like that.

When he first started toying with the strings, he got a frown from the woman running the shop, but once he began to play a song, she stopped. Nothing had been said, so I guess she wasn't that annoyed. It's not like he was trying to play a rock concert with the thing. He was just strumming softly, making a sweet tune that was rather pleasant.

"Well?"

Beatrice turned from the window and smiled. CJ's gaze rose, and with an appreciative smile, he nodded.

"Yep, that's the dress."

Beatrice looked at CJ with mild amusement.

"What?" he said, a little taken aback. "She looks great in it."

"I agree." Karina offered. "But I don't think you were being asked."

He shrugged and turned back to looking out the window.

"Your grandfather will have a fit."

I looked at the white lace that covered the soft tan material.

"I guess it does look like I'm naked underneath. It's a shame, I really like it."

It was soft and flowed around my body. The boho-style wedding dress was delicate and beautiful. It accentuated but gave room to grow, which was necessary. That is unless we were married tonight.

Beatrice sighed with a sympathetic smile.

"I like it too. Alright. Let me work on your grandfather."

"You know what I like just as much as this dress?"

She was intrigued, probably already aware that I was up to no good. The smile on my face was always a giveaway.

"What's that, darling?"

"This dress over here."

"It's quite pretty," she offered.

"Do you think that Karina would like it?"

The shoes that were in Karina's hands dropped, and her eyes widened.

"I think she might. Maybe you should ask her."

"Well?"

Fumbling, Karina picked up the shoes and put them back on the shelf.

"I thought you were marrying, you know, out of

town."

"Carsten made arrangements for you and CJ to join us. After all, Evie's family will be going out of town as well."

"So, want to be my bridesmaid?"

I don't think that Karina could have agreed as fast as what she did. It was surprising that she didn't start crying, though I suspect that when she engulfed me in an overbearing hug, she might have shed a tear or two.

"I take it that you want to?"

"Of course I do."

"Good. Do you like the dress?"

"It's cute."

Karina bit her lip, taking a sly glance at CJ.

"I have to talk to my father about them," I said softly. "They're all half-witch and I don't know if it will cause problems for them if they were to go out of town with us."

"Oh," she said softly.

"So, for now, don't say anything. Okay?"

Karina nodded and took the dress to try on.

"Your father was quite determined to get everything on your list. Galeth was not impressed, but I got the feeling that he was only playing the game."

I nodded, but I wondered if it was the right thing to do when I caused so many issues in the place.

"Your father is proud of you, Evie. You can't fault him for wanting to show you off to his family."

"I know. It just seems like everything is getting out of hand."

"Weddings usually do."

There was another little problem that I hadn't thought of until we started talking about the service. Beatrice asked who I would want to walk me down the aisle. It was a tricky question.

My immediate response was Brad. After all, he was there for me when I lost my mother. It might have only been three years, but it was important. He could have refused to take me. At a time when he should be out enjoying his life, seeing the world, finding a partner, and settling down to start his own family, he took on the challenge of a surly teenager.

I could have ended up in an orphanage, but I didn't. Brad was the reason that I was here in this town. He was the reason that my life had been turned around for the better.

The issue that I faced was that there were two more in the argument. Niko would bow out by his own choice, stating that his role was a grandfather, and Beatrice said that he would not expect me to consider him. The problem was that I would. Niko meant so much to me that I wanted him to be a part of the important times in my life.

Then there was the man who was my father. We haven't had a conversation about the future yet, but I got the feeling that he knew that I would ask him to stay in Hades. I didn't hate him. I wanted him to be in my life. He was doing so much to improve my future. He was standing in my corner and had done so every time I needed him. Even when faced with possible rejection, he still did everything he could to keep me safe and give me the best chance at this life.

"I can't decide,"

"The dress?" Beatrice asked.

"No, who will walk me down the aisle. Every single part of me says that it should be Brad, but,"

"You feel like it would strengthen your burgeoning relationship with your father?"

"Yeah."

"Hey, it's Mister Harlwood," CJ said, waving with a wide grin.

James approached the window with a curious frown and then saw me. His eyebrows raised in shock. Moving to the door, he opened it with a smile.

"Perhaps congratulations are in order?"

"Uh, yeah. Grandfather and uncle might have ganged up on him."

James chuckled.

"Can I ask you something?"

"Of course."

James entered the dress shop, glancing around until Karina burst out of the dressing room with her usual bubbly self. She stopped and stared.

"Oh, hey, Mister Harlwood."

"Good afternoon, Karina. I take it that you will be wearing that to the service?"

"Yeah," she gushed.

"A lovely selection."

Karina nodded, quietly turning to look at the mirror.

"Now, your question?" James asked.

"It's likely that the service will be performed *out of town,*" I said, hoping he'd understand. "Because I think my father would like his family to attend."

"Of course. That is standard, though marriages are not really common for," he glanced at the shop owner, then leaned closer to whisper. "Us."

James straightened and looked at the woman. Like she was in a trance, she moved from behind the counter towards Karina to help her.

"I thought you could only suggest."

"That's correct. I suggested she help Karina. What's your question?"

"I can't decide between my father and Brad to take me down the aisle. It should be Brad, right?"

James sighed, giving me a sympathetic smile.

"I can see your dilemma and understand it completely. The man who raised you in your later teen years or the man who created you. I can also see your reasoning regarding your uncle. He has put a lot of effort into hiding you, keeping you safe, and, at the risk of his own life, brought you to this town. He stands beside you without fear, knowing what you are about to face and what is coming for you. He is the ally you've always needed, the trustworthy confidant who has always had your best interest in his heart and mind. On the other hand, there is your father. If he'd had the chance, he would have been the father you desperately needed. If he'd known where you were, he would have taken you under his wing and raised you, loved you, and given you everything you could have ever needed. He would have protected you and even your mother. He does it now. He will always do it. No matter what you say to him, Carsten will always go above and beyond to keep you safe."

"You're not making this any easier."

"I know. I merely point out that both are weighted heavily toward the pros rather than the cons. I suspect that, given the chance, you'd ask your great-grandfather as well."

"But he will refuse," Beatrice added. "Because he knows that it should be given to another."

My head fell into my hands as I groaned.

"I just want an answer that doesn't upset anyone."

"I can give you an answer, Evelyn. If you like it or not, I can't say. In fact, I can give you two answers."

I looked up with hope.

"The first is that you go down the aisle alone. Be honest with everyone. Tell them what they mean to you and how you are struggling to decide what is right. You might find that one will say the other should do it, which might solve your problem."

"And the other answer?"

"That you ask both of them. The building they will use is long enough to accommodate a walk with each of them. Perhaps even the nameless one who thinks he can escape this."

James smirked with a wink.

"Make them draw straws if you want to let fate decide the order."

"Oh my god, you are amazing."

I hugged James, and I think he was a little shocked at the gesture. When I let go, I smiled.

"You'll be there, right?"

"I would be honored to attend. And because we'll all be out of town, I will ensure that everything at the property remains vermin free, if you follow me."

He was being too nice when he called Drakkus vermin.

"Now, if you will excuse me, I have a mechanic to annoy."

When James was gone, the shop owner was free of his suggestion and had returned to the front counter. I joined Karina in front of the mirror. She wrapped her arms around mine, resting her head on my shoulder.

"Are you two now official and not hiding?"

She smiled, and I had to say, it was the sweetest smile she had. Love was a beautiful thing.

"We are," she whispered. "My mother is just worried about the war, and our past doesn't help. She's seen how sweet CJ is because he's always around now that he's protecting us."

"She's seen the real CJ?"

"Yeah. I never thought that I'd date a werewolf. Crazy, right?"

"Puh-lease. Before coming to this town, I didn't know that vampires existed or that I was related to one, partly one myself, among other things. Every part of this place is crazy."

"Okay, ladies. Enough gawping in the mirror. Lots to do, and there's only a few hours left in the day."

Beatrice ushered us into the dressing rooms, muttering about the shops in this town. It wasn't easy living in a town that shut down as quickly as what Hades did.

CHAPTER 41

In front of me were three men who stared like I'd lost the plot. I was holding out three straws that were numbered one to three. All they had to do was pick a straw, and it was their placement in the order.

"If I can interject," Niko began.

"No." I interrupted. "I refuse to decide because you all hold equal value to me."

"I was going to say I will start, so give me the straw with number one on it."

Beatrice smiled as I huffed and pulled out the straw.

"Fine."

"I will also dictate my placement," Carsten offered. "Because we know who should take the final leg of the journey."

He held out his hand with a supreme smile on his face. Taking the straw, he proudly poked it into the pocket of his jacket and turned it so that the number two was showing.

"I understand, Evelyn. If you'd asked each of us for our opinions, we would have all said Brad should do it. However, I also understand your reasoning for asking all of us. I am honored to be included and will graciously accept the second portion of the walk."

Gripping the arms of the chair, I slowly lowered myself into it, amusing everyone at the table.

"Yeah, you're all laughing, but this is your warning that I'm putting all of you on notice. Babysitting duties will be handed out regularly. Get your sleep while you can. I know I will be."

They all had their little chuckle, and even though I was tired and out of breath, I smiled.

"So, how was Galeth?"

"Incredibly annoyed because he finds it frustrating to deal with someone who knows the ins and outs of our world. Usually, when an offer is made, they're dealing with a novice who has no idea what to do or ask for. Like many in the Hallowed Halls, the hierarchy is full of contradictions and confusion. As for your offer, they have agreed to the terms, including the additions that I made."

That was a little startling, and I didn't expect that they'd agree so quickly.

"Although, he balked at the list I handed to him. With a little reminder of the rules and the past, he relented."

"What past?"

Carsten's smugness stilled as his attention turned to me. With a grimace, he shrugged.

"Belial. That whole debacle could have been prevented if they'd listened to Mother. She could feel your power growing and warned them they needed to protect you. They ignored her and chose to focus on the negative side of the situation. That's the reason that I shadowed you in the portal."

At the moment, I was grateful that Anzide was sleeping in the caravan. He was powering down for a couple of hours so that he could continue his nightly ritual of watching over the property and its occupants. With Carsten here to monitor the area, Anzide was able to rest without worrying about what was going on. He had earplugs in to drown out the sounds of everyone talking. I would have preferred to move away from the caravan, but Niko rarely ventured beyond the wall.

"It's the past, and we can move on from it."

"Of course. Galeth was reminded and agreed. The great hall will be available for you and Anzide to use for the service, although I don't know who will perform it. Have you considered that?"

"You don't have priests?"

"No."

"I have a thought, though it comes with an issue attached to it." Niko began. "Wicca is, in some circles, seen as a religion. If the mother of our werewolf friend is so inclined, she could perform the service. The issue is that she would be exposed to all the problems that come with a witch walking into the land of the Eternals."

"She leads a good life, doesn't she?"

"From my observations, yes."

I frowned at Niko.

"You've been watching CJ's mother?"

"All of them, actually. When this war is over, the coven will be returned to me, and I want to know what I face in these new recruits. In fact, they are already a part of this coven, yet we have not seen them. Why is that? If they are to be a part of the coven, they must present themselves to the leader and give their undying loyalty to them. I understand that the werewolves and the witch might not know the rules, but surely the friend that is a vampire does."

"I will talk to CJ about it when I see him next."

Niko frowned at me.

"Or I could send him a message. How's that?"

"Perfect."

Saying nothing but wanting to say so much, I picked up my phone and messaged him. I also sent a message to Karina so that she wouldn't think anything was going on. It was obvious that I wasn't interested, but I was determined not to cause issues.

"I was actually going to ask about CJ and his family.

They are considered a part of the coven, so I'm guessing it would probably be ideal that they're invited. Plus, Karina and CJ are together."

"You are right in suggesting that it would be ideal for them to attend. Ordinarily, coven members attend all functions, but as this is in the portal, it is a little different. Thankfully, there are only a few members in the coven at the moment, so if we can clear the way for them to attend, then you should invite them."

"I can speak with Mother about the suggestion and point out that this lady leads a quiet life and only practices white magic and bases herself deep within nature."

Lifting my gaze, I narrowed my eyes at my father.

"You've been watching her too."

He huffed, rolling his eyes.

"Yes, fine. I might have gone with Niko to see who these people were."

"It's like I don't know who you lot are anymore. You're spying on our coven members."

"Yes, Evelyn, that's our point. They are a part of our coven, and as a leader, it is your duty and, in turn, mine to know who our followers are. You walked in here and said they were members, and we can be grateful that James has selected them for us, but it is necessary to settle our minds with a little reassurance. You can argue until you are out of breath. It will not change how things are done."

"Whatever," I scoffed.

My phone had beeped. CJ had returned my message with his own, stating that they would be there soon.

"Well, I guess that I'm waking Anzide to check their minds."

"I can do it." Carsten offered. "Let Anzide continue to rest."

"It's fine,"

Anzide pushed the door open, rubbing his eyes.

"You guys need a little volume control. Especially miss angry pants here."

"They're spying on CJ and his family."

"I heard."

Anzide sat down, taking my hand. His thumb rubbed over the ring as he smiled at me.

"So, after all that, have we set a date?" Beatrice asked.

I shrugged.

"If I can get an agreement from the hierarchy regarding CJ's mother, then any time beyond that is possible." Carsten began. "Perhaps even as early as tomorrow."

"That might be ideal."

Because as if they knew that they were the reason for the rush, one of the babies pushed against the wall of my stomach. The little limb rose in the tiniest of peaks, highlighting the need to move quickly on this.

"I will go now and see what I can get out of them."

Carsten faded from his chair, and amusingly, perhaps sweetly, he still had the straw poking out from his pocket.

Car doors shutting could be heard long before Anzide said anything. He perked up and looked at Niko.

"Company."

Anzide rose to his feet, moving into the next section of the marquee.

"Are you staying or going?"

Niko sighed, looking to Beatrice for guidance. She smiled, reaching out to his hand.

"It's okay. CJ is such a wonderful boy, which has clearly come from being raised by two great parents. You know that it's not common for werewolves to associate with a vampire, but they are, so that must mean something, right?"

"I will admit that it is a curious situation."

Hearing noises and a conversation, I lifted from the chair and began the slow walk to the door. It had been a long afternoon of walking around clothing shops to buy clothes that would cover this growing belly. As I reached the doorway, my father appeared. He seemed happy, so I guess everything was okay.

"So?"

"Perhaps with our new friends, it would be less repetitious."

Carsten held open the curtain, and we walked out to greet CJ and his family. CJ stepped forward with an eager grin.

"Hey, Evie, Carsten. This is pretty cool, right?"

"Yeah, it sure is."

"Okay, so this is my dad, Julian, and my mother, Eda."

They both said hello, softly spoken but pleasant.

"And my younger brothers, Sebastian and Killian."

He said younger, but they matched him for height. They also looked like him with perfect olive skin and honey-colored eyes. Built like they all ran around with the football team, they towered over little old me.

"Are you guys triplets or something?"

They sniggered, shaking their heads.

"He's just stunted," Sebastian offered. "Wolfies are always big boys."

"I am not stunted," CJ grumbled. "Just ignore them. Behind them is our quiet mouse, Della."

Killian moved, and the vampire friend offered a shy smile. The woman who was after my heart. The woman who told Drakkus to find the tallest tree with the widest trunk and shove it up his ass. She was a legend, in my opinion.

"It's lovely to meet you all." I began. "I'm a little new to this whole leadership thing, so be ready for the craziness."

Because it's only going to get worse.

"This is my father, Carsten, and my partner Anzide. I don't know if Cooper said anything to you."

"I did. I said you were a magic bird."

"She's not a bird, CJ," Karina grumbled as she walked into the marquee.

She nodded at me with a grin.

"Thought you might be doing an impromptu meeting, so I brought my mother with me. She's bringing in snacks."

"Awesome."

I'd only eaten about half an hour ago, but I could definitely snack on a whole lot of everything right now.

"Anyway, technically, I am classed as an Eternal. It's a mixed bag, but the Eternal overrides everything. My father and Anzide are also Eternals."

Guiding everyone to the makeshift wall, I stopped and faced them.

"Beyond this wall are two secrets that you need to keep until the blood war is over. The first is my great-grandmother, who should be dead, according to Drakkus. In her life about town, she posed as Natalia Eastwell, but she is, in fact, Beatrice Corbin."

Stepping out from behind the curtain doorway, Beatrice said hello to everyone.

"You must be a shapeshifter," Eda offered.

"I am."

Eda seemed quite impressed.

"I didn't think I'd ever get to meet one."

"We are few in numbers, but we do exist. Mostly in Europe, though."

Pulling back the curtain, Beatrice waited for me to pass through before letting everyone in.

"And this is the second secret."

Niko stood, and I could see the shock on their faces. They knew what was in front of them. It was obvious that he was not human.

"My great-grandfather, Niko Corbin. Someone who should also be dead. Because of the blood war, he cannot return to the leadership. When it is over, I will be passing it back to him. We're telling you this so that you understand the changes that will happen in the future."

After everyone said hello to Niko, Julian turned to me.

"I can understand that if you doubt us, Evelyn. James said that you have issues, and I am not surprised. We've been burned by those who would have us believe the lies they tell us. We opened our minds to James, and we let him in without fear to ensure that we were completely honest. It is something that we will always offer. There are no malcontents in our family, and if there came a time when something bothered us, we would say something to you or to Niko."

"I am grateful to hear that, Julian. Please, find a seat at the table."

Niko and Beatrice had been busy searching for more chairs. I stood at the head of the table with Anzide and Brad on one side and Niko and Beatrice on the other. Once I sat down, everyone followed, which was a little weird.

"We asked you here for more than just to meet you. Anzide and I are going to marry, and because my father has many relatives, we agreed that it would be easier to go to the portal to wed. Those who manage the area have stated that they will allow safe passage for all immortals we invite, but we knew that you would hold an issue with that, Eda."

She nodded.

"So, I will pass it over to my father, who has spoken with the hierarchy regarding the subject."

Carsten cleared his throat, leaning forward on the table.

"They have stated that a new policy has come into effect. Each individual will be assessed as a case-by-case situation. I assured them that I have already conducted an inspection of your mind as well as the other individuals in your family. They are pleased with that and have cleared all of you to continue in their lives. You will not be subjected to any form of repercussion for your love or the creation of your children."

Eda and Julian looked at each other with relief. Julian gripped Eda's hand with a smile.

"See? James said coming here would be the best thing we could ever do."

Eda smiled.

"With that in mind, would you be interested in attending a wedding held in the portal?"

Eda and James looked at me curiously. Even Sebastian and Killian were a little confused.

"Are you sure?"

"You're a part of our coven."

Eda smiled. "We'd love to."

"Great, because I have a question for you as well."

"Okay," she said cautiously.

"You practice Wicca?"

"I do."

"Would you perform the service?"

She became quiet as the smile stalled. Her sons leaned forward, looking like they desperately wanted to know her answer. Della nudged Eda, who blinked hard.

"I can. I mean, I would love to, but don't you have

priests?"

"We don't," Carsten interjected. "You have been approved to perform a binding if you accept the offer."

"Yes," she said eagerly. "I can do that without a problem."

"Great. So, how's tomorrow for everyone?"

Silence hit the table as everyone stared at me. I certainly knew how to make a room quiet.

CHAPTER 42

I stood near the grandest of doors, nerves fraught while desperately clinging to Niko. Beyond the double doors inlaid with gold was a family I'd never met. Rows of my uncles, aunts, cousins, and a grandfather that I wouldn't know, even if I fell over them on the street.

I'd walk down the aisle while they looked at me, the stranger they were related to, the woman who caused chaos in their perfect world. Would they look at me with curiosity, love, or hatred?

The door opened, and Beatrice slipped out, quietly shutting the door again.

"Okay, so do you remember the plan?"

I nodded. We'd stayed up late discussing many things, but passing me to the next in the line was something that kept their attention for a while. I left them to it, preferring to go through the service with Eda. She agreed to keep it simple because, in the portal, time moves differently, and time was something that I did not have. No one knew if I would maintain the Earth time while I was in the portal or if it would speed up the pregnancy. The book said five months, but it never specified what would happen if the mother shifted between the areas.

"Alright then. I will see you both in there. Don't be too long."

Beatrice opened the door, and in her place, a servant stepped out. He would open the door when we approached, then close it behind us.

Niko faced me, taking my hands.

"My darling Evelyn, you have accomplished so much in the short time I have known you. In the coming days and weeks, you will continue to progress in your path, learning so many grand things. You will become a wife and mother. You will join my beloved Beatrice to be a powerful matriarch. All of it pales when compared to the love that you have shown me, and the faith that you gave me when you removed the brick. You trusted me when you knew nothing about me. I could never repay the debt that I have accrued. In that one moment, you changed my world. You returned me to this life, to my love, and to my family. I am proud to be your great-grandfather and honored to be included in your life."

"You know it's mean to make a pregnant woman cry on her wedding day, right?"

Niko smiled with a nod.

"I love you too," I whispered, hugging him hard.

Pulling away, I wiped the tears. Resting my hand on

Niko's forearm, we walked into the grand hall. Karina was behind me, fluffing out the dress, ensuring it was perfect.

"See you down there," she cooed.

The vibrant woman was already on her way, gliding down the aisle as if she owned the place and enjoyed the attention. I was looking for the nearest bucket to carry with me in case the nerves became too much.

Beatrice was standing near Carsten. The plan was that when we reached them, Niko would pass me to my father and then continue down the aisle with Beatrice, almost as if they were a part of the wedding party. It was an interesting way of doing it, and I hoped it worked.

My father didn't have a partner. I said he could ask a sister if he liked or a friend, but he said that one idea would cause a mini war to break out and the other was not appropriate in this situation. So, Mother was waiting with Brad.

Reaching Beatrice, she smiled and hugged me. I saw happiness in her eyes, but there was a hint of sadness as well. It occurred to me that she probably remembered when my grandparents married, that is, if she attended the wedding. Poor Niko didn't get to watch his daughter marry.

Niko and Beatrice began the path after Karina, leaving me to continue with my father.

"So, this is your family?"

"Our family."

There were at least a hundred people looking at me. It was unsettling and crazy to think that I was related to so many people.

"I spent years thinking that it was just me and *her*."

Was she my mother anymore? I don't know. The past was always going to be there to haunt me, but knowing the truth and how easily she could have changed everything was not easy. It soured the memories even more.

I had to grow. I wasn't going to forgive her for not doing the right thing, but I could let it go. Focusing on the good moments with her might seem wrong, but if I was ever going to get past it, I had to find positivity somewhere.

"I know, and I have spent all this time trying to change things. Perhaps together we can create a way to locate youngsters so this doesn't happen again."

I looked up at my father and smiled.

"I'd like that."

We were getting close to Brad and Mother.

"I know that it's probably not the right time, but when the war is over, I was hoping you might want to stay in Hades."

"Nothing would give me greater pleasure. Thank you for letting go of the past and accepting that it was not what you believed it was."

I nodded, trying not to cry. I'd be a blubbering mess by the time I got to Anzide if I wasn't careful.

Mother stepped forward as Carsten moved to the side. Her robes were pristine white, and her usually scattery and unkempt hair was in a tidy bun. Passing the staff to Brad, Mother gripped my shoulders, looking at me with a smile which made me think that she believed I was up to no good.

"Today, you stand before your kin, knowing them as strangers no more. You have always been of the first line, but today, you know that it is the truth, and it is acknowledged by your kin. This is the family that has been waiting to meet you for eighteen years. Welcome to the family."

"Thank you."

I think.

She nodded firmly and turned to take back her staff. Carsten handed me to Brad for the final part of this journey. It was taking longer than I expected, but then, I didn't know that Mother would have something to say or that Carsten and Niko would get all soppy.

"You know, when the lady from child services rang to say that because I was your only living relative that she could locate, and I could take you in, I didn't think that this was where we would end up three years later. Crazy, right?"

"You've got that right," I muttered.

"Look at us. Two lost souls from the wrong side of the tracks. Vampires, shapeshifters, werewolves,"

"Biblical creatures and blood wars."

"We can run for the doors, right now. Give them all the middle finger while we're hightailing it to a little island in the middle of nowhere. Vampires can't swim, right?"

I grinned at Brad.

"I don't think that's correct. Besides, you're a vampire now."

"Damn. I suppose that we should just keep going, then. This aisle is the longest I've ever seen. Who built this place?"

I chuckled, unable to hide my amusement.

"Someone that knows how many relatives I have, apparently."

We were almost at the end of the aisle. Karina waited with so much eagerness that I think the smile was now permanent. Anzide watched with love and happiness. Cooper was behind him. I thought it was sweet that Anzide suggested him for this role. Things were still new between us, but nothing was going to change. I could see that he was always going to be around. That aside, they were getting along really well. I'd seen them standing at the fence line facing the house. Anzide was pointing at it, and I guess they were talking about the changes we might make.

Cooper wrapped his arm around Anzide, almost strangling him. The wild grin was amusing. Cooper said something, and it made Anzide smile even more. With a hearty pat with his free hand, Cooper stepped back. Yep, they were solid friends now. God help us if Cooper and Karina break up.

The thought of problematic relationships made me think about Brad and Nora. Niko said that vampires always considered a long future when they started a relationship. Both Brad and Nora were new to the world of being a vampire. Did that mean that it applied to them as well, or was it not the case?

I turned my head to look at Brad. All that I've wanted for him was to be happy. His life had become chaotic when I was thrown at him. A surly teenager who, despite the issues, missed her mother. She didn't cope with the stranger, who was supposedly her uncle. She didn't like having to move yet again.

Things improved when I realized that Brad wasn't like my mother. He cared, and he wanted me to find peace with the world. We didn't move as much as what I used to when I was with my mother. Life was a fraction more stable.

"So, there's something that we need to discuss."

"And now is clearly the best time for it. So, what's up?"

Brad cleared his throat, giving me his patented sheepish smile.

"Nora's pregnant," he whispered.

"Oh my god, Bradley, you tart."

"Says the woman pregnant with twins."

Naturally, I rolled my eyes. It seemed the obvious thing to do.

"You're the only one who knows, so don't say anything."

"Even Karina?"

"Yeah. I think Nora's going to tell her soon."

So, I really was getting a cousin.

"Glad to hear that kneeing you didn't stop the production."

"Evie," he grumbled.

He was blushing, and I giggled.

"I'm glad that you're my uncle."

Brad smiled at me.

"And you're going to be an awesome father," I whispered.

"Thanks. I suppose you're an okay niece."

He chuckled before leaning in to kiss my cheek.

"I'm kidding. You're amazing. Now, be nice to him. He's a newbie, apparently."

Brad offered my hand to Anzide, and when I looked at Brad, I saw a smile, but there was something else there, too.

"Good luck."

Anzide held my hand as I stepped closer.

"What was that?" I whispered.

"Just one of those fatherly conversations that ensured I behaved myself."

"Of course. Was it one or three that ganged up on you?"

"Three," he murmured.

I rolled my eyes. It made me wonder what they said to him.

Eda stepped forward.

"Good afternoon, friends and family. Please, be seated."

As everyone sat down, I looked around the vast room. The front rows on either side were filled with my family and our coven, as well as James. Beyond that, it was nothing but a sea of unfamiliarity.

"We welcome all who have come in peace and love to witness the union of Anzide and Evelyn. Together, we celebrate the love they have for each other and the bond that they have created. Today, you will bear witness to their union, represented by the exchanging of rings and handfasting. Bring forth the rings."

Cooper patted his pocket, frowning as if he'd forgotten them. Giving his mother a goofy grin, he reached in and pulled them out of a different pocket. She subtly rolled her eyes and took the bag from him.

Last night, Eda had borrowed them for a little while, leaving the property. She took the rings to the witches' circle and charged them under the moonlight.

Carefully, she opened the white satin bag and placed each ring in our waiting hands.

"With this gold, Anzide and Evelyn show their union, love, and connection to each other. It is a promise to protect, to nurture, and to love unconditionally. Wear them as a symbol of your promise to each other."

As I slid the ring onto Anzide's finger, I thought about our conversation yesterday. I would have been happy with just the ring Anzide gave me, but he said that he liked the idea of what a wedding band represented. There were no expectations for either of us, but we agreed that it was something we wanted.

"Anzide and Evelyn have selected a simple binding verse that represents their love today and into their eternal future together."

Reaching to the table, Eda pulled the long rope that we'd hurriedly created last night. It was a mixture of everything she and Nora could find in their homes. Ribbons, string, and thin rope. It was colorful, and I thought it was perfect. Each of the different types of material could represent different parts of our lives, the people in it, and how our future would be interwoven with them.

Anzide and I clasped our hands.

"Repeat after me, together. With this bind, I will entwine your hands into mine."

Anzide and I smiled at each other as we repeated the words together.

"For I will be yours, and you will be mine, until the end of time."

We repeated the words again as Eda continued to wrap the bind around our hands. She tucked the end in under the binding and then raised her hands.

"We have heard the commitment that Anzide and Evelyn have made to each other. If anyone should disagree with the union, speak now or forever hold your peace."

There was silence, which was just as well. I think that there would be a brawl if something was said. Would I be the instigator? Perhaps.

Eda smiled.

"So it is done. Anzide, Evelyn, you have stood before your family and friends to declare your love and commitment to each other. I now proudly state that you are bonded as partners, equal in life and love. Go forth into your future with happiness and cherish every moment you share. Seal your bonding with a kiss."

Both of us were grinning like we were seconds away from giggling. Anzide leaned forward, kissing me softly.

It was beautiful and crazy, just like everything else in our life.

CHAPTER 43

I didn't expect that a party would erupt like it had, but I probably should have. After the service ended, the chairs were shifted, and tables were added. A dance floor was created, and staff started bringing in meals. They were efficient and fast, serving what seemed like fifty tables within minutes.

We ate, we talked, we laughed. I got to meet a lot of my family and, of course, my grandfather. In Haureth, I could see a lot of myself. The more I looked around at the figures in the vast room, the more I was grateful that I'd accepted my father. He was giving me the family that I'd always craved. Sure, I had Brad, Niko, and Beatrice but this was something else. It was a family on the grandest of scales. I didn't have a family tree. I had a family forest.

After dinner, we had dessert. Not only was it the cake we'd cut, but a wide variety of little cakes, tarts, cookies, and pies. They'd set up a vast table full of sweets and candies, plus another that was full of fruit.

My feet were tired after dancing with Anzide, so I

helped myself to a pile of candy and fruit, as well as a few little treats from the dessert table. And, of course, this girl had to have a piece of her wedding cake. It was tradition, right?

My feet were up, and Anzide was next to me, picking away at his own plate of food. We were at the far end of the room, which had a broad balcony. It was the strangest view, and it blew my mind when Anzide told me they'd created a window that reflected a view of space. I couldn't reach the window, I couldn't alter it, but I had an insane view of the galaxy.

Hearing a noise, I turned to the sound of the glass door opening. Music flowed out as Karina slipped through the door and closed it again.

"I was going to ask why you're sitting in the dark, but now that I'm here, I can see why. That's one crazy-ass view, right?"

"It sure is."

She sat down and began unwrapping the little candies that were from the table that I did not go to. It was designed for the vampires, and I don't know how they did it, but Karina was eating a blood candy.

"So, apparently, I'm going to be a big sister."

"We're not alone."

"At this point, I don't care."

For a bubbly person, it was not the view that I expected. I glanced at Anzide, and he pursed his lips with a smile. No doubt he was in her mind and could see what was troubling her.

"I guess that Nora must be pretty happy."

Because she seemed happy every time I looked at her. To be fair, she was either eating at the table with Brad or dancing with him. They were still in the new love phase, so it was only natural to see them both smiling.

"I suppose."

"You seemed pretty excited a few days ago. What changed?"

"It's really happening. I guess that it didn't occur to me that it would. Don't get me wrong, I'm happy for them, but it just feels,"

"Like you're being left behind? Forgotten? That someone is taking over your world, you're no longer the center of your mother's life, and you'll struggle to get her attention?"

Karina looked up at me and nodded grimly.

"You know, Brad felt the same about Anzide. If there's anyone that understands what you're feeling, it's him."

"I guess. The problem is that they're also talking about the future. Specifically, the house that Brad's buying. They've already talked about us moving in before the baby is born. I know that they're not going to kick me out or anything,"

"Because Niko would have to fight me to be the one

that gave Brad a smack across the back of his head if it happened. His would be a verbal one, but I prefer to ensure that everyone knows my thoughts in the most physical way possible."

Karina giggled.

"Yeah, that. I just get the feeling that it's going to be like a little bubble of the two of them until the baby is born, and then it's going to be the three of them. I'm going to be like this third wheel that's welcomed to stay but looked at like I'm overstaying. And, like some bizarre twist, I'm forced to endure a conversation where she asks if things are progressing with Cooper. I mean, we've barely started dating. We're both still in school, and she's spent the entire time up until that point stressing about him being a monster. Then she goes and throws that at me. It just makes me think that she's trying to gauge my thoughts about moving out."

"Perhaps a conversation is what you need."

Karina yelped as she gripped her chest, staring at the darkness near the balcony.

"What the freaking hell?"

Niko walked over and sat down.

"I told you that we weren't alone."

"Yeah, but I thought you meant the couple down there. Not mister blends into the shadows and stays silent while I spill my guts out everywhere."

"I apologize if my presence was not obvious enough

for you, but I was here because this view is something I may not get to see again, and it is truly breathtaking. Before we discuss your mother and Brad, I want to ask you if you've thought about your future. Do you intend to remain in Hades, or will you go to university for a few years?"

"I don't know. Cooper said there was a scout at the last training session, and he was looking for the next big thing. He was watching Cooper a lot, apparently."

"Does that mean that if Cooper was scouted, you'd follow him wherever he moved to?"

Karina shrugged.

"I ask because my question was about your future, yet your answer was uncertain, and then it shifted to be all about Cooper. It leads me to think that there is a lot of confusion. If you planned to follow Cooper, you wouldn't care what happened with Brad and Nora because you wouldn't be here. So, either you think that Cooper is not going to be scouted, will refuse to remain here, or that you won't follow him. Let's start with answering that one."

"Cooper said he's not going to accept any offers. Para's can't be exposed like that."

"A wise assessment that is true. If something happened on the field, thousands could see it, whereas here in Hades, it would be hundreds at most. The obscuris veil will help him hide anything like a broken leg that instantly repairs. Outside of this town, he's not going to have that kind of help. If the world sees this young man with a broken leg one day and a fully repaired leg the next, they're going to ask questions. Now that we've established that Cooper is not your issue, what else is there? Do you feel like Brad has taken over as the top priority in your mother's life?"

Karina shrugged, giving a vague nod.

"It is understandable, but can I point out that your mother would have felt the same about Cooper? You mentioned that she was stressing out about him being a monster. It is possible that it was her way of coping with you growing up and finding your feet in this wide world. She would know that when paranormals fall in love, it's rare to have major issues that become catastrophic. Nora would have looked at you with Cooper, and she would have seen the future easily. It would explain why she was trying to gauge your thoughts, subtly searching to see if you had figured it out or what was happening."

"Yeah, I guess," she murmured.

Karina looked at me, and I gave her an awkward smile. Niko was way better at this than I was.

"There is a thought that has occurred to me, and I don't know if you'd considered it."

"Oh?"

"A place of your own. Think about it from an outsider's perspective, one that has seen how quickly love can form, and once that happens, entire worlds can shift. She sees that you've started dating Cooper. It might progress, but it could fall by the wayside and become nothing. It is unlikely though because you're both a part of the coven and she probably thinks that you'd want to avoid any problematic interactions with Cooper if the relationship failed. So, she thinks you're planning for a long future with him. He's been staying with you and Nora has seen that he's a nice boy, he's well behaved and he is everything that she hoped you would find in a partner. Then, she looks at those around her. She looks at the friend you've made and how Evelyn's getting married and about to have children. She wonders if you're going to get clucky and yes, I know that you've got tests and you've got all these things going on, but look at our darling Evelyn. She lives to ignore everything that is deemed normal, and with her as an example, it's only natural that your mother might think that it's going to happen."

I poked my tongue at Niko, which made him smile.

"The writing is on the wall, right? This is only going to end one way. What does a mother do when she is faced with something like that? She thinks. She plans. She formulates. She speaks. Brad comes along and says sure, we've got the funds in the coven bank account, and once I get the okay from Grandpa, we can swing this."

Wait, what? I frowned at Niko, and he ignored me with his smarmy smile that said he was up to no good again.

"So then Grandpa sits down with an old demon friend," James said as he emerged from the shadows.

Karina didn't jump with fright, but she did scowl at me. I shrugged.

"I told you that we weren't alone."

Rolling her eyes, she waited for James to sit down on the seat next to Niko.

"And he agreed to extend the spell he'd placed over the coven bank account for a little longer so that a house can be bought."

I gasped, looking at Anzide.

"Corbin Avenue," I said with a wide grin.

The trio opposite us looked at us like we were crazy.

"We were talking about buying all the houses in the street for our kids because the house only has three bedrooms, and we've already filled them. We thought it would be cool to call it Corbin Avenue."

Niko had a dubious frown on his face as he nodded slowly. Then he turned back to Karina.

"There is more to the situation, though. It will belong to the coven, and you will pay rent, but that money will be considered a mortgage payment. Once you've repaid the purchase price, it will be your house. It is up to you if you decide to take this offer jointly with Cooper."

"You do realize that if you offer it to one coven member, you have to offer it to all, right?"

Niko turned as he nodded.

"Yes, we discussed that as well. As much as a street full of coven houses is a nice idea, it isn't wise to be so centralized. Nora has agreed to create a plan for the town with the houses that are currently for sale with the agency. Once I have returned to the world, I will be able to access my bank account, which has grown beyond my expectations. We will hold a coven meeting after the war, but the offer will begin with those who are a part of the coven at this moment. In time, we can revisit the situation based on the vampire and how long they've been a part of the coven. Essentially, I see this as a reward to those who have stood by you and will continue to do so in the coming days. A house that comes with an interest-free mortgage and an easy going repayment schedule. We can begin with you if that is something you'd like, Karina."

"My own house?" she whispered.

"If that is what you desire. Don't mistake any of this as an attempt to boot you out the door. Your mother has been making herself quite upset regarding the whole subject, and despite Brad's efforts to reassure her that you will always have a place in their home, she knows that it's only going to cause problems. They have discussed an extension, a granny flat, and even converting the room above the garage. Your mother wants to talk to you about it, but she fears that you will react adversely, damaging your relationship with Brad and their unborn child possibly even causing issues with Evelyn and the coven. She will always want you in her home, but your mother understands that at some point, her baby bird has to stretch her wings. It's difficult to know what to do when there are so many unanswered questions. Like I said, perhaps a conversation is what you need."

CHAPTER 44

It was a new day. No honeymoon for me or Anzide. It was back to business. For today, that was the sparring room.

People leaned in, whispering to each other as I walked through the portal. It was crazy to think that I was probably related to all of them, if not most. Carsten walked next to me, proudly showing off his daughter without a word said. The smile on his face and the kick in his step said he was one happy daddy.

As we drew closer to the stairs, I watched in amazement as people began rushing to the other stairs. There was already a long line along the corridor. People leaned against the rail to watch me. There was an element of excitement in the air. It was palpable, like a thick veil in the air.

"Are they going into the viewing room?"

"They are. That's the queue for the nosebleed section, and it's a first come, first served. Beyond that, they can line up at the windows. It's an appalling view, but for the desperate, anything is better than nothing."

"You'd think that they'd build something to cope with everyone. I guess that would take a brain cell or two."

Carsten smiled at me as we began to walk up the stairs.

"It was built when there were fewer of us. They've been busy."

"Yeah, I guess they have," I murmured, looking at the crowd.

There wasn't going to be enough space. Slowly, the darkness consumed the glassed walls, creating a cover that would alter whatever situation we created. Given I was going up against a vampire, it would be the night sky.

Carsten logged us into the sparring room while I suited up. Pulling a coverall suit from the shelf, Carsten gestured to the spell chart on the wall.

"Familiarize yourself with what is on the board. Think about what you can use against Drakkus. You might even want to think about spells that you can create for yourself. In this environment, we can talk about it and practice it straight away. Maybe even bounce ideas off each other, and create perfect spells. I've booked the afternoon for you so you can relax and think about your approach and what you want to try out."

"Well, I was actually thinking about it this morning. Kannon has been adamant that Drakkus is going to win. I think he will be there. I mean, he said that he'd be standing over my dying body, so there's that."

"And with that, we can assume his parents will be there. Any thoughts on the other followers?"

"I met a few vampires who were acting as guards, but nothing specific. Did you talk to James?"

"He mentioned that he walked through the coven house, but there weren't many vampires there. I think to get any real idea about the numbers, you'd need to be there when he's holding a mandatory meeting. James said he would keep an eye on it, but to be realistic, he can't give us every single minute of the day, nor should he. James wants you to be the leader, but he needs a degree of separation from the clan."

"What about you?"

"I am different because I am related to the leader. It's a gray area that we are using to our advantage."

The door opened, and a man entered the sparring room. He gave us a nod and waited.

"Evelyn, this is Horatio, and he is a spell creator like yourself. When you are fully immersed in our world, you will work closely with him to learn your trade. He will be one of a few teachers that you will learn under."

I said hello with an uneasy smile. Horatio appeared to be a no-nonsense kind of guy.

"He's here to help you. I spoke with him about your issue and how you can enter this room and face off against me, but it doesn't give you a real view of the situation you could face. So, he thought about it and created a spell for you to go against. Horatio, if you will."

With another nod, he stepped forward. The walls of the room darkened, and the view of the forest returned. Horatio's legs parted into a firm sparring stance, and his hands clasped at the far left of his body. The right hand waved through the air, and with a gush of powdery black wind, the forest filled with shapes. Bodies of varying height and size. With a curl of his index finger, the last figure emerged. This one stood out from the others.

Moving his legs together, Horatio nodded and left the room.

"This is a rough guess on how many Drakkus has in his coven based on what James has seen around town over the past few weeks. The prominent figure is a representation of Drakkus. Each of these shapes will move, flee, and attack, but Drakkus will be much more brutal towards you. Before I say the word to start the fight, tell me your plan."

"Well, I suppose that without Drakkus telling them what to do, most of those vampires will either leave Hades or come crawling for forgiveness. I think that I would like to try and keep as many followers as I can get, for Niko's sake."

"Even if they are the ones that took part in the treachery?"

"I don't think any of those vampires are around anymore."

My father looked at me curiously, tilting his head to the side.

"James would have entered their minds once Hannah left. He would have seen who knew. If there was anyone that was worthy of death, he would have asked to include them in my list."

"Yes, I suppose that James has already started the search. You might find that a few vampires will go missing if they were involved. Okay, so you want to weed out those who you want to spare from the bloodbath. That means that you need to separate them from Drakkus and the Lothaire family. Do you recall anything from the list that might help?"

My mind sorted through the images like a fast filter, stopping when I reached the Ring of Fire spell. It was a fire that would burn tall as soon as it was shot out. All I had to do was cast the spell around the people I wanted to trap, and it would remain high until I lowered it. That is, once I figured out how to make my hands do as they were told.

"Ring of Fire," I offered.

My father nodded with an appreciative smile. Raising his hands, he created a mini scene between us. With his finger, he curled it around the figures that represented Drakkus and the Lothaire's. It flamed blue, casting a soft hue over the darkened figures.

"A good selection. So, you cast the Ring of Fire to encase Drakkus and the Lothaire's. What next?"

"Well, the Lothaire's haven't done anything seriously wrong, so I can't legally destroy them. The most that I can do, according to Niko, is banish them."

"Would you attend to that first or last?"

"Last. I want Kannon to see me win. I want him to know how wrong he really is."

"And you should attend to them last as well, regardless of the issues you have with Kannon. I indulged in a little bit of light reading last night, and according to the law that the European vampires follow, there is an order that must be maintained. From the leader down to the lowest subordinate, that is how you accuse, judge, and sentence. Curiously, though, you can undertake the trial for the Lothaire's as a group rather than individually. Their crimes are exactly the same so there is a ruling that states that any members within a family that are charged with the same crime, and are likely to be found guilty or innocent as a group, can be judged as one. Thoroughly fascinating, you should read the series when,"

Carsten looked at me and then at the belly that was a little more prominent than it had been the last time he saw me.

"You probably won't have a spare moment for a while. Well, I'm sure it can wait. Tell me the plan after the Ring of Fire."

"Beyond the trial and Drakkus is found guilty, I have to kill him. I don't want to get too close, so I need to create a sharp implement to impale his heart, then remove his head."

"Well, start with the first before thinking about the big picture. You have this area," Carsten said as he enlarged the smaller version of Drakkus.

His finger circled the heart area on the figure.

"However, there is a slight dilemma with this situation. The physiology of a vampire is slightly different in this area. The gaps between the ribs are narrower. If you plan to impale Drakkus, your strike range goes down to this."

Carsten scrubbed out the circle and created another. This time, it was more like a thin oblong.

"What can you create?"

It had to be thin, but it could be wide.

"A sword." I offered.

"Remember, in a youngling like yourself, a spell draws from the surroundings that they can pull easily to them. We cannot wait for time to pass so that you can age and learn how to draw minerals from the ground."

"Okay, so I could form it into ice."

"Interesting. It has an element of rigidity, but you would have to remain mindful that ice can be broken or melted. You would have to actively maintain a high level of frost to ensure that the body temperature doesn't destroy the blade, but it can be done. Okay, I like it."

The small figure was impaled by a long ice shard.

"Do you think you can draw enough water to create

and maintain the ice blade between yourself and the target?"

I nodded. Holding up my hand, I felt the pull in my fingers as I dragged the water to me. My hand felt incredibly cold as it began to form the ice. It didn't take long for the blade to rise into the air. Long, sharp, deadly.

As soon as it was created, I sent a shot of warmth through it. Water dropped to the leaf litter below my hand.

"Well done. So, we've established that you will impale Drakkus with the ice blade, which leaves us with the final blow. I assume you don't want to get too close with that either?"

I shook my head. The further I was away from him and the blood-spurting mess, the better. Carsten moved in front of me, forming a sword made of wood. He held it at arm's length and then moved forward.

"With a sword," he said, moving to the side of the sword that hung in the air next to me. "This is how close you could get. Is that something that you can handle?"

"No."

The sword disappeared as my father moved back to face me.

"Then you need to think of a weapon that is effective at a distance. Alternatively, you can create something like a wooden sword and send it flying through the air. You would have to be fast, but if the wood had a sharp edge, it could work."

"What about a whip?"

"There are no cows here or in Hades to make leather."

"I could make it from something else."

"Like?"

"How about the moon?"

My father was silent as he stared at me.

"Evie," he said softly. "I don't want to discourage you, but younglings should harness the products available to them in their environment. Calling the moon to you is no small feat. Not only is it a celestial body that has its own rules when it comes to interacting with this land, but it is so far away. It would be easier for you to call iron. I won't stop you, and the idea certainly has merit,"

Carsten paused, looking at me with fear. A soft smile filled his face.

"You know what? The moon is up, she's shining bright, and you are stronger than others who are at your stage of learning. Go for it. Are you ready to begin the mock fight?"

I nodded. Carsten let go of the miniature version of these figures, then stepped back.

"Final check."

"I'm good to go. Call it."

Carsten smiled at me.

"Pumpkin pie."

I frowned but was quickly distracted by the advancing figures. Throwing out the blue flames, I watched as it surrounded the figures, subduing them. They could not go beyond the flames.

Taking a moment, I calmed myself down now that they were contained. Drawing water from the air, I sliced through the chest with ease. Now, all I had to do was call the moon to me, to make it obey my request. I looked up at it and wondered if I'd bitten off more than I could chew.

CHAPTER 45

Carsten sat on the floor with me. A blanket over our shoulders protected us from the cool night air, and several underneath us gave warmth instead of cold backsides.

To give me a degree of tranquility, we were in the dining room of the house. The frame hid the stars, but our old friend, the moon, was visible in the sky to my right.

We were outside as Carsten suggested that meditation would help me connect to the moon. If I wanted to perfect the whip, I had to visualize a line between us. We were here because no matter how much I tried, I could not make the moon submit to me.

I suspect that Carsten wanted to say that it was okay and that I expected too much of myself but probably thought that it was better to be encouraging. The only thing that he said in the sparring room when I gave up was that I could always use the ice to do the job. I accepted it but wondered if I could get the ice sharp enough. It's why I said that I wanted to try to connect to the moon.

Carsten warned me against anything physical. Not only was I not ready for it, but he knew that there was a vampire sitting in a car a few houses away. We were being watched.

I wanted to say that I was surprised, but in truth, I wasn't. If I had the ability or the followers to watch the enemy, I'd take that path. Learning everything I could was something that I needed.

With a heavy sigh, I opened my eyes. My father was already looking at me with a smile.

"I know. You yearn to practice with the real moon but can't because of the audience. I have an idea. It will work in the sense that you will be able to create a connection, but it's problematic because of the location."

"Where?"

"The forest connects to the next town. Drakkus won't extend his spying beyond the borders when he knows that everyone he wants to watch is right here in this town."

"So, what's the problem?"

"You are the leader of this town. Technically, you shouldn't leave if you're in the middle of a blood war. The portal doesn't count, if you're wondering."

I was, actually.

"Will he know?"

"Yes. There is always a connection between the two parties. Usually, neither notices it, and I've not found any instances where a vampire has been able to detect it in any other circumstances. The only time anyone has noticed it is when one leaves the town. Unfortunately, it seems we are in a bit of a bind here."

"Yeah," I muttered.

Carsten stared at me for a moment and then smiled.

"Give me a moment."

Closing his eyes, he sat in front of me, unmoving and silent. When they reopened, his smile grew.

"Okay, I did a quick scan of the area, and our friend is the only one. Now, we can wait until he gives up and goes home, but I have a feeling that a replacement will move into the spot, so, with that in mind, I did a little alteration myself. There is a shield over the car that has a view of us that you could almost say is like a recording. I will know if the shield is broken, and it will remain there until I remove it. I'd suggest that you focus and get this done because if he's a smart one, he will figure it out pretty quickly. So, off you go. Onto the grass and give that whip a crack."

Flicking off the blanket, I stood and walked onto the grass. Carsten remained at the house, leaning on the frame.

With a swish of his hand, a shape appeared on the lawn. It was tall like Drakkus, made from a dark crystal-like sand, and shimmered in the moonlight.

"Focus your mind, don't worry about our friend. I am monitoring him, and I am watching the land as well. If something changes, I will tell you to stop. Okay?"

I nodded and took a deep breath in. Settling my mind, I remembered what my father said. Focus. Visualize a line between myself and the moon. I didn't have to be accurate. I just had to see it.

The line was formed, and I could feel the energy buzzing through me. My arms were the first to tingle, and soon, my fingers felt as if I had pins and needles. With my right hand, I curled my fingers and formed a circle as if I were holding a whip.

I could feel it growing, taking shape. When my hand burned with a frostiness that was nothing like I'd ever experienced, I knew the whip was ready.

Opening my eyes, I threw the line out with a flick. The sound of the whip cracked, but it was the most pathetic sound I'd ever heard. It was difficult to see the mark on the dark figure, but the essence of the whip left a trail behind, highlighting that I'd left a gash along the body.

My lips twitched with disappointment. If that happened when I was going against Drakkus, he'd complain that it hurt but would, unfortunately, still be alive.

"Again," Carsten called out.

The dummy reformed and was no longer marked. I formed the whip faster and put more swing into it. As the long line of glistening white curled through the air and flicked against the body, a crack sounded. This time, it was better, sounding like it should.

The mark was longer but still over the torso. I wasn't aiming high enough, but at least this time, the whip was long enough to cut through the figure.

"Better. Go again."

It was difficult to avoid letting out a frustrated huff. Instead, I exhaled slowly and took the time to refocus. I thought about where my issues were and knew that I had to lift my arm higher.

When I was ready, I flicked the whip and watched as it took the top of the head off. I'd gone too high. Groaning, I rolled my head back, which amused my father.

"By the time you're done with him, he'll be a dozen pieces on the ground."

"Yeah, thanks for that."

Carsten walked over to me and gripped my shoulders.

"You are overthinking it and not focusing on where you need to. Form the whip and dictate where it needs to be. Every part of this spell is yours to decide. You are the creator. You are the one who sets the rules and forms the boundaries of the spell. Once more for tonight."

I nodded, and Carsten stepped back. Going through the motions again, I focused on where I wanted the whip to land.

As the long white line flicked out, I watched it pass by the figure. The crack was loud, and it made me wonder if it was enough to alert the distracted vampire that something was going on here. I hoped not.

It seemed like time stood still as I watched the whip dissipate, and the figure stood as if nothing had changed. Then, the head slowly slid from the body, and a clapping echoed. Slow but not taunting. It was one of muted jubilance.

When I turned to my father, I saw that he was ecstatic but trying to play it down. I don't think he was trying to make it seem like it was nothing but probably closer to keeping me level-headed so that I would continue to improve my craft.

"Well done, Evelyn. You have shown remarkable skill, and you should be proud that after only a few attempts, the spell has succeeded in its real world trial. That beautiful beast up there, she's a difficult one to command. This is why Galeth was tripping over his feet to ensure you agreed to the placement. He also knows that the darker side of this life was always lingering, especially if Belial gets his hands on your power. You would be in a submissive state, easily coerced and controlled while he held all your power. He would have become near-on unstoppable. With you accepting a life within the Hallowed Halls, Galeth can ensure that you will always have mentors watching over you, caring for you, and ensuring that your power grows in the light, not in the darkness."

"Yeah, I guess he would have been freaking out."

"To be fair, Galeth could scratch himself and freak out."

I chuckled, thinking, as horrid as it was, it would be funny to see.

"Now, we will repeat this lesson every night to ensure that you get as much practice as you can. Moonlight whips are not exactly a new spell, but they are so hard that no one ever bothers with them. Unfortunately, it also means that no one teaches them. As for mastering it so quickly, it is one of those situations where you can't claim the spell as your own, but you can certainly claim success. I might add that there are only a few in all of our history that have ever been able to achieve this milestone. Making that one up there do your bidding, that's a mighty feat."

I watched as the figure crumbled into nothing. As much as I felt tired, I wanted to practice more. It wasn't going to happen, and I don't think it was because Carsten had grown bored of it. I think it had everything to do with the vampire in the car watching this property.

There was a sinking dread inside of me that this was going to boil over soon. Something was in the air, nipping at me and whispering that it was only a matter of time.

"And you should know that because you are what they call an unstable and untrained creator, the Soldiers of the Hallowed Halls will always have someone watching what you do regarding the spells. They will see the attempts, make a notation, and it will become a part of your record. You showed control, you listened to your teacher, you were focused and you learned from your mistakes. There were no outbursts, no damage, and no issues. All these are things that will work in your favor. I know that it's only a couple of attempts, but it shows that you're not as unstable as what they think you are."

"My emotions played heavily into what happened with the house."

"It is understandable. In their own way, those in the Hallowed Halls know that the situation was out of control, and they are partly to blame. Had they explained the situation better, the outcome might have been different."

I looked at my father with a raised eyebrow and a grin.

"Are you sure about that? Remember, they were taking Anzide from me."

With a soft laugh, he nodded.

"Yeah, I guess nothing would have changed."

Wrapping the blanket around my shoulders, I wandered back to the marquee. Anzide was seated in the section at the far end of the area. We'd purchased flywire to keep the bugs out but raised one of the panels to look beyond the canvas walls. It was sectioned off from the rest of the area so Niko could still walk around if the panel was raised.

Anzide unzipped the panel and waited for us to enter.

"That was amazing. For as long as I've known they've existed, I've always wanted to see a moonlight whip. Never thought I would, though."

"Evelyn has shown remarkable talent with her skills.

She will be a formidable foe on the battlefield."

Carsten smiled, continuing through to the main section of the marquee.

Anzide watched for a moment, then turned back with a grin. Pressing his hand to his heart, he patted it.

"Beating so hard. I was on the edge of my seat. Watching you is incredible. I've seen you stand up to Audrey, Kannon, Drakkus, the Nephilim, Delray."

"Belial."

"Yes," his eyes widened. "Belial used to be so powerful, and you trapped him in a spell."

"Used to be?"

Anzide shrugged as he sat down. My hand was in his, following him to the lounge.

"The restraints subdue power, but as punishment, he was literally, in every sense of the word, stripped of his powers. So were my parents. They are pretty much useless eternals now. In a place like that, it's not a good thing. Enough of them. This is the Evie show."

I hummed a soft chuckle, snuggling into his arms.

"It's always the Evie show, silly boy."

CHAPTER 46

Karina and I were seated in the lunchroom as CJ entered through the swing doors. I tipped my head in his direction, wordlessly telling Karina that there was something interesting. She looked over her shoulder, turning back with blushed cheeks. CJ had seen her looking at him and given her a smirk in return. Slowly, her eyes lifted to me and my amusement.

"Don't say anything," she whispered. "But maybe he might not have slept in his own bed last night."

I grinned with a waggle of my brows, and her cheeks flushed just a little harder.

"Evie," she chided.

"Hey, I'm the one that's pregnant with twins. Pretty sure it's obvious that I've been sharing my bed as well."

Karina gave me a one-shoulder shrug as she lowered her gaze to the meal in front of her.

"Are you okay with what happened?"

Her eyes bolted up, staring at me like I'd said something shocking.

"Of course I am."

"Okay, well, you're just acting odd, that's all."

"We talked about it for a while, and I said that the past is behind me and that I'm going to pretend he was my first. I was worried, but he was so sweet and kept saying it was okay to stop. He wouldn't be mad or anything. Coop said that he'd even be happy just to lay there."

A soft smile filled her face.

"It kind of felt like it was the right time, you know? To move on and grow. I'm glad that we did."

"Well, I am happy that you're okay with it and that it went well for the both of you."

"Oh, it went well, alright."

"Too much information." I cooed.

The cheeky thing grinned as if she had a dirty secret. I'm sure she did. I just didn't need to hear about it and then have to face CJ.

The man of the hour crossed the gap between the servery to our table with great strides, taking the spot next to Karina. He leaned in and whispered something in her ear. Whatever it was, it had to be either amusing or scandalous because the smile grew so large I saw her fangs.

"You are going to blush yourself to death."

Karina scoffed, pressing her drink bottle against her cheeks.

"Hey,"

I looked up and saw one of the footballers moving towards our table with his tray in his hands.

"Mind if I join you guys?"

Karina shrugged, too busy scarfing down her fries. CJ smiled at the guy who had decided that next to me was his ideal seat. Anzide's eyes narrowed, but he remained in his position, leaning against the nearby wall. If he'd listened to me and just appeared, this wouldn't be an issue.

"It's Evie, right?"

"Yeah."

"Danny."

I nodded, saying nothing else. I wasn't prepared to invite danger like that.

When another footballer appeared at the table with his tray in hand, I knew that it was only going to get worse. CJ and Karina moved to one end, which was great, except that I was distracted by watching them move for the other guy that I didn't notice another had appeared. He sat to my left, making me the Evie filling in a footballer sandwich. I felt so tiny.

Anzide was not a happy boy at the moment. I had to give him credit. He hadn't moved or said a word. The glower was mighty, but the lips were still. At first, I thought it might have been jealousy, but then I realized that these guys were on the football team, the same team that Kannon had been on. These were his friends. Would they act on his behalf?

I looked around the table and realized that the answer was no. They were more interested in eating the mountain of food on their trays and discussing future games. When Audrey walked past, Danny commented that it seemed as if she'd had a bitchectomy, which made me snort my drink. The one on my left thumped my back until I choked out that I was fine. Karina merely smiled, quietly eating her lunch.

It was a curious turn of events. I'd gone from sitting at the table by myself or with Karina to this. A table that was full of footballers, Karina and me. Clearly, Kannon had a lot to do with it, and now that he wasn't here, they didn't care. It gave me hope that the rest of the school year wouldn't be so difficult. Also, a lot of these people would remain in this community. Sure, a lot of them would go to a larger city to find work, maybe university. Some footballers might get a contract with one of the big teams. Anything was possible, but for those who liked living in a small town, they'd stick around. What might start as a casual lunch in high school could become a friendship that continued for a lifetime. Well, their lifetime. I'd always be around.

The thought of always being in Hades made me smile. It also caused a few wayward thoughts. When I saw James emerge from the kitchen and move towards the swing doors, I knew I needed him to answer a question.

Upending my drink, I packed my tray and stood from the table. Karina frowned with what I assumed was a burning curiosity.

"I'll catch up with you later."

Dumping the empty tray on the stack, I made a beeline to the doors and caught up with James. Anzide lingered, keeping his distance.

"Something bothering you, Evelyn?"

"I was just thinking about the odd change in the dynamics of the footballers now that Kannon's not around to influence their opinion."

James nodded like it was not unexpected.

"And then my mind began to wander as it does, and I thought about the future. Like the long-term future and how many of those people in there will become a part of this community and, in a way, friends."

"How do you hide from them when this youthful appearance will not change?"

"Exactly."

"Well," he hummed, clasping his arms behind his back. "Everyone who is in this kind of situation finds their own solution, whether it is moving around every so often or moving away altogether. However, we have an advantage that the immortals don't have. Well, I suppose the witches could conjure something if they thought about it. However, it would not be as amazing as what we can create. For myself, I use a range of spells. The first is that I have a veil around me that if a mortal looks at me, they see me, but they don't overthink what is in front of them. I also use a mild aging spell. You can't see it because as an Eternal, you can only ever see my true nature. However, the mortals see a man who is in his late fifties. I am going to continue in this role and this life until I reach an age where retirement is acceptable in their minds. Then, if I wish to continue in this role in my next persona, I will do so. For you, though, it might be a little different. When everything is done, and your life has settled, consider learning the veil spell. It will serve you well in your older years when those around you will expect to see you age."

A teacher turned the corner and began the short walk down the corridor towards us. James stepped aside, smiling at the man as he passed. His eyes remained pinned as the teacher passed through the swing doors.

"Interesting to notice how the mood changes when one student is removed. It's like happiness has returned. How has Miss Hartley been treating you?"

"Far better than previously. She's keeping it subdued, but Audrey's making a solid effort to keep me happy."

James nodded.

"I am not surprised."

"I'm a little confused about Audrey and Kannon. Anzide checked her mind and found they met six months ago, but it didn't make much sense. She came to the town when she was young and Kannon was born here."

"He might have been born here, but the story his parents told me was that they only recently moved to the town. They even had transfer documents. I should have checked, and it is a mistake I will not repeat, but I was wrapped up in a lure actually working. I suspect that in the previous graduates, Drakkus lost his spy and was forced to send another in."

"Have you had anyone acting odd or any new applications?"

"No to both, thankfully. I'm sure he's obsessing about the war. Once it is over, I won't have to worry about spies, but will monitor the paranormal activity within these walls. You'd be surprised what children see."

Surprisingly, my father turned the corner and smiled when he saw us.

"Ah, all three of you together."

"Is something wrong?"

"Well, yes and no, but I do need to talk to all of you, right now if possible."

When some students emerged from the cafeteria, James gestured to the corridor.

"Let's return to my office where the environment is more controllable."

Once we were in the safety of James's office, and he'd created the veil to hide everything we said, I sat down. Lately, I've noticed that I need to sit more. My pace had slowed, and it felt like I'd eaten too much. Heartburn had become my new constant.

"Okay, so I think that the Europeans have arrived. At least, one has. I've been tracking all of the vampires in this town at Niko's request so that we can monitor anything like a large cluster or unusual behavior. I passed an unfamiliar face on the street, and I knew he was a vampire. Beyond that, I can't say, as everything else was blocked."

"Which can mean only one thing. He's got an Eternal helping him. It's likely to be a demon soul feeder. Angels rarely associate with vampires."

"Do you find that troubling?" I asked.

"Only if they intend to stay here permanently. My presence is obvious to other demons if they enter this town. Whoever it is would know that there is an expectation that their time in this town is limited. Most honor that, and few push the boundaries. If the demon had any sense, they would approach, and state their reasons for being here and the expected duration of their visit. As this is likely to be related to the blood war and most Eternals know that a residing demon will influence the vampires to their desires, the other demon is unlikely to show their face any time soon. Their goal is to shield the vampire as they conduct their investigation."

"So, they're watching us?"

"They are."

"Are we going to be in any danger?"

"It would depend on what they think. This war has dragged on for far too long. Drakkus doesn't have much of an argument that would benefit his reason for delaying it, but you certainly do. You're still in school, you're trying to learn how to run a coven with limited resources and experience, and you're also learning how to control the powers that have come with your newly found identity and of course, those little bundles of joy. There is a degree of leniency that can be given, and I'm sure you'd happily argue about it, given your history. If not, then you can always utilize your father's help to fight."

James leaned forward on the desk, giving me a stern look.

"And remember that this vampire has an Eternal helping him. No matter what kind of Eternal we are facing here, they would receive the same alerts like everyone else. This person would know exactly who you are and what's happening in the portal. If it were me in that position, I would state that this young lady is from the lineage of the first creation. She is young, untrained but she has incredible power waiting to be unleashed. I would also warn against antagonizing her as the records show that she has no qualms in using her powers against her enemies."

Yeah, I guess that was me in a nutshell.

"I have no doubt that any and all information would be passed onto the vampire. He will be warned that going against you is an extremely dangerous thing to do. You are strong-willed, you stand up for what is right, and you do not back down easily. This vampire will not pick sides, but he will lean heavily towards you. It also helps that the Corbin clan are the true leaders of this land."

"So, now what?"

"Now, you train with your father, and you learn how to conduct the trial with Niko. It is imperative that you get it right because I guarantee that the Europeans will be watching."

CHAPTER 47

Beatrice had duties to attend to for the festival and suggested that she could drop us off in town to begin the long day of baby shopping. At the moment, it was just Anzide and myself, but it would change later on. When she was done with her duties, Beatrice would join us. Karina was also going to be here at some point, though I don't know when exactly. She said that she had a test to study for and Nora wasn't letting her out until she'd clocked a few hours. I knew that Karina was eager to go baby shopping, so I said that we would start with the big ticket items, and by the time she was ready to join us, she could help pick clothes and other little things.

Anzide was looking at the prams at the moment, frowning at one of them. He lifted the swing tag to show me.

"Are they serious?"

"Having children is expensive."

"Yeah," he said, sighing.

"Do you like it?"

"It's alright. When will we use it, though?"

I shrugged. It's not like we went on walks or did groceries. Beatrice liked to do the grocery shopping. Personally, I think she liked to do it because it gave her time away from the property. As much as they kept saying everything is fine, I knew it was a struggle. The sooner the house was built, the better. I could say the same about ending the blood war, but for now, I was focusing on the one thing that had a strong visual presence in our lives.

"Maybe if we take them somewhere?"

Sighing heavily, Anzide moved further along the row.

"How about we just get it and not worry about how much it will be used?"

"Sure. What else did Beatrice put on the list?"

"Car seats. Cots. Bassinets. Change tables. The list is endless."

Anzide looked exasperated when he turned to me.

"We don't even have the house yet."

"Sure we do."

"It's not in our name, and you can't live in it until this stupid war is done. Where are we going to put everything?"

Pulling him closer, I wrapped my arms around his neck.

"There is room in the marquee. We don't have to get the big items just yet. We'll start with what's needed in the beginning."

Anzide was panicking about it, but the reality was that we were close to finalizing the purchase of the house anyway. Because we were paying cash and there was no mortgage over the property, it was going to be done quickly. It had been inspected, and while there were issues, they were only minor. Between building the coven house and the repairs to our home, Henry was going to be busy for a long time. We were yet to inspect the other house, but that was happening soon, too.

"You know that we're closing on it next week. We can organize for everything to be delivered the next day."

"To an empty house."

I huffed and frowned at Anzide.

"Well, we can go furniture shopping today if you like."

Because I was in the mood to test lounges. The kind of testing where I'd lay down with my feet up, eyes closed, and perhaps even snoring. I suppose that we needed to find a bed too. Testing the beds might seem inappropriate if my mind was in the gutter, but it wasn't. All I could think about was how much I really wanted to sleep for several hours.

He shrugged and took the scanner from me. With the barcode recorded, Anzide picked the pram that apparently wasn't that expensive.

Row after row, we looked at everything, decided what we wanted, and scanned it. The list that Beatrice had written out for us was long, pilfered from a baby store website, but perfect because they'd thought of everything. The bonus of this store and its registry scanner was that anyone could come in here and buy from it. Apparently, that was necessary because they were already having heated discussions about who would buy what for their grandchildren. My father was probably trying to make up for the past when he wasn't around, and of course, he believed that he didn't search hard enough.

Niko and Beatrice were undoubtedly pretending that these were their first grandchildren. I don't think they were trying to dismiss Brad or my mother. I think that the pain of the past was too much for them to deal with at the moment. It's not as if Brad was going without anyway. Niko suggested that his car needed an upgrade to cope with the changes, and because he conducted duties for the coven, a large portion of the funds could be taken from the money they'd been accumulating. Brad wasn't thrilled, mostly because he wanted to focus on the rebuild and two new houses.

By the time Karina arrived with Cooper, we'd reached the nursery linen section. Karina held up a sheet set with a grin on her face.

"So, what do we think of barnyard animals? Have we decided on a theme for the nursery?"

Anzide groaned. "That's a thing?"

"It is." Cooper offered. "You need to get a mood board happening or something."

Anzide frowned as he turned from Cooper to me.

"Mood board?"

"Well, I suppose deciding on what color to paint the walls would be ideal so that we could get it done quickly. The room will need to be aired out to get rid of the paint smell. As for the theme, I think that at the moment, something is better than nothing."

"Well, barnyard animals are an easy theme to stick to and pretty standard for kids' stuff."

"Yep."

I scanned the set and ticked another thing off the list. We were almost done, which was great because I was ready to sit down.

It was lunchtime before we walked out of the store. We hadn't finished, which frustrated Anzide who commented that he couldn't believe that two little beings needed so much stuff. The woman behind the counter said we could return to add more to the list if we wanted, which was great because I was tired.

We decided to try a little takeaway shop at the end of thc block. After ordering lunch, we found a table, and I thoroughly enjoyed getting off my feet. Karina pulled another chair over and made me put my feet up. It was awkward and a little uncomfortable, but it felt good to stretch out.

While we waited for our meals to be made, I stretched my shirt over the mound that seemed bigger than it was this morning. One of the babies stretched and pushed a limb against the wall of the womb.

"As amazing as it is, that is weird to see." Karina offered.

"I know, right? There are living things in there. They survive in the goop and grow from almost nothing into,"

"Screaming poop machines?"

Pursing my lips, I nodded. We were about to have two poop machines. I didn't regret nor would I ever wish for a different life, but I knew that Anzide and I were way out of our depth here. It made me grateful that we had Beatrice and Nora. I suppose Eda would be equally as helpful, perhaps even Della.

"You know that you're going to be okay, right?"

I shrugged and glanced at Anzide because she was clearly talking to him.

"It's going to be rough. You'll have a lot of sleepless nights, and you'll be walking around like a pair of zombies, but like everyone else, you'll just keep truck'n. Power on and keep going. And if it gets too bad, then the neighbors will be more than ready to take over."

"That's all well and good, but if they're screaming the house down?"

I expected Karina to respond, but it was Cooper who leaned forward on the table and offered advice.

"Then you check their diapers. If they're clean, then you stick a binky in their mouths. If that doesn't work, then feed them. And if all of that fails, then give them a cuddle, walk around, go for a drive, sing to them, and give them a bath in warm water. There will be an answer."

With a narrowed eye, I looked at the curious one. Cooper shrugged with a grin curled into one corner of his mouth.

"Killian was a monster who screamed the house down. I had a front row seat to everything my parents did to appease him."

"Well, who would have thought you'd be a baby expert?"

He shrugged, then turned his head to look at Karina. I saw the smirk and the wink, even though he was trying to hide it. Nothing could hide Karina's pink cheeks and the shy smile as her gaze lowered.

If I could predict the future, I'd happily wager that these two will be married and pregnant really soon. Their parents would make them wait until school was over, and if college was in their future, that would come first, too. It was clear that Nora expected Karina to pay attention and learn as much as she could. As for Cooper's parents, I'd say that while they appreciated that he was athletically talented, they wanted him to focus on his education as well.

It was a curious situation, now that I think about it. According to Karina, Cooper was talented enough to be scouted by a major league football team. If he was offered a deal, would he go?

"So, what's the plan for life after school?"

Cooper's head turned to me, giving a vague shrug. Karina was quiet, which was not surprising. I suspect that she feared that Cooper would leave and not come back.

"I was actually talking to Henry."

"The builder working on Evie's house?" Karina asked.

"Yeah. He said there is so much work available now that they've opened up the new estate. Plus, James mentioned that he was going to throw out a lure, so it sounds like Henry and the other builders are going to be busy. I asked if he'd let me help out, and he agreed. After school, I'm going to be doing a couple of hours of work. Mostly stuff like cleaning up but he said that if I put in the hours, I can start an apprenticeship next year."

Karina stared, and I moved my foot to nudge her side. She blinked hard and smiled.

"That's awesome."

I could see that Anzide was thinking about what Cooper had said.

"Hey," I grumbled. "You're on baby duties, so don't be getting any grand ideas that you can run away every day."

"I could try."

"Yeah, you try and see how long you spend in the dog house."

"Oh my god," Karina gasped. "You totally need a

dog."

"I think we've got enough on our plate at the moment."

"Speaking of plates," I muttered, pulling my feet from the chair.

Lunch was on its way to the table, which was just as well because I was starving. With Cooper distracted, I looked at Karina, giving her a questioning smile. She grinned, rolling her eyes. Yep, Evie was now a mind reader, and she knew that her bestie had a mini freak-out about Cooper leaving town.

The thought that had come out of nowhere hit me. In my mind, thinking about everything that had just happened and Karina's reaction, I'd called her my bestie. It had come naturally, and it kind of blew my mind that it had happened. I guess that I had a demon to thank for that. He'd clearly seen the issues I had regarding the past, the many towns that I'd lived in, and the long trail of forgotten friendships. Now that I'd finally settled, it was time to start again, and in a town that was filled with treachery, it was never going to be easy.

CHAPTER 48

It was game night. Not so much a game night in the terms of battling against other teams but a friendly round against a high school football team from a neighboring town. Beatrice told us that they were doing a lot of raffles, and it was the Heritage Trust's job to sell tickets to the crowd as they entered the gates. The proceeds of the tickets would go to a few charities.

I had a list of the prizes which Beatrice had given me. She said that I could try and win something if I wanted. Beatrice even pointed out a couple of businesses that she thought I might like to check out, some before the birth and some after. At the moment, I was eyeing off the spa pamper package. I'd happily soak my feet for a few minutes. I might fall asleep, but at least I'd be relaxed.

Because Cooper was on the team, we were going to the game to support him. As much as I didn't want to go near the football field, it was slightly better now that Kannon had been booted out of the school. Audrey was now secretly on my side, so she wouldn't be making her snide comments anymore. So, I guess going to the football field wasn't so bad now.

It was also the town fair, so there would be plenty of things to do after the football match. I was eager to get out into the town that usually had a bedtime of sunset and see what it was like during the evening. The most I'd seen was looking out the window at the bed and breakfast before we moved here.

Main Street had been blocked off from early this morning as vendors set up their stalls. The park near the town center would have lots of rides and a sideshow alley. I have never been to a fair, so it was obvious that I was excited to go.

My mother never cared to go to one and probably didn't have the money for it either. She seemed intent on never spending the inheritance. When I was younger, I found it disappointing, but as the years passed, I gave up hoping that she'd take me. Now, I was going to take myself.

Seated on the chair, I pulled my shirt tight over my belly. By the time the next town fair rolled around, these babies would almost be a year old. It was a crazy thought, one that I was excited and scared about. A year into this new life. Would it be good or average? I hope that by this time next year, I will be accustomed to life with twins, and maybe we could take them to the fair. It definitely had to happen, if only to put the pram to use and maybe get out of the house. Was I worried that we'd be a pair of zombies? Yep.

Beatrice's alter ego was a part of the Heritage Trust, so she was rostered on to attend to duties early in the evening. She said she'd picked that time, knowing that once everyone was through the gate, she would be free to enjoy the night. Her job would be done, she could sit with us for the remainder of the game, and when it was over, she could wander around the fair with us.

Niko had decided to remain here rather than going out to feed. He figured that everyone would go to the fair so the pickings would be slim or intoxicated. So, he had a stack of swatches on the table, ready to be gone through. I think he secretly liked the idea of building and decorating a new home. It didn't make it any easier, but it had lessened the anguish I felt.

"Well, I'm off."

Beatrice lifted her bag onto her shoulder. With a kiss goodbye to Niko, she changed into her alter ego and began to walk out of the rear section of the marquee.

"You guys want a lift?"

"Not me, I'm going with Nora, who will be here any second."

"Or us. I think Karina would be heartbroken if she didn't get to cram into the backseat of the car with us."

Natalia chuckled, and with a wave, she was out the door. A wave of aftershave floated with Brad, and I coughed.

"Good Lord, Bradley. Are you trying to make the woman sick, or are you hiding that you didn't shower?"

"Neither. I showered, and it's not that much. Come on, Nora's just messaged me that they're on their way."

By the time we reached the driveway, Nora was turning into the street. I had to smile when I saw Karina with a pair of demon horns on her head, red face paint, and wearing a football jersey. She got out of the car and turned around, showing me that she had the number ten.

"Did you steal that from Cooper?"

"Nah, he had a couple of spare ones."

We climbed into the back, and as Nora backed out of the driveway, Karina started showing me everything in her bag. She'd managed to collect banners and buntings in the team colors and had large plastic trumpets. If she blew that thing in my ear, she would be in trouble. And relegated to the far end of the bleachers.

Nora parked in the real estate car park. There weren't many available on the street, so this was a good option. As we crossed the road, Karina called out to Cooper, who was standing near the side fence of the school.

He turned with a smile, but I could see that something was odd about it. When he approached us, Cooper turned back to whatever it was that had his attention.

"Are you excited?" Karina said eagerly.

Cooper frowned, giving an uneasy shrug.

"What's wrong?"

"I just saw Natalia talking to Drakkus. Isn't she, you know,"

"Yeah," I interrupted.

"Well, he took her by the arm and dragged her further down the street. They turned at the next block."

I looked at Anzide.

"Do you think he figured her out?"

"Yep."

We had to save her. Facing Nora, I hoped that this would work.

"Do you know where my father lives?"

"The house across the road?"

"Yes. Please go there and tell him that it's time. Then collect the unseen one."

"I'll drop my location," Karina said as she waggled her phone.

Nora nodded, took Karina's bag of bunting, and plastic trumpets, and rushed back to her car. The rest of us began the pursuit.

"Is this it?" Karina said, wide-eyed.

"He's taken my grandmother, so yeah. I'm sick of the nonsense, and I want this done before I get any bigger than I am now. I get tired easily, and it needs to happen now before the lethargy hits me even harder or my belly becomes too big. Or worse. I don't want to be in labor when this happens."

Karina nodded. I knew she was worried about that,

too.

We couldn't see Drakkus anywhere, but Cooper was sniffing the air. He'd found something because we were moving with purpose and definitely in a direction. It wasn't long before he stopped. Karina almost ran straight into the back of him.

"In that alley," he said softly. "I can only detect two. There is a lot of fear in the air, plus anger."

"Mom just messaged that your dad is on his way, and she has just loaded the unseen package. I just dropped her and your dad the location."

"Good. Let's go."

Crossing the road, we entered the alley. It was poorly lit but well maintained. No litter or boxes, just an industrial bin. It looked clean and new, probably only just delivered.

Drakkus had Natalia bailed up against the wall. When he turned and saw us, Drakkus gave a malevolent smile. One hand pressed against Natalia's shoulder, pinning her to the wall.

"What a pleasant surprise, Evelyn and her friends. You're just in time for the confession. Natalia was just about to tell me everything."

"No, I wasn't." she hissed. "I've got nothing to say to you."

"Of course, you don't, so perhaps I will fill in the details so you understand how obvious you are. At first,

I thought that you were in a relationship with Brad. It seemed the only logical solution considering you were at the caravan constantly. We put a watch on your house to see how often you returned. You haven't been back there in a long time, which certainly grew my curiosity. I was positive that you were with him until the newest resident turned up, which by the way, was well done. I don't know how you managed to get rid of Hannah, but kudos to you, Evelyn. That truly was a remarkable effort."

I wasn't about to offer any form of gratitude for his praise, nor was I about to tell him how I did it. Just a cold stare. Curiously, though, he didn't mention the dead followers. I suppose that he didn't care about them, given how easily he killed Jess.

"And the obvious began to grow. Brad and the new woman, going out on dates together. Even seen holding hands and kissing. You cheeky thing."

Brad quietly seethed next to me. Clearly, he had no idea that they'd been watched. It was rather foolish. I would watch my enemy if given the chance, and he should have assumed it would be the same for Drakkus.

"But that left me with the curious woman that was hanging around your property but, by appearances, not in a relationship. She was a peculiarity, and I thought about her appearance and her time here in Hades. Natalia Eastwell emerged from nowhere and managing to gain a place on the board of the Heritage Trust, something that is quite a feat for anyone, let alone an unknown person. Then, she manages to persuade them to place the Corbin house into the care of the trust. Why did this nobody care about a house that should have meant nothing to her? I never truly understood why, and over the years, I have done all I can to stop her from entering the Corbin house. I thought she was some kind of fanatic or perhaps a looter. Anyway, she was a vampire that refused to enter my clan. The only vampire in this town that wasn't under my control."

"That's because you're a psycho," Natalia hissed.

She tried to move but couldn't. It was just one hand, but it looked like he put a lot of pressure on the spot.

"Now, now. It's not the time for name calling. Is it Beatrice?"

Drakkus laughed.

"I tried to figure out why I couldn't kill you and how our best attempts to get the job done were pointless. Vampires sent to take you down turned up dead at the edge of town or hidden in the forest somewhere. I grew tired of losing members, so you were put on the proscribed list. The more I thought about you and this entry into the town, your efforts regarding the house, and your refusal to join my clan, the more I began to realize that you were not normal. I thought about Niko and how the two of you could create a female together. He was just an ordinary vampire, but you're not, are you? You're a shapeshifter and that's how you could create a female with a vampire. It made sense that you would return to your family, and once I realized that, everything began to fall into place. So, with that in mind, I'm going to keep you hostage until Evelyn hands over the leadership. If she wants you back, then she has to pay the ransom."

Drakkus took hold of her arm and dragged her out of the alley. Behind the shops was a thick forest. It would not stop me, not when he was attacking my family again.

CHAPTER 49

The forest was sparser than the one behind our property. Instead of vegetation around the trees, it was mostly leaf litter. It appeared as if the area was maintained.

Drakkus stopped when figures emerged from behind the trees. There were a lot of vampires waiting for us.

"Evie," Cooper whispered. "I have a present for you."

I looked at him and saw his family.

"Did a location drop with a nine-one-one message. Ready to see some wolfy action?"

"Uh, sure. Just remember that I have to kill Drakkus to end the blood war.'"

"We know, and we're only here to thin the herd."

Cooper stepped out of our little lineup to the amusement of our enemies. His father and two brothers also joined him. Their clothes began to rip from their bodies as the skin rippled. Fur emerged, and their faces changed shape, elongating into snouts.

As the growls that sounded remarkably like delight came from four werewolves, a collective gasp passed between the vampires in front of us. Cooper howled, and most of the vampires took off except Kannon and his parents. I shot a bind out at them and pulled the three of them to the nearest trees, pinning them to the trunks.

Cooper remained, but his brothers and father took off after the fleeing vampires. Drakkus was horrified, clearly misjudging the company I kept. He knew they were werewolves, so why did he look like he'd seen a ghost? Had he never seen one in the flesh before? They were huge. I understood why Cooper, his brothers, and their father were tall. The werewolf alter ego was even taller. And broad, too. They towered over us.

Teeth gnashed, drool dripped. It was scary to see Cooper in his alter ego, but I knew that I was safe. I didn't fear him.

Hearing footsteps behind me, I turned to see Carsten and Nora.

"Good evening, Evelyn. I see that you're ready to end the war. Your delivery is waiting for the cue to approach. I will be here should you need support or guidance, but I will remain hands-off unless you are in dire distress. This is your show, and I will take from your guidance. Good luck, and remember what we have discussed."

He leaned down to whisper.

"And your other delivery is waiting for your final blow. Be ready for it."

Carsten lifted upright again and smiled at me.

"Go get him, tiger. I believe in you."

Stepping forward, I wiped my clammy hands on my jeans and prayed this went well. As much as I'd practiced this moment with Niko, I was worried that I would screw it up.

"I, Evelyn Newton, leader of the Corbin clan and the rightful ruler of the town of Hades, make a claim under the code of vampires that you, Drakkus Fleming, have broken numerous laws that include the crime of murdering your own kind. Punishment for said crimes is instant death, administered by the ruler of this town. Do you have anything to say in your defense?"

"Well, I think that you should at least prove that I have, in fact, murdered vampires. Where is your list, Evelyn? You don't have one, do you? Why is that? It's because I have never murdered anyone."

"You're wrong. I have a witness that says differently."

This was the gift that my father brought to the battle. The only way we could guarantee that we could get her to wherever we needed her with such little time was with the help of my father.

Audrey stepped out from the line that was hiding her. Kannon's eyes widened when he saw her.

"I present Miss Audrey Hartley, who has agreed to give evidence. Please state what you saw, Audrey."

"On Tuesday afternoon, four pm, I was at the Fleming clan house with Kannon Lothaire. The leader, Drakkus Fleming, demanded that Kannon show his loyalty to the clan and his leadership by executing his aunt, Jessica Lothaire. When Kannon refused to do it, Drakkus Fleming became enraged. He lunged at Jessica with a knife and stabbed her."

She paused. Despite what my father had done for her, the memories were still there. Audrey remained focused on bringing Drakkus to justice for Jessica. What happened was wrong, and Audrey knew there were other ways to deal with problematic vampires.

"Then he removed her head."

I looked at Kannon. His head was hung low, but it quickly changed. Anger burned on his face as he looked at her.

"You bitch," he growled. "You promised to keep the secret."

"And you promised to keep your dick in your pants, yet here we are. I will not share you or anyone. I don't need a liar in my life, just like I don't need a cheater. We're done, Kannon. Have a nice life, loser."

And in true Evie fashion, Audrey turned and walked away with her hand in the air, giving Kannon the one-finger salute. She'd just moved a rung up the ladder, in my opinion.

She'd done as I had asked. Provide the testimony, end her association with the Fleming clan, and, in a way, taken my side of the conflict. I urged her to remain as neutral as possible to avoid blowback from any of the other vampires that might survive the showdown.

A mockingly slow clap echoed through the forest, followed by a taunting laugh. Drakkus took a step closer. The fool had let go of his captive, and as she changed shape into a bird, Beatrice flew away and appeared next to me. This time, she was in her true form.

The smile on his face fell, and he was no longer amused. Drakkus scowled.

"All this time, you were in front of me, and I could not see it."

"'That's because you're an idiot. There was a reason that Niko and I didn't want you anywhere near our daughter. You're a fool, and you don't deserve anything in this life, but you think that the world owes you everything."

This could go on all night, and I had better things to do. I could also see that Drakkus was getting antsy. Remembering Niko's warning about how flighty Drakkus could be, I threw out the Unholy Burn. Like I'd been taught, it formed a ring around my enemy. Or, in this case, enemies. Kannon and his parents were bound to a tree within the circle.

The flames rose high around the rear of the circle and were tight enough to ensure that he couldn't jump through them or over the wall to escape. If he was foolish enough to even touch the flames, Drakkus would regret it. No, scratch that. He would be dead. It was quick and efficient.

Rather than entering into a ridiculous monologue like Drakkus had, I dealt with the issue swiftly. Shooting out a Frost Storm, I watched the icy blade cross the gap between us and slice into his chest. Letting the flames die down now that he was impaled, I stepped closer. Running my fingers over the long, cold blade, I ignored the mocking laughter.

"Surely you know that it's not enough, right? Can she do the job, or will she fail because she's so sweet and innocent?"

"Oh, I wouldn't say that Evelyn is innocent," Niko said as he emerged from the shadows. "Sweet, though? Absolutely."

I smiled at him and turned to face the shocked Drakkus.

"Niko," he whispered.

"Did you really think he was dead?" I asked with a pout.

"I'm not," Niko said, resting one hand against Kannon's throat as he leaned his body.

Kannon was gasping for air, and Niko didn't care at all.

"And I've spent all this time ensuring that she was prepared to take you down in the most legal way possible. That's done, and she's proved your guilt, so now we are here at your execution."

"But I am still alive."

"That is true. She did learn from your mistake."

And with that, I threw out the Moonlight Whip. The long white whip that glowed like the moon curled around the gap and flicked against his body. As the crack of the whip echoed through the forest, his eyes rolled back, and the head slipped away.

The whip receded, and I could feel my legs giving way. Anzide caught me.

I was shaking.

"It's over," I whispered with a sob.

He wiped the tears with a soft smile.

"And it went exactly as it should. You were perfect, my love. Now, you have two jobs to attend to before the hour strikes."

Anzide helped me to my feet while holding me to ensure I didn't collapse again.

"I, Evelyn Newton, leader of the Corbin clan and the rightful ruler of the town of Hades, make a claim under the code of vampires that the vampires known as Eddios Lothaire, Iralya Lothaire, and Kannon Lothaire, have broken numerous laws that include the crime of collusion with the enemy against the true leader. Punishment for said crimes is permanent banishment from the town of Hades, administered by the ruler of this town. Do you have anything to say in your defense?"

Niko removed his hand from Kannon's neck. He shook his head.

"I require a spoken answer, please, Mister Lothaire."

"No." he snapped.

"And you, Eddios?"

"No."

"Iralya?"

"No," she whispered sadly.

"Then let it be known that I, Evelyn Newton, leader of the Corbin clan and the rightful ruler of the town of Hades, permanently banish Eddios Lothaire, Iralya Lothaire and Kannon Lothaire from the town of Hades. Banishment will begin at sunset this coming Sunday. If you are found within the town limits after six p.m., then you will be in breach, which is a punishable offense."

I pulled the bind away and let the three of them free. It was a tense moment, but I had a werewolf at my side, as well as two Eternals who were ready to shoot them into the sky, giving them a free flight into the next town. That is, of course, if they could beat the vampire that was itching for a little retribution of his own. Niko was pacing like he had a lot of anger to unleash.

Kannon was still angry, but Eddios put a firm hand on his shoulder and urged him to leave the forest, taking the long path through it rather than trying to walk through the wall of people behind me.

"And now, the finality," Anzide whispered as he helped me turn.

Facing Niko, I smiled. This was the moment that I'd

been waiting for. It wasn't that I didn't like ruling. I just felt uneasy about it. I was not a vampire, and I didn't think that I was the right person for the job.

"Let it be known that I, Evelyn Newton, leader of the Corbin clan and the rightful ruler of the town of Hades, abdicate my rule in favor of the return to the rule of the oldest living member of the Corbin clan, my great-grandfather, Niko Corbin. May his leadership be long, just, and always for the wellbeing of his followers."

"I accept the offer of the position of leader of the Corbin clan and the rightful ruler of the town of Hades."

The sound of cheers rang, and if that wasn't enough, fireworks began shooting up and bursting in the sky above us. It was like Hades was celebrating the return of the true leader.

"My first order of business is to place my second in charge. That is my beloved wife, Beatrice Corbin."

With a flick of his hand, he called her to his side.

"And our master of coin, my grandson, Bradley Newton."

Brad gave an uneasy smile and a nod of acknowledgment. He always had been a man of many words when it came to things like this. The focus was on him, and he wasn't a fan of that.

"As well as senior leadership roles to my great-granddaughter Evelyn Newton and her partner, Anzide, who has no surname because he's Nephilim."

"Eh, just call me a Newton too."

Everyone chuckled.

"So be it."

Niko turned to face those who remained. They were a mixture of creatures. Four werewolves, a Wiccan witch, three turned vampires, and an Eternal. I wasn't sure what my father's plans were, but I knew that Niko would always include him for my sake.

"And though you are not all vampires, I extend a continuing invitation to remain a part of this clan and this town. In the coming days, I will consider each and every one of you and what you have done to support Evelyn in her journey to free us from the enemy. Words cannot convey the gratitude that I have for all of you and what you have done for her and, in turn, me. Now, I think it is time to get rid of a body and then go home."

I never thought that I would consider that to be such a great statement. Yet here I was, mere steps from a headless corpse, and I was the happiest I'd ever been.

It was over.

BONUS CHAPTER 1

A SUNSET WITH NIKO

Stepping out of the marquee, I saw Niko had climbed the ladder and was standing on the second floor of the house. The frame was up, the joists were in, and the subfloor was down. I could actually envision the house now, and it made me feel so much better. There was light at the end of the tunnel.

The things that Henry and his team finished today meant that we could walk up there. Well, some of us were allowed to. Apparently, pregnant women had to stay on the ground with their feet firmly planted, definitely not climbing ladders or wandering through a construction site. Was this pregnant woman going to listen? Absolutely not. Did she ever? No, definitely not.

Niko reached the edge of the house, grasping the frame. When I saw him close his eyes, the contentment was obvious. The golden rays of the sunlight shone over his features, bathing him in a rich orange hue. A smile filled his face, and I realized that until now, he'd had to hide and probably missed the sunlight.

It wasn't common for vampires to willingly accept the

sunlight, especially if they'd been hidden from it for over sixty years, but Niko was old enough to cope.

And now, he was able to step outside of the safety of the caravan and walk beyond the walls of the marquee. He could walk around the property at a leisurely stroll without fear of anyone seeing him. No longer bound to the shadows, he was free to walk around the property. He was free.

It might have been hormones, but when the statement entered my mind, tears slid down my cheeks. Out of everyone here, he's suffered the most. He sent his wife and daughter away to protect them, only to learn it was pointless. Victoria still died. Running from a monster created an irrational fear in her that she would pass on to her daughter, but at the end of the day, my grandparents still led a reasonably normal life. Brad showed me the photos of his childhood. It was a good one, and he said that my mother would have had a happy childhood as well.

But all that time, Niko was trapped behind a wall, wondering what happened to his wife and daughter. He never got to see Victoria grow up. Never saw her marry or become a mother. Niko never knew the wonder of becoming a grandfather for the first time. He could have been there in the moments after my mother and Brad were born, holding them and enjoying those precious moments.

Everything that has happened in our lives, it could have taken place in this town. If Drakkus had accepted what Niko and Beatrice wanted for their daughter's future, none of this would have occurred. I struggled to understand why he was so adamant that he was given Victoria's hand in marriage. Why couldn't he accept that Niko and Beatrice said no? Why wouldn't he wait until Victoria was an adult? He could have easily approached her, formed a friendship, and then a relationship if she was willing.

I guess that was the problem. Would she be willing? What if she said no? What if she hated Drakkus? Arranged marriages were uncommon in vampire culture, but as the leader, Niko could have searched for a husband for Victoria to strengthen his leadership. Instead, he chose to let Victoria grow up without the burden and find her own path of love. It would be the decision that would lead everyone in this town down a dark path which they would not emerge from for over sixty years. Lives would be lost, a family would be broken apart, and a coven would be destroyed.

I wouldn't second guess Niko and Beatrice's decision. They were saving their daughter from a monster. The cost was high for their choice but probably not as high as what Victoria would have paid if they'd agreed.

As I wiped away the tears, I realized that there was another side to this situation. If the events didn't happen, then my mother wouldn't have spent years wanting to return to Hades to finish the war. She wouldn't have accepted her fate and laid down with a biblical creature to create a war-ending daughter. I would not exist.

It was a wild thought, one that I didn't know how to handle. For Niko's sanity, I would lay my life down. He would get angry at the concept and the ease at which I could do such a thing, but he didn't see things from my perspective.

It was then that I realized that perhaps I was wrong about who suffered the most in this life. We all felt the weight of those dire actions. We all suffered. Perhaps not as much as the person next to us, but in a way, each of us had a burden to bear.

Putting on a happy face, I crossed the lawn and began to climb the ladder before Niko could scold me. I still earned a frown, which I was used to.

"Evelyn, do you wish to cause distress to those who love you?"

"No, but I'd like to enjoy the sunset with you."

His face twitched with what I could assume was anger and love. Pulling lawn chairs over, he opened one for me and helped me into it. Life was not easy, and as much as I wanted to be here, I dreaded the climb down. My gusto and stubbornness were about to be my downfall. It was guaranteed that I would be scolded for climbing the ladder as they helped me down.

Satisfied that I was temporarily subdued and safe, Niko opened the other lawn chair and sat next to me.

We were now lower than the sun. It shone over the forest, creating a view that could only be described as majestic. The shadows of the deep fall colors were a mixture of rusts, oranges, and even a few green trees that stubbornly refused to change were framed by the golden glow. It was like nothing that I'd ever seen before. When I looked at my future home, I saw that it would have the same view. It made me even more grateful that we were able to make this happen.

"I can see why you picked this place."

"It's a beauty that is breathtaking. When I first came here, I knew that this was the place where I would settle and create a family and a coven. I would wake happily each night for an eternity. It's a shame it didn't last."

Niko sighed softly, then gestured to the lawn.

"In the days before everything happened, Beatrice would lay a rug on the lawn, and we would spend the evening gazing at the stars. Back when we didn't have any issues. Life was simple. We were happy and care-free."

"You could have that again. It won't be the same, but life is what you make of it."

Niko looked at me with a smile.

"Wise beyond your years."

"My teachers are to blame."

He chuckled, thoroughly amused because he knew that he was one of them. I could say that Niko was the teacher who instilled morals in me. He was a dutiful leader who had a good heart.

"You changed everything."

Niko looked at me curiously.

"I hated moving, and this place was deathly boring. I couldn't wait for Brad's employer to call and say we had to leave. It was like all of the fun had been sucked out of the town, and what remained was a dull little place. It felt as if everyone was waiting for trouble to brew. All I wanted was to return to one of the towns we'd been to, even if I was the outcast loner or the town had the worst crime rate for the entire state."

"Been to a few?"

"More than I'd like to admit. Brad won't either, especially not now that we know he was unemployed."

A grin curled in a corner as I let out a half-hearted laugh.

"He picked those places."

"Sometimes we see the surface but not what is beneath. It can be a fault, but in some instances, the layers beneath might not be what they seem."

"Yep, just like this place. It's still a boring little town with nothing for teenagers to do. It's still full of vampires and oblivious humans, but it's okay."

"Just okay?"

I shrugged.

"I guess so. I mean, it's getting better, and the more I explore, the more that I can see the charm of the place. The reality is that you made this place better. In those days, I found a sense of happiness that I'd never felt before. I wanted to stay. Even when faced with danger, I still wanted to be here."

I nudged my shoulder against him, beaming a smile at him.

"You have always been the best part of Hades."

Niko smiled, getting a wistful look on his face.

"Thank you for that, Evelyn. It would seem that we all have our own interpretation of what makes this place great for us. For me, I have found that the world has changed dramatically in my absence, but there was one thing that would always remain the same."

And it played out in front of us as if Niko had a magical command over them. Brad had dragged out the newly purchased barbeque while Carsten, Anzide, and Cooper were hauling out the tables. Beatrice, Della, and Eda had arms full of platters, laughing as they talked. Nora wasn't far behind with Karina as they carried out the buns and condiments. Sebastian, Killian, and Julian brought out the bench seats for everyone to sit on.

"This is what I crave in this life. A coven that is a family. It's the strangest coven I've ever encountered, but it is pure perfection. Look at the connectivity between them, see how they interact with each other, and watch the happiness that grows. You gave that to me, Evelyn. As I am yours, you are mine. The best thing in Hades."

Wrapping my arms around his, I laid my head on his shoulder.

"If you had a crystal ball or some way of seeing into the future and knew what was going to happen, would you change it?"

There was silence for a moment, and a raspy *no* escaped.

"Why not?"

"Because you would not exist," he whispered.

Niko cleared his throat.

"It's painful to look back now that we're on the other side of everything. We can easily look at the past and wonder *what if,* but I know what would have happened. I would have killed Drakkus, then there would be no blood war, I would not have sent Beatrice and Victoria away, and there would be no imprisonment behind the wall. I would not have seen you."

"It would have been a better life."

"You can't say that's entirely true. You also fail to see that in this life, there is a wonderful young woman who has changed so many lives for the better. She stood up and declared that the Nephilim were being treated poorly. She gave them back the rights that they should have always had. Not only that, but she is a masterful creator of spells, and if the whispers are true, it would seem that she is like nothing they have ever seen. For someone so young, she is powerful, and it is widely believed that she will become the greatest spell creator to ever exist. She rattles cages and demands answers to questions others fear to ask. She wants the best for everyone because she knows that they deserve it. Who would have done that if she wasn't around to do such things?"

Niko shifted, and I lifted my head to look at him.

"What kind of monster would I be if I robbed this world of you?"

I was stunned, to say the least.

"So, to answer you again, no, I wouldn't change a thing."

BONUS CHAPTER 2

LELA & LEVI

After the dozens of photos that were ordered to be taken, Karina glowered at her mother. Poor Nora was being given a lot of suggestions, and it was escalating into an argument. Even when she was in front of the camera with Karina, orders were being barked. Brad was becoming a monster.

Since it was out in the open that Nora was pregnant, the soon-to-be father was doting on her to the point where Karina said it was like watching someone get smothered. Niko intervened. Now, things were still intense, but for the first time father had taken a step back and accepted that Nora was only a few months pregnant. The labor was a long way off, and like all mothers, Nora was doing a great job at growing a healthy baby.

As for this nightmare, it was the night of the winter ball. The Christmas holidays were just around the corner, and as a celebration, the school was holding this event.

We were all dressed up for photos in the new house. It was an interesting sight because Karina was the only one who wasn't pregnant. The rest of us were either showing, had a slight pot belly, or looked like a beached whale. Yep, I was huge, and I still had a couple of weeks to go.

Eda and Julian walked in the front door with Cooper. While they began taking their photos, I waddled to the kitchen for a breather and to find the antacids. Taking one, I stuffed the packet into Anzide's pocket.

He offered a sympathetic smile.

"Want to know who the culprit is?"

"Sure."

Placing his hands on my belly, Anzide closed his eyes and searched.

"It's our little man. He's riding high and pushing everything up."

"Yay. Tell them to move down a fraction."

"Can't. There's no room in there."

"I know. I can feel my organs being squished into oblivion."

Julian called out to us. Apparently, the limousine had arrived. I began the slow waddle through the living room that was partially furnished. We were running out of time, and I couldn't decide what I liked. Anzide didn't make it any easier. If I pointed something out, he'd say that it was great or it would work well in the room. I wanted definitive answers for one or two items. Not everything that we looked at.

Reaching the garden steps, I lifted the soft pink lace of my dress with one hand and held Anzide's arm with the other. It was a gorgeous dress that Beatrice pointed out. The split over one leg was a little too high, but she put a few stitches into it and fixed the problem.

I was eased into the back of the limousine to a chorus of have fun and behave ourselves. As if I could do anything else with this giant mound in front of me.

Karina and Cooper were behind us, eager to start the night. I was keen, too, provided that the heartburn stopped. As for how long I would last, only time would tell. Of late, my bedtime has been regular. Nine pm, on the dot. I was alert one minute and drowsy the next. I'd go to bed, and within seconds of my head hitting the pillow, I would be asleep. Of course, it wouldn't last long. The lack of space meant that I had a smaller bladder capacity.

Cooper was such a goofball. He was at the far end of the limo with Karina, annoying her with the layers of black tulle around the skirt of her dress. She was giggling despite the frown she was trying to give.

Her dress was gorgeous. Perhaps a little risque with the low back and sweetheart neckline, but with any luck, the thin straps across her back will hold.

It didn't take long to reach the town hall where the ball was being held. The red carpet spanned the entire length of the path that led to the front door. Through the window, I could see the flash of the photographer. Once we had our photo taken, it would be time to celebrate the end of this journey.

The line was long, but it didn't take much time to reach the hall. The photographer was benevolent, allowing us to take a group photo in addition to the couples photo. I liked that he agreed.

Entering the hall, I dragged Anzide out to the dance floor. It was a little awkward with the giant mound between us, but we were determined to have fun. Our babies would be here in a few weeks, and once they were in the world, time away for fun would be limited.

After one song, I was beaten. Anzide helped me through the crowd to the drinks table.

"Test it first."

He took a sip and shrugged.

"Tastes like punch."

"How sad. Where's the local demon to spike it?"

"I doubt he'd do that."

Sipping the drink, I ambled over to the side of the room so that I could sit down. This was my life now. Do something, sit and rest for half an hour. And, like life liked to kick me when I was down, I felt the need to go to the restroom.

"Gotta go."

Anzide was used to me and my yo-yo-like behavior. Helping me out of the seat, he called out to Karina, who was at the drinks table. When I got too big and sometimes needed help, Karina told Anzide that she was the maid of honor in all things and he wasn't permitted in the restroom because it was still a no-go zone for the dinky pinky club members. He found it amusing and enjoyed her distaste when he said there was nothing dinky about it.

I winced, feeling odd. My odd little penguin waddle was made worse by the strange sensation. Karina looked at me peculiarly. Giving her a hurried flick of my hand, she followed me to the bathroom.

"I need to pee. I think."

"You think?"

Karina squinted an eye at me. I pushed through the door to see Audrey standing at the basin, applying lipstick.

"Hey Evie!" she said eagerly. "You look gorgeous. That color is so pretty on you. Hiya Karina, I love your dress. Super sexy."

"Uh, thanks, Audrey. You're looking great, too."

She smiled at us, and I looked at Karina. Her eyes were downward.

"So, either you've lost control of your bladder, or your waters just broke."

I looked up and saw Audrey and Karina staring at me.

"Oh, my goodness. Are you in labor, Evie?"

"Yeah, I think I might be. Karina, can you find Anzide, please?"

She nodded, fleeing through the door with speed. Audrey took my arm and helped me move away from the mess. Taking a stack of paper towels, she dropped them to the floor and began cleaning up the mess. I never thought that I'd see this.

"Do you know what you're having?"

"A boy and a girl."

"That's so cool. Picked names yet?"

"Lela and Levi."

"Oh, they're sweet names. Are you excited?"

"More nervous than anything. The pain hasn't started yet."

Picking up the towels, she dumped them in the trash and cleaned her hands.

"So, will you be going to the hospital, or do you have to go somewhere else?"

"For the safety of the babies, I'm going somewhere else."

She nodded, looking a little sad.

"But if you'd like to visit, I can get Karina to let you know when I'm home."

Audrey smiled as she took my arm again.

"I'd like that."

We began to walk to the door. I guess she was helping me out of the place now.

"I just wanted to say thank you for standing up for me, showing me that what Kannon was doing was wrong, and, you know, keeping your side of our deal."

"Niko said that you haven't visited him yet."

Audrey nodded as she opened the door.

"Dad said that I should get this year done, be finished with school, and then do it. I think that he wants to talk to Niko as well, to you know, apologize for ratting him out."

"Niko understands the control that Drakkus had over everyone."

In the distance, I could see Anzide walking at a fast pace around the dance floor to get here.

"And now that the risk of the Europeans visiting is over, you should visit my father. He said that he can help with your memories."

"At the moment, it's okay. I know that it happened, but I can't really remember it or see what went on. I guess that I can talk to him when I visit."

Anzide stopped in front of us, puffing as if he'd run here.

"Well, this is it. You're about to become a mother." Audrey gushed. "Good luck."

Audrey wandered off into the crowd, leaving me with

a quietly frantic Anzide. Karina and Cooper were hot on his heels, as was James, reaching us within seconds.

"You said I had time," I groaned, feeling a wave of pain hit me.

"Well, to be fair, most Eternals only have one child, so they would have based the gestation upon what they've seen. It is extremely cramped in there. You seem to enjoy doing things differently."

Karina giggled at James's dry assessment of me.

"I will deliver Karina and Cooper to the property."

"You can't leave the ball," I whined. "Stay and visit when the night is over."

"Not a chance," Karina grumbled. "I plan on being there for everything. So, suck it up, princess."

James smiled as he shook his head. Karina was a woman who knew what she wanted and wasn't afraid of making it happen, much to the amusement and, sometimes, bewilderment of those around her.

Taking Anzide's hand, we moved to a hidden section where we could enter the portal.

"I sent a message on the group chat. Your father is going to deliver everyone to the waiting room."

I nodded, feeling a dull pain growing. Stopping, I leaned on the wall near the message board. When I focused on the pain, I realized that I'd been feeling it all day and ignored the signs. It felt like every other day. The aches and the pains. What I didn't notice was that it came and went in waves. They were subtle enough not to notice at first. Now though, I saw it all. I've been in labor since this morning.

When we appeared at the reception desk in the hospital, the nurse looked at us.

"You two are a little overdressed for the occasion, don't you think?"

"You're hilarious, Tess."

"I know. How long have you been in labor?"

"The past few minutes, I have been aware of it, but I think all day."

Anzide frowned at me, and I shrugged.

"I've been in some form of pain for pretty much all of it."

Tess moved the wheelchair out and eased me into it.

"It's alright. You're not the first to miss the signs, and you won't be the last."

She pushed me into the delivery room. Moving the curtain around, Tess helped me out of the chair and urged Anzide over.

"Help undo the dress. I'll go and get a gown. You might want to get comfortable."

He watched as she moved around the curtain.

"That sounds ominous. How long do you think this will take?"

"I don't know."

Gripping the edge of the bed, I hoped that the pain would pass quickly. It had stopped and started again, which wasn't a good sign. I hadn't timed the gap, but I knew it was small. It would seem that I'd missed quite a lot.

"Good evening, Evelyn," the doctor called out. "Tess informs me that you're in the final stages of labor. Is it okay to come around?"

"Sure. I mean, I'm still in my dress, but why not? You're about to get an eye-opening view of the south end of town anyway."

The doctor chuckled as he pushed the curtain aside a fraction.

"Never heard it called that before, but it's certainly an interesting way of putting it. When Tess returns with the gown, you can change, and then we can have a look and see how dilated you are."

"I'm thinking *fully* is the term that you will use."

Hearing footsteps, the doctor looked around the curtain.

"Ah, Tess is here. I'll give you a moment and then return."

Swapping with Tess, the doctor remained on the exterior while Tess helped me into the hospital gown. With my dress laid over the back of the chair with Anzide's jacket, Anzide and Tess helped me onto the bed. Then it was time for a visit to indecency town where everyone got to have a grand old time looking at me.

Tess looked, and with pursed lips, she tried to smile. Yep, I was there. She called the doctor in, and he took one look and lifted his gaze to me.

"Well, you're fully dilated to the point where you're actually crowning."

"Seriously? Why is there,"

I paused and felt a sharp pain shoot through me. Gripping the edge of the mattress, I felt the pain push hard against my body.

Mild chaos had erupted. The curtain was pushed back, and extra staff flooded into the room. Equipment lined the far wall waiting for the babies to arrive.

Tess guided Anzide to sit beside me, prop me up, and hold me as the need to push grew dramatically. It felt like my body was being ripped apart.

There was no time for fear. No thoughts about the power I held or the risk that I could unleash a lot of deadly things upon this place and these people. I'd gone through this issue with my father, and he helped me plan for any potential problems, but nowhere in that planning did we anticipate the labor being so quick that I would walk into the place already crowning.

"Keep going, Evelyn. Give us another big push."

With everything that I had, I did as the doctor asked. Tears mixed with sweat, I cried out as the burning pain seared through my body.

Everything faded when the sound of crying echoed loudly. One slimy little girl was pulled free and lifted onto my chest. Lela was not impressed at being rubbed over with the towel or the change of environment. The room was warm, but I couldn't imagine it would be the same as life in the womb.

We had a moment of respite. Anzide wrapped his arm around me as he traced his fingers over our little girl's head. All the while, I was being poked and prodded.

Tess eased the baby off my body after a few minutes, handing her to Anzide.

"It's almost time," she said softly. "You can take her over to the table. The nurse will help you wrap her up."

It seemed like a blur. A fog had descended, and I felt as if I was floating aimlessly. Almost like I was back on the lake in that stupid boat.

Feeling something warm grip my hand, I found the light on the island. The sounds of the room came back to me, slamming me with demands from the doctor, a wailing baby, and the reassuring words of positivity from Anzide.

Yet again, I complied. I didn't think that I had the energy to push another child out. But I did. Through the agony that seemed unending, the pain that felt like my skin was ripping, and the white-hot burning that surged through my body, I pushed.

Our son was born, and like his sister, Levi was not

impressed. I had to say, I agreed with both of them. This was not fun, but when I looked at them and at Anzide, I knew that I'd do it over and over again. It was the family that I'd craved for so long. It was a love that would always be there, unending and eternal.

FROM THE AUTHOR

Thank you for reading. I hope you enjoyed the book as much as I loved writing it. If you would like to read more, please check out my other books.

Please also consider signing up to my newsletter to be up to date with all future releases.

www.tmwatkinsauthor.com

ABOUT THE AUTHOR

TM Watkins lives in Brisbane, Australia with her family. She spends her days contemplating the next adventure for her characters and her nights writing about them. Her life as an author began on Wattpad and Radish Fiction under the pen name xMishx.

To join the mailing list, please sign up at

www.tmwatkinsauthor.com

www.ingramcontent.com/pod-product-compliance
Lightning Source LLC
LaVergne TN
LVHW050910080826
845145LV00001B/40

* 9 7 8 1 7 6 3 7 1 9 5 4 5 *